5/12

D0428708

THE ORDER

DON'T MISS THIS OTHER TERRIFYING TALE
IN THE WORLD OF

BOOK OF CAIN

# DIABLO

## THE ORDER

# NATE KENYON

BASED ON THE VIDEO GAME FROM
BLIZZARD ENTERTAINMENT

**G**
**GALLERY BOOKS**

NEW YORK • LONDON • TORONTO • SYDNEY • NEW DELHI

G

Gallery Books

A Division of Simon & Schuster, Inc.

1230 Avenue of the Americas

New York, NY 10020

First Gallery Books hardcover edition May 2012

GALLERY BOOKS and colophon are registered trademarks of Simon & Schuster, Inc.

For information about special discounts for bulk purchases, please contact Simon & Schuster Special Sales at 1-866-506-1949 or business@simonandschuster.com.

The Simon & Schuster Speakers Bureau can bring authors to your live event. For more information or to book an event, contact the Simon & Schuster Speakers Bureau at 1-866-248-3049 or visit our website at www.simonspeakers.com.

Designed by Alissa Amell

Manufactured in the United States of America

10 9 8 7 6 5 4 3 2 1

Library of Congress Cataloging-in-Publication Data is available.

ISBN 978-1-4165-5078-5
ISBN 978-1-4516-4566-8 (ebook)

*To, Abbey,*
*my little girl,*
*who may someday gather*
*the courage to read this . . .*
*but not yet.*

# PROLOGUE

# MEMORY

*Tristram, 1213*

The boy thrust his hands into his wool tunic as if to warm them, although the blaze from the fire was hot enough to curl the soft down on his cheek. He was narrow across the shoulders, and his face was thin and drawn even at this young age, so he looked far older than his eleven years. He wore a satchel across his neck made of deer hide with a heavy book tucked into one pocket, which pinched him and made red marks on his skin. He didn't much care about that, or about what the others might have said about him. He had no real friends. He was a natural loner, at home with his texts, and he liked it that way.

The firelight flickered and danced across the other children, who sat with faces rapt and shining, upward-turned in spiritual ecstasy as if the figure telling stories before them were the archangel Auriel herself, come to walk among them.

No. That wasn't right. The boy shook his head slightly in disgust. Perhaps a few years ago he might have made such a comparison, but not now. The figure who spoke with such confidence was simply his mother, a mortal with no higher knowledge than any other regardless of her bloodline, and if the archangels existed at all, they certainly would not waste their time coming to this forsaken place.

A log popped, sending a sharp blaze of sparks up into the night and making the others jump. Smoke swirled and drifted around their heads, bringing an acrid, bitter smell that masked the stench of the barnyard below. She had them in her grasp, as always; the elders of the village might roll their eyes as she passed, and the innkeeper and town guard might whisper behind her back about a touch of madness, but the children would always come to listen, and they would believe.

Until they grew older, Deckard Cain thought, and opened their eyes to the truth.

"The last Prime Evil and youngest brother, Diablo, the Lord of Terror, was the strongest of all, and horrible to behold. It is said that those who gazed directly upon him went mad with fear. But the Horadrim never ceased in their pursuit. Once Tal Rasha had been entombed forever with the Lord of Destruction beneath the deserts of Aranoch, Jered Cain led the remaining mages through Khanduras, battling Diablo's minions at every pass." Aderes glanced at each child in turn, holding their gaze in her own. When her glittering eyes found his, the boy looked away, as if searching for something far beyond the reach of firelight.

His mother's tone might have faltered slightly, or perhaps she was just catching her breath. "The Horadrim with their powerful magic did great damage to the demon's army. But Diablo summoned thousands more of his terrible servants from the Burning Hells to fight for him, and finally Jered decided to make a stand. The archangel Tyrael had formed the Horadrim for a single purpose, to contain the Prime Evils and banish them from our fair lands, and he would not let them fail."

Aderes Cain's skin held a waxy sheen, her coal-black curls damp against her forehead. She had the blank-eyed stare of the damned. Deckard had heard this story many times before, and it got larger and more impressive every time she told it. He knew all the twists and turns. Now would come the moment when she shocked the young children by revealing that the heroic mages had made their stand *right here in these lands,* and the very ground beneath their feet had run black with demon blood. Her voice would grow even louder as Jered and his Horadrim brothers fought back wave after wave of monstrous creatures, finally imprisoning Diablo inside the soulstone and burying it deep beneath the ground, where it still lay even today.

The legend used to thrill him, but he was no longer a young child, and his mother and her growing madness had become something uncomfortable for him. He had more important things to concern himself with now, and he could not bear to listen anymore. When she turned away for a moment to address the others, he slipped back from the circle and faded into the cool night.

The air was moist, and it was much colder away from the fire. Deckard walked barefoot across the slick grass, gathering his tunic closer around his thin frame. He could see his breath in the air, and it seemed to rise up out of him like a creature not made of this earth. Somewhere near the barn below, a man cursed as a sheep screamed at the slaughter, and the sweet-sour smell of blood came, carried by the breeze. Fog eddied around the trees at the edge of the forest, and a chill danced down the back of Deckard's neck like ghost fingers. He shivered and made for his home, not fifty steps away.

Inside, two lanterns were lit in the small entry, but he did not pick one up, remaining swaddled in darkness as he padded noiselessly to his room. He knew the way by heart. It was cold in the house, too, colder than he would have thought it should be. His fingers touched the binding of the book in his satchel, caressed it, but he did not draw it out, not yet, choosing to let the moment linger deliciously, like a drunkard withholding the taste of wine for a single moment more before bringing the chalice to his lips. It was a book on the history of Westmarch and the Sons of Rakkis, a scholarly text, nothing like the things his mother liked to read: those stories of noble heroes and impossible worlds above and below this one, their inhabitants always dancing just out of sight. The stuff of folklore.

He wanted to be alone for a while. It was only moments later that he heard the door open again and his mother come in, dropping her heavy wooden clogs on the hearth. Soon she would start a fire and put the kettle on for tea, and he would hear her tuneless humming as she sat in her rocking chair to knit or read. But he was wrong; instead she came straight for his room, and he barely had time to tuck the book under his bed and sit down before she knocked on the door and came in.

"Deckard?" She held a lantern up against the darkness, squinting at him. "You left the circle before I was finished." In the warm yellow glow she looked as if she were unraveling, her hair wild and tumbling down over her shoulders in heavy curls. She had a gray streak just beginning, Cain thought, by her right temple. He hadn't noticed it before.

"I've heard the stories many times. I was tired and needed rest."

"They're not just stories, Deckard. Jered is your blood, and you—you are the last of a proud line of heroes."

"The Horadrim."

"That's right. Direct descendants of the great mages, tasked with protecting Sanctuary from the demons that stalk this world. You know this."

Cain shrugged. He did not like to look directly into her eyes, not quite sure of what he might find there. He sat for a moment in silence, and then: "Why didn't you let me take Father's name?"

He didn't know why he'd said that. His father had died a few weeks before of a wasting disease, after working in the tanner's shop for most of his life, first sweeping floors, then as an apprentice, and finally the last two years as head of the shop. He hadn't been much for talking, and it had been a rare thing for him to show any emotion at all. Deckard was not much like him, or maybe he was.

His mother put the lantern down on the bedside table and sat next to him. She reached out to touch his shoulder, and he turned just the slightest amount, enough to make her withdraw her hand as if scalded. "You're hurt and you're angry," she said. "I understand that. But it won't bring him back."

He stared down at his fingers clasped in his lap, then felt the straw under the covering that had become gray and threadbare in places through many washings. This had been his bed since he had left the crib, in the same room, in the same modest home and the same town. *Nothing ever happens here.*

When he glanced up, his mother's eyes were shimmering in the lamplight. "I loved your father, in my own way. But it is not my destiny to turn away from the name I carry, nor is it yours. The scrolls say that someday the Horadrim will rise up again when all seems lost, and a new hero will lead them in battle to save Sanctuary. Do you understand? You are meant for bigger things."

Cain clenched his fists. "Bigger things? The Horadrim are all gone, so you became a storyteller to fill the emptiness. But the people of Tristram are laughing at you. Look around you, Mother! Where are your angels, your demons? Where are your heroes? The Horadrim are long dead, and the town's no different for it!"

He stood up and went to the tiny window, his entire body trembling. *You are the last of a proud line.* He wanted nothing to do with that nonsense, not anymore. He wanted to be left alone to read his own books.

The night was heavy and moist, and the fog had grown thicker. He could see it pooling under the lights hung on posts, obscuring the muddy ground. He heard his mother get up, but he did not turn around at first. Only when he heard the crackle of flame did he whirl to find Aderes with his book in her hand, holding it against the open lantern as the brittle, dry pages caught fire, his mother's eyes like pools of orange and yellow that reflected the heat back at him.

With a gasp he leaped forward and grabbed it from her, beating it against his chest until the heat seared him and he dropped it to the dirt floor and stomped it out, then stood there, chest heaving. "What have you done?"

"This one is not part of your destiny," she said. "Your proper texts are with Jered's belongings, when you choose to read them. I kept them for you."

He stared at the remains of the book on Westmarch. The pages were seared and blackened, beyond saving. A rage built up and caught in Deckard's throat. "Your demons live inside you, Mother, and nowhere else. I promise you that. If they're coming, as you say, let them come. Why don't they show themselves, if such things exist?"

A strangled cry escaped his mother's mouth, and she clasped her hand to her lips. She took a stumbling step backward. "Be careful what you wish for, Deckard. You don't know what you are asking for with this—"

"Let them *come*!"

The sound of his shriek filled the night, echoed back to him, then died away. For a moment the world seemed to cease its motion, and Deckard felt a draft circle his bare legs like an ice-cold caress. His body tingled with equal parts excitement and fear, a momentary longing for something to change, anything that would take him away from this place. He knew that if it did not, he would end up like his father, working in the tannery or selling meat to the occasional wanderer who still came to gape wide-eyed at the old Horadric monastery as it settled into ruin. He would die here, and his bones would sink into the earth and nobody would remember when he had lived or perished.

"I want to believe," he said, suddenly very tired. "But I can't."

His mother shook her head. "Then I cannot help you," she said. "You are already lost." A sob caught in her throat. She turned and fumbled with the door, leaving the lantern on the table as she walked out of his room.

Part of him wanted to go after her and tell her he was sorry, that he hadn't meant those things he had said, but his legs remained rooted to the spot. Perhaps he had meant to say them, after all. The lantern flickered, as if the breath of an unseen presence had touched it. Shadows danced upon the wall, and for a moment he thought he heard a whisper: *Deckaaaard . . .*

He spun to face the little window again, open to the night. The air coming through it was icy and seemed much colder than it should have been. He went to it and peered out, squinting to see more clearly. There was nothing outside at first but the dark and the fog, and then movement came from the direction of the fields. He flinched as a stray dog slunk quickly away with a soft whine, looking for scraps, disappearing on its way toward a cluster of houses.

Cain looked up the hill at the old monastery that loomed over the town like an ancient, empty husk, something used up and abandoned. He gathered his tunic around him and shivered, momentarily in awe of his own hubris. In his heart, he prayed for something to happen that would derail him from the path he saw clearly open to him, but he knew that it would not. Real life was not like those myths.

He picked up the pages of the book on Westmarch, and the blackened edges crumbled to dust in his hands.

*Let them come.*

It would take another fifty years, but Deckard Cain's wish would be fulfilled.

PART ONE

GATHERING SHADOWS

# ONE

*Ruins of the Vizjerei Secret Repository,*
*the Borderlands, 1272*

In the great, dark depths of what followed, there would be little time to reflect on the moment when the crumbling of the line between this world and the next began to accelerate out of control; the explosion on the mountain was like two warriors rushing toward their doom, swords flashing by in the blink of an eye, seeming to emerge unscathed until they began to stumble, bloody mouths opening, mortal wounds bringing them to their knees.

But perhaps that moment was here, held within the endless, baking heat of the Borderlands, with the ruins hovering just out of sight. When the two travelers neared the top of the final dune, they might have heard a ringing, like a piece of metal struck with a hammer and vibrating at a pitch just out of hearing range that set their teeth on edge.

The pair paused for a drink of water. Sunlight shimmered off the endless sands, baking their skin. The younger one, a proud knight of Westmarch, wearing golden armor and bearing a red shield, spat a yellow stream and wiped his shining face with a rag, then drank deeply from the canteen before handing it to his companion.

The older man, who wore a gray, hooded tunic belted around his waist and a rucksack across his back, shifted his walking staff to his other hand to accept it and took his fill. The belt was etched with strange designs the color of dried blood. He was thin enough to blow away in the wind, and his wild, white hair and long beard made him appear slightly mad, but there was a strength to him that had grown more apparent the longer they traveled together. He walked slowly but at a steady pace, no matter the time of day or night, and the young man had often found himself scrambling to keep up.

The old man pointed to their right, where the sand held a slight depression that ran in a line for about twenty feet before disappearing again. "That marks a place where a thresher surfaced to feed," he said. "They become more aggressive as evening falls. We must be very careful."

The end of the slight depression was speckled with dark red spots. *Blood.* The young man had heard about the threshers, terrible beasts like dragons with monstrous teeth and claws that could tear a man apart. He could fight with his sword against anything made of flesh; it was the creatures not of this realm that posed a far greater threat, he thought, although he had never met one in person. But looking at the old man and knowing something about the scars he carried, the young man thought his companion might be able to hold his own against those just as well.

After a moment's pause, they continued on, and at the top of the very next rise, they found what they had been seeking.

Twin columns rose up out of the sand in the distance like jagged teeth, their tops ending abruptly as if snapped off by something inhuman. That could be so, Deckard Cain thought, if this was in fact the entrance to the ancient ruins of the Vizjerei repository.

He could only imagine what sort of horrors might have visited this place in years past, looking for sorcerers' blood.

They had been traveling for days and had left their mules at the last town to continue the final part of their journey on foot. Mules would be of little use on this shifting sand base. The location Cain and his companion sought was remote. He had no doubt that these ruins would have remained well hidden for many years more if this young warrior had not brought him the obscure Zakarum texts now safely nestled in his rucksack. The Ancient Repositories of the Vizjerei in Caldeum were far larger and better known among mages, but this one, if it did indeed exist, could be even more important.

It had been a very long journey. After the narrow defeat of Baal at Mount Arreat and the destruction of the Worldstone, Deckard Cain had been unable to convince his traveling party that the immediate danger to Sanctuary was not over. Far from it, in fact, if everything he had read and understood in the Horadric scrolls was true. The archangel Tyrael himself had warned him of it, before he had been lost. Cain sensed a subtle change in the world that mirrored the prophecies, a disruption in the delicate balance between the High Heavens and Burning Hells that had existed for centuries. The loss of the Worldstone was devastating, and left Sanctuary open and vulnerable.

To make matters worse, Cain had begun dreaming again about his childhood and his mother's stories, waking in a cold sweat nearly every night. He fought against endless armies of darkness with nothing to protect him, or sat hunched and broken in a cage hung from a pole while monstrous creatures taunted him. And he relived things even worse than that: ghosts from his past that he had thought were buried forever.

He hadn't dreamed like this since the fall of Tristram. His own guilt over those events consumed him; he had been too late to stop the demonic invasion of his own home, as self-absorbed as he had been back then, and he had been too late to change what had happened on Mount Arreat.

Cain's companions remained insistent on celebrating their victory, returning to loved ones and picking up the pieces of their shattered lives, and he could hardly blame them. He, however, had nobody waiting for him, and with Tristram destroyed he had nowhere to go, so he set off looking for the pieces that would fit together to reveal the pattern underneath. If the invasion was truly coming, he would need help: the Horadrim had been formed to battle evil but had since faded away into history. His mother's voice echoed back to him from years before: *Jered is your blood, and you—you are the last of a proud line of heroes.*

Akarat started down the slope of sand toward the columns, but Cain held his arm. The paladin was trembling, full of the energy and recklessness of his age, which masked his more delicate senses that might have otherwise given him pause now. But Cain felt it, like a faint sour smell on the wind.

The scent of danger.

Akarat unsheathed his sword in his eagerness to charge down upon whatever was waiting for them. "We're exposed here," he said. "It's better to move quickly. I'll protect you from threshers or sand wasps. Besides, we might find nothing at all."

"We should watch a moment longer," Cain said. "The texts warned of a spell that shields the repository from sight. By all rights, these columns should not be visible to us. Something has weakened it."

He did not say more about what he was thinking: *If there are such valuable artifacts hidden here, there may well be other powerful forces guarding their secrets.* He knelt in the hot sand and removed his rucksack, searching inside for a particular object. This young man reminded him of another he had known years before, an old friend who had descended into hellish catacombs in an attempt to save Tristram. That hero had paid dearly for his overconfidence, as had all of Sanctuary, and Cain had been unable to save him.

*If I'm right, it's you who will need protection,* he thought.

He removed the object, something like a looking glass with an amber lens, and held it to the light. The sun was falling to the horizon, giving the air a more deeply yellow tinge. They had no more than an hour before darkness fell, and the best thing to do would be to set up camp now and explore the ruins in the morning. But Akarat had spoken the truth; they were exposed here, and neither one of them wanted to face what might come out of the sands as the shadows deepened.

He stood up, trying to ignore the bite of pain in his back and the throbbing ache in his knees, a constant reminder of his age. How had this happened? It seemed only moments ago he was a boy playing fetch back in the fields, watching out for cow patties in the long grass or stealing eggs from Grosgrove's henhouse. Ah, how fickle life was, drifting through your fingers like this forsaken sand, gone before you could catch it . . .

Cain's own self-doubt crept back in. Most of his life had been spent in selfishness and denial, living among his books and ignoring his own past. He had waited fifty years to embrace his destiny, and in the process had helped destroy everything he had held dear. Could he even consider himself Horadrim at all?

He was no hero, despite what his mother had always told him. The thought of everything resting on his frail old shoulders was terrifying. Something terrible was coming, something that would make the previous attacks seem like child's play. Nobody he had spoken to about the demon invasion believed him, except for Akarat; they all thought he was a doddering old fool at best, and dangerous at worst. The people of Sanctuary went about their daily lives and rarely sensed the intrusion of angels and demons into their world. Life was hard, but it was mundane.

They hadn't seen what he had, hadn't dreamed his dreams, or they might have felt differently.

The paladin grunted. He had sheathed his sword again but was shifting from foot to foot. When they'd been in Westmarch, he had been eager to hear Cain's stories, insisting they stay up long past when old men should have been in bed; but now, out here and close to battle, he wanted action. The young paladin was named after the founder of the Church of Zakarum himself, and it seemed to be a fitting name for him. Although young and headstrong, he was both a true believer and a zealot.

Cain muttered several words under his breath, a brief incantation to activate the power inside the artifact, and handed it over. "Look through the lens at the ruins," he said. "Quickly now, before it fades."

The young paladin raised the glass to his eye, and his sudden intake of breath was enough for Cain to know the artifact was working. "By the Light . . ." he said softly. He lowered the glass, staring down at the ruins, then raised it again. "Incredible." He handed it back to Cain, his eyes wide with wonder.

The old man peered through the glass. The lens coloring gave the entire scene a tinge of orange, like a fire burned just out of sight. The remains of a massive structure and its surrounding grounds spread out below them, just beyond where the two columns marked the entrance. More columns in various stages of decay marched in twin lines to what had been the front doors of a temple. Broken walls rose to where they had been torn away by some great explosion many years ago. Huge stone blocks, chipped and worn from the drifting sands, lay half buried where they had fallen.

Cain scanned the scene carefully and lowered the glass. Once again, all that was visible to the naked eye were the two columns. The spell that had protected these ruins was powerful enough to last centuries, but it was weakening now. The real question was why.

There was no stopping Akarat, however. He was already

twenty feet down the slope, moving as quickly as his armor allowed. He glanced back at Cain, the excitement on his face touched by the warm glow of the sun before he descended into shadow.

"Come on, then," he said. "It's right before us! Do you want a written invitation?"

# TWO

## *The Hidden Chamber*

The air was cooler near the ruins. The reveal spell held within the looking glass had faded away by the time they reached the massive columns, but the two travelers had no need for it after they had passed the entrance.

The two columns cast deeper shadows across their path like black lines drawn in the dust. Beyond the shadows the veil gradually lifted away, and the ruins of the secret repository loomed all around them, coming into view like the rise of mountains through the mist. Broken stones thrust through the sands, swept clean in places by the wind. Ancient carvings of runes covered the sides of the larger blocks, marking this as a place of great Vizjerei power. Cain felt his heartbeat quicken, the palms of his hands growing moist. He could feel it thrumming beneath his feet, deep within the earth.

Or perhaps, he thought, he felt something else.

There was darkness here. Although the sun still touched the tops of these rocks, it did not warm them. Even the paladin sensed it now, his steps faltering as they moved deeper into the ruins. Before them lay the remains of the temple, its entrance covered in rubble, what was left of the roof all but collapsed upon itself. Massive timbers reached toward the sky like the ribs of a giant beast. This was where the ancient texts would have been kept, if they had existed at all. But it would be dangerous inside, possibly unstable.

A sound reached their ears like the rustling of leaves. Akarat stopped and drew his sword. "Do you hear it?" he asked. His voice was quiet.

Cain nodded, stepping to the young man's side. "There may be something else here with us, after all," he said.

"Like . . . what? An animal?"

"Perhaps," Cain said. He could tell that the paladin was both scared and excited, and trying hard not to show it. Stories of demonic attacks were one thing, but actually facing something most people thought was only a legend was another. Cain knew that all too well.

The sounds swirled faintly around them, almost fading away before returning again like waves on a beach or the hushed muttering of a crowd. A curious prickling sensation warming his skin, Cain held his staff like a talisman as he moved ahead on the broken path, Akarat close behind. "Close your ears," Cain said, "as if you were deaf. Should you hear voices, do not listen to them."

"I don't understand—"

"If something foul is present, it will try to corrupt you, find your weaknesses. Ignore anything it tries to say. Whatever it is, I promise you are not meant to hear it."

He reached the edge of the tumbled rocks at the entrance to the temple and peered around them, looking for a way in. There was a space just large enough for a man. Darkness loomed beyond the narrow passage that was the height of his shoulders. Cain swung his rucksack down again and found a crumbling spellbook, searching the brittle pages for the right words. As he said them aloud, the glass sphere at the end of his staff came to life, taking on a blue glow and lighting the space within.

Beyond the reach of the wind, where the sand began to fade, the drifts held the faint impression of a footprint. Either a man, or something that walked like one, had passed through this place not long ago.

He tucked the book away and turned to the paladin, who stared at him and the glowing staff and back again, mouth agape.

"Magic? True magic?"

"A simple spell, nothing more. Like the looking glass, held within the objects themselves. I simply have the knowledge to unlock it. This is a place of sorcery, chosen, at least in part, because of the power in the soil. A spell is more useful in a spot like this."

"Are you really the last of the Horadrim?"

Cain considered how to answer. "What I learned, I learned from books," he said finally. "It's a forgotten order. If there were any others left, they would surely be more prepared than I am, and would have made themselves known by now."

"So if you are the last, what then?"

"I must do what I can to stop what is coming to Sanctuary." Cain shrugged. "And pray it is not too late." *And may the Heavens help us all*, he thought, but did not say it.

Akarat glanced to his right and left, as if waiting for something to pounce. "There is much of this world still to know," he said. At that moment he looked like a boy who had just walked in on something he shouldn't have seen and was trying to make sense of it. He hadn't noticed the footprint.

Cain put his hand on Akarat's shoulder. "Have you ever been in battle?"

"I—I've fought many times," the paladin said. "I've patrolled the city, and in the ring I've proven my skill—"

"Not in training, or on patrol," Cain said gently, "but against those who would run you through, if given half the chance. Or worse."

Akarat shook his head, his eagerness betraying his attempt to appear more confident. "There have not been many opportunities since I came of age."

"I forget that. The battle on Mount Arreat occurred years ago. You would have been no older than . . ."

"Ten years," Akarat said, his eyes bright. "I remember hearing the stories from the men who returned. I wanted to be like them."

"There's no shame in that." Cain smiled. "The world has been calmer, at least on the surface, since then. But it will give you an opportunity soon. For now, I want you to guard this entrance." When the young man started to protest, he shook his head. "I am an old man, not very strong. I cannot fight with a sword. But I am not wearing armor, and I'm slender enough to squeeze through these smaller spaces and find something that may help us, if given the time to do so. You'll do me far more good out here, making sure nothing can surprise me from behind."

Akarat set his feet and took the hilt of his sword with both hands. "I won't let you down," he said.

Cain smiled, but when he turned back toward the darkness, the smile faded. Again he was reminded of the hero whom he had once known in Tristram as King Leoric's oldest son, and who had later been known as the Dark Wanderer. He had said much the same thing before descending into the depths of those cursed caverns beneath the cathedral. Cain had tutored the boy himself and had loved him—at least, as much as he had been capable of love, back then.

He ducked his head to enter the makeshift passage. Inside the narrow space, the height required him to shuffle forward with his shoulders slumped and knees bent, turning sideways to slip through a tight spot as the rock brushed against him. The pain bit into his back again, an invisible and constant enemy.

*Perhaps I shouldn't have come in myself,* he thought. *Perhaps this is a younger man's task, after all.*

But only a few feet farther in, the makeshift passage opened up and dropped away. He held up his glowing staff to see more clearly. A set of rough-hewn stone steps led down into the earth. They were in good shape; the lower levels of the temple had apparently survived the building's collapse. More footprints marked the dust, several going up and down. It was impossible to know how long they had been there.

The smell of mold and dust drifted up to him, like something from a tomb that had been opened up after many centuries. He heard the faint rustling again and peered into the deeper blackness, but saw nothing.

Deckard Cain descended slowly, the air growing much colder as he went. The stairs ended in a stone floor. His light revealed a large chamber supported by massive wooden beams and strung with thick cobwebs. There were runes of both power and warning carved into the beams. Cain read them with increasing apprehension. These were the marks of the followers of Bartuc, a Vizjerei mage who had lived many centuries before and had been corrupted and overcome by bloodlust after summoning demons to do his bidding. His clashes with his brother, Horazon, had been the climax of the ancient Mage Clan Wars and led to the deaths of many thousands of people.

If this had been a repository for Bartuc's army, whatever Vizjerei artifacts he found here would be infused with demonic magic. They would be suspect at best, and possibly very dangerous.

Had they made a terrible mistake, coming here?

Cain flinched as dust or sand sifted down from above his head and something large and black skittered along a beam and disappeared. It was too large to be a spider, and no rat could have clung sideways to the beam like that for long.

*Better not to look too closely at such things . . .*

In the center of the room, something sparkled in the light. The dust had been brushed away here, exposing an intricate, circular pattern of runes carved in rock. A portal, to where Cain could only guess. Set at its center was a jewel the color of blood. Someone had tried to remove it, scratching the floor with deep grooves, but had apparently given up. Cain knelt next to the stone, studying the runes carefully. What he read made his heart race. Then he spoke several ancient words of power to release the jewel and slipped it into his sack.

He made his way across the floor, following the footprints to an alcove in the far wall. Rotted boards clung to supports, the last remains of an ancient library. This had been a ritual chamber, many centuries before, used to summon things from beyond the human world. A portal to the Burning Hells themselves, perhaps. The shelves were empty now. He saw a speck of yellow underneath a splinter of wood and bent to pick up a corner of parchment paper, curled and speckled with mildew.

Something moved in the shadows to his right.

He whirled, holding the light up. For a moment it appeared as if the shadows themselves were alive, bunching and swirling like ink in water. At the same time, a voice like the distant moan of wind drifted through the empty room and raised the hairs on the back of his neck.

*"Deckaaaaarrdddd Caiiinnnn . . ."*

Cain felt a strange doubling, a memory of a night many years before, when he was just a boy. A whispered voice calling to him, just like this. He backed away, fumbling in his rucksack with one hand, holding the lighted staff with the other against the darkness. Already he was doubting himself: had it just been the wind moving through the broken remains of the building above him, a trick his mind had played after so long in the sun?

The voice came again, a sound like bones scraping together in the grave.

*"Your ghosts are many, old man, and they are active."*

A grating of metal over rock seemed to come from everywhere at once. Once again a pool of black smoke thickened and then dissipated, only to reassemble somewhere else: a shape carrying a sword, the form of a man, but with eyes that glowed red with the fires of Hell.

Cain knew what this was, yanked from the depths of his own mind and used against him: the image of the Dark Wanderer himself, conjured up to weaken his resolve. The smoke-shape swirled and shifted, reforming into two indistinct human shapes, one taller and clearly female, one small and delicate. Shock raced through Cain's limbs as an older, familiar memory fought to surface. He closed his eyes against the darkness as the yawning pit of despair opened within him, threatening to pull him in.

*You must not listen.*

"A storm is coming," a voice said, from the direction of the stairs. "We need to seek shelter—"

Whatever lurked in the chamber gave an audible hiss of pleasure as Akarat stepped onto the stone floor, blinking in the light, a look of confusion on his face. "Get back!" Cain shouted as something uncurled from the shadows and flowed across the chamber toward the young paladin.

But Akarat rushed forward instead like a fool, pulling his sword from its sheath and slicing down with a two-handed thrust that split the shadow in two. The sword hit the stone floor with a shower of sparks. He lifted it and swung the heavy blade sideways to no effect. The darkness flowed like smoke around the young paladin, swirling around his legs and moving upward as Cain knelt in the dust and set his staff down.

The paladin began screaming.

Cain's scrolls spilled onto the stone. *Where is it?* He fumbled through them frantically, finally found what he wanted, and unrolled the delicate paper, shouting the words of power with all the strength he could muster.

The demon shrieked with anger, an inhuman sound that was

cut off at its peak as the scroll crumbled to dust in Cain's hands. The chamber grew brighter, glowing with its own emerald light as a spell bubble formed around the two men. Thrust outside the bubble, the shadow writhed, swirling around an invisible barrier that would not let it pass. Cain caught a brief glimpse of multi-jointed legs, something insect-like about the seething form as it coalesced and drifted apart again.

Akarat crossed the floor to Cain's side, gathering the older man's scrolls and helping him to his feet, then looked at the writhing blackness that now seemed to batter itself against the emerald shell. The young man was breathing heavily, covered in a sheen of sweat. "How . . . how did you do this?"

"An Ammuit spell," the old man said. "A matter of illusion, it will keep us safe for only a few moments."

"You are a true sorcerer, after all!"

"I'm only a scholar who has learned how to use what others have given me."

Akarat turned back to stare at the thing that had attacked them. "What is it?"

"A servant of a Lesser Evil, sent here to guard whatever had been kept in these chambers. You must not listen to what it says or it will begin to twist you inside until you break."

"I . . . I saw things. Terrible things." The paladin shook his head as if to clear it. "About you . . . and about me." He turned back, and his eyes were haunted.

"You must not believe them, my son. We need to leave this place, and quickly."

"I . . ." The young man's face grew dark. "That thing is evil. We have to kill it!"

"It's not flesh and blood—"

"I can defeat it. I must *try*, for the sake of everything holy. The Zakarum faith teaches us to resist all evil things, to fight against them to our last breath. Creatures like this corrupted the high council and murdered Khalim, and turned our temple to darkness! The Zakarum is in shambles because of them." Sweat plastered Akarat's hair against his brow as he raised his weapon and turned back to the wraith. "The archangels will support me in this, I swear it."

*He is already lost.* Cain's heart sank, and a deeper chill settled into his bones. He reached out to touch the paladin's arm. "There is a way to fight demons like this one, but it is not with the sword—"

The shadow congealed into a blackened face with empty eye sockets, mouth gaping wide, hovering just out of reach. Akarat gasped, his entire body tensing as the face began to melt into a mirror image of the young man's own, its features showing shock and then terror as a gaping wound appeared in the specter's throat. Its head tipped backward off the stump of a neck as smoke poured out like black blood.

With a strangled cry, the young paladin leapt at the thing still seething outside the emerald shell. A brilliant flash of light illuminated the chamber as he passed through the spell's protective barrier, and Cain threw his arm up to protect himself and fell back, but not before he caught a glimpse of the paladin's sword slicing through empty space.

The light crackled like a lightning strike as Akarat screamed again and was suddenly silenced. It seemed that the world had stopped for a moment, that time had shifted back upon itself again, sending Cain hurtling backward to other days that he did not want to remember, dreams filled with the shrieks of a young child lost and alone. The spell broken, darkness filled the room until the old man held up his staff again and slowly regained his feet. The orb had lost some of its brilliance, as if the shadows themselves had begun to absorb the light from it.

The blue glow revealed the paladin still standing upright, his back to Cain, his body slumped. He had dropped his sword on the floor, his arms hanging motionless at his sides.

"Akarat," Cain said. He took a step forward, consumed with dread. The young man did not respond; only his shoulders moving slightly up and down indicated he was still breathing.

*We must leave this place. I was wrong, coming here.*

An icy cold draft caressed Cain's face, bringing along a foul stench of death. When he touched the paladin's arm, a chill spread through his fingers.

The young man turned at his touch, but the face that greeted him was no longer Akarat's.

Leathery skin stretched tight over a swelling brow and cheeks, and the lips were cracked and bleeding. What had been Akarat's eyes now regarded him, from puffy pockets of flesh, with glittering hatred. Cain thought of cold, dead things rotting away in a nameless grave, and he knew he must not look, must turn away now and run, or the darkness would creep into his own soul and blacken his blood.

*"We have been waiting for you, Deckaaaaard Cainnnn."*

"Release him," Cain said.

*"We think not."* The thing smiled, exposing long, canine-like teeth sharpened to points. *"There's so much to do, to prepare for the coming."*

He tried to think of what he had in his sack to assist him, but he had no spell for this, no magic artifact to drive the demon away. Without spells or artifacts, he was lost; he had no magic of his own.

*"Last of the Horadrim,"* the thing hissed, mocking him. *"You are nothing. And you are wrong. Look around you, at the footsteps, the missing scrolls. Others of your kind have been here, and failed. Why should you be any different?"*

*Others?* He glanced at the shuffling footprints around the chamber, some of them his and Akarat's prints, but some unfamiliar. A faint thrill of hope lifted him from his despair. Yet he knew it was impossible, knew in his heart that he was the last.

Nothing this creature said could be trusted. *The demon lies. You must not pay attention.*

*You are the last of a proud line of heroes.*

"Akarat," Cain said firmly. "I am speaking to the man inside this shell. You must fight it, my son. You must fight against the thing that has taken you."

"*Our master comes,*" the creature said, licking its bleeding lips. Its breathing rasped heavily in Akarat's chest, the smell coming from it like that of a thousand rotting corpses. "*The true lord of the Burning Hells. He will be upon you soon, and your death will be slow and painful. Perhaps he will make you a slave, forced to serve him forever. We know many others of your kind who are with him now.*" The demon grinned at him. "*Even those you know and love.*"

"Akarat. Listen to me. Do not let it win. You are in control. You hold the power within you!"

The skin on the demon's face rippled, and it hissed as if in pain. Cain held up his staff between them, and it recoiled from the light. "Release him!" Cain shouted.

The creature hissed again, and for a moment its face became Akarat's again, the young paladin blinking in bewilderment at Cain before his features twisted into something ugly, and he was gone.

"*The boy is not strong enough. And neither are you.*" The demon took a step forward until its foot touched the sword Akarat had dropped. It bent to pick up the weapon, looking at the blade shining in the blue light. Then it looked back at Cain, grinning once again. "*Shall we use this one? Small cuts, perhaps. A thousand of them.*"

Cain stumbled, fumbling in his pack again with one hand, his trembling fingers moving over the texts within, searching for something that might help him. His other hand ached where it gripped the staff, the only thing that seemed to stand between him and a slow and painful death. Akarat was lost, he knew that

now, and already he mourned for the man he would have become, while the demon raged before him.

*If it only knew that I have no power of my own, and this staff is
nothing magical at all without a spell to enchant it . . .*

Immediately he regretted thinking such a thing, but it was
too late. The demon's smile grew wider, and it took another step
forward. *"Not a real Horadrim, after all? Of course not. Your weaknesses betray the truth."*

Cain stumbled backward into the ancient chamber until he
neared its center. "Stay away!" he shouted, brandishing the staff.
The blue light contained within the globe flickered, began to
dim. The grin grew wider still, as if Akarat's twisted face would
collapse into it, a black hole that would consume all light and
everything good in the world.

*"Do you know what you have begun? The Heavens will burn, Hor-
adrim. The scourge of Diablo and his brothers will seem like days for
celebration compared to this. Our master is all-powerful, and he will
tear down the walls of Sanctuary until the ground trembles and splits.
Caldeum will burn, the archangels in the High Heavens will fall, and all
of Sanctuary will be ours. And you will be too late to stop it.*

*"So pathetic. Your savior is so close, hidden among thousands in
plain sight not three days' journey from here. Yet you know nothing, see
nothing."*

Cain fell to his knees. His hand found what he had been
searching for, and he curled his fist around the dark jewel pried
from the rune-inscribed circle on the floor.

*"Where are your angels now, old man? Where are your heroes for
you to hide behind as they ride into battle? Is this all you have? This boy
you have given to us to mask your own selfishness and pride? You are
worthless. Just like your forebear."* The demon lifted the sword in
both hands and stood over him, cackling, and Cain recoiled,
scuttling backward on his hands as he dropped his staff, the
glowing globe ticking across the floor until it came to rest a few

feet away. *"We have changed our minds. Not a thousand tiny cuts, but only one, to separate your head from your shoulders."* The demon cocked its head, as if listening. Whatever it heard made it cower like a beaten dog. When it spoke, it was not to Cain, but to someone hidden from mortal eyes, and the sound of its voice had changed to a pathetic whine. *"We thirst for blood. Why is it not time?"*

Then it spotted Cain's hand gripping the stone. Cain moved as if to hide it, but the demon made a lunge with the sword, chopping down at Cain's wrist so quickly he dropped the jewel in his haste to move away from the blow. The sword missed his flesh by inches.

*"You thought you could banish us with this?"* It picked up the stone and held it aloft, the blood-red jewel glittering in the blue light, then took another step closer. *"It holds no power without the runes and the magic to awaken it, old man."*

"I—I command you to leave this body—"

*"Silence!"* The demon raised the sword again in one hand, the jewel still clutched in the other. Cain glanced down at the stone floor. *One more step . . .*

The demon shuffled forward, hatred etched into its features, unaware that it had walked directly into Cain's trap. Quickly he spoke the words of power, read from the runes he had committed to memory, the words leaping to his lips in a suddenly clear, strong voice. The demon glanced down, surprise plain on its foul face as the circle of runes where it stood began to pulse with a fiery light and the jewel it still held came to life.

It howled in anger at what Cain had done, and along with the rage there seemed a new expression of begrudging respect. *"Trickery!"*

But Cain could take no satisfaction in that, knowing that he had sentenced Akarat to death.

The portal that Bartuc's followers had used to summon demons from the Burning Hells opened with a burst of red light. The demon screeched as the jewel clutched in its hand matched it in brilliant color, the sword clattered to the floor, and Akarat's outline disappeared, fading like the afterimage of the sun in men's eyes as they blinked against their own blindness.

"Back to the Hells with you," Cain said to the sudden emptiness as the portal snapped shut again. His entire body ached.

*Akarat, my son, forgive me.*

He climbed slowly to his feet and regained his staff. The blue glow was nearly extinguished now. The demon was gone, but so was his companion, and they had found nothing. Akarat had perished in vain.

Deckard Cain climbed the stone steps alone, squeezing his way back through the narrow passage and out again into the open, where a storm had come up over the ruins and now threatened to drench everything in sight. He carried Akarat's sword, along with a heavy heart. He had failed once again to do enough to keep those close to him from dying.

Dark clouds hovered overhead, and the wind tugged at his tunic. The light was fading swiftly.

*I must hurry.* There still might be something to salvage from this trip, and he would do anything in his power to honor Akarat's memory by finding it. Cain skirted the edge of the ruined main building, following more footprints. In the back, among the broken columns and shards of stone he found a path to what might have been a garden of some kind many years before. In the center of an open space stood the remains of a fire, along with abandoned packs and three broken walking staffs.

Cain's pulse quickened. Whatever had happened to those who had come before him had happened here; whether they had lived or died was unclear, but they had clearly brought up whatever they had found in the basement chamber and made camp before being interrupted.

Something fluttered in the wind, half buried in a drift of sand. He walked over to find a spellbook. *Vizjerei.* Demonic magic, Bartuc's work. Old enough to be from the temple. There was something important here, after all.

He scanned the sand for more. A few steps away and near a partial design drawn in the sand he found another, this one a book of Horadric prophecies.

He stood for a moment in shock. Horadric texts, here, in this place? How? The pages were torn, pieces missing, the words barely legible. Cain cradled it tenderly, with reverence, as he did all texts. They were precious to him, all of them like his children. But this one stood above the rest.

A crest of arms appeared, burned into the first of the pages like a brand. A sign of a great lineage, and a testament to the text's immense value. It appeared to have been written by Tal Rasha himself, one of the first Horadrim tasked by the archangel Tyrael to hunt down and imprison the Prime Evils.

Cain flipped through it, his heart thundering in his chest. What was still legible told of another war coming between light and dark, one that would make all others pale in comparison. *And the High Heavens shall rain down upon Sanctuary as a false leader arises from the ashes . . . the tomb of Al Cut will be revealed, and the dead shall lay waste to mankind—*

A noise made him turn. A sand wasp flew about ten feet away, its heavy abdomen and stinger hanging low as it ducked and darted across the ground, hovering near the abandoned packs. Cain remained still until it moved on, then went to see what had drawn it there.

Inside the packs was rotting food, which had surely brought the wasp, but also more texts. He set the stack gently on the ground and looked through the texts one at a time as the sky rumbled overhead, the moist wind bringing the scent of rain. They were an odd mixture of Vizjerei, Horadric, and Zakarum writings, and he could not make sense of how anyone would have gathered such a collection—or why they would have left them here.

Cain read through them, a familiar rush of excitement building as he flipped the fragile pages. As he lifted the second one from the bottom, it felt different in his hands. This text was much more recent: a reproduction of a spellbook, barely a year old by the looks of it. The workmanship was sound, the pages newly bound and transcribed. It also appeared to be from the Horadrim.

(*Look around you, at the footsteps, the missing scrolls. Others of your kind have been here, and failed . . .*)

Deckard Cain's mind raced. There had been a lot of false Horadric texts spread across Sanctuary over the years, but this one appeared to be more authentic than others he had seen. He studied it more closely, paying attention to the prose style of the words, the music of the language itself. He became aware of the energy held within it, the book seeming to vibrate at a pitch just beyond normal human perception. The more he read, the more confident he became that this was an accurate reproduction of an original text. Finding it with the other, much older volumes made this even more likely.

Who could have had access to these books? Was there some kind of organized effort to bring the mage clans' magic back to these lands?

He thought of something else the demon had said. *Your savior is so close, hidden among thousands in plain sight not three days' journey from here.* The closest place of thousands was Caldeum, the largest trade city in Kehjistan. That was also a place where a book of such quality might have been manufactured or sold. And there was something else, *someone* else, in Caldeum—someone he had been meaning to check in on for a long time. A friend from the dark days of Tristram, a responsibility he had been avoiding. This would give him a good reason.

*You must go to Caldeum.*

The voice was so strong that for a moment Cain saw Akarat standing there in plain sight, golden armor aglow, his eyes shining with an inner light.

*The fate of this world lies in the balance. You must go.*

Cain blinked, averted his eyes, and looked back again. There was nothing before him but the wind whispering across the rock, as the first, fat droplets of rain began to fall.

Deckard Cain took Akarat's sword, its weight strange and awkward in his hands. He was no fighter, and a blade like this was useless to him. He stuck it deep into the sand, leaving it standing like a small monument for others to see. Then he gathered the texts he had found into his satchel and made his way through the strengthening rain out of the Vizjerei ruins, climbing the sand dunes as quickly as his old body would allow. He thought of resting for the night, but a voice kept urging him on. There was no time to waste.

The battle for this world had begun.

# THREE

## *The City of Caldeum*

The girl, bone-thin and barely older than eight years, emerged from a rusted sewer grate as the sun touched the tops of the streaked copper domes and tall spires of the city. The world was drifting down toward night. Brown hair hung in strings across a pretty, pixie-like face streaked with dirt, bangs cut short to ease the time between already infrequent washings.

She crouched in the shadows of an alleyway. The wind shifted, and a fine mist from Caldeum's man-made waterfalls touched her face. The water thundered in the distance. She muttered something under her breath, and a young woman passing by gave her a startled look and a wide berth, clutching the folds of her peasant's dress to her waist; she had been so still among the shadows that the woman hadn't noticed her there. The girl glanced at her with little interest. She was used to others avoiding her presence, as if the very sight of her made them shiver.

What was happening nearby kept her attention. The girl watched the activity around the trade tents that had been pitched in the sand beyond the city walls. Her mother had told her not to come here, but the trade fascinated her, so many different kinds of people milling around shouting at each other—peasants with carts loaded with fabric, vegetables, and meat; city guardsmen standing watch with heavy swords and shields; merchants bargaining for lots; nobles in their silk robes; and servants trailing behind tending to their needs. Caldeum was a city full of color and heat, despite the tension that people seemed to feel lately, as if something terrible was about to happen. But she, alone and filled with a restlessness she could not understand, lived apart from them, among very deep, dark shadows of her own.

The smell of food wafted upward from the tents, and the girl's stomach rumbled just before an old man in tattered clothes stumbled into the street near her, as if appearing out of thin air. His hair was a mass of tangled, filthy curls, his beard long enough to touch his chest. He carried a cloth sack bulging with his personal belongings over his shoulder, and it was large enough to make him stagger from side to side as he went. She tensed as he weaved into traffic; surely he would be run down, but as he dropped the sack in the street and planted his feet, glaring at the carts and packbeasts, they all cursed and drove around him, parting like water around rock.

The old man mumbled to himself, but it was too quiet for her to hear the words. He rummaged in his sack for a moment and held up a bolt of cloth, the remains of a tunic. *The end of all days* was scrawled across it in blood-red letters. He pulled it over his head and held up his wrinkled, filthy hands, as if to testify.

"Beware the coming of the evil ones!" the beggar shouted, his voice as ragged as his clothing. "It begins with the fall of the mountain and the opening of the gate, and it will end with terror and death! The sky will turn black, the streets fill with blood!"

A group of boys were gathered across the street. One of them elbowed another and pointed at the old man. They laughed and went out to meet him, forming a loose circle. "Get out of the road, old man," one of them said. "You'll end up with that beard caught in someone's wheel."

The beggar's head bobbed back and forth, his gaze darting between their faces. "You are doomed. The Dark One is powerful, I tell you. He will raise a demon army! The dead will walk among us!"

The boys laughed again, rolling their eyes at each other. "You *smell* like a dead man," one said. "Maybe you're confused." Another picked up his sack, and the beggar's hands began to flutter like birds, reaching out for it as the boy tossed the sack to the side, narrowly missing a woman and her child, who scurried past, eyes averted. The beggar tried to get his belongings, but the boys closed in, forcing him back and cursing at him. As the old man reached out again, brushing their arms, one of them shoved him. He stumbled and nearly fell.

The girl could not stand it anymore; their cruelty was like watching a monstrous wave approaching from the shore. She set her small shoulders and stepped out from the shadows. "Leave him 'lone," she said.

The boys turned to stare at her. "Well, look at that," the lead boy said, sauntering over to her. He was larger than the rest, at least a foot taller than she was, and his eyes were piggish and cruel. "He's got a guardian angel, after all. Or maybe *you're* the walking dead he's going on about?"

The girl's heart beat faster as the rest of the boys left the old beggar and approached her. "What do you want with a fool like that?" Pig-Eyes said. "He your boyfriend or something?"

The girl glanced through the boys at the old man, who had gathered his sack and was wandering away from them, muttering again. The wave she had felt building had broken momentarily like water on rock, and for a moment she allowed herself some relief. But then Pig-Eyes was shoving her shoulder with a pudgy finger.

"Hey, I'm talking to you."

The others snickered, grinning at each other. The fun was

about to really begin, those grins said. Time for Pig-Eyes to do his thing.

"I don't like you," the girl said. "You're all ugly, inside here." She touched her thin chest.

Pig-Eyes narrowed his gaze, the grin fading away. "Well, you're ugly on the outside," he said. The tone of his voice had gained an edge. "I seen you before, haven't I? Leah, you are? Where's your crazy mother? Servicing the men at the tavern again, is she?"

The other boys whooped and guffawed, slapping each others' shoulders, but Pig-Eyes didn't look away from her face. "Listen, I don't like you either," he said softly. He poked her again. "Understand? Nobody does. You're a sewer rat. We should toss you in the fountain, wash off the stink from those filthy tunnels you crawl around in, but then we'd sell no tickets to the show."

The others laughed again. *Sewer rat.* She hated when they called her that. "Don't touch me," she said, and when she looked into his gaze with her own, he took a small, involuntary step back. Her eyes held a glittering darkness, a depth that made others turn away in discomfort. She did not know why, only that others found something unsettling in her, and at the strange things that sometimes happened when she was around. She was like a divining rod for bad luck, it seemed. But that would not hold this one at bay for long, especially not in front of his friends. He would try to hurt her, things would get out of control, *she* would get out of control, and she did not know what would happen then . . .

A crow *cawed* above them, circling the group and settling with a flap of black wings about twenty feet away. It cocked its head, beady eyes studying them, and hopped to where a dead rat lay in the sun. A wagon went by, the wheel dangerously close, and the crow hopped away and then back again, peering at the flattened mess of guts and fur before pecking at a long, wet strand, tearing and pulling it up off the hot dirt like a worm before tilting its head back and gulping the meat down.

Leah's stomach churned as the crow cocked its head again, its black eye staring right through her, *I see you, little one,* and she began to feel as if that eye might open up enough to swallow her whole, just like the raw, red flesh the bird was eating.

Her body trembling, she clenched her hands into tight fists, ready to fight, but the boys were distracted for a moment by the crow, and she took the opportunity to dart underneath Pig-Eyes' arm and up the darkening alley, running hard. A moment later someone gave a shout, and she could hear them coming after her, their running feet like thunder as the blood began to thud in her ears. Somewhere below them she heard the old man's hoarse voice screaming out his prophecies of the End of Days, and in her mind's eye she saw the crow staring at her as if she were next on the dinner menu.

*Something terrible is coming.*

For a moment she did not know if the voice was from the crazy beggar down the street or from her own head. A chill ran down her spine, and she shivered as she ducked into another, narrower alley between the backs of a bakery and a dress shop, swerving to avoid a drunkard fumbling at a woman's breast in the dark amid a muttered curse and more shouts from the boys. *Something terrible.* She did not know why she thought that, but it was there, all the same, flapping over her like the wings of that crow. She had heard the voice inside her head before, and it was not at all like her own. She had often wondered if everyone had these voices that spoke up every now and again, or whether she was alone in that, too.

The alley opened into a larger street with more foot traffic, and two soldiers watched her from the other side with their hands on their swords. With luck, they would spot the boys running and stop them, but she could not count on it. She swerved right, into the cool, shadowed doorway of a smoke shop, the smell wafting over her like rich, mossy earth. She knew the city well, knew that this shop ran deep and had another door in back that led to safety; the boys might know too, but they did not know what lay beneath it. By the time they figured out what she'd done, she would be gone.

As she darted through, ignoring the startled shout of the proprietor, she tried to get herself to relax. Nothing had really happened, nothing that would cause her trouble as long as her mother didn't find out.

The grate was neatly hidden by shadows on the other side of the shop. She pushed it aside and dropped soundlessly into the blackness of the sewer hole, sliding the grate back into place above her head. She knew these tunnels better than anyone, and their darkness and close walls comforted her. She had played in them for as long as she could remember. This one would lead her safely home.

*You're a sewer rat. We should toss you in the fountain, wash off the stink.* She angrily brushed away tears as she dropped to the floor and padded silently forward, her eyes already picking out dim shapes from the faint light that filtered down from the grates above. She would not let them get to her, not like this. She had endured the odd looks and jeers most of her life, feeling like she did not belong, and today was no worse than others.

But in the end, it was not the boys' taunts that stuck with her; she could not get the image of the old man out of her mind, the haunted sound of his voice, and the black-eyed crow peering at her from the gutter as it bent to feed.

Its beak tearing at dead flesh.

*Something terrible is coming.*

What that might mean she did not know, but she felt its arrival like a foul stench on the wind.

By the time Leah emerged from the sewers and reached her home, the last of the day's light was bleeding from the sky, and the air had cooled enough to make her shiver. The boys had given up the chase long ago, and she had calmed down enough to begin to question her own sense of doom. Today was like any other; the beggar was a crazy old man, nothing more.

But when she opened the door, her mother was waiting, her eyes holding that glittering edge Leah had come to know and dread. Gillian snatched her arm and yanked her inside. "Where've you been, child?" she hissed, shutting the door and throwing the bolt. She looked around as if expecting someone to jump out at them. "Playing in those damned sewer tunnels again? You're filthy. You can't go wandering around at night alone!"

"I—I'm sorry," Leah mumbled. "I was visiting . . . Jonah." This was the owner of the small shop where they got their eggs and milk; for a moment, Leah was afraid that her mother would realize that she had returned empty-handed, but Gillian didn't seem to notice. She had always been absentminded, and some in town might even say she was crazy, but her strange ways hadn't used to feel so unsettling. Lately, though, things had changed. Leah rubbed at her arm where Gillian had gripped her with fingers like iron and thought of the crow again, talons razor-sharp and clutching at raw, reddened flesh.

Gillian cocked her head, listening to something out of sight. She muttered under her breath and pulled Leah farther into the room, backing them away from the door as if waiting for someone to come through it at any moment. "They're watching," she said, suddenly dropping to her knees in front of the girl and gripping her arms forcefully with both hands. "They're *everywhere*." Her voice dropped a notch. "They want you, Leah, and if they find you, you're never coming back from that. *Never.* Understand?"

The urgency of her pleadings made her sound more pathetic than dangerous, but Leah was frightened, all the same. This was different than the boys outside, but it was no less worrisome.

The air in the room had cooled, and a charge seemed to run through them both. Leah nodded, clenching and unclenching her fists, although she didn't understand anything at all. *Who is watching? Those boys, or someone else?*

Gillian shuddered and dropped her hands as if they had been scalded. She stood up, putting a hand to her head, wincing in pain.

"Shut your mouth!" she shouted, whirling, her rage directed not at Leah but at something unseen, unheard. "She's just a girl. She doesn't mean for it to happen!"

The chill deepened. Something rattled like plates on a table. Gillian turned back to her, eyes wide and frightened. She grabbed Leah again by the arms and shook her, hard enough for the girl's teeth to snap together. "Stop that!"

"I—I didn't—"

"I don't believe them," Gillian whispered. "What they're saying. You're a good girl, Leah. Aren't you?"

Leah nodded again, looking around the shabby room with its weathered table and chairs, soot-encrusted fireplace, and threadbare rug, so worn and dirty it had lost all color. There was no help to be had here, nobody to hear her scream. Her tongue probed a raw spot where she'd bitten her cheek. She felt something building within her, as if a strange and unknown part of her had been asleep but had begun to stir, and she thought of the dreams that came to her in the middle of the night of a world that could not be real yet felt as vivid as any place she'd ever seen with her own eyes.

"The dead are restless," Gillian said. "The demons, ready for blood. They *want* it, Leah. They *bathe* in it. They—"

The lantern hanging in the kitchen flared brightly. A bowl tipped off the table and clattered to the floor, puckered green apples rolling across bare wood before coming to rest at their feet. Gillian jumped away from Leah, arms out as if warding off a blow. Then her mouth set in a hard line, and her eyes flashed with anger. She grabbed Leah again and pulled her roughly out of the room and down a short hallway to Leah's bedroom. "I won't have that happening in my house, you understand me?" she snapped. "I won't have it. You stay in here until I say so."

"Mother, please—" Leah felt tears welling up in her eyes.

"Sometimes I think you're a demon too," Gillian whispered, but her eyes were unfocused, and Leah didn't know whether she was talking to her or to someone else. Then she slammed the door, and Leah heard the bolt slide shut.

Leah rested her head against the cool wood and wiped her tears away. She could hear her mother rattling pots in the kitchen, muttering to herself, but the words were too muffled to make out. She did not know what was going to happen to her. But Gillian did not return. After a while Leah lay down on her bed, curled up on her side, and closed her eyes.

Some hours later, Leah awoke to darkness. The house was silent at first, and she did not know what had made her stir. Through her window the moon was fat and full, a bloated yellow tick hovering above the city's massive copper domes in a cloudless black sky. She had a vague memory of more unsettling dreams, monsters chasing her through wild lands full of fire and magic. Her mother had warned her about these dreams, saying she must not confuse them with what was real, but the stern voice she used had always made Leah uneasy. Perhaps Gillian was afraid of the madness that was slowly creeping up on her.

*Going crazy.* That was what was happening to her mother,

wasn't it? Hearing voices, talking about demons and blood and death. Gillian had taken an abrupt turn for the worse, and for the first time, the girl wondered what might happen to her if her mother could not take care of her anymore. She had never known her father, and Gillian refused to talk about him; for all Leah knew, she had been born without one, and no other family had ever come to visit them in Caldeum. She didn't know much of anything about where she had come from; she knew only of some distant tragedy in her mother's past that had led them many miles from where they had been, unmoored and alone.

She heard a creak from somewhere down the hall. A faint line of light under her door brightened and then faded again, as if someone was moving around out there with a lantern. She got up and passed silently to the door, pressing her ear against it. Her mother was arguing with herself in a harsh whisper that was getting louder; her creaking steps became faster as she paced back and forth. Again, Leah could feel something building both within her and without, a crackling energy that was so terrifying she could hardly breathe. She shrank away from the door as the light brightened under the crack, climbing up onto the narrow bed, clutching her knees to her chest and rocking.

Gillian shrieked in the hallway, her voice startlingly loud in the quiet house. A small, animal moan escaped Leah's mouth as the bolt was thrown back and her door swung open, crashing against the wall. Gillian stood framed by the lantern she held up, swaying slightly in her night robes, her hair a wild, ghostly aura around her head. "Come here, child," she said. When Leah did not move, her voice grew needle-sharp. "You need to *listen*. I'm talking to you." Her mother smiled, but there was no warmth in it. It was almost as if her mother wasn't there at all, as if she had fallen into a trance. "There's something important we have to do."

Leah didn't know exactly what happened next—as Gillian entered the room, the world seemed to stretch and fall away and go dim, as if someone else had taken control of Leah's senses. The next thing she knew, she was in the hallway, her mother's sweaty hand on her arm, propelling her ahead, and when the rapping came at the door, she didn't know whether it was real or inside her head.

Gillian froze halfway into the living room, a haunted look on her face. The remains of the fire crackled in the hearth as a log shifted. The lantern's flame sputtered and threw shadows that danced across the gray walls.

The rapping came again, louder this time. Gillian sighed, dropping her hand from Leah's arm, and her entire body sagged as if releasing something she'd been holding tightly inside. Whatever darkness had fallen over them had broken. "S'late," she muttered. "Who might that be?" Her eyes suddenly focused on Leah's face, her trembling shoulders. "What's wrong with you? And what are you doing out of bed? Fetch some water while I get the door."

She set the lantern down on the table and pulled her robes around her thin frame. Leah did not move, her legs rooted to the floor as her mother reached for the knob and swung the door open.

An old man stood there in a gray, hooded tunic, white hair and beard long and unkempt, a walking staff in his hand and an old, battered pack over his shoulder. For a moment she thought of the crazy old beggar in the streets, but this man was entirely different. His dress was strange, and he seemed to be carrying a heavy burden. But his features were ancient and kind, and his eyes seemed to twinkle like stars in the shadows of his face.

"Gillian," he said. "I'm sorry to call so late, but I've been traveling for days, and I didn't want to wait."

Leah's mother stood absolutely still, seeming to not even breathe for a long moment. Her hand slowly drifted to her mouth. "Deckard? Deckard Cain? Is that really you?"

The old man smiled. "I believe so, although the dust of the road is thick enough to make one question it." His gaze left her mother and settled on Leah. "It's been a long time. I wonder if I might come in?"

Gillian said nothing at first, as if struggling to find the right answer. *Let him in,* Leah thought, *please,* although she wasn't sure why. There was something about the old man, something comforting. And anything would be better than being alone with her mother now.

"Of course," Gillian said finally, stepping aside. "Forgive me. I don't know where my . . . mind is."

The old man put his hand on her shoulder. "Thank you," he said. "We have things to discuss, after all, do we not?"

She nodded, meeting his eyes, and something unspoken seemed to pass between them.

Then he stepped through, and Gillian closed the door softly behind him, shutting out the night and whatever else might be lurking out of sight.

# F⊕UR

## *Gillian's Residence, Caldeum*

Deckard Cain stepped into the shabby home, looking around at the nearly colorless walls, the chipped and scratched old table, and the filthy hearth, his heart sinking in his chest. The protective spell that Adria had placed over the house and its inhabitants had still been active, and he had found them only because he knew precisely where to look. But everything inside was too tired and worn. There was a tension in the air that was palpable.

He had come to Caldeum because of what had happened at the ruins, but he had also come to visit an old friend and fulfill a promise, and had hoped to find everything well. But Gillian was not the same woman he had left here a few years before. She had aged far more than she should have; formerly young and beautiful, with a laugh that could infect a room, she had gone puffy and soft, her hair graying and brittle as straw. Her eyes had become haunted and bruised, and an air of neglect hovered around her, as if she could barely remember to care for herself.

It was no real surprise, he thought, considering what had happened to her in Tristram. What had happened to all of them. But with guidance from his Horadric texts, he had known better how to manage the madness that threatened them, while those few others who survived the demon's carnage were left exposed, broken and lost.

"I'll get you something to drink," Gillian said, waving at the table. "Please, sit. Leah, did you fetch that water?"

Cain took the opportunity to study the girl as she moved into the tiny kitchen area and took an earthen-fired cup from a dusty shelf, dipping a ladle into a wooden barrel. She was thin, long-limbed, and coltish, as if some parts of her body had begun to outgrow others, her hair was cut short and uneven, and her nightdress was tired and gray. But she had an elegance about her, even beneath her layer of dirt, an inner thrumming of energy, and he could tell she would be a stunning woman someday.

*Like her true mother.*

This was the real reason he was here tonight. He had neglected it for far too long. He glanced back at Gillian and caught her watching Leah too. He could not tell whether her eyes reflected love, sadness, or fear.

Leah returned to him with the cup, and he took it with a smile that felt awkward and stiff. He had never been good with children—even years ago, when he'd been a much younger man and had run the one-room schoolhouse in Tristram, they had been like foreigners who spoke a different language that he had never bothered to learn.

"Thank you, young lady," he said. He took a sip of water, which was lukewarm and tasted slightly metallic, but good all the same on his parched throat. "I must say, you are quite different than I imagined you."

The girl's eyes widened slightly.

"This is . . . Uncle Deckard," Gillian said. "We knew each other in—in the town where we grew up."

"Pleased to meet you," Leah said, putting out her hand. Cain hesitated, then took it, feeling the small bones in his own, as delicate and light as a bird's wing. At the same time he felt the strength coiled within her, and he had to bite back a gasp of surprise and refrain from yanking his hand away. This was no ordinary little girl, but he could not tell what sort of magic she held, or what its purpose might be. Still, it unsettled him, the way a glimpse of movement in a dark alleyway at night would make one pause before entering the shadows.

Cain released his grip. Now was not the time for this, but he made a mental note to study the girl further when he had a moment. She intrigued him, and her true lineage made him even more curious about what sort of gift she might have been given.

Gillian put her hand on Leah's back and propelled her toward the narrow hallway. "Now, off to bed with you. We have things to talk about that would bore you to tears, and it's late."

She waited until Leah had closed the door to her room. "What are you doing here, Deckard?" she asked, returning to the table. She did not sit down and kept her hands at her waist, clenching and unclenching them as she clutched the folds of her nightdress.

"Wonderful to see you, too, Gillian."

She smiled, but it did not reach her eyes. "Forgive me. But it's been years, with no word, nothing at all. I thought you might be dead."

"I have business in Caldeum, and I wanted to check on you and Leah."

"Your business tends to be dangerous."

He nodded. "That it is. I'm searching for the makers of this." He reached into his sack and pulled out the reproduction of the Horadric text. "I found it among the ruins of a Vizjerei repository."

Gillian lifted the book in her hands, then turned it over and studied the binding. "There's a bookseller in town named Kulloom—he often drinks at the tavern where I put in my hours serving customers. He might know where a book like this was made."

"Thank you. I'll try him."

"It's important?"

"The fate of Sanctuary itself may hang in the balance."

"What do you mean?"

Cain hesitated, wondering how much to say. Most of the citizens of this city would have laughed him right through the front gates if he told them what he feared, but Gillian had seen demons with her own eyes, and seen her town destroyed by them. "I have reason to believe that the rulers of the Burning Hells, Belial and Azmodan, are preparing for an invasion. The destruction of the Worldstone has affected our world in ways we cannot understand, and has left us vulnerable. Think of Tristram, Gillian. The horrors that descended upon us. The madness we suffered . . . I cannot let that happen again! We must learn as much as we can before it's too late."

"You always got right to the point." Gillian stared at the Horadric symbol on the cover of the book, seeming to drift away. Her hands clenched harder, and the haunted look in her eyes returned. "I hear them," she said softly, as if speaking to herself. "Whispering. All the time, inside my head. They won't let me rest. They tell me terrible things. They want me to . . ." She stopped, her lip quivering.

"What is it that they tell you? What do you hear?"

Abruptly she put her fingers to her mouth, looked at Cain as if surprised by his presence, then whirled and went into the kitchen, busying herself with her back to him. "I'm a silly old woman," she said. "You must be hungry. Let me get you something."

"You're hardly old. Where is your laughter, Gillian, your love of life? Where has your spirit gone?"

She stopped, muttered something, put her hands on the counter to brace herself, and made a muffled sound, her shoulders shaking. Cain got up from the table and went to her. She turned and pressed her wet face to his chest, silent sobs wracking her body.

It broke his heart to see her like this. He stood awkwardly for a moment and put his arm around her shoulders. He could feel her tears wetting his tunic, the bones sliding under her skin. He had never been much comfort to anyone, had always been more comfortable around dusty books and scrolls than people. But it didn't seem to matter much to Gillian; after a minute her sobs began to ease, and she stood back and wiped her face with her sleeve. "I don't mean to be rude. You must think I'm crazy."

"The girl," he said. "She doesn't know?"

Gillian shook her head. "I've told her very little. It's so hard. I'm . . . afraid of her, Deckard. There are things . . . things that happen when she's around. Adria—"

"Is surely dead." Cain put up a hand as if to dismiss the thought. Gillian had raised Leah as her own, just as he had hoped she would years ago, after Leah's real mother had left her in Gillian's care. "A witch may be powerful, but her reach does not extend beyond the afterlife. And Adria did not mean harm to anyone. There's no reason to think there is anything to fear. If Leah has inherited any of her talents, she has had no training, no knowledge to shape them. She is innocent."

"Adria once frightened me. Her child frightens me more."

Cain thought of his reaction to Leah's touch, and suspected many others had had the same response. The girl would need someone to help her understand her own gifts, and suspicion and fear would only cloud the waters. "You need to resist this feeling. It comes from what happened at Tristram. Such close contact with corruption and death can affect the mind. But you are stronger than you think."

"I don't know if I'm strong *enough*," Gillian whispered, tears welling in her eyes again. "I'm just a barmaid. I'm not meant for this."

Suddenly she stiffened, cocked her head, as if listening. Cain reached out to touch her shoulder, but she moved away abruptly, making a soft, strangled sound in her throat before picking up the loaf of bread she had been preparing from the counter. "Enough of me," she said more firmly, the quaver in her voice evening out. "You will eat something, and then get some rest. You're welcome here for as long as you need to stay."

Cain took the bread she offered him and returned to the table, chewing the stale loaf while he studied Gillian's back as she continued to busy herself in the kitchen, violently attacking the dirty pots with a scrub brush as if she might wash away all that had happened like so much dirty water. His heart ached for her, and for all the people who had been left behind, forever haunted by those terrible events, driven mad by the demonic contact. Most had been killed outright; perhaps, Cain thought, they were the lucky ones. Gillian's physical deterioration surely mirrored her inner turmoil. Diablo's contamination continued, even after the Lord of Terror was long gone.

He considered whether to push her some more, and decided it might make her condition far worse. He was worried for the girl. When he had learned that Adria had left her in Gillian's care, letting her remain here had seemed to be the only option at the time; he had been concerned with much larger, more important things, and he had meant to come to Caldeum to see to her when the world had settled again. But then the battle with Baal near Harrogath had destroyed Mount Arreat, and things had taken a very dark turn. He had become distracted by the ominous signs of gathering evil (perhaps he had let it happen far more easily than he would admit), and the years had passed so quickly.

Looking around this place now, and seeing Gillian's odd behavior, he wondered if he had made the right choice.

*Deckard Cain stood before the shelves of the ancient library, the light from the small lantern barely enough to make out the spines of the Horadric texts that sat like mute witnesses to his failure. The wind howled outside like a living thing, battering itself against the thick stone walls of the cathedral; icy drafts blew like the breath of ghosts against his bare shins, and dust swirled and danced beyond the flame.*

*He took a book down from the shelf and sat at the desk, where he scanned the lines of print with a trembling finger. The more he read, the more it confirmed all that he had found in Jered Cain's writings. His heart was full of regret. It could not be. Yet it was: everything his mother had told him, all her stories of demons and angels that he had dismissed as folklore for these fifty-some years, chronicled here, in careful detail like a book of forgotten histories rather than myth.*

*His mother's voice echoed back to him through the years:* Jered is your blood, and you—you are the last of a proud line of heroes . . .

*Every logical fiber of his being cried out against this. He was not wired to accept anything he did not understand. He was a schoolteacher and a scholar, not some mad dreamer. Yet the events of the past few weeks could not be denied.*

*An unearthly moan drifted up from somewhere far below his feet, followed by the faint rattling of metal. Deckard Cain tried to convince himself that it was the wind whispering through empty chambers. He shivered and pulled his tunic tightly around his thin shoulders.*

*Tristram was in shambles. King Leoric had lost his mind and was surely under the influence of something powerful and black at heart. Cain could only guess, from what he had read, what that thing might be: Diablo himself, the Lord of Terror.*

*He took his battered journal from the pack around his waist, and bent to write. But the words would not come, not tonight.*

*Cain rubbed his aching, bleary eyes. He had been awake for more than twenty hours. The flame inside the lantern sputtered as a fresh draft of air washed over him, and a moment later he heard the sound of a door opening. He looked up to see a young woman hurrying down the aisle toward him, a heavy cloak wrapped around her sleeping gown to ward off the icy cold.*

*"Gillian," he said, finding his staff and getting to his feet. "What are you doing here?"*

*The barmaid's pretty blue eyes were wide with fear. "The soldiers have returned from Westmarch," she said. "Our army has been all but destroyed! There are so few left. And now the king's men have gathered against them."*

*"Where is Aidan? Has he come back with them?"*

*"I don't know."*

*Cain's fear deepened, swirling within him like smoke. While Captain Lachdanan and his army were battling the Westmarch forces, King Leoric had taken to executing some numbers of the townspeople he had deemed responsible for the disappearance of his son. The depth of his bloodlust knew no bounds. Dead birds falling from the sky, ghostly apparitions in the night, butchered livestock, accounts of strange and horrifying creatures wandering the edges of town—all of this paled in comparison to the corruption of men's souls, the blackness of their hearts.*

*"And where is the king?"*

*Gillian shook her head. "Nobody knows. But the men are coming here, Deckard, to the cathedral. You must leave this place!"*

*"But the texts—"*

*She put her hand on his arm, tugging at him. "We can come back later for them."*

*"I have waited too long, Gillian. So many years, absorbed by my own selfishness and small-mindedness, refusing to see the truth about the darkness that lies beyond our world—"*

*A sound like a distant scream echoed upward from the catacombs beneath their feet. Gillian recoiled, terror whitening her face as she clutched at the cloak around her shoulders. "We must go now. Please, Deckard!"*

*He nodded, returning his journal to his pack, along with the books he had been reading, and picked up the lantern, handing it to Gillian.*

The last of the Horadrim. *His mother had seen it all. How could he have been so blind?*

*Another noise reached them, this one from outside, the sound of men approaching in a hurry. Cain looked at the barmaid. "We'll leave by the rear door," he said, taking her hand. "This way."*

*There was no time. A shout came from the antechamber, and the clank of armor and heavy footsteps echoed through the soaring hall. Cain blew out his lantern, plunging them into darkness and pulling Gillian down with him, behind a row of pews. She gasped, her fingers entwining in his and clutching at him as a line of men ran into the room, the first of them turning to clash with their swords against the others who followed. Cain recognized the king's men, pursued by Lachdanan and the remains of the royal army of Khanduras. Brother against brother, battling through the very halls of the cathedral!*

*He searched for the king's eldest son but did not see him. The fight was fierce. Grunts and cries mixed with the clank of metal. A pew shattered as the leader of the king's guard was thrown backward, skewered through the throat. The horrible sound of his last gurgling breath reached Cain's ears, and the coppery smell of blood filled the room. As quickly as it had begun, it was over. The moans of the dying rose up and were silenced with the blades of the remaining soldiers.*

*"Bring a torch!"*

*Lachdanan stood in the shadows of the aisle, breathing hard. A soldier approached him. Cain and Gillian crouched lower as torch flame washed the stone walls with light and threatened to expose their presence.*

*"Where is the Black King?" Lachdanan's eyes were wild and glittering in the light.*

*"We believe he is somewhere below us, sir, in the catacombs."*

*"Lead me there. He must pay for his sins. Quickly now!"*

*The soldier nodded. The group of them set off, passing no more than ten feet from where Cain and Gillian were hiding. Lachdanan had been a friend once, but something told Cain that they must remain out of sight. When the men had passed through the chamber on their way to the stairs leading below and the cathedral had fallen back into darkness, he stood up, looking at the carnage with a terrible sense of outrage and loss. Blood pooled in the aisle, black in the shadows, while the bodies steamed in the cold.*

*Dread filled his heart. How had it come to this?*

*Gillian stifled a cry. Cain turned to find a figure looming over them, eyes like the fiery pits of Hell, the stench of death in the air.*

*Behind the figure stood a woman holding hands with a small boy, their eyes watching him with a mixture of sorrow and reproach.*

Cain awoke to darkness, momentarily confused by the power of the dream. Much of it had happened like that, except for the end; why had he imagined that figure?

And the woman and child . . .

Cain cut off the thought abruptly, aware of a distant threat looming over him like boiling thunderheads. He had made himself a bitter promise many years ago. He would not think of them. *Never again.*

He wiped his wet face with the sleeve of his tunic. Something had awakened him. He listened to the ticking of the hearth near where he lay on the floor, his old bones aching from the hard boards underneath his back.

The sound of someone moving and a soft mutter of voices came from the hall.

Cain slowly got to his feet and found his staff. There was just enough moonlight coming through the window to avoid running into things. He shuffled forward, stopped, listened again. Nothing.

Leah's door was open. He walked to the end of the hall and peered in. Gillian stood at the foot of the girl's bed, staring down at her and whispering, slowly swaying back and forth, her arms at her sides.

"Gillian," he said softly. She did not seem to hear him. Moonlight filtered through the window, falling across the bed. For a moment, a shadow seemed to pass, darkening the room, and Deckard Cain imagined huge, black wings flapping across a cloudless sky. Gillian turned abruptly and walked past him as if he weren't there, her sightless eyes open and staring, as Leah muttered wordlessly in her sleep and turned over.

Cain followed Gillian down the hall, where she entered her own room and closed the door. He stood there waiting, but nothing happened, and eventually he returned to his spot on the floor before the hearth, where he lay for a long time without sleeping, troubled thoughts crowding his head, waiting for the dawn to come.

# FIVE

## *The Black Tower*

Two hundred feet above the ground, in an empty room of blackened stone, a solitary figure watched the ruined landscape as the sun dipped below the horizon. The wind slipped through narrow, glassless window holes, rippling his robes and threatening to tear his hood from his head; he held its edges in his long, bony fingers. The man's flesh was translucent, blue veins running just beneath the skin like threaded tattoos. This was as much as he cared to expose to the air. It would not do to reveal his face, even here, even when he was alone. He no longer revealed that unless darkness shrouded him from any prying eyes.

It was a small price to pay for immortality.

The Dark One turned from the window. He thought of dead things clawing their way loose from a muddy grave. Creatures such as these rarely left his thoughts these days. He had departed the land of the living long ago, but he was not deceased; and as such, he existed between two worlds, bound to that very thing which had freed him. A strange paradox, to be sure, at least for now. But the dark magic of the ancient Vizjerei sorcerers had taught him that he could harness the same forces that controlled him, in time.

There had once been days when he had not been so utterly confident. He had been treated like scum, ignored, beaten down, and considered next to useless for most of his younger years. But with the help of the true lord of the Burning Hells and the ancient texts he had consumed voraciously as soon as he could get his hands on them, knowledge had turned to power, a revelation to him, and it had vindicated his feelings of superiority. He was a kind of royalty, if truth be told, meant for much bigger things. This was his destiny, to bring the world full circle and exorcise the plague of humanity that had come to control it.

Now it was time for another meeting.

His skin already prickling in anticipation, he swept out of the chamber and down the stairs, his robes flowing like black water across the stone. He had come to look forward to these meetings with a mixture of terror and awe, and an almost religious fervor overtook him; he trembled with it like a small child faced with death for the first time.

He remembered the moment his lord had come to him, a momentous, life-changing event, although he hadn't quite grasped its full significance then; he had been hurrying home through the streets of Kurast with a package for his master, a powerful and cruel Taan sorcerer known for beating his servants, and he had been terrified of tasting the whip for being late, when a beggar woman had gestured to him from the shadows of an alley. He had hesitated, wary of the woman's sheer bulk and her filthy state of dress, but there had been something in her eyes that compelled him.

His master would surely beat him, but that was nothing new. He was well accustomed to the lash of the whip. He had gone to her, and that moment had changed his life forever.

"Lɪft ðə vel frəm hɪz ajz," *the beggar woman whispered, her cracked, peeling fingers caressing his cheek, and her gaze held him still, paralyzed, only dimly aware of himself as the power flowed from her and through his limbs. "Awake, my son."*

*He tried to speak, but could not. Every muscle in his body had gone rigid, cords standing out in his neck. She wheezed, her smile exposing toothless gums, and whispered something else he did not understand. She pulled up his sleeve and traced the pattern of a rune into the flesh of his arm, and his skin grew hot, her touch like an iron brand. He smelled his own scorched hair and fat as it sizzled and popped. The woman's eyes consumed him, and he fell into them like pools of water.*

*Those yellow eyes shone with a light that was not human. They held a sly confidence, and they were infinitely powerful in a way that made him come unmoored, set adrift from himself.*

*The creature behind those eyes was no beggar woman. It was capable of anything.*

*He felt another world opening up to him somewhere far beneath his feet. A part of him left his body behind and tumbled down, down into the fires of Hell, down into the depths where things gibbered and screamed, terrible things that he could not face and that yet compelled him to look. There were monsters without skin, their tendons, muscle, and threaded veins exposed, and others that looked like fat, wriggling leeches. There were red-faced imps with dirty claws, and monstrous, bloated, corpse-like things that moaned and shambled on clubbed feet. Creatures with tangled, stringy beards screeched at him and swung their bloody scythes. He felt as if he were drowning, his skin split and his soul yanked from his body, tethered to something monstrous, and he shrieked soundlessly from the pain as, somewhere far above, the woman clutched his flesh to her filthy, stinking breast with hands like gigantic iron claws; and as he tried to scream once again, a monstrous form rose up before him, towering over the rest, uncurling like a serpent from the swirling smoke, its three-horned head focusing a series of unblinking yellow eyes upon him.*

*"What you have come to understand about the world you live in is a revelation," the beast said. "You are the most rare of humans: one who can see through the illusions that others have built. Sanctuary is not the place they would have you believe, but you are not blind to their games. Because of this, you have been chosen."*

*The beast went on, igniting something in him he had barely known was there. Sometime later he hurried home and took his lashes from the sorcerer for being late, and many extra for good measure, as the man's package had been lost somewhere in that alley. But he barely felt the pain, and he did not cry out. The sorcerer eventually stepped back from his bloody work, wary of the difference in his servant boy: the orphan who had been taken in from the streets was suddenly a man. The power the sorcerer had always sensed in him had begun to manifest itself.*

*From then on, the beatings ceased. He left the sorcerer's home soon after, aware that everything had changed for him after that moment in the alley. The scarred brand of the rune that had been etched into the skin of his arm confirmed this. His soul had been bound to another, a thing of nearly infinite power: something inhuman.*

*It would be another few months before he fully understood the truth. The Lord of Lies himself had chosen him.*

*He was a servant of Hell.*

The Dark One reached the bottom of the tower stairs. Below the main floor were other, hidden rooms. He opened a panel and exposed a second staircase that descended into gloom.

Moist air wafted up from below. He stood for a moment and listened. A moan echoed through the blackness, followed by the clank and rattle of metal, bringing a prickle of excitement to the back of his neck.

The staircase curved around the massive, hollow center of the tower, and his nails made scraping sounds as he let his long, skeletal fingers trail along the stone of the core, feeling the energy thrumming beneath his touch. The stone was feverishly hot and coated with a luminescent moss. As he continued down, the glow of torchlight grew brighter, and he could hear more shrieks and moans of the damned. Finally he emerged into a hallway with arched doorways leading off it on both sides. These chambers had been carefully designed, their stone floors containing a grate and piping that focused the energy of the inhabitants' suffering to the building's center shaft, down to the reservoir far below his feet.

The Dark One walked to the first doorway and entered the chamber. Torchlight flickered, making shadows move across the stone walls. He liked to sneak up on his prisoners and watch the fear in their faces as they found him standing there, his power over them absolute. This one was hanging by four chains running from the ceiling, their ends embedded in the flesh of his shoulders and upper arms, so that he looked like a puppet suspended by thick strings. The man's head was down, his long hair obscuring his face, and his body sagged against its own weight. He might have been already dead, except for the slight rise and fall of his chest. This had been a villager from Gea Kul, known for a spark of natural magical ability in days past, a raw energy that had never been cultivated. Until now.

The Dark One slipped across the stone to the man's side like a ghost. The man was relatively fresh, had not been drained as fully as some of the others. *Perfect.* He reached out with one claw-like finger and caressed the man's cheek. "Awake, my son," he whispered, thinking of the beggar woman in the alley.

The villager jerked and raised his head. Terror registered in his pale gray eyes and he tried to scramble backward, but the chains with their cruel hooks held him fast, and he screamed, his outstretched arms straining against his weight. The Dark One smiled, delighted at the man's spirit. The Lord of Lies would find this one quite suitable, indeed.

"*Lift ðə vel frəm hiz ajz*," he whispered. As he began the incantation, the torches on the wall flared up, washing the room with light, and the man's flesh glowed white-hot with the mark of the sacred rune. Others seemed to sense the building energy, and more shrieks echoed through the stone hallways like the gibbering laughter of the damned. The man on the hooks jerked once again, his head whipping back and forth and his entire body going rigid, muscles standing out in his arms and neck; then his head fell forward, eyes closed, and his breathing grew slow and deep.

The room grew darker again, the walls retreating into blackness. When he raised his head again, the man who had been inside that human shell was gone. Yellow eyes, fierce and full of intelligence, fixed themselves upon the Dark One's face. The trace of a smile touched the possessed man's lips.

Power radiated outward in waves. In spite of himself, the Dark One shivered, remembering that day many months ago in the alley, and many others since. He was once again in the presence of his lord, ruler of the Burning Hells.

He waited until Belial was prepared to speak. The Lesser Evil's voice, when it came, was deep and powerful, a rumbling of stones that came from within the human's chest and seemed to resonate everywhere.

"Our time comes quickly. You are ready."

It was a statement, not a question. Nevertheless, the Dark One nodded. "The constellations will align in less than a fortnight, as you and the texts have foretold, and we will enter the month of Ratham. Our servants have been busy. The chamber is filling quickly now."

Belial gave a slight nod. "Yet the girl remains hidden from us. Do you know what this means?"

"The spell that protects her is powerful—"

"That is no concern to us, not any longer. I have intervened."

The creature smiled. "She will be revealed soon enough. You will not fail."

Once again, it was not a question. The Dark One dropped his gaze, his throat dry; he wondered if he dared make his doubts known. All his life, people had underestimated him. He did not need any assistance. He had everything under control, and besides, the girl might not even exist.

He felt the immense power thrumming beneath his feet. He imagined the warren of chambers far below, the lost buildings and dusty rooms and those lying dormant within them, waiting for their leader to call them back to life. Waiting for *him*.

"Are you sure this is necessary? I . . . I am confident that it is only a matter of time until I find her—"

"Have I ever misled you? Have I ever given you any reason not to trust what I am saying?" The yellow eyes were lighter now, full of mirth, and the smile had grown wider, the voice more serpentine and playful. But the Dark One knew the power behind those eyes, the promise of violence. One did not question the Lord of Lies; his authority was absolute.

"Of course not, my lord."

"I have chosen you because of your rare gift of sight, and the blood that runs through your veins. The blood of kings. I have shown you this, given you proof of who you are, in spite of how you were raised by those who had no knowledge of it. But there are others who would lead our army, should you prove yourself not worthy."

"I will not let you down."

"I have no doubt of it." The yellow eyes blinked, and suddenly the Dark One was no longer in the stone room beneath the tower. The walls dissolved around him, and he was standing upon a vast, empty plain with a city in the distance, the sky above blackened by boiling clouds. The parched and cracked ground exploded upward as legions of the dead tore their way free, climbing to their feet and standing ready for his command. Beyond them rose the tower and the gigantic, looming shape of the Lord of Lies, king of the Burning Hells, a beast so monstrous and powerful it was like looking into the sun.

The vision was gone as quickly as it had come. The Dark One stood gasping and shaken by the strength of it, his entire body buzzing with excitement. It hardly seemed possible that a poor orphan child from Kurast could become the most powerful person in the world, yet that power was at his fingertips. Belial himself would walk these lands, and the Dark One would lead his army upon Caldeum and would take his rightful place as the ruler of Sanctuary, ushering in a new era in which humankind was in its proper place. He shivered, and thought of the revenge he would take upon those who had wronged him.

"Find the girl. Bring her to me before the stars begin their pull and Ratham begins, and all this will come to pass. Our call for ancient blood must occur precisely on the first day of Ratham, as the sun touches the sea. There is much to do, but you will prepare everything perfectly before then. If you do not . . ." Belial's voice trailed away for a moment, and the possessed human shell grew silent. But the eyes were still blazing with light, and they fixed upon the Dark One's face. "If you do not, I will need to use other means that you may not find so rewarding."

The Dark One climbed the stairs once again, more slowly this time. Belial had left his presence without another word, returning to the fiery depths from which he had come and leaving the villager from Gea Kul bleeding from the eyes and nose and mouth. The man would be useless now; the feeders would have to bring others, and there were few left nearby. They would have to step up their work in Kurast and extend it beyond the city's borders.

*Soon, Caldeum will be mine.* Their plans were moving quickly.

He had sensed the disruption in the balance between the Heavens and Hells for some time, but more recently he had felt other forces at work. An energy was building far across the land, led by that damned old fool Deckard Cain. Something powerful in its own right was gathering against him, mirroring an epic battle of years ago, and he did not like the feel of it.

*Find the girl.* The Dark One remained unsure what the Lord of Lies intended for her, but the prophecies in his most ancient texts told him the same thing: a young one hidden somewhere, not far from here, held the key to everything he had worked toward for so long. Yet she had been hidden by a spell that could not be broken, it seemed, no matter how hard he tried. There was powerful magic at work.

*Where is she?*

The Dark One reached the top of the tower's ritual chamber, returned to the narrow window slots, and peered out. As the last of the sun's rays sparkled on the horizon, his eyes began to tear, and he squinted against the pain. He could not tolerate such bright light. A creature of darkness, he had evolved from the sorry, ragtag bunch that had been his disciples, casting them off long ago. *Horadrim.* What a silly game they played. He had no need for them anymore. He had outgrown them; they were weak, mindless, limited in what they could do. They did not understand him or his talents, did not recognize the true power hidden within the demonic magic of ancient times. The strength to command the very creatures that haunted human nightmares. The power of the Hells themselves.

Beyond him, the land spread out like a wasteland of death and destruction. The sea lurked at its edge, flat and deadly silent, the slumbering beast of a thousand tentacles, the home of bloated corpses and watery graves.

He spoke words of power, a call that carried into the coming night, and raised his arms to the sound of wings.

A murder of crows flew by the windows, their black bodies flashing by before they whirled and returned, landing on the narrow sill and hopping inside. Thirteen of them came, all large, fattened birds, a glossy sheen to their feathers, their bright eyes studying him. "Come here," he whispered, and they hopped toward him, briefly taking wing again with a flutter before settling on his outstretched arms and shoulders. He felt their sharp talons digging into his flesh beneath the robes; relishing the pain, he looked at them all fondly as they stared back, heads cocked and waiting, their cold, bloodless stare bringing chills.

"My eyes," he said, "my ears and heart and lungs. Fly for me now, this night. Spread your wings across this land, from mountain to sea, city to desert. Search to the ends of the lands. *Find her.*"

The largest crow, the size of a dog, opened its beak and cawed, a raw, brutal sound like the screech of stones on metal. The others took up the call, and the stones echoed back their cries in a thunderous cacophony that seemed to shake the stone floor. The Dark One dropped his arms, and the birds took flight, swooping once through the chamber before slipping through the window cracks and out, into the night.

He stepped to the window and watched them go, spreading out in all directions. Soon they were invisible against the dark sky. The Dark One imagined them as an extension of him, and he watched through their eyes as the ground wheeled by far below, felt with their minds as they studied the alien landscape and the things that moved upon it, searching for their target.

She could not hide from this, not for much longer, whatever spell might surround her. He would bring her here by the first day of Ratham, one way or another. His destiny foretold it.

Sanctuary would fall, and he would rule the new world, reborn in the shape it should have always been. There would be hell to pay for anyone who stood in his way.

# SIX

## *The Bookseller's Tale*

The next day Cain awoke to the smell of freshly cooking bacon. His stomach rumbled loudly as bright sunlight filtered through arrows of dust. The end of stale bread the night before had been the last meal he had eaten in some time, and he was starving.

He rubbed his eyes and sat up. Gillian was busying herself in the tiny kitchen, humming tunelessly as the meat sizzled on a flat iron that lay across the fire.

"You're awake," she said when she spotted him. "It's about time. You slept like the dead. I sent Leah earlier to fetch us something good to eat. We don't have bacon and eggs often, but this is a special occasion. We don't get a visit from Uncle Deckard every day."

"You didn't have to go to the trouble," Cain said, getting to his feet and stretching until his back cracked. He was too old for this sleeping on the floor business. "Let me offer you something for it—"

"Nonsense." Gillian waved her hand at him. "I'm not about to be thrown out on the street, you know. I have gahah tea."

Cain nodded his thanks, and sat at the table while she brought him a steaming mug. He sipped the hot liquid slowly, embracing the warmth that spread through his limbs. Gillian's mood was so different from when he had arrived, she appeared to be a completely new person, and he wondered if she even remembered her sleepwalking incident from the night before.

"Where's the girl?"

"Oh, she likes to wander. She'll appear when the food's ready, I'm sure." Gillian set a plate full of eggs and bacon before him, and he began to eat, the hot food making him smile with pleasure in spite of the vestiges of the dream that still clung to him like spider webs.

Leah did not appear, however, and after he had eaten his fill, Cain said good-bye to Gillian and set off to find the bookseller Kulloom. She had given him directions to the man's shop, which wasn't far, but Cain's feet ached from his long walk through the sands of the Borderlands, so he stopped to wrap his blisters in gauze that he bought from a woman selling cloth on a street corner. The woman was old, with a back twisted and hunched from disease, and she would not look at him, as if frightened of his presence. He was a stranger in town and dressed differently, although with a city as large as this, that should have been a common occurrence. *Odd.* Others seemed to act the same way as he passed, avoiding his gaze, all of them walking quickly, heads down and purposeful.

The city was going through its paces, but there was no happiness here. Although the sun was shining brightly, there was a cloud over Caldeum.

Cain reached the bookseller's shop, but the thick wooden door was locked, and the shades were drawn. As he knocked, receiving no answer, a man sweeping the front steps of the grocery next door took notice. "Looking for Kulloom, are you?" The man squinted at him and hooked a callused finger over his shoulder. "Not much business for him these days. I'd wager you'll find him drowning his sorrows at the Searing Sands Inn. Probably boasting of his supposed adventures, the sot." The man cocked his head, looking Cain up and down. "You might think twice about visiting there, with that look of yours. They don't take much to your kind."

Cain thanked him for his advice, and set off in the direction the man had given him, wondering what he had meant by *your kind*. A few blocks down he found the inn, a shabby, dark place with camels and mules out front and the sound of music coming from within. When he entered, the smell of stale ale and hot food washed over him. He was surprised to find the tavern was nearly full, even at this hour. In contrast to the streets outside, there was life here. But the energy was nearly frantic, almost as if the people here had been told they were to be executed tomorrow, and they were determined to make their last day count for something.

As the people began to notice his presence, the organ music faltered, then stopped. All eyes turned to him, except for one fat man sitting near the bar, who continued to gesture wildly and speak loudly to a group of others. Eventually, even he realized the place had gone mostly silent, and he looked at Cain with indignation.

Cain set his staff on the sticky floor and stepped forward. "I'm looking for a man called Kulloom," he said, to nobody in particular.

"Well, you've found him," the man commanding an audience said, his face flushed red. "What's the meaning of this? I have important things to relate to these fine people."

"Gillian told me to seek you out. I have business to discuss."

The man's face grew guarded, and a few other patrons muttered something to one another. "He's no priest," the man said, his eyes sweeping over the room. "Look at the state of his tunic. Just a wanderer." He looked back at Cain, and gestured to an open table near the back. "Come on, then. Have a seat, and we'll talk."

Cain nodded, and made his way behind Kulloom through the

dim tavern to the table, watching the man's considerable bulk waddle side to side. "Never mind them," Kulloom said, when they had sat down and the conversation around them began to come to life again. "You look a bit like Zakarum to the uneducated masses; that's the trouble." He shook his head. "No-good snakes in the grass, those priests, and the nobles from Kurast along with them." He studied Cain's face with slightly bleary eyes, and his voice was slurred by drink. "But you're not a member of the order. I've been to many a place in my time, and I recognize a necromancer when I see one. Am I right?"

"I'm afraid not. Just a wanderer, as you said a moment ago."

"Well." Kulloom waved his chubby hand, as if it was no longer important. "And when you mention that woman's name, it's all the worse for you. People here think she's lost her mind, raving on about the end of the world. The owners don't want her waiting on the customers anymore. And that girl . . ." He shook his head. "She's bad luck. Do you know that after she came in here once, the bar nearly caught on fire? Gillian had her in the back, and a stove flared up. It took some quick thinking by yours truly to put it out."

"They are in your debt, then."

"Precisely. I can't buy my own drinks here anymore, which is half the trouble." Kulloom sighed. "It's far too easy to drink and reflect on what's past, rather than work my shop. The truth is that business has dried up. The emperor has brokered a deal with the trade consortium council, and the members of the former Kurast government have been accepted into our ranks, with Asheara and her mercenaries providing some . . . err . . . assistance. But it's all smoke and mirrors, you understand. It's only a matter of time before things begin to crumble." Kulloom's face glistened with sweat. He brought his mug to his purple lips and took a long drink of ale, wiping his face with his sleeve. Then he leaned closer across the table, lowering his voice. "It's not just here in our fair city that things are falling apart. I've traveled across Kehjistan, and by the looks of you, you have too. Perhaps you know what I mean? The world is changing, and not for the better. I've seen things . . . things that would make you tremble in those sandals of yours." Then he sat back and regarded Cain with some newfound suspicion, as if a thought had suddenly penetrated his addled brain. "How do you know Gillian? And what's your business with me, anyway?"

"I'm an old acquaintance of hers, and she recommended I speak with you. I'm interested in your expertise." Already Cain was beginning to wonder if he would get anything at all of value here; Kulloom seemed like more of a drunken lout than a clever businessman. But if he dealt in rare books, there was still a chance that Cain might glean some morsel of information that would help him. It was worth the risk, he decided, although he would have to be careful what he shared about his own intentions.

He reached into his rucksack and removed the reproduction of the Horadric text he had found at the ruins. He had covered it in cloth, and when he unwrapped it to reveal the symbol on the cover, Kulloom's eyes narrowed. "Where did you get this?" He stared at Cain. "Are you Vizjerei? The Zakarum are more tolerant of the mages these days, but it remains a dangerous place for those who don't take precautions."

"I follow the teachings of the Horadrim, and I believe this book is a copy of a genuine ancient text. I need to know where it was bound."

An odd change seemed to come over Kulloom. His eyes grew distant, his face slackening and losing some of its color. When he spoke, his voice was almost completely without inflection. "Horadrim . . . It was said by many people that they were long dead, if they existed at all. But I've heard differently."

A surge of excitement ran through Cain. He reached back into his pack and removed a nugget of gold, which he placed on the table between them. He had no Caldeum currency, so this would have to suffice. "Tell me what you know."

Kulloom did not seem to notice the gold at first. "In one of the trade tents below the city several weeks ago, I met a merchant who had come from the south, a man of considerable learning and experience. He told me of a group of men who called themselves Horadrim and were led by a sorcerer who had amassed great power. The rumor was his purposes were dark, however, and he was preparing to summon something terrible to our world. What his goal might be, the man I met did not know. But the people were afraid."

"Afraid of what?"

"Their dreams. It was said that this man, or whatever he had become, had been corrupted by a creature more powerful than anyone could understand. This creature's tendrils are already spreading across our lands, in the form of ghoulish creatures that visit the people in the darkest night and steal their souls while they dream, leaving soldiers of evil in their places. The merchant saw the fear on people's faces, and once . . . he witnessed one of these ghouls, in a trade tent some distance outside Caldeum's walls, beyond the hills. He would not speak more of it, only that it was horrible, and that it still haunted him."

Suddenly Kulloom focused on Cain. He reached out with a fat-fingered hand and grasped Cain's wrist. His flesh was clammy and slick with sweat, and as he pulled Cain closer, he seemed like a drowning man, fighting to keep his head above the rising waves.

"You must *do* something," he said. "You must find these men and stop them . . ."

The man's grip was like iron. Cain resisted the urge to yank his arm away. He waited, but Kulloom said nothing more, and as the silence lengthened and the two of them sat together like partners in a strange dance, the room began to quiet again, and heads turned their way.

Kulloom blinked. The intensity seemed to run out of him as he sat back in his seat and noticed the gold nugget for the first time. He snatched it up in a meaty fist and folded his arms across his chest, and when his gaze reached Cain's face once more, he was again bleary-eyed with drink.

"Tell me more about this group that calls itself Horadrim," Cain said. "It does not make sense that they would be in league with evil. That is not the way of the order."

"I'm sorry, but I was told nothing more." Kulloom shook his head. "Lost myself for a moment there, with my stories, but that one's got no ending. I tend to get carried away, damn the ale in this place. I've said too much, haven't I? Scared you silly."

"Not at all," Cain said. He sat back and studied the man. "You've been most helpful."

The conversations around them slowly began again, as people realized there would be no bar fight today. The barmaid brought Kulloom a fresh mug of ale, which he drank from greedily before slapping it down and waving for another. "This book." Kulloom tapped the text still lying on the table. "Cheap workmanship, not something I would sell in my shop. Most likely from Kurast. But I could get others, if that's of interest to you."

"Kurast? I thought the city was abandoned."

"It's a den of thieves, and worse." Kulloom took another swig of ale. "The people there make the patrons of this fine establishment look like angels." He gave Cain a smile, but it was not a pleasant one. "There's no rule of law in Kurast, and it attracts those who prefer to operate away from the emperor's prying eyes, so to speak. I have a contact who could make some inquiries—"

"I'd rather speak with whoever made this book in person." Cain reached back into his pack and withdrew another gold nugget, this one larger than the first. Kulloom's eyes widened as

Cain placed it on the table. "This is yours, if you can give me a name."

"If you go there, ask for Hyland. I don't know if that's the name he was born with, but that's what he goes by these days. He's what passes for leadership in that hellish place." Kulloom picked up the second gold piece and tucked it into his pocket. "In Kurast, you may find out more about this group of mages and the creatures their master commands. I have to warn you, it's no place for an old man. The people there will take what they can from you and leave you to die on the road. And there are other things . . ." He shrugged. "Things that are not so kind."

"I can take care of myself."

Kulloom studied him, his eyes growing sober. "Off with you, then," he said finally. "I have things to do."

"One last question." Cain had been thinking of the other Horadric text he had found at the ruins, the one that had appeared to be penned by Tal Rasha himself. Something nagged at him about the passages he had read—a name he did not recognize, even with his vast knowledge from years of scholarly study. "Have you ever heard of a man called Al Cut, or where his burial chamber might be?"

Kulloom shook his head. "I have not. But burial chambers are not pleasant places. Perhaps you would do well to avoid them."

Cain looked at him for another long moment, trying to sense whether anything else was hidden behind the man's hooded eyes. If there was, he could not see it. Finally Cain thanked him for his time and stood, gathering his book and staff. As he turned to go, Kulloom called back to him. "And be careful with that woman you're with," he said, as the conversations again dried up and heads turned to watch. "The girl, too. She's not right in the head."

"Aye," someone else said, a balding man with a bulbous nose and blackened teeth. "Tales of demons and black magic and dead men walking the earth. It's enough to make your hair fall out."

"You have little enough as it is," Kulloom said to him. "Now let's have another drink and forget this nonsense for now. Some of us have to go back to work soon."

Several of the patrons laughed, and one of them slapped Kulloom on the back. But the man did not smile or take his gaze from Cain's face. Cain nodded and left the man to his small group, the sound of more laughter and raised voices already drowning out Kulloom's final words, which might have been a further warning, or simply a dismissal.

Cain emerged onto the street, blinking in the bright sun. The buzz of excitement that had begun inside the tavern still consumed him. He wondered how much of what he had learned today was trustworthy, and how much was the drunken rambling of a man who couldn't find his backside with both hands. Kulloom was nothing like he had expected from what Gillian had told him, but it was clear that she was no longer welcome in that place. If so, her funds would surely be growing short. He felt a lingering sense of guilt for leaving her burdened with a child who was not her own, mixed with a growing concern for Leah. Without the proper training, whatever natural power she held could very well destroy her. But what could he possibly do? He had nothing to offer a young girl, and had little use for children in general. When he'd been a teacher in Tristram, his job had been to impart the wisdom he had learned over years of solitary study, but the children had been frustrating and difficult. They did not want to listen to his lectures, nor did they care much about the books he cherished so deeply.

And there were far more important things for him to worry about these days. Kulloom's words came back to him: *You must do something. You must find these men and stop them . . .*

Stop them from what? What did they have to do with these ghouls that were supposedly haunting Sanctuary? The rest had been left unsaid. Too much, in fact, but Cain had sensed that Kulloom knew little else and he was wasting his time trying for more. The thread he had picked up inside the tavern was tenuous at best, but the idea that a group of rogue sorcerers was operating somewhere to the south filled him with renewed purpose.

*Horadrim.*

Kulloom himself had used the word, but he had hardly seemed to realize the import. Almost in spite of himself, hope lightened Cain's steps: could it be true? Could there really be a link between these mages and the teachings of the Horadrim? It seemed impossible. All he believed, all he had read, and all the accounts he had heard over the years led him to believe the way of the order was long dead.

Surely, Kulloom and his merchant source were mistaken; these particular men, if they existed at all, were more likely simply an offshoot of a Caldeum mage group. Underneath all this was the warning Kulloom had given him, and the idea that the purpose of these men was more sinister in nature. The Horadrim had been tasked with saving Sanctuary from Diablo and his brothers, commanded by the archangel Tyrael himself. It was hard for Cain to believe that any true follower of the order would become involved in the dark arts.

One thing was clear: whether it was a dead end or not, he knew he had to find out more, and whatever answers there might be would be found in Kurast.

*The tomb of Al Cut.* Cain worried the phrase about in his mind like a small dog with a bone. He had never heard of anyone in history by that name. There must be more to the prophecy, but the ancient text had ended abruptly, as if there was more contained in a second volume. He could not make sense of it, but he had the feeling it was important. The answers might lie in the missing volume.

As Cain hurried down the street as fast as his poor feet would take him, he had the feeling he was being watched. He whirled around, expecting to find that Kulloom or others from the tavern had followed him out, perhaps bent on braining him with his own staff before taking the rest of his gold; but the street behind him was empty, save for a man and his child, who were walking with their heads down, ignoring him. The two turned a corner almost immediately and disappeared from sight.

The sun beat down on Cain's head, washing the buildings on either side with bright light. He had the strange sense that he was alone in Caldeum, that all the other people had winked out of existence at once, and he was the only one left alive in all of Sanctuary. He imagined creatures among the shadows, the city falling into ruin as undergrowth began to reclaim all that had once been human. The illusion was broken when a mule-drawn cart clattered into view and a group of men exited an inn, talking loudly and gesturing to each other.

Nobody had been watching him, yet he still felt eyes boring into his back as he turned once again to go.

# SEVEN

## *The Burning*

Cain spent the rest of the day exploring Caldeum, searching for any more information about the group of mages who called themselves Horadrim. He tried to keep his excitement from becoming too evident, but the people seemed to shy away from him, refusing to speak, and those few who did looked at him as though he had sprouted two heads when he mentioned Kurast. It was a dead city, and full of murderers and rapists, he was told, no place for an old man like him.

He grew more and more discouraged as he went, and the idea that there was any connection to the Horadrim or its teachings began to seem a desperate hope. He had been amazed by the idea of it as he left the pub, but as the hours dragged on without another lead, he became more convinced that Kulloom had been mistaken, or had simply told Cain what he wanted to hear to get the gold nugget that had been promised to him.

Later in the day he was questioned by three of the Iron Wolves, all of them large, muscled men in ornate gold-and-silver armor and carrying heavy swords. Luckily they did not go so far as to search his rucksack, or he might have been thrown in jail; it was clear that significant tension existed in Caldeum between the leaders of the mage clans, the Zakarum, and the trade consortium council, which was now a mixture of Caldeum and former Kurast nobles who had fled that city when it fell to Mephisto and his demonic forces. The people were terrified that the darkness and corruption of Kurast had spread to Caldeum, and perhaps there was something to it. Because of this, allegiances were everything, and the guards had little use for an old man who may or may not have been a rogue sorcerer.

After a warning to finish his business and move on, they let him go, and Cain returned to Gillian's home as the sun dipped below the city walls and night fell.

He did not know what to expect when he arrived. Gillian's mood that morning had been such a stark contrast with the night before, it was almost as if he had been dealing with two separate people. The house was dark and silent, and when he knocked, nobody came for so long he thought Gillian might have gone out. Just as he turned to go, the door opened, and he found her standing in the shadows, her face gray and lifeless.

"I spoke to your friend Kulloom," he said after he had entered and set his staff down. "He's an interesting man."

Cain smelled something familiar on the air that he could not place. The smell turned his stomach. Gillian had swung the door closed, but had not otherwise moved. "He's not my friend," she said. "I wasn't entirely truthful with you, Deckard. I don't . . . work at that tavern anymore." She glanced to the right and muttered something under her breath, as if speaking to someone else, although the room was empty.

"I see. How are you going to eat?"

"I—I make do."

Gillian's voice was strained. Cain went to light the lantern on the table, cutting through some of the gloom. Gillian shrank away from it as if the flame might leap out and scald her. Her gaze darted left and right, scanning every corner of the room.

Her face was shiny, her eyes ringed with dark circles, and her mouth continued to move as if she were about to speak, but she said nothing.

Judging from the state of the house, she could not have much money left, and that, along with the stress of taking care of a child, may have been more than she could bear. What had she said to him last night?

*Whispering. All the time, inside my head . . . they won't let me rest. They tell me terrible things.*

Close contact with demons often drove a person mad, and it could have an effect years later, like ripples growing in a pond.

Gillian refused to look at him. One hand was behind her back.

"What do you have there?" he asked, keeping his tone casual, although his sense of alarm was growing.

"Nothing." She took a step back and shook her head.

"Let me see it, Gillian."

She shook her head again, holding her other hand out, as if to stop him. Her back was against the door now, and he caught a flash of something shiny as she shifted her body. She seemed to be fighting a great inner battle. Her face crumpled, her lip trembling. A tear slid its way down one cheek; then she shook her head again, and abruptly her expression changed, growing hard and angry. "No. *No.* You leave this house right now, Deckard. You're no longer welcome."

"I think you should sit down. Let me get you some tea."

"I don't want any tea! You would probably enchant it to keep me quiet. Isn't that what you do? Your kind likes to bury things in the past and keep them there. Like what happened to you in Tristram."

"You don't know what you're saying."

Gillian's expression changed again. Her voice grew lilting, almost playful: "I grew up with him, don't you remember? Until he disappeared—"

"Enough!" Cain shouted. "Do not speak of that." His rage and self-loathing boiled to the surface, and he made a move toward her. Gillian brought her hand out from behind her back.

She held a large knife, its edge stained red.

Now he knew what he had smelled when he entered the house: the coppery scent of blood.

"I was cutting meat," she said. "For our dinner. Chopping it up."

"Where's the girl?"

"She's sleeping. They told me I must not disturb her." Gillian suddenly smiled, and it was a wide and predatory smile, like a snake about to swallow a mouse. Her eyes went glassy and rolled back into her head, showing the whites.

The room seemed to revolve around Deckard Cain, walls bowing like giant lungs taking in a breath. The child! He had left another innocent one alone and in danger, focused on his own pursuits while blood was spilled. He cursed himself for his blindness and stupidity, his uselessness in reading the signs that had presented themselves plainly to him yesterday; Gillian was sick, quite possibly dangerously so, and he had ignored the warning signs. Just as he had always done.

His past tried to force its way back in, nearly overwhelming him. This time, he must act before it was too late.

*Your kind likes to bury things in the past and keep them there.*

Cain grabbed the lantern and limped to the hallway as fast as he could, light bouncing against the floor and ceiling and sending dancing shadows across his sight. Leah's door had a latch on the outside, but it was halfway open. He entered the room, his heart racing, and stopped short. The lantern revealed an ordinary scene, the girl curled on her side on the narrow bed, her face smooth and peaceful. There was no blood, and she was breathing regularly.

He gave a great sigh of relief. Gillian had been cutting meat for their meal: that was all. There was nothing to worry about; Leah was fine.

That might be so. But it did not explain Gillian's odd behavior, and it did not change the fact that they were clearly on the edge of losing everything, with money running low and tension in the home rising quickly. It did not explain the voices in Gillian's head, or the fear she had for Leah.

*Like what happened to you in Tristram . . .* Cain heard a noise from behind him, and he turned to see Gillian enter the bedroom, the knife in her hand.

She did not appear to see him. As she approached the bed, the temperature of the air in the room seemed to drop. Leah sat up, eyes still closed as if asleep, and as Gillian raised the knife, a crackling energy leapt between them, and Gillian was thrown violently into the wall by some invisible force that reached out a giant hand and swept her aside.

Cain recoiled in shock. He had seen nothing, and there had been little warning, but some kind of strange magic was at work. Leah was like a puppet with its strings being pulled, her head weaving back and forth in a strange, hypnotic dance. He thought again of the touch of her hand, the feeling of power coiled within her, a strange magic that threatened to burst free, with unknown consequences.

*What is this?*

Gillian stood up, going at the bed again. Leah's eyes opened, and she screamed in fear, shrinking back as the knife was torn from Gillian's hand by that same invisible force, clattering onto the floor.

"Evil ones!" Gillian shouted, spittle spraying from her mouth as her eyes rolled wildly. She kicked and scratched at something that seemed to hold her in place. "Child of the witch! Your black ways will not save you much longer! The dead are coming for you!"

Fully awake now, Leah seemed powerless to stop whatever was happening, as if her own body was beyond her control. Her frantic gaze went from Cain's face to Gillian's and back again.

Cain had to end this quickly, before it was too late.

He set the lamp down, reached into his pack, and removed a vial filled with a white powder of Torajan jungle tree root and bone mixed by a priest of Rathma. He uncorked the vial, poured the powder into his palm, and blew it into Leah's face.

The girl sighed, her eyes rolled back into her head, and she slumped back onto the bed, unconscious.

Quickly Cain turned toward Gillian, who had been released from whatever had been holding her and was going for the knife on the floor. He threw the remains of the powder in her direction, and as it drifted over her, she dropped like a stone, her legs buckling loosely as her head hit the wall with a heavy thud.

The house was suddenly silent as the energy left the room all at once. Cain checked Gillian's pulse where she lay and found it hammering at an unbelievable speed, her breath coming in fast, shallow gasps. His guts crawled. The necromancer's powder was a gateway to a plane between the living and the dead—not enough and it would cause visions and confusion in people who remained conscious, but too much could be far more dangerous, sending people to a place from which they might never return. He had not been able to measure the amount he had used, but there was no way to change that now.

He went to the bed and checked Leah, who was sleeping soundly, her pulse steady, her face calm, almost angelic. An unexpected surge of emotion washed over him: this little girl was in the grip of something she could not control or understand. She did not know her own history and had just awakened to the woman she thought was her mother attacking her with a knife. Whatever was happening was not her doing, and she was both confused and terrified.

He had to find a better way to protect her. He had to *help* her, somehow. But he was no hero: he had proven that time and time again, and what could he do with a small child like this?

He was an old man with enough problems of his own. If he did not find the key to stopping the evil that was coming to Sanctuary, none of this would matter, and they would all be dead, or worse.

Leah's pulse remained strong. Cain managed to get his hands under Gillian's arms, but carrying her was nearly impossible. His knees and back screamed at him until he finally gave up. Leaving her where she lay, he picked up Leah and her clothes and shoes and carried her through the gloom to the front room, where he set her as gently as he could on the rug before the fireplace. He lit a second lantern from the embers still glowing in the fireplace, washing the small room with light and banishing the shadows that seemed to pool around them. Leah did not stir.

Back in the bedroom, Gillian's breathing had eased, and her heart had slowed its frantic pace. Cain managed to get her off the floor and onto Leah's bed. Then he closed the door and threw the latch.

Satisfied for now, he took the knife and went back to Leah, going over in his mind what had just happened. The girl's power seemed to be defensive, reacting only when she was threatened, but it was stronger than a simple spell. He had never seen anything quite like it before. Leah's real mother had been a powerful witch, and it was possible she had passed her abilities to her daughter. But witches were not mages. Trained sorcerers were able to control the elements in similar ways, harnessing their power to influence the physical realm, but it took years of training to control such things. For a small girl like this to do so—and to do it without a conscious knowledge of the craft—was shocking. And potentially very dangerous.

There must be someone who could provide better counsel. Almost in spite of himself, Cain thought of the mages Kulloom had mentioned. If they were studying the ways of the Horadrim, perhaps they would be able to help. True Horadrim would understand her gifts and be able to guide her through the stormy waters she would enter as she grew to adulthood.

*They may not even exist,* his own mind insisted. *But you, old man, are just a scholar playing at these things. You are no mentor. Without them, what hope do you have?*

The smell of blood was still thick in the air. He looked into the kitchen and found the carcass of a large rat. It had been decapitated and partially disemboweled, as if Gillian had been preparing it for their meal.

Too exhausted to be disgusted at the thought, he swept the remains into a refuse barrel and sat down in the chair, watching Leah's sleeping form. The powder would keep her under for at least another couple of hours, but he would have to decide what to do with her and Gillian before then. This situation could not remain the way it had been, yet he could not think of a remedy.

The burden of this new responsibility bore down on him like a heavy weight, and his dream from the night before drifted back to him: hiding in the shadows of the Zakarum cathedral with Gillian, and turning to find a monstrous figure looming over them, the other woman and child close behind. He'd imagined a look of reproach in their eyes, an accusation that he had tried to bury for nearly fifty years: *Why couldn't you save us?*

That was not how it had really happened. There had been no hulking figure, no unsettlingly familiar woman and child. King Leoric had been slain by Lachdanan, but things had only worsened after that. Lachdanan had been cursed, and the townspeople began to disappear. The madness creeping through their little town and the strange sounds and glimpses of demonic creatures had sent many of the people who were left fleeing, and brought adventurers from across the land, looking to become heroes or intending to pillage the riches they had heard were hidden under the ancient Horadric building.

One by one, in spite of Cain's warnings, these wanderers had descended into the depths of the catacombs, and their screams had echoed back through the dark corridors as they had perished against the black hordes of Diablo.

Cain had been wracked for so long by guilt over his lack of faith, his insistence on turning away from his own mother's teachings and the ways of the Horadrim. He had read obsessively through the early morning hours, poring over every shred of information he could find and joining others at the Tavern of the Rising Sun to recount the histories. But he was too old and frail to have been able to go himself to face the demon hordes, and he had not been able to make the others understand what they were up against until it was too late.

More warriors had come, some of them more impressive than others. But everything had seemed hopeless until the king's oldest son had returned from the disastrous attack on Westmarch: Aidan, who had left seeming like little more than a spoiled child, had come back an accomplished young man. Cain had barely recognized him, and it had swiftly become a measure of respect for Cain to refer to Aiden as simply "the hero." Cain had explained what he had learned from Jered's texts and those he had found in the cathedral, trying to warn Aidan about what he would find in the catacombs below the old structure.

But nothing could have prepared the young man for the horror of what was to come.

*The corridors of the inn were dark and empty, whatever ghosts that lived here now silent and still. Cain found Aidan sitting on the edge of the bed, his head cradled in his hands. He was dressed in full armor, his heavy sword at his side.*

As the old man entered, Aidan looked up, and for a single moment Cain saw beneath the young man's carefully constructed shell: a mixture of anguish and white-hot rage twisted his handsome features.

"My father is dead," he said, "my brother missing. The entire town is in shambles. How can you tell me to wait?"

"I did not mean to make light of your loss," Cain said, as gently as he could. "But before you go down there, you must better understand what you are facing—"

"I understand enough." The young man stood and took up his sword, running it into its sheath. He was calm once again. "The demon responsible for this abomination must be sent back to the Burning Hells. You've said so yourself." He crossed the room and put his hand on Cain's shoulder. "I am not the scared boy you once knew, my friend. I have studied and trained with the best teachers in Kurast. I have fought the brave soldiers of Westmarch. I will face the demonspawn, and I will strike them down one by one until I find the source and let him taste the edge of my blade."

"The depths of these catacombs will be overrun by legions of demons, lesser ones and those more powerful," Cain said. "Lazarus has led many of the people to their deaths. There will be . . . those you know, those you have loved, back from the dead and horribly changed. They may eat human flesh, desecrate the bodies of those in their path. Your father may be one of them."

Aidan's eyes grew dark, flashing with anger. "Lazarus is a traitor, and I will have his head before I am finished. I will do whatever it takes to drive these hellish forces from Sanctuary."

"And your brother, Albrecht." Cain placed his own hand over the hero's own, interrupting him. He needed to make the young man see the truth, before it was too late. "What will you do, should you have to face him? He may have suffered an even more terrible fate. It is possible he is corrupted—"

"Then I will strike him down, too. It is my duty to end his suffering."

"At least allow others to accompany you. There is a rogue from the

Sisterhood of the Sightless Eye who is of sound spirit, and a Vizjerei sorcerer—"

A horrible, wrenching scream split the night. Aidan rushed to the small window, then ran from the room. Cain followed as fast as he could manage, his old legs aching as he descended the stairs and emerged to find Aidan kneeling over a wounded woman, another form standing nearby with a pitchfork drenched in blood. It was Farnham, who had followed Lazarus into the catacombs and returned unable to speak of what had happened. After bouts of drinking, he had tried several times to return to the depths, and it appeared he had finally succeeded, only to return again to the surface, bringing someone along with him.

"Help her!" Farnham pleaded helplessly. He looked around in a near panic. "Where is the healer, Pepin?" His arms were covered in what appeared to be bite marks, and his scalp had been torn, a flap of skin and hair hanging by his ear. He did not seem to notice his own wounds, but remained fixated on the woman.

Cain moved closer. The woman's pretty face had been split from cheek to jaw. For a moment he thought it was Gillian, but this one's figure was slimmer, more girlish. Farnham's daughter, no more than sixteen. There were other wounds to her torso, gaping slashes as if from a cleaver. Aidan had put his hand on her face, trying to hold the flesh there together, but she twisted her head and moaned, and his fingers slipped in the blood.

Abruptly her body convulsed upward, spine arching as she began to shake. The skin of her face slid away, exposing the bone of her jaw, and fresh blood flowed down her neck. Aidan tried to hold her still again as Farnham rushed forward and Cain stepped in front of him.

"What happened," he said, "in the tombs? You must tell me."

Farnham shook his head. Drops of blood spattered Cain's face. "They followed Lazarus to their doom, along with the other fools. I went down again and found my daughter alive. The rest are dead. They're all dead. Ah, the earth is cursed; the creatures down there are abominations!"

"Who did this to you?"

"The Butcher and his blade," Farnham said. "He slaughtered most of the people himself. I faced him again, but we managed to hide until we could escape. I've seen his killing room, filled with bodies and surrounded by those who still walk upright. But they are not human, Deckard." Farnham's bloody fingers clutched at Cain's tunic, leaving streaks of red. "They . . . bit me."

The girl on the ground made a gurgling, choking sound. Farnham cried out and left Cain to kneel at her side, holding her hand. Aidan stood up, his eyes telling the story: she was lost.

Cain took him aside. "She may rise again, after her soul departs," he said quietly. "I will get Farnham away from here. You must do what is necessary to end her suffering."

Aidan nodded. "And then I am going down into those tombs to end this," he said. "The terror must stop now."

An unearthly howl rose up from the direction of the cathedral, echoing across the dark, empty landscape and sending chills down Cain's spine. The howl was followed by a shuddering thud, and the chittering laughter of the damned.

Something moved in the shadows of the woods, something large and inhuman.

Cain looked around at the abandoned town, the only home he had ever known. His own house was only a few steps from here, the same home he had grown up in with his mother, and where she had told him her stories of Jered Cain, Tal Rasha, and the Horadrim, heroes who had battled the Prime Evils to the end.

His destiny, unfulfilled. So many had died because he had refused to listen, had ignored his mother's warnings and the books that had lain gathering dust while he pretended to pursue more intellectual pursuits. He had not believed in such things as demons, but their time had come, nevertheless. The weight of his guilt was crushing.

I have let you down, he thought. I have let you all down, and now there will be hell to pay.

The smell of smoke drifted over him. The town was burning . . .

Deckard Cain awoke with a start, the image of the dying girl still fresh in his mind. He had fallen asleep in his chair, watching over Leah; he could see her in the flickering light from the lantern, still lying motionless on the rug near the hearth.

Something was wrong. The lantern's wick had gone out. But the smoke and the light of the flames from the dream still lingered.

*Tristram didn't burn. Not then.*

Alarmed, he snapped more fully awake. The flickering light came from the hallway.

Cain stood up and moved as quickly as he could manage. Smoke was pouring from around the door to Leah's bedroom, flames licking the dry wood like demon tongues. Already he could feel the heat on his skin. He muttered the words to release the spell he had set on the door, then edged closer, trying to reach the handle. The heat was too strong to get close enough.

He had left the other lantern burning inside the room. Somehow, it had set fire to the wood. And now Gillian was trapped.

"Gillian!" he shouted. There was no answer from within.

Smoke swirled around his head, entering his lungs and making him cough. The taste was bitter on his lips. He tried to cover his face with his sleeve, but it didn't help, and he felt himself growing light-headed.

"What's happening?"

Leah stood behind him, her little face white, eyes wide with fear. She had dressed and put on her shoes, and her voice held a hint of barely restrained panic.

"The house has caught fire," Cain said. "We're in terrible danger."

"But my mother—"

"She is beyond our help," he said. "The heat is too strong for me to enter the room. We must go now."

Leah shook her head, her hands clenched at her sides. "No! We can't leave her!"

"There's no time to waste, Leah. Don't be foolish." Cain went to her and tried to direct her back to the front room, but she stood as solid as a rock. He felt the need to do something, calm her in some way in order to get her outside, but he didn't know how. He was used to giving advice to men who were going into battle, men who were logical, reasonable, who understood something of the risks and could make a decision based on facts. What did you say to a child in this situation? *Gillian is likely dead, and we will be too if we do not act quickly?* How did you deal with such a horror?

A rumbling noise shook the house, and something shattered in the kitchen. Leah had squeezed her eyes shut, her body beginning to tremble. Cain felt the same strange drop in temperature he had experienced earlier in the girl's room, when Gillian had come at her with a knife, and a charge in the air like an invisible presence prickled his skin. Wood popped and groaned all around them, and a great whooshing noise came from the closed bedroom.

Something else shattered from the direction of the fireplace, and almost immediately Cain saw the reddish light of flames dancing across the hallway walls. He rushed to the other room and found the second lantern had fallen to the floor, splashing the nearly dead embers of the fire with fuel, which had ignited. A line of flames ran across the floorboards to the table.

If they did not hurry, they would be cut off from the front door.

Cain returned to the girl. She was still standing rigidly where he'd left her, eyes closed, hands clenched. Her skin was shiny with sweat. He got the feeling she wasn't really there anymore, as if something had swept in and carried her away, leaving her body behind.

Had she done that, knocking over the lantern? What was happening to her?

As he took her by the shoulders, he had the chance to wonder for just a moment whether it was a good idea to touch her before the shock hit him like a monstrous wave of fire, shooting up through his arms and throwing him backward. He caught a glimpse of Leah's eyes opening, that same confused, frightened look in them that he'd seen when Gillian had attacked her in her room, and at the same time he felt something else across a vast ocean of space. A presence, Cain thought, that was not purely human, soaring overhead with huge, black wings, sensing them somewhere close, but not quite finding them.

Then he hit the wall, the shock running up through him like a thousand ants biting his skin. Somehow he managed to keep his feet, the familiar pain in his back returning tenfold. Leah shrank from him, shaking her head, her hands up and waving as if she could push away everything that was happening to her.

It was all too much for her to bear. Her eyes rolled up into her head, and she slumped to the floor, unconscious.

Whatever strange energy that had possessed her was gone now, and Cain managed to pick her up and put her over his shoulder. He returned to the front room and found his staff and rucksack in the thickening smoke, the weight of Leah's body making him stumble and nearly fall as he picked them up. Relief washed over him after he had his books and artifacts, but it was short-lived.

The flames were growing quickly, the heat getting fierce. Orange fire began to run up the walls to the ceiling. Cain could not seem to find the way out. Things appeared to fall away from him, the room growing impossibly long, and he thought of a bird's gaze darting back and forth as it looked for a worm: a black crow the size of the city, spreading its wings to block out the sun.

As Cain stumbled again, nearly overcome, the door to the

house crashed open, breaking the spell and letting in cool, fresh air. The black, flapping wings faded away as a giant bearded man with his arm covering his nose and mouth fumbled through the smoke toward them.

He grabbed Cain and half-dragged him and the still-unconscious Leah toward the open door and into the night.

# EIGHT

## *One for the Madhouse*

Outside the small home, a crowd had gathered. Men were passing buckets of water down a line, trying to douse the flames that had begun to spread through the windows to the roof before they could jump to other houses next door. Other people simply stood and watched, shuffling from foot to foot, muttering to each other and pointing.

The man who had pulled them to safety introduced himself as James, a blacksmith who lived a few doors down. Cain thanked him for his help. "Smelled the smoke," he said. "Lucky for you, I don't sleep much." He gestured toward Leah. "You mind if I take her off your hands and have a look?"

"I'd be grateful."

James took Leah from Cain's shoulder as if she weighed nothing at all, putting her gently on the ground. He opened her eyelids, listened to her breathing, and stepped back. "She's not burned; nothing else seems wrong with her."

"It wasn't the fire," Cain said. "I'm afraid she suffers from hysteria. The stress was too much for her."

James nodded. "I've got a daughter about her age," he said. "Lives with her mother across town. We don't see each other much." He shook his head. "Her mum and me, we weren't good for each other, and that's the truth. Now, this one," he said, pointing at Leah, "I never took to what people said about her or her mother. Sometimes people who stick to themselves get accused of being things they aren't, and that's a shame."

*Gillian.* In the madness of the fire, Cain had nearly forgotten about her. He looked at the small house, where the townspeople continued to work frantically with buckets of water and seemed to have gotten the blaze under control. But the windows were black with soot, and smoke still drifted from the roof. She could not possibly have survived it.

He was nearly overcome with a sudden weariness, and desperately wanted to find a place to sit down and rest his aching bones. But he knew better. More of the townspeople were staring at them and whispering. It would not be long before the rumors spread. He was a stranger, and they already seemed suspicious of him. That, combined with his recent arrival at Gillian's home, would make them wonder what had really happened tonight.

For some reason he thought again of that winged creature searching the wastelands and beyond, looking for him even among the blackened and smoking bones of the house, and he wondered if the presence he had felt as the fire had closed in had been real, or only imagined.

A commotion came from somewhere behind the building. Cain heard a woman's voice, ragged and shouting. He asked James to stay with Leah for a moment, and hobbled toward the sound with his staff, his heart in his throat.

As he reached the corner of the house, a small crowd of people met him there, two large guards holding a struggling woman by the arms. Cain stopped short. It was Gillian, her nightdress torn and black with soot, her graying hair loose and tangled around her shoulders. She looked like she had lost her mind, he thought, and that was probably not far from the truth.

"Caught her down the street, trying to run," one of the guards said to those who had formed a circle around the new group. "Crawled out the window in back, says she started the fire—"

*"Burn in Hell!"* Gillian shrieked, spittle flying from crusted lips. "I did it; yes, I did. To burn away the sin, rid us of the evil here. Blind fools, all of you! The end of the world is coming! The skies will turn black, and the earth will vomit up abominations!" She fought the guards holding her, twisting in their grip and trying to claw at them like a howling cat. The guards held on with both hands, but even at nearly twice her size they were nearly yanked to the ground.

"Hold her, damn it," one of the other men said. He was clearly in charge, a petty nobleman of some kind, still in his sleeping robes and far from home. His face was puffy, and he looked cross. Cain wondered if he had been pulled out of bed himself. *Pardon the interruption.* The man walked over to Cain and poked him in the chest. "Who are you?"

"Only a simple wanderer," Cain said. "I knew this woman many years ago, in a town called Tristram. I sought her out for shelter when I reached Caldeum."

"You're no wanderer," the man said, glancing at Cain's staff and rucksack, his eyes narrowing. "Tristram? That's the place that was abandoned a few years back after Leoric went mad. Lots of stories there—none of them made any sense. But I don't trust a soul from that place. Beggars and thieves, all of you."

"He's a demon from the depths of Hell," Gillian hissed. "Don't be fooled." She gave a strong yank of her arms that nearly freed her before the guards gripped her again. She stopped and looked into the distance, as if listening, and then smiled, exposing her teeth once again like a predator about to pounce. "We are all tainted. We are born from demons; our souls are black from their stink. I can smell them. And they will return to claim us."

The nobleman ignored Gillian's words, although the rest of the smaller crowd shuffled uneasily on their feet and murmured. "What's wrong with her?" someone shouted. The nobleman put up his hand to quiet them.

"This woman here," he said, jerking a thumb at her, "she's been trouble for this city. Her daughter too. Started a fire once before, at a pub. They're strange ones; people don't like to be around them. This blaze is under control now, but the next time we may not be so lucky. We can't leave her and her daughter here alone."

"She faced a terrible tragedy in our hometown," Cain said. "Many lives were lost there, and her spirit and mind were broken. I ask you to have pity on her."

"She could have burned down the whole neighborhood," a woman said, clutching her shawl around her bony shoulders. She was older, her face sunken, dark circles around her eyes. Her voice was frail and trembling. "And the girl's a witch. Everyone says so."

Cain looked around at the faces staring at him. The commotion and Gillian's raving had attracted an even larger crowd; more had gathered quickly from the street, and he began to be concerned that they'd get violent. They were frightened, and Gillian's lunatic actions were making things worse.

"Ask him about his own secrets," Gillian said quietly, her voice now filled with a soft cunning. The predatory smile had not left her face. "Ask him why those closest to him left him alone. Why they *disappeared*."

"Gillian," Cain began, stepping forward, "you must stop this nonsense—"

She lunged at him so quickly the guards holding her nearly lost control. "*Horadrim*. It means nothing, not anymore. Evil sorcerer! I trusted you, but you are a vessel for *him* just like the rest. *You* know what's coming for us, don't you? Fire and blood and the dead clawing their way from the ground, the way they did in Tristram. The earth will split, and hell will spew forth! You know it to be true! You have *seen* it, as I have!"

More mutters mixed with uneasy laughter rose from the crowd, cries about Gillian's madness growing as the villagers condemned her state of mind. Clearly, she had lost control, people said. It was time to put her away for good. Gillian's head whipped from side to side, and the rest of those near her shrank back, as if the power of her gaze would contaminate them.

"I hear them whispering; they tell me things, terrible things, about Adria and her daughter. She is cursed!"

Cain took another step, close enough to touch her. When he reached out to her shoulder, she froze, trembling. Her skin felt hot enough to scald him.

Abruptly her eyes filled with tears as she sagged between the arms of the guards, and the Gillian he had known so long ago seemed to surface for a moment. "I'm . . . sorry," she whispered. "I am lost and confused. They . . . they told me the child must die. I had to do it. I could not stop them anymore. Help me, Deckard, *please*. Make them stop."

"Hush now," he said quietly, squeezing Gillian's shoulder and releasing it. Then he turned back to the nobleman. "What would you have me do?"

"There's a madhouse in the north end of the city," the nobleman said. "It may be appropriate, in this case. We cannot have her among the public. Many people are worried enough about their own lives, and her screaming about the end of the world only makes things worse."

The nobleman had folded his arms across his chest and seemed ready to march them both off to the gallows as an alternative. The crowd murmured, many heads nodding in agreement. Cain looked around again at the faces surrounding them, all of them openly hostile and suspicious. A great sadness filled him, a sense of the loss of one of the few people who remained from his life many years before. Gillian needed more care than he alone could give. Her encounters with demons had corrupted her mind and soul, perhaps forever; she may well still be possessed by them. She had seen things that nobody else here in the crowd could have possibly understood, had faced down her own demons and lived to tell about it. People had been ripped limb from limb in front of her, babies eaten by the ravenous undead, heads impaled upon stakes by gibbering imps who had bathed in the townspeople's blood. Yet the strength within her, the nobility of her inner battle, would remain lost on the people around her now. Only Cain knew the truth: she was more of a hero than any of them could ever dream of becoming. The great tragedy that followed her like a black, looming cloud would finally be her undoing.

Cain wiped a tear from his eye. There was nothing more he could do for her. He still sensed the anger and fear in the crowd, and the danger of real violence was growing. But he had promised Adria years ago that Leah would remain safe. He could not abandon that promise now.

He gave the nobleman a short nod. "I will keep the girl," he said. "I know of relatives who will take her in."

"You will leave the city immediately?"

"At first light."

The nobleman seemed to consider this for a moment. If he doubted Cain's story, it was too much trouble for him to admit it. Finally he nodded. "Be gone with you both, then," he said. "The fire is out, and these fine citizens need to return to their beds." He turned to the crowd. "Go home, everyone."

"No." Gillian began to writhe and kick again, and her shouting filled the night air. "How could you? Deckard!" The two men dragged her away from the rest of them as she began to fight harder. "You will see!" she screamed. "You have been blind, but you will all see soon enough! Caldeum will be filled with Hell itself, and you will wish I had burned it to the ground!"

As they reached the street corner, Cain heard one of them grunt and curse as Gillian landed a blow, and suddenly she was free. Bedlam washed over the crowd as she rushed back toward Cain, her hands raised above her head and her fingers curled like claws, face blackened with soot, her eyes wild. She looked like a true madwoman, and men and women shrank away as she appeared to be ready to murder them all.

But as she reached him, time seemed to stop as she sank against his body and clutched him close, her breath hot against his ear. "Go to Kurast," she whispered. "They are waiting for you there, Deckard. Your brothers. Take Leah and go, please, and search for Al Cut! It is our only chance."

Before he had the chance to react or say a word, the guards were upon her. They yanked her brutally to the ground, turning her on her face and pulling her arms behind her until she shrieked in pain. "Wait!" Cain shouted, but they ignored him, pulling Gillian to her feet again and dragging her away. He stepped forward to follow, but the nobleman grabbed his arm, and the crowd closed in again, their voices raised in anger and fear.

The guards turned the corner, disappearing from sight. Then he heard a muffled thud, and the screaming ceased. Cain ached for Gillian to the very core. The Caldeum madhouse awaited her, full of the worst cases of the insane and the damned, those who were locked up and harnessed, chained to the walls, their voices ragged from shouting. They were drugged and beaten, and he had heard that some doctors there still practiced the barbaric rituals of years before, drilling holes in skulls to release pressure and dull the spirits of those who could not rest.

His heart breaking, the old man almost went after them again, but he knew he could not. There were far larger things at stake, and no matter how he felt about Gillian, he could not allow her situation to distract him.

What had her last words meant? *They are waiting for you there, Deckard. Your brothers.* And what about the rest of it? She had mentioned Al Cut. Had he said something to her about that name when he had arrived? Or did she know something more than she had told him?

The crowd had remained for a few moments, waiting to see if anything else would happen. But now that Gillian was out of sight, the energy quickly dissipated, and people began to drift away in small groups.

The nobleman released Cain's arm, and took one more look at him. "If I return here in the morning and find any trace of you," he said, "I will have you thrown in jail, and the girl can go beg on the streets."

"Your generosity is overwhelming," Cain said.

"Watch your tongue!"

Cain took a single step forward until no more than a foot separated them. In spite of the man's bulk, he was very short and squat, and Cain towered over him. "I believe I have, thank you. But there are other judges of character who may not be so forgiving. You should ask yourself what's coming for you, in this life or the next."

The nobleman blinked, a bit of color draining from his face. For a moment it seemed he might grab Cain with his own bare hands, but he had been spoiled by years of soft living. He shook his fist in Cain's face. "Tomorrow," he said. Then he turned and walked away.

*Leah.* Cain rubbed his face with his hand, trying to return some feeling to his suddenly numb flesh. His bones ached with exhaustion, and his mind worried at this new problem. Gillian had clearly entrusted her to him. But what on earth would he do with the child? His thoughts returned to that moment inside the burning house when Leah's eyes had squeezed shut and her hands had clenched, the energy surging from her, shattering the lantern and rattling the walls. This was no ordinary little girl. And he was not equipped to deal with her.

Along with that thought came the memory of the presence that had seemed to sense the disturbance and seek it out, the black, flapping wings, and he wondered if they had barely escaped something far worse.

Deckard Cain made his way back around the corner of the house to the front, where a handful of people remained, watching the last wisps of smoke drift up from the dark interior. The door was still open, but he could not tell whether it was inviting him in or letting something out. Several men with empty buckets emerged, their faces grim and black with soot. They stomped down the steps and past him without a word or a second glance. They were protecting their own homes and families, and were interested in nothing else.

Leah was awake. She stood huddled next to James, impossibly small next to such a giant. He had taken off his cloak and draped it around her thin shoulders. Cain felt a burst of warmth for the man who had quite possibly saved their lives. Whatever else had happened here tonight, James had shown them that there was still some kindness left in the world.

The big man spotted him and turned. "She woke up just a moment ago," he said. "Seems perfectly fine to me. I had her wait here, avoid that commotion." He jerked a thumb toward the area where Gillian had been dragged away. His eyes showed Cain that he had heard more than he would say. Cain nodded.

He went and stood before Leah, looking down at her. The girl said nothing, clutching the cloak with both hands. Her face was streaked with soot and the remains of what might have been tears, but she retained a bit of stubborn grace as she stared back at him in silence.

"You will come with me," he said stiffly. "Your . . . mother is no longer able to care for you due to her illness. We will find a safe place for you soon enough, and arrange for funds that will help support you until you reach an age where you can provide for yourself." Then he added, awkwardly: "I'm . . . sorry."

If Leah heard or understood him, she did not acknowledge it, her wide, dark eyes unblinking. In that moment Cain felt the ghosts from a day long past crowding in, among them a child who had stood before him much like this.

"You can stay with us tonight," James said, breaking the spell. "Things will seem clearer in the morning."

Cain realized he had been holding his breath, and he let it out in a slow hiss. He shook his head. "It's better to leave Caldeum now," he said.

James frowned. "It's still dark, and she's got nothing but the clothes on her back. The house is full of soot—"

"Thank you," Cain said, "but I will get her what she needs." He put a hand on James's shoulder. "You have done more for us than we have the right to ask. But we have been ordered to leave this place or face a jail cell, and I have urgent business in another town that cannot wait."

For a moment the big man seemed about to protest, but then he shrugged. "If you insist," he said. He looked at Leah. When the girl tried to hand him his cloak, he waved it away. "Keep that until you find one that fits you better. It's a lucky one, you know. Saved my life once. Maybe it'll do the same for you."

Leah pulled the cloak back around her shoulders. It fell well below her knees, long enough to be a dress on her. Cain shook James's hand, then turned to Leah. "It's time," he said. "No sense in waiting any longer."

Leah followed him obediently enough. If leaving her childhood home gave her any pause, raised any depth of emotion, she did not show it. As they made their way toward the city gates,

Cain looked back only once and found James staring after them, still in the same spot where they had left him. He raised a hand in the man's direction, but received nothing in return.

Outside the gates, a breeze picked up grains of sand and sent them skittering across the nearly empty road with a sound like fingernails across a board. The trade tents, empty now, flapped in the wind like the wings of gray birds disturbed in their sleep.

Cain led the way, Leah a few short steps behind. Now she dragged her feet, staring down at the dusty road, her head hanging like a convicted prisoner headed to the gallows. But she did not speak or utter a sound. Several guards looked the strange pair up and down but did not move to stop them. They were trained to keep the wrong people out of Caldeum, not prevent them from leaving.

The sun was beginning to lighten the sky, bringing a slight tinge of warmth above the mountains in the distance. They passed a small group of weary travelers in a mule-driven cart, the back piled high with colorful cloth. A small boy sat cross-legged on the top of the pile and stared somberly at them as the cart wobbled by.

A short distance farther on, they reached a fork in the road. Cain stopped, leaning heavily on his staff. To his right the road ran toward the sea, and held more travelers and was well worn; to his left, another road led toward Kurast, this one rutted and empty, weeds beginning to sprout through the dust.

*Kurast.* A dead city, full of rapists, murderers, and worse. What kind of place was that for a child? Yet they must go there, for the road to salvation led through it, if he was right; in Kurast, he would find an answer to the mystery of the book and the mages calling themselves Horadrim, who were there or somewhere just beyond. Cain hardly dared hope that they existed. But if so, they might be able to help with whatever was happening with Leah. And they might just hold the key to saving Sanctuary from eternal darkness.

As the two figures stood at the crossroads, it seemed as if the lightening sky turned black again, and a chill swept through the land, and Deckard Cain felt that same monstrous, unseen presence fill the night like a black cloud blotting out the stars. He thought of the protective spell that Adria had cast over her daughter's whereabouts so many years ago, a spell that had remained intact until Cain appeared on Gillian's doorstep. Even after that, it had held its magic. But the fire had changed something, had damaged the spell somehow, and now, whatever might have been looking for them had a window to peer through.

The voice of the demon in the Vizjerei ruins came back to him: *Our master comes . . .*

The chill crept into Cain's bones and settled there, turning his aching knees to blocks of ice and sending a shiver through his body. Quickly he laid his staff down in the dirt and fumbled through his rucksack, the little girl just behind him all but forgotten in the urgency of need, his fingers like fat, dead things that would not obey his command. Finally he pulled a scroll free and cradled it in his hands as his heart raced in his chest and his blood thumped in his ears. An artifact left to him by Adria, saved for such a time as this.

*They will find you before long, and if they do, this quest is over before it even begins . . .*

His voice slowly gaining strength as he went, Cain uttered aloud the words of power from a scroll of misdirection and protection he had gotten from Adria long ago, casting an invisible cloak over them to hide them from sorcerers' eyes, at least for a short time.

For so many years, he had denied the existence of Horadric power, banished the truth of his ancestry to the depths of dusty, forgotten trunks and musty, book-lined chambers, fought against his mother's teachings, refusing to see behind the veil of what he perceived as madness. He had lived in denial, putting his trust in scholarly pursuits of a more mundane nature. But the world of magic, of demons and angels, had always been there, waiting for him to find it, the struggle of good against evil, playing out as it had for centuries, an eternal battle for control of Sanctuary and the souls of those men, women, and children who lived their lives in blissful ignorance. The power of evil was always present, and always close, like the hot breath of a beast upon his neck. Cain himself had tasted it long ago, and had spent the rest of his life trying to shut away the horrible memory, at least until the invasion of Tristram and the rise of Diablo had forced the truth upon him.

But darkness could not exist without light. Humankind was a study in contradictions, a mixture of the two, and the power to push back the darkness was there, as he knew well now; he had seen it in action many times, and had seen the things that battled against it.

As he spoke, the chill left the air, and the sky began to brighten again, until finally the words ended and Cain returned the book to his sack and picked up his staff. He was only an old man, but he had learned enough during his long years of study to keep them safe. For now. He could only pray that his search would lead them to others who were capable of far more than this. The battle that had begun in the hidden Vizjerei ruins had been fully joined, and who knew what hell might come, and how far they would all have to go before its end.

"Come, Leah," Cain said. "It's a long road ahead, and we must go as far as we can before night falls."

The two travelers set off together as the sun came up over the mountains, making their way toward the dead city, and whatever else might be waiting there for them.

# PART TWO

# DARKNESS
# DESCENDING

# NINE

## *The Cavern in the Hills*

He watched the two figures walking in the dust, one tall and thin, the other smaller and ten steps behind. They did not appear to be on friendly terms, although they were clearly traveling together. From this distance their features were impossible to make out, but he knew that the tall one was an old man and the smaller one a little girl.

A thrill ran through the young monk's body. He had found them. It had taken him months of fighting through false leads and misdirection; even now, across the vast plain just beyond the city's edge, their figures were indistinct, wavering as if viewed through a wall of water. It was not simply the heat that rose as the sun baked the ground through the swirling dust. There was magic surrounding them, and only Mikulov's intense focus and signs from the gods allowed him to see them at all.

He crouched down behind a large boulder and wiped a thin trickle of sweat from his eye. His breathing remained calm and even, his heart rate steady, but he was not satisfied with his state of being. Although he had waited for this moment, his reaction was unsettling, and thrills of excitement and beads of sweat were signs that his body was not in perfect harmony with his mind. His masters would have been disappointed. The Ivgorod monks held a legendary control over themselves created from years of study, and in moments of stress their minds often left the physical realm and ascended to a higher state of being, becoming one with all things, as the Patriarchs had intended.

Mikulov slipped silently away from his hiding place, working his way back into the hills. He moved like a ghost among the statues of dusty rock and withered trees; even the small, lightning-quick lizards that sunned themselves in the baking heat never moved at his approach. He would wait until the man and the child were away from the city before he revealed himself to them. The gods would provide the time and place.

The Patriarchs had taught him that he was a weapon, a living, breathing instrument. Through him, the Patriarchs would destroy the foul influences that corrupted this world. He must be willing to accept that destiny, and act upon it.

Mikulov had entered the Floating Sky Monastery as a young boy, as countless others had before him. He was quickly singled out from his peers because of his natural abilities of speed, agility, and a sharp mind, and his masters spent the next fifteen years with him, teaching him the ways of the gods, the tactics of battle, and the path to salvation. The gods were in all things, his masters said. They taught him to meditate for hours on end, to seek the quiet center of being, where self-consciousness dissolved and the human mind became one with all things, built to serve the Patriarchs.

But Mikulov had always been restless. He was not well suited to endless contemplation, and it was against his nature to be patient, although in his masters' minds, patience was everything. He struggled mightily with this, until one day his studies led him to an ancient book of prophecies, and everything changed.

Through the book, Mikulov became familiar with the Horadric order of mages who had battled and conquered the enemies of this world so many years ago. Ivgorod's own prophecies seemed to predict the Horadrim's role in a coming battle, one that would eclipse all others in scope and horror: a battle that would usurp the will of the gods. It wasn't long before he began to dream about this war between the gods. Although vague at first, his dreams were unsettling, and left him each morning with a feeling of unease and loss he could not overcome.

Over the following months, the dreams became worse, and far more specific: visions of the dead walking the earth, commanded by a terrible man with a shrouded face.

*The Dark One.* This man was consumed by a hatred that burned as hot as the sun, and he would lead Sanctuary into oblivion. But beneath the surface was something else, something far more ancient and deadly, that commanded the Dark One to act. If he were not stopped, the ancient entity would rise up and consume everything in its path.

Mikulov continued his studies with an increased sense of urgency, convinced that the war was coming sooner than anyone understood. The signs were everywhere, and the prophecies he uncovered foretold an event that would occur on the first day of Ratham, the month of the dead, when the stars would align in a moment of terrible power and destruction.

A lost city would rise, and with it, Hell would come to all of them. The gods had foreseen it.

Eventually his masters began to see the signs as well, and interpret them. The world's delicate balance had been disrupted; a secret plague was descending over Sanctuary; evil was bleeding into the world, its minions becoming ever bolder, darkness spreading across the land. But in spite of his pleadings, the Patriarchs' instruction was clear: it was not yet time to engage the enemy, and he was not ready.

Ivgorod monks simply did not defy their masters, and Mikulov spent many nights struggling to know what path he must take. He looked for signs from the gods. The dreams continued, growing in intensity, but the Patriarchs still would not act. Finally, in spite of his own turmoil and terrible sense of loss, Mikulov decided to leave the monastery and search out the Horadrim on his own to offer his assistance.

It was a life-changing decision, one that he knew might very well lead to his death. The monastery was the only true home he had ever known, and his masters would never welcome him back again. The Patriarchs might even order his execution. But he was haunted by what he saw when he closed his eyes at night, and he knew that he must act or his life would no longer have meaning. Either way, he would cease to exist.

If this was his path, he must take it. The gods would not rest until he did.

He set out on his journey with a heavy heart. Finding any trace of the Horadric order turned out to be more difficult than he had anticipated. The order had vanished from Sanctuary, the last of their kind apparently having died out long ago. But eventually he found that the demonic uprising that had spread to Kurast and Mount Arreat several years before had begun in the former Horadric monastery in Tristram. From there it did not take him long to find Deckard Cain.

This was his only link to the Horadrim, and Mikulov would not miss his chance. He followed the old man in secret for months, losing his trail in one place only to pick it up again somewhere else. More than once he was close enough to see Cain, but the time was not right to make contact.

He listened to the gods as they spoke to him through the

wind, the rain, the rivers, and wildlife. He would engage with Cain when they chose for it to happen.

Perhaps soon, in the hills above Caldeum, he would get his chance.

There was evil here.

Mikulov sensed it, hovering somewhere out of sight. The wind whispered it to him as the sun's rays gave a momentary pulse of heat. The lizards scurried to safety, puffs of dust marking their passage.

With a breath of air, the gods instructed him to look up. Far above his head, carried by the hot winds rising from the desert, black birds were circling.

A sense of great danger overwhelmed him. The ground ahead offered him shelter. He slipped between two large slabs of rock and into a dark, shadowed crevice, away from prying eyes.

The air was even warmer in here, and the crevice ran deeper into the hill than he had thought. Mikulov advanced slowly as his eyes adjusted to the gloom. His sense of menace had not subsided once he had entered the narrow cave. In fact, it had gotten worse, and as he moved ahead, he felt his consciousness expand, a dreamlike haze falling over his heightened senses.

Before him he found a set of ancient, rough-hewn steps descending into the darkness, and he began to walk down, his hands out before him, feeling the moist air. Thick, rope-like cobwebs brushed his face. There was some light coming from below, enough for him to see, and the walls fell away from him as he continued, so that he had the sense of entering a vast, open cavern far below the surface. There were both great wonders and terrible dangers down here, an entire world underground, and he thought of giant spiders spinning webs across piles of rotting corpses, lurking in the shadows of dusty alcoves with a thousand glittering eyes and fangs bared and dripping, waiting for fresh blood.

The stairs seemed to continue forever. Mikulov lost track of how long he had been descending, and stopped wondering where the walls and ceiling of the cavern had gone. He had the feeling that far above him stretched a night sky littered with stars—not the sky of his own world, but that of another dimension or time. The gods would speak to him through this canopy of stars and show him the way to salvation. Somewhere below he would find the answers to all that he had been searching for, but he knew those answers could destroy Sanctuary.

He looked below and saw a wagon wheel of old, leaning buildings, the ground littered with fallen stones, silent and still, with dusty, broken streets running like spokes in all directions, and sensed that among the shadowy corners and forgotten rooms lay moldering corpses, their bony, empty sockets staring lifelessly ahead for time without end.

The lost city.

Mikulov slipped on silent feet through a crumbling stone arch. The city stretched before him, as if frozen for eternity as it had fallen, centuries before. A temple loomed to his left, its doorway open and pitch-black. Beyond it was a wide boulevard that had cracked in two, and the crevasse that yawned like a toothless mouth was glowing, as if the fires of Hell were beneath it.

Something moved in the shadows of the temple.

Mikulov glanced at the open doorway. For a moment, nothing happened, and then, moving with strange, jerking steps like a toddler just learning to walk, a creature emerged from the darkness.

It was human, or had been once. What little clothing remained hung like ribbons from the creature's shoulders. Shards of gleaming white bone thrust through strings of leathery flesh. Its face was little more than a skull with wisps of hair and skin and grinning teeth, but it stared forward and then turned back and forth as if searching blindly for something.

It paused, its empty eye sockets focused on Mikulov.

As it stood outside the temple, another emerged from the dark, this one with more shriveled meat on its bones, then another and another. Mikulov turned to see other corpses gathering all around him, lurching forward with bony hands up and grasping. He turned back, but more had gathered behind him, cutting off the stairs to safety, and as he stood there in shock, he could hear the thunderous sound of thousands of skeletal feet marching through the streets, just out of sight.

Mikulov darted through the closest of the risen dead, feeling their cold bone-fingers kissing his shoulders before he slipped beyond them and ran ahead. As he approached the wide boulevard, he heard a shout and saw a group of people surrounded by horrible, ghoulish creatures that scampered upon all fours like dogs, their flesh pale and withered, their balding skulls gleaming. The people were cornered, their backs against the stone wall of a building. There were about six of them, one taller and thinner than the rest, his long, white hair wild around his face.

Deckard Cain.

Mikulov stood helplessly as the creatures closed in on the small circle. More of them approached on all sides, too many to count. Just beyond them stood a shadowy figure in a black robe, his features hooded. *The Dark One.*

The creatures fell upon the group. A thin, high scream cut through the noise of marching feet, the sound of a little girl in terror.

Mikulov ran forward as the ground began to shake, and stopped short as the crevasse before him suddenly widened. Something gigantic began to climb out of it, monstrous, armor-plated claws rising up and bracing it on both sides and a three-horned head emerging with yellow eyes burning like pools of fire. The creature rose up and towered before him, impossibly huge, more eyes opening like glowing orbs, shining like the fires of Hell itself, and its gaping maw opened, showing bone-teeth in a glistening jaw.

There was no use in fighting such a thing. He averted his eyes. The sound of deep, jarring laughter brought him to his knees as he waited for it to descend upon him.

The feeling of rough stone beneath him brought him back with a sudden jerk, and Mikulov found himself staring at a blank wall. For a long moment, he kneeled, motionless; the heat of the narrow cave he had entered was oppressive, making it difficult to breathe.

He gathered himself, got to his feet and glanced around. The cave was no more than ten feet long, and ended abruptly. There were no stairs, no cavern beneath him. Nothing he had seen was real.

Mikulov closed his eyes, seeking peace. As the images faded, he began to feel the gods once again: the whisper of sand across rock, the cry of a small animal in the distance, the heat on his skin. He allowed his pulse to return to normal.

The vision had been stronger than any that had come before it. He pondered its purpose. The gods had shown him this for a reason, but he did not know whether what he had seen would come to pass, or whether it had a different meaning that they required him to understand. Surely such a cursed place did not actually exist, and the creature that had loomed over him was so terrible it could not be flesh and blood. The thing's laughter, the evil in its burning eyes remained with him even now, and he could not shake them.

Finally he opened his eyes. The narrow cave was still there, the walls still solid and eternal. Mikulov ducked back through the opening and into the scorching sun, looking up at the cloud-less sky. Through the rippling heat, he could see that the birds had gone. His sense of immediate danger had passed. But a fresh feeling of urgency drove him forward.

His back itched where the tattoo that marked all Ivgorod monks extended from his neck halfway down his body. When he died, this tattoo would tell his life story through the eyes of the gods. He prayed it would reveal a victory against the plague that would soon descend upon Sanctuary, and that he would live long enough to see its completion.

But he would need help in the battle, from those who had fought such a plague before. If there were any Horadrim left, Deckard Cain would know how to find them. The little girl would play a central role as well; the prophecies had foretold it, but they spoke only of her strange power, and did not say how it would be wielded.

One thing was clear: he had little time left now. Ratham was nearly upon them, and the Dark One was preparing to strike.

Mikulov slipped through the baking heat, back toward the road to Kurast and his ultimate destiny.

# TEN

## *Out of Caldeum*

The road was empty, abandoned, the rutted tracks overgrown with a nearly colorless grass that looked like the hair on a stray dog's back. It had been a main thoroughfare at some point but had long since fallen into disrepair. The road led through the dusty, windswept plains that surrounded Caldeum, past huge slabs of rock like sleeping giants and the monstrous skeleton of some ancient creature, its bones bleached white from the sun, then rose with the land as Cain and Leah began to ascend the slope of a hill.

Leah stopped on the top of an outcropping and looked back at the city. The sun was now higher in the sky, and the light sparkled off the waterfalls and copper domes like a tumble of jewels in the desert. Tears glimmering in her eyes mirrored the prisms of light.

*My home.*

She mouthed the words silently to get a feel for them, although they meant little to her. A sense of hopelessness fell over her like a smothering blanket. The truth was, although she knew the web of streets and buildings and sewers by heart, she had never felt much at home anywhere, other than in the tunnels beneath the streets. She was an outcast, even among the people of Caldeum, where she had lived her entire life. The city might have looked pretty from up here, but she knew the dark and dirty underbelly, the cruelty of the people, the filth that gathered in forgotten corners and swelled and changed until it grew into a ravenous beast, waiting to swallow you whole.

At least, that was what Gillian used to say. When Leah thought of her mother, an even more complicated set of conflicting emotions washed over her, a terrible, gut-wrenching loneliness mixed with terror that was so strong it threatened to overwhelm her. Her mother was not well: that much she understood. She remembered the paralyzing fear of two nights before, Gillian rambling about demons bathing in blood, and later dragging Leah from her bed, whatever terrible thing that might have happened avoided only by the arrival of the old man; and last night, the smoke and the flames and confusion, and the dim knowledge that somehow her mother had been responsible for the events that had led to the burning.

Leah had other memories that chronicled Gillian's descent into madness. But she was the only family Leah had ever known. She had been there when nobody else had cared, and there had been good times too. Enough of them to matter.

*She is my mother.*

And that, the little girl realized, was everything. The simple fact that she was gone was enough to hurt like the deep slice of a knife. She felt shattered inside, completely lost and alone.

What would happen to her now? What would happen to Gillian? Where had they taken her?

Panic flooded to the surface, and Leah swallowed against the lump in her chest. *Where was her mother?* She turned to ask the old man—Uncle Deckard, she had been told to call him, although she had never received any explanation of how they might be related—but stopped before the words had left her throat. He was walking slowly up the track, leaning on his staff, his back to her. A good distance away now and growing smaller as he went.

She kept her mouth shut, cutting off the words and watching him go. He was strange, stiff and formal, and intimidating in the way a strict teacher might be in school. But Leah seemed to make him nervous. She could not understand why, but he acted as if he was afraid she might do something unpredictable at any moment, like burst into song or stand on her head or start running around screaming at the top of her lungs. Gillian had seemed to trust him, but what if he meant to sell her into slavery, or worse? She knew enough about wizardry to recognize a spell when she heard one, but she did not know what kind of spell he had uttered shortly after they had set off on their journey. And nothing had happened anyway. If he was a sorcerer of some kind, he must not be a very powerful one.

*What if he practices dark magic? What if I am to be a sacrifice to the demons my mother always said were coming for me?*

The thought sent chills down her spine. She had tried to forget what her mother had said, but the words kept forcing their way back into her mind.

*"They want you, Leah, and if they find you, you're never coming back from that. Never."*

Standing there on the rock, she felt as if the entire world was gone, and what remained around her was nothing but dust. She remembered the circle of boys who had teased the old beggar in the city before turning on her. *I'm like that old beggar,* she thought, *with nobody to care about me and no place to go.* She wiped at the tears that trickled down her dirty cheeks, smearing the soot that still clung to her skin, and fought against the sudden urge to go running after the old man and throw herself at his feet, even if he was almost as scary as anything else on this terrible, deserted road.

A flapping sound roused her from her trance. A huge crow

had taken flight and was circling overhead, its wings as wide as her own outstretched arms. She shivered, the memory of the crow from the street coming back to her, the way its sharp beak had pulled at the dead flesh, how it had cocked its head and stared at her with beady eyes, strings of gray meat still dangling from its maw. That led to the idea of something else watching her, a being much more powerful and deadly.

*Something terrible is coming . . .*

It seemed as if the sky had darkened, a shadow falling over the land. Leah clutched James's cloak and ran off the rock and along the deserted road, chasing the old man up the hill until she was close enough to feel a bit better. For better or worse, he was the only one who could protect her now. She did not know whether he cared enough for that to matter.

They camped for the night on the hard ground under the stars, Leah shivering under the cloak, and were up again at dawn. The old man gave her a few bites of bread and sips of water from a small canteen. Hours later, the sun was falling in the western sky, and still he walked on at a steady pace, speeding up slightly on downward slopes, and slowing down when the track climbed more steeply.

They had passed no one since the fork in the road, and had said little to each other for most of the day. The silence had grown into its own separate presence, like another person walking with them. Leah's throat felt like dry stone. She had long since gone numb. Her stomach rumbled, and hunger pains bit deeply. She had had nothing but the bread and water, and her companion seemed to be oblivious to the very idea of food.

Eventually they came to a river carved into the dusty ground, its banks steep and covered with reeds. The road led to a wooden bridge that looked treacherous to cross. Underneath it the water ran black and silent. Beyond the bridge the ground rose more steeply through a rock-strewn hillside, and larger, more menacing mountains loomed in the distance.

"We'll find a place to camp here," the old man said. He turned to look at her, leaning on his staff, and she saw the exhaustion etched in his features, deep lines around his mouth and along his brow. He did not seem so scary now, his tall, skeletal frame more fragile than imposing.

Who was he, and where was he taking her? She wanted to ask these questions, but her fear of him kept her mouth shut. They left the road and walked a short distance along the riverbank, looking for a flat place. Dry grasses hissed across the bottom of James's cloak as Leah followed Cain to a copse of trees that grew near the bank. They were thin and spidery, their limbs nearly bare, but the ground underneath them was dry and soft, and they provided some privacy from any prying eyes.

The heat on the dry, open path had been overwhelming, but under the trees it was shaded, and a bit cooler. The old man set his rucksack down near a flat rock. Leah approached him cautiously, ducking under a low-hanging branch. It was darker in here, and she allowed herself a brief moment to relax as her eyes adjusted to the shadows. He sat down on the rock with a heavy sigh, crossed one leg over the other, and rubbed gently at his foot. She noticed it was wrapped with cloth underneath the worn sandal. The cloth was spotted with blood.

"I noticed there were burris reeds growing at the water's edge," he said. "They're tall, with gray fuzzy tops. The root makes a good salve. Would you mind fetching some?"

Leah left the cover of trees and ran to a place on the river where the reeds grew thick. She made her way down the slope, avoiding the muck at the bottom as best she could, and thrust her hands into the water, bringing it to her mouth and sucking greedily. It tasted slightly gritty and metallic, but delicious. She drank her fill until her belly rumbled and grew heavy, then plucked several reeds from the soft ground. They came up easily, their wormlike, puffy-white roots dangling from her grasp as she climbed back up the bank and returned to the trees.

Cain laid the roots on the rock, pulled another round rock the size of a fist from the ground, and rolled it across them a few times until they had been crushed into a milky paste. Then he sat down, carefully removed his sandals and the cloth wrapping his feet, and spread the white salve of the root across his raw patches of flesh, hissing slightly as if it burned him. After a long moment, he sighed and closed his eyes. "I believe there's an element in this particular plant that numbs the pain, and the salve protects and dries out the damaged flesh so it can heal properly. Pepin helped heal many wounds like this in Tristram, after the . . ." He glanced at Leah. "I suppose you're hungry. We need to eat to keep up our strength. Look in my rucksack; I think there's some bread left."

Leah needed no further invitation. She searched his sack and found a small end of a loaf under a bewildering number of books; small, mysterious boxes; and scrolls. Cain watched her devour it, and shook his head. "We should find you something more than that," he said.

Leah followed him back down along the banks of the river to a place where a bend harbored a slow, calm pool. A tree growing on the bank spread its roots across the pool's edge, creating a warren of shadows and a tangle of black tentacles within the muck. He filled a small water pouch from his sack, then took out a scroll and kneeled on the riverbank under the tree and read the runes inscribed upon it. Then he took the end of his staff and dipped it into the water.

A crackling, blue light shot off into the depths, and a fat, silver fish began to emerge from the murky gloom beneath the tangled roots, floating to the surface, motionless.

"Take it, quickly now," Cain said softly. Leah reached down and scooped it up. Its body was soft and slippery. Another emerged, this one small and sleek, then another, the largest of the three. She pulled them out, one at a time. Cain stood up slowly, wincing as if his body pained him. "The words give the wood a charge, which transfers to the water. It relaxes muscles and paralyzes the fish for a time. The charge is not very powerful. But it's far easier than baiting a hook, and it's gotten us our supper. Now gather those up, and let's make a fire."

They returned to the area under the trees as the last of the light faded from the sky. She put the fish next to the large rock, and Cain built a fire pit from smaller rocks and piled dry grasses and sticks inside. The air quickly grew colder, and she found James's cloak and wrapped it around her shoulders once again, grateful for its warmth and now-familiar smell.

The old man was clearly some sort of wizard. There were mages in Caldeum, but she had rarely seen any kind of magic other than simple street tricks, and his abilities intrigued her, despite her distrust of him. He dug into his pack again, sprinkled some sort of powder on the fire pit and struck a flint. Sparks flew and ignited the grasses, and the powder crackled and popped, smoke rising from the pit as tongues of flame began to lick hungrily at the wood.

Cain laid a flat rock across the top of the circle as the fire rose higher, and set the fish on it. Leah sat a few feet away from him as the delicious scent of them filled the night air. Her stomach rumbled again, even more loudly, and the heat from the flames warmed her hands and face. She began to relax, and that led to an unexpected trembling, and then great, shuddering sobs tore through her, a torrent of tears streaming down her cheeks.

The old man sat for a long time in silence, as if he hadn't noticed. "I'd expected this earlier," he said finally, without looking at her. "I know it's difficult, for a young one, but you must remain in control. You're having a physical reaction to trauma, now that the immediate danger has passed. It's perfectly natural, nothing to be afraid of, Leah."

"My—my mother, she's—dead?"

"No, Gillian is not dead," Cain said. Now he looked at her, and there was something in his eyes she could not read. "And she's not your mother."

That made her sit up, the shock of what he had said stopping her tears abruptly. She waited, heart pounding, mouth dry.

"I've been debating how much to tell you about this, but I see no reason to wait. Regardless of your age, you should know the truth." The old man was watching her intently. His eyes sparkled in the firelight. She imagined two burning coals buried in the depths of black wood. "Your real mother was a woman named Adria from Tristram. A woman with very unique gifts."

"I—I don't believe you."

"Adria and Gillian came to Caldeum together, to escape Tristram, where we all lived. Adria gave birth to you here, but she was never one to remain still for long. She was not the type to care for a young child. Gillian had become better settled in Caldeum; she was safe enough, and she seemed to be the best option to care for you, since Adria could not, and I . . . well, I was quite ill equipped for the job, even after I had been freed from my bonds."

"You're lying!"

"No," Cain said, his voice growing firm. "I'm afraid not."

"Yes, you are!"

"Leah, you must remain calm—"

"I—I *hate* you! Leave me alone!" Leah burst into fresh tears as the fire abruptly flared up with a crackling hiss. She stood and stumbled away from him and the now-nauseating smell of cooked fish, her hands outstretched in the darkness, remembering the look on Cain's face, the way his eyes shone in the firelight.

She felt branches brushing her skin, and she thrust herself through the trees and into the cold night air, running blindly through the grass, her body threatening to bring up the hunk of bread that now sat like a stone in her belly as her mind went over the words again and again in her head: *She's not your mother . . . she's not your mother . . .*

A rage built inside her. How could he say such a thing? Everything she had been feeling, all the hopelessness and terror and loneliness, crashed over her once again. Of course Gillian was her mother; it was impossible to imagine anything different. Yet . . . hadn't she always felt alone in a way that she could never understand? Hadn't the boys always teased her about being an outcast, a girl with no ties to anything and no place to belong?

She remembered a violent storm that had come up over Caldeum when she was a very little girl, the wind whipping through the valley, picking up the tents and throwing them against the city walls. Gillian had hurried home, clutching Leah's hand tightly as drops of rain as fat as grapes had begun to fall, exploding all around them, and then hail, hammering copper rooftops like drums and shattering glass. Gillian had lifted her up and run with her, and Leah had clung on for dear life until they reached the house, where Gillian had sung to her and stroked her hair, promising that the storm would pass soon and everything would be fine. A mother's promise.

*Your real mother was a woman named Adria . . .*

*No.* Leah clenched her fists, digging her nails into her palms as fear, frustration, and anger ripped up through her and exploded. She was just a little girl; there was no real way for her mind to process such a thing. A scream tore itself from her throat, expanding into the night, building ever larger until it seemed to overwhelm everything else, and her vision was filled with floating spots of light as she tripped and fell headlong to the ground.

The scream echoed back to her as something huge cracked and groaned nearby, and a great, thundering crash shook the earth. Leah clutched her hands to her head and curled herself into a tight ball, but the world seemed to be imploding around her as her entire body tingled and the pain made her scream again.

Dimly, she heard someone calling her name, then more words spoken aloud in a commanding voice, and the noise and the shuddering thunder ceased all at once.

# ELEVEN

## *Dreams of Tristram*

I dreamt of the death wail of a small child tonight.
It tore up from the depths, shattering the windows
of the decrepit cathedral. As I started awake, it became apparent that it was actually the shriek of
Diablo's tortured end. Unable to return to sleep after such an unsettling cry, I ventured outdoors to
await the warrior's return. He finally emerged,
covered in blood—much his own, much his enemies'. I am greatly relieved that he survived the
ordeal, and that these horrible events are now in
our past. But my mind is troubled, for could this
not have been avoided if I had not dismissed my
legacy so lightly?

*Deckard Cain looked up from the pages of his journal, and the passage
he had written just days before. He sat at his old desk in his mother's
house, the room empty and still, the ghosts that had haunted him finally
silent for now. The sun had come up over Tristram for the first time in
what felt like weeks.*

*He considered how to continue. The next journal entry should have
been joyful. Outside, those few who had survived the carnage still cele-
brated, their hoarse shouts cutting through the thin morning air. I*

should be out there with them, *Cain thought.* Diablo has been defeated, Aidan has emerged victorious from the catacombs, and the demons that had been vomited up from the depths of the Hells have scattered. I should be rejoicing over the end of the plague that has consumed us for so long.

*Yet he could not. The town was in shambles, the streets splashed with blood. The devastation overwhelmed and saddened him. Fire had torn through a portion of the properties, leaving smoking ruins behind, and some of the buildings closest to the cathedral had been ripped from their very foundations, their wooden walls jumbled like a pile of matchsticks.*

*The town might never recover. And all of it was his fault. Worse than that, doubts had begun to nag at him once again. He was terribly afraid that this was not the end, after all.*

*Cain sighed, and rubbed his aching eyes. The last remaining citizens of Tristram might not want to admit it, but deep shadows still darkened this place. The ground was cursed, and it would be better to burn it away completely like a cancerous growth, rather than let it spread. He looked around the little room at his piles of old books, memories of days long past: most of them histories of Sanctuary and its people, or attempts at scientific method, dry accounts of the bare facts, and none of the real truth that lived behind the veil. But there were other books here as well, those he had gathered more recently from the Zakarum cathedral. These books recounted a far different history: angels and demons in Sanctuary, their very blood mingling and changing over centuries, all mortals descended from them. Some of these legends were similar to those his mother had told him, years ago. Others he had never heard before.*

*There was no denying the evil they had faced here, not anymore. But could he believe all the rest as well, everything in these books? Was it all true? If so, he was a scholar who had focused on the wrong things for all these years. His entire life had been a lie.*

*He could not breathe in the little room. He needed space. There was something he must do, and it could not wait any longer.*

*Abruptly, Cain pushed away from the desk and stood, avoiding his more familiar staff and grabbing another that leaned in the corner. Evil seemed to pulse from it like a festering wound, and the old man held it away from him as he shuffled to the front door and out into the sunshine.*

*From the direction of the center of town, a wisp of smoke twirled upward into the blue sky. He could not tell whether it was from the celebration or from a fire that burned unchecked. Either way, the flames would help him accomplish what he needed.*

*Someone was playing a flute, and others were singing. Instead of a light and joyful song, Cain thought, the sound was like the mournful cry of a forgotten dove, its lover dead and gone.*

*He made his way forward, past his neighbors' homes. Pepin's house was dark, the door leaning half open. A single, bloody handprint marked the entrance. He did not look inside, afraid of what he might see. As the town's only healer, Pepin had done so much for the people of Tristram. The saddest story was of Wirt, a boy who had been abducted by demons and nearly killed before the blacksmith Griswold had rescued him, but not without a terrible cost. Wirt had been badly wounded, and Pepin had been forced to amputate his leg and install a peg leg in its place.*

*Wirt's mother had died of grief before he had been found, and Wirt himself had grown bitter and withdrawn. His unspoken crush on Gillian did not help matters, either; she had been blind to his affections, and his heart was broken. Cain was not sure what had happened to the child, but he feared the worst. A boy with a bad leg had little chance of outrunning the things that wanted to claim him.*

*He approached the center of town. The remaining citizens had built a bonfire in the center of the street, and several men were piling more wood upon the flames, coaxing them higher. Cain counted perhaps fifteen or twenty people, most of them older or infirm, those who had had no choice but to barricade themselves in their homes and try to wait out the storm. Ironically, besides a few other brave fighters, they were the ones who had survived.*

*Farnham, the father who had lost his daughter to the Butcher, sat* apart from the others, his face red, eyes bleary from drink. Dark blood-stains still speckled his shirt. He looked up as Cain passed him, grunted once, and took a swig from a bottle of something amber-colored and foul.

Cain approached the fire, and the others parted to let him pass. Several of them eyed what he held, and shrank back, as if witnessing a snake charmer with a deadly cobra. He spotted Aidan on the other side of the flames, huddled motionless and watching from within the shadows between two buildings. He had changed from the armor he had worn in battle and had long since washed away the blood that had caked his skin after he had returned from the catacombs. But the weight of what he had done was still heavy around his neck. A more permanent mark from the battle had scarred his formerly smooth forehead like a brand.

Cain's heart sank at the sight. Aidan had emerged victorious, but that victory had taken a severe toll on him. He was a different man than he had been before. His own brother, Albrecht, had been possessed and deformed by Diablo himself. Albrecht had been only a child. Cain knew that his terribly mutated body would have returned to its original form upon his death. Although Aidan had spoken little of it since, witnessing his brother lying there on the bloody ground, killed by his own hand, must have been worse than fighting any demon.

Cain remembered tutoring Aidan in the king's quarters, a slight, dark-headed youth full of life and promise, although Cain hadn't appreciated it then, as self-absorbed as he had been. At the thought of those days, a darker, far more terrible secret tried to push its way back in. He fought it back with effort, and focused on the present.

He looked down at the staff in his hand. A cursed thing. Aidan should have been the one to do this, he thought. The rightful heir to the kingdom of Khanduras, and the leader who had saved all of Sanctuary. But he had refused, for reasons that remained unknown. Cain would have to carry it through.

He reached the fire. "Citizens of Tristram," he said. "You have peered into the abyss, and you have survived. But none of you have avoided a terrible loss. The Prime Evil Diablo is dead, but what he has brought upon this town still lurks, in the shadows and within the hearts of all of us. Never forget what has happened here. Never allow such evil to surprise you again."

He looked around at the faces surrounding him: the wounds on the bodies of several people raggedly sewn shut, puffy, dark circles under their eyes, the blank looks of those who have seen more than their souls could bear. All of them had lost loved ones, and all of them were suffering. "I give you the staff of Lazarus," he said. He held it up for them to see, ignoring the ache in his back and the pain in his knees. "The traitor who betrayed us all and awoke Diablo from his slumber will not haunt us anymore."

Cain tossed the staff onto the flames. The fire seemed to rise up and embrace it with a dull roar. He stumbled back from the sudden heat, feeling the hands of others catch him and hold him up. For a moment he sagged into them, welcoming the support. Perhaps he would not have to do all this alone, after all.

The tortured wood gave off a sound like a high, hissing scream. It popped and cracked, emitting a green smoke that rose up into the air and swirled higher. The flames began to blacken it before the pile collapsed and it disappeared under the glowing embers.

Cain sighed. He had meant to give a rousing speech, a way to put a ceremonial end to their misery. But it felt hollow to him. Lazarus was dead and gone; his staff was only a piece of wood, and it burned like any other.

He tried to move away from the hands that had been holding him, but they held him fast. He turned to find the familiar, round face of Griswold the blacksmith, his bald head shining in the sunlight. "Old friend," Griswold said, "stay a while, and drink with us."

Cain smiled, but something about Griswold unsettled him. The blacksmith had been a fierce ally in the fight against the demon plague, helping forge weapons and armor and wading into the battle himself, using his bulk and brute strength to shatter the skulls of imps and siege beasts until suffering a terrible leg wound. But his eyes were distant now, his meaty hands clutching Cain's upper arms. A vague threat of violence clung to him like a foul odor.

Cain glanced back across the fire at Aidan, who had not moved. "Aye, he's a brooding one," Griswold said. "Not been the same since he's returned from below. He speaks little, and does not socialize with the others."

"He's suffered."

"As have we all." Griswold's gaze grew distant. "I hear voices, in the night. Keeps me from my bed."

"Demonic contact can have long-lasting effects," Cain said.

"Suppose that's what it is," Griswold said. His fingers tightened, digging painfully into Cain's flesh. Then he shook his head and released Cain's arms. "Go speak to the boy," he said. He took a bottle from someone's hand and drank deeply before tossing it aside. "He could use some wise counsel. And have some ale. We're here to celebrate, after all."

Cain skirted the fire, moving away from the small crowd. Something was not right. Diablo had been destroyed, his minions dead or scattered. The danger was over.

Then why did he have this unsettled feeling growing inside him, like a black, creeping sickness?

He reached the shadowed place between two buildings and peered in. Aidan was gone. A moment later he heard a muffled voice from somewhere beyond, and he stepped into the dark, walking carefully without his staff, moving away from the sounds of the crowd and the fire. It was isolated in here, and he felt the hairs prickle on the back of his neck before he emerged into a side street.

Aidan stood with a woman about fifty feet away, under the shade of a large tree. Cain stopped short at the building's edge, something telling him to remain hidden. He watched the woman touch Aidan's arm, and Aidan bent to speak to her, and then the two of them moved away, out of sight.

The light was dim under the tree, and they had left quickly. But Cain

*would have recognized the mix of grace, beauty, and raw power any-*
*where, the way she moved, seemingly gliding over the ground. The*
*woman with him was the witch Adria.*

*A new sense of unease fell over him, but he dared not follow the two.*
*He had more important things to do. He had vowed to never again let*
*his own lack of dedication to his Horadric studies destroy others' lives.*
*He would return to his texts, today, and search for answers to his name-*
*less fear. He would not rest until he knew the truth.*

*When he turned back to the alley, a small boy stood before him,*
*hands clasped at his waist, his face mournful.*

*"Why did you leave me?" the boy said. "Why?"*

Cain awoke with a jerk, stifling a cry. The fire he had built had
died down to embers, casting shadows that seemed to move
among the low-hanging branches of the trees.

Cain's fingers crept toward a hidden pocket in his tunic,
where a single sheet of brittle parchment lay nestled apart from
his nest of other treasures, close to his heart. He caught himself,
his heart thudding in his chest. *No,* he thought, remembering the
boy's face in shocking detail for a moment before pushing it
away from his mind. *Not that. I cannot bear to go back there again.*

He took a deep breath and let it out slowly. It was the incident
with the girl that had brought on his dream, almost certainly. He
should never have told her about her mother in that way. He had
handled the entire thing terribly. He did not know how to deal
with children: how much did you share with them, and how
were you to bring up such difficult subjects? Thank the archangels it hadn't been worse.

After Leah had run off, he had chased her out of the trees,
and had felt the crackling energy of whatever strange power she
held inside building toward a horrible end. If she hadn't tripped
and fallen, who knew what might have happened? He had found

her lying motionless and unresponsive on the ground near the river, and carried her back to the fire, where she sat slumped forward in shock.

He was finally able to get her to eat a bite of the fish, and she tore into the rest with her fingers like a starving animal. After she had eaten, she had started asking him questions, quietly at first, then with more conviction and urgency.

She had wanted to know everything. Cain had done the best he could, while trying to be sensitive to her situation. Adria had arrived in Tristram shortly after the troubles began, and had quickly become well known among those who had remained for her abilities with potions and enchanted objects, and her gift for foreseeing future events. In fact, it was that gift which saved her life when Tristram fell. But the last thing Cain had heard was a report of her death many months ago, somewhere in the Dreadlands. That had brought more tears from Leah, and one last question:

*"Did she . . . look like me?"*

Cain stood up, shuffling around the fire to where Leah lay on her side under James's cloak, her eyes closed now, her face peaceful and smooth. She looked so small and helpless. How could he have treated her this way? What was wrong with him? Was it really so hard to take care of children, to be sensitive to their particular needs? Or anyone else's needs, for that matter—his focus on his studies was a form of selfishness he could no longer afford.

For the first time, he considered turning back, finding shelter somewhere in Caldeum or beyond, as far away from Kurast as he could get.

*You need to continue your search, Deckard.*

His mother's voice was so clear and strong within his own head that he looked around in the dim firelight, as if he might see her standing there. Of course he did not, yet he had the feeling that Aderes Cain was somewhere just beyond his senses, her passion for the Horadric cause keeping her bound to the mortal realm forever. Whatever its source, he knew that the voice in his head was right: they were no longer welcome in Caldeum, and to run from his destiny would only serve to prolong the inevitable. He had to keep going, tracking down the slim lead on the possible mage group in Kurast, searching for the answers to the questions raised by the books he had found at the Vizjerei ruins.

*The tomb of Al Cut.*

Who was Al Cut? The mystery nagged at him like an aching tooth. He wanted to find people with the right information, and shake them until it all came out. Hell was coming to Sanctuary. It was simply a matter of when.

Cain looked down at Leah. The mage group in Kurast might be able to help her control whatever strange power she had building within her, and for that reason too he must continue. He sighed, feeling that the burden of all he carried might be too heavy to bear.

*Help me make the right choices for her, and for all of us.*

James's cloak had fallen away from Leah in her sleep. He pulled it back up over her shoulders, and she stirred briefly, and was still.

Something moved outside the ring of trees. The sound of panting came faintly from somewhere in the direction of the river, as though from a large dog or wolf, then a scratching, like nails on wood. Cain returned to the glowing embers, stirring them with a stick until flames sprang up, and piling on more wood until the fire began crackling and the camp grew bright enough for him to see more clearly. He went to his rucksack, looking for some kind of protective artifact or scroll, but he could think of nothing suitable. If whatever creature was out there wanted them, he was helpless to stop it.

Somewhere in the distance, an unearthly howl rose up, melancholy and haunting, before drifting away to silence. Nothing else happened. After standing quietly for some time, listening, Cain took his seat. Lulled by the warmth of the fire, he was eventually taken over by sleep once more, and thankfully he did not dream again.

# TWELVE

## *The Walled Town*

The next morning dawned bright and cold. A thin layer of frost covered the ground outside the trees. Leah's skin was pale, and she had dark circles under her eyes. Cain gave her the last of the fish for breakfast, keeping only a few small bites of skin for himself.

They did not speak of what had happened the night before as they gathered their few belongings and left the camp. But a greater shock awaited them just outside. A tualang tree at least a hundred feet high had fallen directly across the bridge. Its branches lay splayed in all directions like some kind of monstrous squid, and the wooden planks had cracked at the bridge's center and collapsed into the river. The water boiled and rushed all around it, partially flooding the banks.

It had been too dark to see last night. But Cain had heard the thundering sound of the tree falling. He had felt the pulse of energy from her. *If this was her doing, what sort of immense power does she wield?*

"Just some bad luck," he said aloud. "The tree is old, the trunk rotted. You can see the damage there, by the root." He stepped around broken branches that littered the ground, feeling the muck under his sandals, studying the problem more carefully. The river was too deep and too strong to swim, and there was no sign of any other bridges or shallow areas within shouting distance. They might be able to walk the trunk to the other side, if they could avoid the branches and keep their balance.

He warned Leah to stay away from the sap, which was irritating to the skin, and used his staff to keep his feet steady as he climbed up onto the tree and began to navigate through, pushing branches aside and squeezing through others, one step at a time. He was reminded of the narrow, rocky passage in the Vizjerei ruins, and that made him think of poor Akarat, and his terrible fate; for a moment he almost imagined the paladin just ahead of him, urging him forward. But of course nothing was really there, and when he glanced back, he saw Leah close behind, her small face somber and determined.

The bridge groaned ominously, pieces of its structure tumbling into the raging rapids. Finally Cain reached the end, where the shattered trunk sent thick splinters of wood like spikes in all directions, and as he climbed over the trunk, a large splinter caught at his tunic, scratching deeply into the skin of his side. A burning pain raced through him before he pulled himself free and limped to the ground. Cain touched the spot and found traces of blood.

Leah jumped down lightly a moment later. All at once, with a shriek and a great, earth-shaking crash, the entire structure collapsed into the river. Plumes of water shot thirty feet into the air, the surface churning and boiling as the two travelers were instantly soaked through by the spray. Cain stumbled backward, his heart in his throat. A few moments earlier and they would have been killed.

One thing was certain: there was no turning back now.

They kept to a steady pace as the sun rose in the sky and banished the last of the night's chill. Cain used his staff to bear as much of his weight as he could, but his feet were growing worse, and his knees and back were threatening to give out. And now he had a new wound, which had begun to throb dully. He felt unbearably old.

As the morning stretched into afternoon, the road began to climb slowly into the hills. It had not taken a direct route to Kurast, instead going east to the river before taking a turn to run south. Rising above them in the distance, the mountains ran down the length of the land as though across the back of some giant sea monster.

Cain found the going even tougher here as the heat swelled, the ground rockier and more rutted than before. It was well past noon now; they had finished the last of the water from the small pouch, but there was nothing on the horizon to indicate a place where they might stop for more. They hadn't seen a single soul since they had left Caldeum.

Three hours later, they passed a well-worn footpath that branched out to the right and disappeared into the hillside. Just beyond it they came to a steeper pass cut into the hills that had been overrun with boulders. The two cliff faces on either side were nearly sheer, and the rockslide was almost thirty feet high between them.

The two travelers stood at the foot of the rock-strewn track. The road was completely blocked.

He consulted a map from his rucksack. The path they had just seen should lead them around this pass. They could rejoin the road a few miles farther on, as it looped back. "We'll take the long way around," he said. "Come on."

Leah didn't move. She stared at the slide, her little face screwed up in concentration. "There's someone here," she said.

Cain leaned on his staff and studied her. "Why would you say that?"

She shrugged and looked around at the hills that seemed to

loom over them in the sunshine. "It's scary out here. I feel like there's someone watching us."

Cain stopped to catch his breath and look around. He had had the nagging feeling for some time now that they were being watched as well. He scanned back down in the direction they had come, and gazed at the hills above them, looking for some kind of hiding place where a man might take cover. At first he found nothing—no movement, no sense of a presence lurking anywhere. But then he thought he heard a very slight sound, like the scraping of something against rock.

A stream of pebbles trickled down the embankment.

*The people there will take what they can from you and leave you to die on the road*, Kulloom had said. *And there are other things . . . Things that are not so kind.*

Cain glanced at Leah, who was continuing to stare up at the pile of rock, her face ashen. It would not do to spook her. Even if they were not alone, whatever might be watching could be some kind of animal, or it might be someone perfectly harmless, who simply preferred to remain hidden.

*No reason to think it might be something . . . unnatural.*

"I'm quite sure we're alone, Leah."

The little girl did not seem convinced. She crossed her arms and hugged herself. "Why haven't we seen more people? And where are we going, anyway?"

"A city called Kurast."

Leah's eyes grew wide. "That's a bad place."

"Now, Leah—"

"My moth—Gillian told me it was haunted. Why would you want to take me there?" She took a step away from him. "You—you want to sacrifice me to some dark magic, don't you?! You don't want to help me at all. You're . . . you're a sorcerer who summons demons! Mother told me about people like you!"

Leah's gaze went from side to side. Cain tried to offer reassurances, but he was at a loss for words; speaking more plainly or offering a logical solution, the way he might when dealing with an adult, did not seem to work with her.

He took a step forward and immediately knew he had made yet another mistake, but it was too late. Leah bolted back down the road for the path like a frightened rabbit, running as fast as her little legs would carry her.

"Wait!" Cain hobbled off the road after her, but the path was steep, and his knees began to protest more loudly. He thought about the long road he had ahead of him, the dangers he would face, and the problems a little girl could cause if she would not obey him. He watched her growing smaller as she continued up the hill, and kept on as quickly as he could, leaning on his staff for support, calling out to her again as she crested the top and disappeared.

Fresh panic washed over him, along with the memory of those lost and never found. The path seemed to widen and change before him, and for a moment he saw, with horrible clarity, an overturned wagon, one wheel still spinning, bright red blood splashed across its spokes as it flicked lazily around in the sunlight.

Cain blinked, wiping away the vision. He swallowed back a shriek of terror; his hand was in his sack again, fingers touching the folded paper in the hidden pocket. He withdrew his hand as if it had been scalded.

The path was empty, a desolate stretch of parched ground. The breath wheezed harshly in his lungs, and his throat grew tight. Why did children never listen, even when it was for their own good?

The day had turned darker by the time he neared the crest. Cain spotted her in the growing gloom. She was sitting on a rock a few feet off the path, head in her hands. At first he thought she was crying, but when she looked up, her face was dry.

"It's no use," she said. "I've nowhere to go, and nobody to help me."

Cain stopped, leaning over on his knees, trying to catch his breath. His heart was like a runaway horse galloping through his chest. A wind came up, ruffling Leah's cloak and bringing a chill deep into Cain's bones.

Finally he straightened. "I'm trying to help you, Leah," he said, as he got his wind back. "But you can't . . . run off like that. You must understand that there are things . . . the road to Kurast is a dangerous one. A child could disappear in an instant, with nobody to witness what happened!"

"Are you trying to frighten me even more?"

Cain gathered himself for a moment, regaining control. "I am simply telling you the truth. It is my way, to speak plainly. There is evil in this world, things you cannot imagine. There are goat-men and demons and creatures even worse than that. It's best to be cautious and prepared."

Fresh shock whitened Leah's face. For a moment he thought she might cry again, but she simply stood up off the rock, and when she looked at him again, her face was full of a child's righteous anger. "Gillian used to talk like that too," she said. "You're strange. I don't think I like you much." She pointed down the other side of the hill. "I want to go *there*. Maybe they could help us."

A small town seemed to squat in the valley below, ringed with a high stone wall and jungle, heavily fortified and partially hidden by a mist that had arisen suddenly and had begun creeping up the hillside. The town appeared dark and lifeless at first, but then a single light flickered like a beacon through the mist and seemed to dance, as if someone with a lantern was moving through the streets.

In his panic, Cain hadn't even noticed it. He should have been relieved, but the bouncing light only served to deepen the sense of isolation, and after another moment it flickered again and went out.

He consulted his map again, but the little town did not appear on it. He peered through the gloom at the path they were on, which led down the other side of the hill and through the trees. It wouldn't take them long to reach the gates. If they hurried, they could be there before the stars became visible.

Something about the entire scene worried him; there was a weight to the air, a sense of foreboding that he had learned over the years not to ignore. But they had little choice, he thought. Without food or water, they would not get much farther.

"Come on then," Cain said, starting down the hill. "No sense in waiting here any longer. Let's see if they're hospitable."

Another gust of wind swept over them, stronger this time. The wind brought the foul smell of rot along with it, like a stagnant bog, as the mist swallowed the ground below. When he glanced back, Leah was following him, clutching the cloak tightly to her throat.

The muscles of Cain's thighs trembled with fatigue as he descended the steep path. He had not eaten since the few morsels of fish skin that morning, and although his body had been trained over his many months of wandering to expect this kind of treatment, he knew that it was only a matter of time before he would not be able to take another step.

*You are an old man,* he thought, as he had dozens of times already during the past few weeks. *You should be dozing on a farmer's porch somewhere with a cup of tea, not out in the wilds searching for demons.* As he walked, the boy from his dream the night before stayed with him, but of course it had not really happened that way. The boy had been gone for decades.

By the time they neared the town, night was close. They walked down a wide, gravel road flanked by tall, spindly trees nearly bare of leaves. The iron gates to the town remained shut, but two large men materialized from a well-concealed door in the stone wall. The guards were as tall as Cain and nearly twice as wide. They wore leather-trimmed breastplates and held double-bladed battle-axes.

The deepening gloom bled the color from the air. The mist was thicker here. It clung to the ground and swirled around the guards' legs, making them appear to be floating apparitions cut off at the knees.

The two guards stepped closer together, blocking the way to the gates. They said nothing, their faces impassive, vaguely threatening.

"We have come many miles, and seek lodging," Cain said. "We are unarmed and will pay for food and a bed to sleep in. We'll be on our way in the morning."

Cain went to his rucksack for a piece of gold, but the guards swung their axes into fighting position and stepped forward, ready to attack.

A shout came from behind the gates, and several figures materialized from the thickening mist. Two more guards released the locks and swung the gates open with a loud, squealing scream of metal as the guards stepped aside, standing at attention.

The man who walked through the gates was tall and cadaverously thin, with long, black hair swept away from his forehead. He wore expensive silk robes and gold jewelry on his fingers, and his smile was wide and friendly. He spread his long arms, as if welcoming home a favorite family member.

"I do apologize for these two," he said, and waved a hand in the direction of the guards. "We are not normally so suspicious, but the times demand it, I am sorry to say. I am Lord Brand. You are on your way to Kurast?"

"We are," Cain said, introducing himself. "And in need of your hospitality."

"And you shall have it." Lord Brand's gaze swept over Leah, his glittering eyes seeming to linger upon her face for a little too long as his smile widened further. "Who might this be?"

"My niece," Cain said. "Forgive me, but she is hungry. We've come a long way, and have not eaten since this morning."

A howl went up from somewhere beyond them, the sound echoing through the valley, bringing chills to Cain's spine. Brand looked to the trees, his smile fading, and he stepped aside, motioning them forward. "You'll stay at my manor," he said. "We should get behind the walls. These days it is not safe to remain outside after dark."

The guards fell in behind as the small party walked through the gates and into the town. A dozen townspeople waited there with their lanterns held high. They all wore the same shapeless, gray clothing, and all of them stood with slack faces, their skin the color of their clothes. They had the skeletal look of the terminally ill, with sunken features and filmy eyes. Several of them muttered under their breath as if to themselves, and their gaze did not meet Cain's as he passed. He wondered what strange illness might be sweeping the little town, and considered turning back with Leah and taking their chances in the jungle.

But the strange procession had its own momentum. He was swept along as Brand took the lead, and the sound of the gates clanging shut behind them rang through the empty streets like a harbinger of doom.

# THIR+EEN

## *Lord Brand's Manor*

A few lights flickered in the windows of houses as they proceeded toward the center of town, but Leah did not see anyone else, and after a few minutes she dropped her gaze to her own feet and simply followed along behind Deckard Cain.

She had begun to regret asking him to come here. Something about this place made her terribly afraid, but she did not know why. Lord Brand acted friendly enough, but he looked strangely tall and misshapen, with his arms and legs so long and thin, and his smile made him look hungry.

The streets reminded her of home, with their looming stone houses and storefronts and narrow alleyways that seemed to lead nowhere. But Caldeum had been full of noise and activity during the early evening hours. There was no life here, nobody out shopping or headed to the local tavern for a drink and a meal. The townspeople walking with them muttered to themselves like madmen, their faces looking as though they hadn't slept well in months. She was only eight years old, but she was perceptive for her age; Gillian had always told her that she could read people better than most adults. And what Leah felt about this place made her stomach churn.

She risked a glance at Cain, who was just ahead of her. He was favoring his right leg more heavily now, leaning on his staff with each step. When they had first met, he had seemed impossibly old to her, with his wrinkled face, white hair, bushy eyebrows, and long, stringy beard, and now he appeared to be about to collapse.

*What if he falls down dead here, in the middle of the road? What will become of me?*

At the thought of that, Leah's fear became a near full-blown panic. She had run from him earlier because she had thought he was dangerous, but as odd as he was, he had done nothing other than try to protect her so far. Without him, Leah would be entirely alone. Now they were surrounded by people she trusted even less, and the old man was the only thing between her and starvation, or far worse.

She had had terrible dreams last night, of monsters that attacked her. She stared at the dark alleys on either side, imagining things watching them. Goatmen with glowing eyes and bloody mouths. Demons, looking for blood. *They want you, Leah, and if they find you, you're never coming back from that. Never.* A sewer grate beckoned, its iron bars like teeth; she imagined claws wriggling up through it, grasping at her feet.

Another howl rose up from somewhere in the distance. The small procession stopped abruptly, and Leah stared at what appeared to be a small castle. It had its own stone walls and gate, a smaller ring inside the town's larger one, and was built on the highest point of land, so that it appeared to loom over them. There were so many angles, turrets, and roofs it was impossible to make sense of its shape, and Leah became dizzy and looked away.

Lord Brand turned to face them with another broad smile. "My home," he said, as two of the guards opened the gates and stepped aside, standing at attention. "The Brand manor. You are most welcome here, for as long as you like."

Something about his voice brought deeper chills to Leah's spine. She glanced around at the houses that huddled against the night, and for a moment she was sure she saw movement in the shadows, something that slithered like tentacles, but when she focused on the spot, there was nothing there at all.

Cain and Leah followed Brand and the guards through the gates and up the huge, sweeping front steps, leaving the other townspeople behind. The double doors of the manor opened with a slow screech, revealing a cavernous entry hall with an enormous fireplace at the far end and a fire roaring in the hearth. Torches blazed on the walls, illuminating a series of elaborate tapestries hanging by iron hooks. A breath of air guttered the torches and set the tapestries fluttering, their shadows moving across the stone floor like black wings.

The fire seemed to do little for the cold, which made Leah shiver and draw her cloak more tightly around her thin frame. There was a strange smell in the air. She looked up, but the ceiling arched so far above her head that she could barely make it out. She clutched her arms to her chest and tried to think of warm summer days, but the darkness closed in again, making her want to scream.

Brand's footsteps echoed as he led them through the hall. They seemed to walk far longer than they should, but when Leah glanced back, she was surprised to find that they had barely moved; the entry doors were just a few steps away.

Eventually they reached another large room, with an enormous wooden table set for a meal. A gray-haired woman who might have been about Gillian's age stood muttering to herself. Brand clapped his hands, and she immediately scurried off.

"We were about to sit down for supper," Brand said. "Fill your bellies, and then I would be pleased to hear more about your travels."

Leah sat down with Cain at one end of the table. A few moments later the servants returned with heaping platters full of steaming food: whole chickens skewered on blackened sticks; thick, juicy slices of red meat; asparagus; potatoes; and loaves of warm bread. In spite of herself, Leah's stomach rumbled, and she and Cain sat down at one end of the long table and dug in as Brand settled across from them and watched intently with his fingers steepled before his nose, the ghost of a smile still on his face.

The food was strangely tasteless, but Leah didn't care; it was hot, and there seemed to be an endless supply. She tore into a leg of chicken, juices running down her chin, and ripped off a chunk of bread to mop up the pool of salty broth on her plate. The potatoes burned her fingers, but she ate them anyway, and washed them down with a mug of wine.

Next to her, Cain ate in silence. Brand never took a single bite and simply watched them without comment, occasionally gesturing to the servants to bring more of one thing or another as supplies ran low.

Leah ate until she could not eat another mouthful. The remaining strings of meat on her plate were too rare and oozing pink fluid; she swallowed against the gorge that suddenly swelled in her throat, and as she looked around, the room filled with shadows that pooled in the corners and crept like black mist.

"So tell me," Brand said, breaking the silence. "What is your business in Kurast?"

Cain looked up from his plate. His eyes looked glassy in the firelight. "I'd rather not say," he said. "But I can offer you payment for your hospitality." He took out a gold nugget and placed it on the table.

"Fair enough. But I won't take your gold. We don't get many visitors here, but those who come tend to stay for longer than they expect."

"We'll be gone in the morning."

"Perhaps." Brand shook his arms to free them from the cuffs

of his robe, and the fabric fluttered. A deck of cards appeared in his hand. "You look like you're searching for something, my friends. Let me offer you a reading. The cards can suggest a possible future and can help you find the right way forward."

He let the cards drift through his long fingers like water flowing over a drop, deftly flicking one out to the table, then another, and another. They were oversized and thick, painted with bright red and black figures; the first showed a scroll, the next a sorcerer with a serpent around his waist, the third a man on a wheeled chariot being pulled by two mules, one black, one white. "Taratcha is a misunderstood art," Brand said. He stopped the soft rain of cards from one hand to another and placed the remaining deck on the table. "The word comes from *turaq*, which means 'pathways.' There are always multiple paths open to you. There is nothing inherently wrong with the cards themselves. But there are those who shy away from the truth, finding it too difficult to bear." He tapped an upturned card with a shiny fingernail. "The Scroll of Fate. Changes are coming, your destiny awaits you. Forces are gathering on the horizon, something momentous." He tapped another. "You see here, the Sorcerer. I can tell you are under great stress, and time is a heavy weight upon your necks. There are heavy choices to make, but you are resourceful. This quest consumes you, yet you are uncertain about its outcome. The answers may come from within, or from another who can bring about a transformation." He tapped a third card. "Here, the Wheeled Chariot. It moves between spiritual planes. This can represent a great battle that can be won, if you have the strength to see it through. But it requires control over forces that may consume you and opposing needs that may pull you apart. You must overcome these opposites and bring them together in order to triumph. The Wheeled Chariot suggests a great conviction to overcome, but also an inner focus that may destroy others around you."

Brand swept up the cards, then picked up the deck again. This time when he let the cards flow, flicking out one after another, he kept his hypnotic gaze on Cain's face, and the cards seemed to float in slow motion before settling before them, face up. Leah saw a hooded man with wings of light, a warrior swinging a giant sword, and a tall, dark tower struck by lightning. The last one disturbed her; she could see figures falling from the tower, looks of terror on their faces.

"Justice," Brand said. "This is paired with the second card, Judgment. There is a great tragedy in your past that must be overcome, balance restored. You are preoccupied with that tragedy, even as you try to ignore it. But it will be resurrected whether you like it or not. You must face a moment of reckoning for what you have done."

He tapped the last card with the tall building rising up from a jagged, broken plain, its black surface cutting through storm clouds and looming over what appeared to be a city far below. Leah looked more closely at what appeared to be creatures below it, reaching up for the falling men. There was something terrifying about the card, a darkness that spread through the room. The card's contents seemed to change as she watched, growing more detailed, the creatures writhing upon its surface.

"The Black Tower," Brand said, his eyes focused upon Cain's face, a slight smile on his lips. "An ill omen, I'm afraid. Chaos and destruction may come to you. Something long lost will rise again. Along with it, an epiphany and, again, transformation, as with the Sorcerer. This may be brought about by you or another, but it will come, and you will never be the same."

Leah's stomach churned. The card's contents swirled and shifted, and she looked away. For a moment, what she saw did not register to her shocked senses; the food on her plate had changed. Instead of the remnants of a fine meal, the plate held strings of raw, glistening gristle and matted fur, along with a long, hairless tail curled across its edge that twitched once, and was still.

Leah shoved the plate away from her in terror and disgust as Brand appeared to grow in size, looming over the table like some kind of giant. As the room started to spin and it became harder to breathe, Leah began to see him as a monstrous, beady-eyed crow, head to one side, studying them as a bird might study a carcass on the road before pecking at the meat.

A woman came to clear her plate. The woman did not look at her or speak at all, and Leah noticed bruises on her neck, as if she'd been choked. She wanted to scream, but something was wrong with her throat. The room still spun lazily around her, but she could not make herself move. Her body clenched down hard, threatening to throw up all the food she had eaten.

"I don't feel so well," she said thickly. "I don't—I don't think—"

Lord Brand stood up so quickly the chair nearly tipped over. "You must be exhausted from your long journey," he said. "Let me show you to your rooms. We can talk more tomorrow."

Cain tried to stand as well. The old man's eyes were drooping, his body sagging as if he could barely hold himself upright. Leah couldn't seem to focus. She could not move her legs.

More of the gray, lifeless townspeople materialized from nowhere and helped them from their seats, holding their arms as they followed Brand like dull sheep through the huge manor.

The rooms seemed to go on forever, with many archways and doors leading off in different directions. Most of the doors were closed, and Leah heard thumps and low moans coming from behind them. The ceiling lowered itself above their heads, until it seemed they were walking through a narrow tunnel, cobwebs hanging in the corners, the walls dripping with moisture and covered in a strange green moss. She thought she might be dreaming, but the hands holding her up felt real; she looked at them and saw curved, yellow talons, and she tried again to scream but managed only a whisper.

Finally they ascended a stone staircase. The manor seemed to go on forever, the upper hallway receding to a pinpoint beyond these chambers, so that Leah got the feeling she was in some kind of magical structure that might house thousands. When she glanced behind them, she did not see the staircase they had ascended, even though it should have been right there.

The others were carrying her entire weight now, and when she looked at the old man, his head was slumped, his feet dragging along the floor. Darker shadows lurked, and flickering candles were set at far intervals in small recesses in the walls, leading to a set of adjoining rooms.

"Here we are," Brand said, his long arms outstretched, directing them into a sleeping chamber with a four-poster bed in the middle that was large enough for five people. The thought of his touching her made Leah want to scream. "This should suffice. The young lady may sleep here, if she prefers." He motioned to a second, smaller room, connected by an open door.

Cain stumbled, and Brand was at his side in an instant, saying something in his ear in a voice too low for Leah to hear. He led Cain to the bed and sat him down on it. "Sleep as long as you like. We hope you'll be comfortable here."

Leah tried to protest, to say something that would break the silence and make Cain wake up from his trance; but she found herself growing ever sleepier, her limbs being drawn down toward the floor and becoming impossibly heavy, and her eyes closing of their own accord, and she shuffled forward to the other room, nodding. She thought she saw Gillian standing there, waiting with open arms, but it was the Gillian she remembered from years ago, and not the one who had lost her mind and tried to kill them all. This Gillian was kind and gentle, and sang to her at night, and tucked her in as a real mother should.

*Come to bed*, Gillian said, and as Leah climbed onto the soft covers and closed her eyes, she thought for just a moment that Gillian's arms had begun to grow longer and darken, shriveling into something else that slithered up the sides of the bed to wrap her in a black, soundless cocoon, before sleep took her and she drifted dreamlessly through an endless ocean.

# FOURTEEN

## *A Stranger Comes*

Deckard Cain dreamed of fire and blood. He was caged like an animal, hanging from a pole twelve feet off the ground as grotesque, gibbering demons laid waste to the last remains of his beloved Tristram.

They had returned shortly after Aidan had left the town in the dark of night. The siege on Tristram had not been over, after all, and the creatures that had descended upon it were far worse than ever before. They fed on human flesh, tearing the corpses on the ground limb from limb, chasing after those few townspeople who remained alive. The entire world had fallen into anarchy, and he, last of the Horadrim, the one remaining hope of a long and proud line of heroes, crouched impotently in his own filth, waiting to die.

In his dream, a new man appeared; his face was hooded by a dark robe, his back hunched, and he pointed a long, bony finger in Cain's direction. The finger grew into a blackened, twisting sliver of wood, curling toward the cage, wrapping around it, weaving through the bars until they had been almost completely covered. Then the tendril of wood began to squeeze. Metal groaned and popped, and Cain huddled in the center of the cage as everything collapsed around him, pushing in on all sides until he could no longer breathe.

He was consumed, lost, abandoned, and forsaken. He was no Horadrim, and no hero. He would die here, alone, while Diablo's two brothers, Mephisto and Baal, destroyed Sanctuary, once and for all.

Cain awoke gasping into shadows, his body flushed and covered in sweat, the covers of the bed wrapped so tightly around his body he couldn't move. At first he remembered little about how he had gotten there, but slowly the memories began to return, and he recalled entering the strange little town, the residents all walking silently with their heads down, led by the mysterious Lord Brand, and the meal at his table, with its seemingly endless supply of food. After that, all memory was gone.

Cain cursed himself for being so careless. There was evil here, although Brand's purpose remained unclear. What had he done to them? And who was really behind this?

Cain tried to sit up, but could not. His arms were pinned to his sides, his legs immobile.

These were no bedsheets.

The room was lit by the remains of a single candle in an alcove in the wall, sputtering down to the last half inch of wax. The flickering flame sent shadows dancing across the walls. The bed was covered with a mass of rough and tangled roots, pulsing and slithering and tightening like black snakes around him. They had grown right up out of the floor, encasing his body. As he watched in horror, more of them wriggled through cracks in the wood, growing longer and thicker as they slid up the side of the bed and whipped around it to hold him fast, their hairy sides sticking and pulling at his skin.

His staff and rucksack were sitting in the corner, out of reach.

*Leah.* Cain struggled, but the roots only tightened even more until it became difficult to breathe. Where was she? Was she safe?

More shadows fell across the bed. Lord Brand loomed over him, his servants behind him in gray, hooded robes. The people were chanting in low voices, and they held lanterns so that the room filled with an orange glow.

Brand held up a hand, and they stopped at once, standing like statues behind him. Brand was smiling again in that predatory way, and his eyes were bright, searching Cain's features for something that was not clear. "Did you think you would be allowed to go to Kurast alone? To find the answers you seek?"

"Release us—"

"You will remain here, for now. Our master commands it."

"Who is your master?"

Brand looked away, the smile fading from his face. "We are born from darkness, into light, and He shall lead us back to the fires from which this world was forged—"

"Enough!" Cain said. He tried to shout a warning to Leah, but his voice came out as a hoarse cry. The hairy roots slithered again, tightening painfully across his chest. He groaned.

Brand's gaze fixed on his. "You are weak, Deckard Cain. You search for others to do your dirty work for you, yet you call yourself Horadrim. Those who put their trust in you have known only pain. The cards speak the truth: chaos and destruction is coming for you, and you will face a final judgment for what you have done."

Cain reeled, as if from a blow. Brand knew exactly where to strike: Cain's deep fear of cowardice, selfishness, and regret. *I have failed.* Foul demons were at work; he must not let them see his weakness. Yet he had no access to a spellbook, nothing to use that might free him from their clutches.

"How do you know who I am?"

"I know you are an old fool," Brand hissed suddenly, thrusting his head forward like a cobra about to strike. "The plagues of Hell are coming. And they will destroy this world and all it has been, and the gates of the High Heavens will fall. We cannot stop them, but we can avoid the eternal hellfires if we do what must be done, if you are sacrificed, and the girl is given up—"

A high scream came from the adjoining room. Cain jerked his head to the right, trying to see into Leah's room. One of the cultists was standing in the open doorway, his back to them; he stumbled and fell, as if shoved by a powerful hand.

The temperature in the room dropped, and a now-familiar charge tightened the air around them. Lord Brand stepped away from Cain's bed, his hawk-like features registering shock, and then fear, as a great tearing sound came from Leah's room.

Brand's skin rippled. For a moment, his brow flattened, his nose protruded grotesquely, and eyes shrank to beady specks.

Cain sensed movement from the doorway.

Leah stood there among the shattered remains of the roots that had imprisoned her, her head up, eyes blazing. Yet it was not Leah, not exactly; something else seemed to carry her as she strode confidently through the room to Cain's bedside, ignoring Brand, who fell away from her, arms up as if to protect himself. Leah raised her own arms, and something huge and powerful exploded out of her, blue fire licking her fingertips as the roots holding Cain's bed tore to pieces and the cultists were thrown backward against the walls, tumbling like straw thrown by the wind.

Abruptly, Cain could breathe freely again, and he took in great gasps of air, his lungs burning, nostrils filled with a smell that was half copper, half foul bog, a sulfurous stench that made his stomach churn. He climbed from the bed and gathered his rucksack and staff. When he turned back, Leah was still standing there, motionless, and when he grabbed her arm, she turned docilely toward him, her face slack and lifeless. He snapped his fingers before her, but she did not seem to react. Some kind of trance again, similar to the one he had seen back in Caldeum.

But there was no time to explore it further. Already the people on the floor were stirring.

Where the roots had been was a scattering of black seeds. Cain scooped some up and dropped them in his sack, then led Leah to the door and down the hall to the stairs. The entire house seemed to have shifted in the night; the hallway turned a corner, and the stairway appeared farther away than he remembered and curved back upon itself. He fought back the disorientation, and they descended as quickly as possible. On the bottom floor, the layout had changed, and he led them through more hallways than he remembered and past rooms they had not seen.

Finally he found the front doors, and he pulled them open and they ran out, into the frigid night.

The fog was thick, swirling across the ground and shrouding the nearby houses. More townspeople crowded the front walk, chanting, all of them in the same gray robes. As Cain led Leah through their midst, they reached out with grasping hands to clutch at his tunic. But they were slow and clumsy, and he was able to swing with his staff and tear free before he heard a shout. He turned and stared in shock; there was powerful magic here indeed.

Lord Brand had emerged after them, but the manor was no longer there. In its place stood a modest, one-story house, its straw roof sagging inward.

"Run, Leah," Cain said.

The gates were hanging open. He and Leah raced through them, Leah leading the way now. They turned up an unfamiliar street and ducked into a dark alley, Leah running through it to another, wider street, the distance between them lengthening quickly. Cain increased his pace to a hobbling run until his lungs burned with the effort, but Leah was faster, and after another turn he lost her completely in the dark and the fog, and stood panting on a corner, close to panic. Where had she gone?

The town was silent, all windows dark. It appeared abandoned, and Cain had the same feeling he'd gotten back in Caldeum, as if everyone in Sanctuary had disappeared all at once, and he was utterly alone.

A shout came from behind him, and he was about to start running again when he heard a voice raised in an urgent whisper: "This way. Hurry!"

Someone beckoned to him from the shadows of the alley across the street. Cain could make out nothing else but the glint of eyes in the dark. He hesitated as the sound of pursuit grew louder; they would be upon him at any moment.

"The girl is here," the voice said. "She is safe. Please! Come!"

*May the archangels protect us,* Cain thought. He crossed the street as fast as his aching legs would allow and slipped into the alley, ready to face whatever waited for him there.

# FIF+EEN

## *The Graveyard*

It took a few moments for Cain's eyes to adjust as he followed the stranger through the gloom. The person who had spoken to him was a man with his head shaved smooth; he wore some kind of cloth wrapped around his waist, and he moved with a quiet grace, slipping through the night without a sound.

The man led him through the alley to the other side, which opened to a small space between the last row of homes and the stone wall that ringed the town. Leah was waiting for them. She seemed to be in the same trance that he had seen earlier, and did not react to his presence or move in any way.

A light appeared from somewhere beyond the alley. Someone called out, and Cain heard the sound of running feet. "This way," the man said from a trench at the foot of the stone wall. "We must go now."

Cain took Leah by the arm and led her to the trench, which held the end of a clay pipe and a trickle of water, wastewater from the town, most likely; it ran under the wall, through a space covered by iron bars. A portion of the bars had given way, and there was just enough room to squeeze through.

The man disappeared through the hole. Cain helped Leah

down and climbed after her. Brown, foul-smelling water seeped through his tunic and chilled his knees and arms; at the end he had to go onto his stomach and wriggle, pushing his things ahead of him, and the cold ran all the way down his body. There was a moment of claustrophobic terror as Cain's clothes caught on the bars and he didn't have the strength to pull free, but the man grabbed his arms and pulled him the rest of the way.

The scratch Cain had gotten when he had crossed the bridge throbbed dully as he got to his feet and gathered his staff and rucksack. The area where they had emerged was treed and silent, but flat and free of underbrush, and they were able to move quickly.

The icy air made his wet tunic cling to his chest and legs, and he shivered, his teeth chattering, hands shaking. Shadows seemed to flutter all around them, giving the illusion of movement; he heard things slithering, soft thuds and the rustle of dead leaves, the faint crack of a branch, and once, a fluttering of wings over head.

As they reached an open space among the withered trees, the fog dissipated, and gravestones thrust up from the ground like huge, jagged teeth. The stones, which leaned in different directions, had been placed in a circular pattern that led to a round plot in the center with a crypt.

Cain felt a gathering of dark magic that prickled the hairs on his neck. The door to the crypt hung open. Blackness lurked within it.

The man had stopped inside the first ring of stones, holding Leah's hand. Cain studied him in the moonlight that trickled down through the opening in the trees. He was some kind of monk. He had a thick black beard. Heavy wooden beads hung around his neck, armor was bound to his forearms, and he wore boots laced up to his knees. His upper chest was bare, and muscles stood out like cords across his shoulders and arms.

Friendly or not, Cain realized, they had little choice but to trust him. He had given them no reason so far to doubt his intentions, and if Cain's instincts were correct, they were going to need all the help they could get.

As if in answer, a group of shadowy forms burst through the cover of trees all around them. Their pursuers from the town had arrived. Hands grabbed Cain from behind, and others converged on the monk and Leah.

The monk moved with blinding speed, seemingly without effort. It was as if he disappeared and reappeared in another location, slipping through space faster than Cain's eyes could track him, his fists like flat iron anvils as they pummeled those townspeople who dared come within reach. Those who had been holding Cain let him go, and he fell to his knees in the soft ground, looking up in time to see the monk crack two skulls together with a mighty crunch, then drive his foot into the midsection of yet another robed figure, sending it flying at least ten feet backward.

As several more cultists converged on him like mindless puppets, the monk spun and released a thunderbolt of energy that cracked the darkness with a white-hot burst, searing Cain's eyes and making him throw his arm up over his face. When he looked back, blinking away the dots of light that danced before him, the cultists were nothing more than a circular pile of grotesquely seared arms, legs, and torsos. Leah, however, remained unharmed, just a few feet away, still standing immobile as if rooted to the spot, her gaze blank and unblinking.

A scream of anger came from halfway across the graveyard, and Lord Brand emerged from the trees. Brand raised his arms, and Cain felt the ground shift beneath him. Horrified, he scrambled to his feet as something pushed upward through the sod.

A hand and half an arm of decayed flesh emerged, its bony, white fingers wriggling like worms.

Gillian's voice came back to him, from the night of the fire . . . *the dead clawing their way from the ground, the way they did in Tristram. The earth will split, and hell will spew forth . . .*

"We must go, now!" Cain shouted, as the ground began to heave and ripple across the graveyard. The monk picked Leah up and threw her over his shoulder. Cain pulled a scroll from his rucksack and spoke as quickly as he dared, the runes glowing green across the parchment before it began to smoke and crumble in his hands. A distraction for their escape: a spell of elemental magic, easy to conjure, difficult to control.

Crackles of lightning split the night sky, illuminating a nightmare landscape of rotted flesh and blindly grasping hands. Cain did not wait any longer, skirting the edge of the graveyard and avoiding the things that seemed to search him out. The lightning struck the ground in two places, searing flesh and sending explosions of dirt and grass into the air. Another struck at Brand's feet, and he was thrown backward against the remains of his followers.

Cain didn't stay to see the rest. The monk was already gone through the trees, and the old man went after them, leaving the graveyard behind as lightning crashed and shook the earth.

They ran headlong through the jungle, pushing through brush and splashing through another trickling brook, branches scratching Cain's face as he stumbled in the dark. His mind went over and over the scene in the graveyard, trying to make sense of it. How had Brand and his followers arrived there so quickly? Who was he, exactly, and what was his purpose?

*Our master commands it,* Brand had said. He had known about Cain and his Horadric studies, had seemed to know about the impending demon invasion. But he had not answered Cain's question: who was their master?

The monk slowed his pace after a few minutes and proceeded more cautiously and quietly, holding the noise to a minimum. There did not seem to be any pursuit. Sometime later they broke from the jungle. The monk had led them to a hill overlooking the road to Kurast, on the other side of Lord Brand's town. The night sky had cleared, and it stretched overhead like a black carpet peppered with stars. There was just enough light for them to make out the road, a ribbon winding through the valley below.

Cain caught his breath, his sides aching, lungs burning, knees ready to give out. Leah was clinging to the monk with both hands around his neck, and when he set her down gently in a grassy spot, she slumped forward, her eyes glassy and staring at nothing. *She must remain strong in the face of danger.* But as he watched Leah sit like a lifeless statue, his heart broke for her. She was no warrior. She was just a little girl.

"They have not followed us here," the monk said. "We are safe, for now." He put his hands together and gave a slight bow. "I am Mikulov," he said. "From Ivgorod. And you are Deckard Cain, of the Horadric order. I have been following you since Caldeum. It is time we talked of the dangers that are facing us all. We have much to learn from each other, and not much time left."

# SIX✝EEN

## *The Hidden Room*

The Dark One walked the dusty earth. He strode freely among fiends who gibbered and cavorted under a blood-tinged moon, the souls of the damned under their cloven feet. They were the only companions he wanted. This wasteland was his, an area devoid of all green and lush life that grew under the sun—free of all humans, too, at least within this space he had claimed as his own.

Not so far off, sleeping like the dead among the broken and abandoned buildings of the city, were the still-living, breathing husks of men, drained of their will. They were emaciated to the point of collapse, and lived only to serve him, and he took what he needed with the help of his ghoulish soldiers, ruling over them with an iron fist. Their life essence would provide a key element for his grand plans, built upon the extensive research he had done into the ancient writings of the most powerful sorcerers of dark magic. What he was attempting had never been done, not at this scope, and it would require the souls of many thousands of people. It would also require the command of a master of the dark arts, someone with the abilities few had ever possessed.

Someone like him.

As a boy, he had always felt something deep within him that was above the poverty and squalor of his surroundings. He knew that his proper station was above the other boys in the orphanages he passed through, whether they recognized it or not.

He had never known his mother or his father; they had disappeared long before his memories began, and all he had of them was a family name and crest on a scrap of tattered parchment he kept in his pocket. In his daydreams he imagined they were respected, powerful people who had been driven into hiding or killed in a political uprising, forced to give him up as an infant or risk his death. In the string of orphanages he endured beatings, starvation, and nights of sleeping on cold, louse-infested straw; fifteen-hour days of washing laundry in the stream, cutting wheat in the fields, or cleaning out the horse stalls; and teasing from his peers, which often ended in a bloody nose or split lip. He remained silent during these moments, refusing to give in to the urge to run and hide, and the boys eventually found something else to occupy their boredom. When they left him alone, he spent the few precious moments he had learning how to read, and devoured every text he could find.

He learned something about human nature during that time: far too many people, when alone and left to their own devices, were not who they seemed to be. Children were told stories of demons and monsters to keep them in line, but it seemed to him that the real monsters wore human skins.

Eventually, someone else took notice of him. He was older then, and living mostly by himself on the streets. The sorcerer who took him in had an eye for natural talent, and a taste for pain. This sorcerer was not a good man, but a powerful one, and the Dark One learned much under his tutelage. He learned even more through the secret texts he discovered in the man's library and, later, in moldering tombs and forgotten ritual rooms hidden among ancient ruins outside the city, where the sorcerer sent him to gather artifacts from the days when mages ruled Sanctuary.

In one such hidden chamber, he discovered a text that spoke to him more than any other: a genealogy that traced a pattern of births from one of the most powerful mages in history. On the cover of that text, branded into the cracked leather binding, was the same crest from the scrap of paper in his pocket.

The Dark One listened to his footsteps crunching through the broken shells that had washed up onto the shore. His back was hunched, his head thrust forward. He peered out from under his hood. Beyond him lay the water, the smell of sulfur thick in his nostrils. There were things in the shallows, red-skinned beasts that dissipated like smoke, bloody apparitions that screamed soundlessly into the night sky. They had gathered for him, and before long they would be completely under his control. Soon, the Dark One thought, he would rule all of Sanctuary. In the coming End of Days, as the moon turned black and its pull leached the seas from shore, he would transform fully and take his rightful place at the side of the Lord of Lies. And then he would wipe the scourge of humanity off the face of the world, ridding it of the true monsters and paving the way for others to rebuild what was left. This was his destiny.

*Find the girl.*

The words were whispered in his ear, bringing his thoughts into sharp focus. The wind brought him the sound of wings. His scouts were returning, with news. They would not dare come here empty-handed.

The Dark One waited while a giant bird swooped down toward him through the night and settled to the ground with a flapping of feathers that sent wind rippling across the water. As the bird extended its talons, its legs lengthened and grew thicker, wings rolling up like tubes into human flesh, feathers transforming, blending together into a black cloak, beak morphing into a hawkish nose.

The man who now stood before him was skeletal, pale-skinned, and tall, and he held his hands with fingers intertwined at his waist like battling spiders. His cloak was similar to the Dark One's own, and his back was slightly hunched. But there the similarities ended.

"My lord," he said. "I have news. I have seen the girl you seek."

The Dark One smiled. This was what he had been waiting for; the girl and her traveling companion would soon be in his possession. "You have her, then?"

Lord Brand's thin smile faltered, and he broke eye contact. "She has escaped from us, along with the old man. There was someone else who assisted them. In spite of the prophecies, we did not foresee it."

Rage blackened the Dark One's heart, and he took a step forward, his hands clenched into fists. "How could you let that happen?"

"We bound her with black magic, as you instructed, but it was not strong enough. She broke free. Still, we might have had them in the graveyard, were it not for this monk, and the old man. He is . . . resourceful."

"He is *nothing*. Weak and useless, and gravely delusional."

"He raised a powerful storm, my lord. And the spell that had concealed them is still active."

"You have failed me."

"I . . . I am sorry, my lord."

"Let me show you something," he said. He turned away from the pack of ravenous demons and entered the tower with Lord Brand behind him, descending through the hidden panel to the rooms below. This time he passed the chambers where men hung by hooks, going lower, then lower still. Moans and the shaking of chains followed him to a larger room where no torches guttered upon the dripping, moss-covered walls.

The things that gathered there did not like fire, but the Dark One did not mind the darkness; his eyes had also grown accustomed to it, and the moss that encased the walls glowed a faint green, giving off enough light for him to see.

A gigantic, circular stone structure dominated the room, leaving only a ten-foot-wide passageway around it. The structure was like the bulb at the end of a tendril of stone, growing up through the center of the Black Tower.

Archways every few feet allowed access to the passage around the stone bulb. From each of these archways creatures emerged, their pale skin luminous in the faint light.

They watched in silence. "What are they?" Lord Brand whispered finally. His face was drained, his mouth slack as he stared in astonishment. "Feeders? I have heard stories, but I have not seen . . ."

"They were men once," the Dark One said. "The easiest to corrupt, through greed or fear or rage. Now they exist to gather what others possess and bring it here to me, where I keep it safe. This is a weapon, a very rare and dangerous one. And it will ensure our own victory in the coming war."

The creatures crept forward on all fours, their backs twisted and hunched grotesquely upward, their bellies swollen like ticks. One of the creatures passed them, turning a blind, moon face upward, and he put his hand upon its hot, slippery scalp as it hissed with pleasure at his touch.

The creatures approached the bulb, placing their mouths upon a series of small tubes that projected from the stone opposite each archway. Faint, unearthly cries and sobs drifted through the cave, a thousand people in agony. Each of them sighed, quivering, as they released their burden and their swollen torsos withered away to bone and skin.

Lord Brand recoiled as the shrunken, wraith-like husks returned through the archways, making way for more creatures to come forward. They watched in silence as the cycle was repeated and more of them appeared, always more, regurgitating the contents of their bellies into the stone gourd, the cries of the damned drifting through the dark.

"They are loyal servants, and they do not fail me," the Dark One said. "Do you understand?"

Lord Brand nodded. "I do, my lord."

"Good." The Dark One's rage was boiling now, and he could not contain it for much longer. The power churned within him, begging to be released. He gritted his teeth as they returned to the surface and he thought of all who had wronged him over the years. *They must pay for their sins.* For a brief, terrifying moment he imagined his own failure, and a slow death followed by oblivion, his family name and crest once again buried in the bowels of history while Deckard Cain and his legacy lived on.

There were more demons in the surf. The waves moved like oil against the rocky shore as the Dark One turned to Lord Brand. His anger exploded with a white-hot flash as he raised his hands and spoke words of power from the ancient Vizjerei book of spells, summoning the power of Bartuc himself: the Warlord of Blood, master of demonic magic, who had harnessed the power of the Burning Hells to do his bidding.

A bolt of pure energy hit the tall, thin birdman in the chest, opening a smoking, dripping hole in his flesh and throwing him backward to the ground, where he writhed in pain, screaming, as the Dark One strode forward, the power building once again, a delicious wave of euphoria washing over him as he prepared to release it and shatter every bone in the man's body. The demonic specters cavorting about the hissing surf screeched in ecstasy, ready to bathe in the gore, their grotesque bodies pulsating with excitement at the carnage.

"Wait!" The groaning man on the ground held up a hand, the other hand clutching at the wound in his chest. Blood poured over his fingers and onto the sand. "Please. All is . . . not lost!"

The Dark One stopped, holding in the energy like a ball of hot lava in his belly. "Speak quickly," he said, through gritted teeth, his mouth twisted into a grimace of pain and pleasure. He leaned down, pulling the birdman's hands aside and sticking a finger into the wound. "You have only moments to live."

"The old man and the girl are headed for Kurast!" the man screamed. The Dark One removed his finger, and the birdman coughed up a spray of blood. "I am sure of it. We—we can find them again."

"That may be so," the Dark One said. "We may indeed be able to find them again, after all. But I'm afraid you won't be part of the search."

He stood up again, closed his eyes, and released the full fury of his power. Blue fire crackled from his fingertips and laced down toward the birdman, enveloping him. He arched upward, screaming soundlessly as his skin started to bubble and his hair crackled and burst into flame.

The Dark One turned away as the smell of burning flesh wafted across the desolate beach. The demons converged upon the smoldering form, howling with delight, tearing blackened skin from the birdman's limbs with their hands and teeth.

*Lord Brand.* He shook his head. Such a pretentious name for such a useless creature. Birdman was much better. He would return to the Burning Hells to face his master's wrath.

There were others, the Dark One thought, many others who would do his work for him. He thought of the road to Kurast, long, empty, and winding, a very dangerous place. It was not such a wide swath of land to search, and not so far away. Anything could happen there, and a traveling party could be detained and brought to him. He smiled, a sense of calm falling over him as he considered the possibilities. He would have the girl very soon. Perhaps a different approach was needed, he thought, a subtler one of lies and deceit, a manipulation that would use his servants to bring those he was seeking right to his front door. The Lord of Lies would approve; it was time for another meeting to discuss their plans. Time was growing short, and there was much still to do.

The old man would do his lord's bidding, whether he liked it or not. Then the fool would die quite painfully, as his ancestor should have many years ago, and anyone else who stood in the way would die too.

The End of Days was almost upon them all.

# SEVEN+EEN

## *The Road to Kurast*

Mikulov stood on an outcropping of rock, looking out over the landscape that spread below him in the early morning light. The road ran through the valley, and as it grew smaller in the distance, the trees withered, the land growing dull and lifeless before the city of Kurast.

*City of the damned.* They were less than two days' travel away, and what they would find in Kurast and beyond would change his life's path: Mikulov felt certain of that. It had been foretold in the prophecies written many centuries ago, and in his own dreams. He thought of his masters at the monastery, and a pang of sadness touched him; he could never return again. But this was his destiny, and he intended to follow it to the end.

Mikulov brought his hands up and over his head, stretched, standing up on the tips of his toes, and bowed his head. He held this pose for five full minutes, his face serene, his body absolutely still. Anyone watching him might have thought him a statue: they would not have guessed at his inner battle against the impatience that urged him forward. But he knew the importance of peace. It was better to remain calm before leaping to action, even when time was short.

And time was short now, indeed.

The gods would be pleased with his efforts to free Deckard Cain and young Leah. After his vision in the small cave in the hills, he had followed them away from Caldeum, scouting for danger. Once, he had dislodged a group of small rocks, and he had felt sure that Cain would discover his presence as they tumbled down the slope. But the old man had not, and they had ended up in the strange, haunted town. It was then that Mikulov knew he must act quickly. This was the moment the gods had chosen.

His mind cleared of the clutter of sleep, Mikulov relaxed his pose and flexed the muscles of his feet, calves, and thighs, letting the energy he generated move up his torso. The tattoo of the patron god Ytar, the god of fire, seemed to move across his back of its own accord as he stretched his arms forward and down, his skin sliding over sinew and bone. He dipped to touch his forehead to the ground, then looked back up to the gray sky. Storm clouds had gathered on the horizon.

The others would be stirring now. It was time. He took a few moments to gather a welcome bounty he had found growing near the cliff, then climbed down from the rock and padded soundlessly through the clearing, returning to camp to begin the next stage of their journey.

Deckard Cain blinked himself awake, suppressing a groan as he looked up into Mikulov's face. He had barely been able to sleep, consumed with his thoughts of the town and the graveyard, and his dreams were haunted by memories that were even worse. Every single inch of his body ached, and he was in desperate need of a bath. In contrast, the monk appeared as refreshed as if he had spent the night in the emperor's palace.

Mikulov held out a cloth filled with bright red berries. "The gods have provided for us," he said. "They are good, and have healing properties. The ground here has not yet felt the full taint of sickness that has taken Kurast."

Cain glanced at Leah. He had thought she was still asleep, but her eyes were open. The girl hadn't spoken since the graveyard, nor eaten. The berries were safe; he recognized them from his studies on this region, although he had never tasted them before. He took a few from the cloth. Sweet juice flooded his mouth, and he had eaten half the pile before he knew it.

Mikulov's smile grew even wider. "Good, good," he said. He nodded at Leah. "There are enough for two."

His aching knees screaming at him, Cain got to his feet slowly, taking the berries to her. He wasn't sure what they had actually eaten the night before at Lord Brand's home, but the berries seemed to do wonders for his uneasy stomach. "Regain your strength," he said, putting his hand on her shoulder. "We will leave this place when you're ready." Leah took the cloth from him, and for a moment the pain in her eyes was so clear and sharp it nearly took his breath away.

"May I speak with you?" Mikulov asked. He stood a few feet away, hands clasped at his waist. Even motionless, his balance and inner strength were apparent. From their brief conversation last night, before they had fallen into an exhausted sleep, Cain knew the monk had read prophecies written by the Patriarchs and other Ivgorod scholars that were remarkably similar to Cain's Horadric scrolls, and that also warned of the demon invasion of Sanctuary. He was aware of an imbalance in the world that must be corrected. His gods had become restless, he had said.

The Ivgorod monks' combination of religious fervor and calm, centered focus was unique. They were ferocious warriors against the evil that plagued this land. It was good to have one on your side.

Cain thought back to what the demon had said in the Vizjerei ruins: *Your savior is so close, hidden among thousands in plain sight not three days' journey from here.* Demons could be notoriously clever and could not be trusted. But they hid their lies within the truth.

He and Mikulov retreated to a quiet area out of Leah's earshot, and the monk sat cross-legged on the ground next to him. "I don't want to frighten the girl," he said. "But we can't wait any longer. We must go to Kurast."

Cain watched Leah get up and walk away, toward a rocky ledge that broke the cover of dying trees and overlooked the valley below. She climbed the ledge and sat at the top, staring out at something beyond his line of sight. "I cannot take her there," he said quietly. "It's no place for a child, and the events of the past few days have made that clear. I should never have brought her on the road with me. She needs someone who can care for her, and a place she can feel safe."

"You must not turn back now—"

"It is only a detour, my friend. Once I find a home for her, I will return."

"But there is no time," the monk said, putting a hand on Cain's arm. "The month of Ratham is only days away!"

"What do you mean by this?" Cain asked. The month of Ratham was named after the necromancer who had founded the priests of Rathma; he had been a disciple of the celestial dragon Trag'Oul, and a guardian of Sanctuary.

Necromancers had the power to raise the dead.

Mikulov took several narrow, tightly rolled scrolls from a pocket under his belt. "I have seen visions of hidden chambers underground," he said. "They are filled with the dead. And a man, or one who looks like a man, shrouded in darkness. He calls himself the Dark One. In these visions, the man calls the dead to life." The monk unrolled the scroll and spread it gently on the ground. "This scroll is a reproduction of one found in the jungle ruins of Torajan." He unrolled a second one. "This is a Zakarum prophecy from the caves of Westmarch." He unrolled a third. "And this, from the bowels of Bastion's Keep, before Mount Arreat was destroyed. All of them speak of a coming war between darkness and light, and the rising of the dead, an event that will occur on the first day of Ratham."

Cain took the scrolls and scanned their contents. His heart beat faster. Although written in different languages, they all contained references to an army of the dead that would rise as Ratham began. They were important pieces of a huge, complex puzzle that he had been trying to put together ever since Mount Arreat had fallen, and this young man had found them. He felt a slight twinge of jealousy for not having found them himself, but quickly dismissed it as his apprehension grew stronger.

"I have discovered similar writings," he said. "But not with a clear date for such an occurrence. Are you sure these are accurate?"

Mikulov nodded. "They have been verified by our Ivgorod Patriarchs, who are highly trained in such things."

Cain shook his head slowly, once again reading the spidery script scrawled across the brittle pages. If these scrolls were indeed true, then the beginning of the demon invasion was far closer than he had assumed—just seven days away. Even now, the forces of evil were gathering somewhere near Kurast, and their fury could mean the fall of Sanctuary to the Burning Hells, the collapse of the High Heavens, and the end of life as he knew it.

. . . *clawing their way from the ground* . . .

Cain was not normally given to hysterics, and his greatest strength, he had always felt, was his measured, calm approach to crises. Study the problem, evaluate the solutions, and choose the best path. But the events with Lord Brand had disturbed him more than he had thought possible. He kept seeing the hands of rotted flesh and wriggling bones that had punched up through the graveyard sod.

*Seven days.*

The monk was waiting patiently for him to speak. "This Dark One," Cain said. "Lord Brand, in the walled town, mentioned something like this, a master who commands him . . . perhaps it is the same person."

"I have no doubt of it. This man is consumed by hatred and jealousy, and it fuels him. But he is commanded by another, something far more evil. I have seen them both, in my visions of the secret place, hidden underground. A creature so huge and terrible, it is difficult to describe . . . it had armored claws and three horns, and yellow eyes like lamps."

*Belial.* Cain sat back, thunderstruck. He had suspected as much for some time, but this drove it home: the Lord of Lies was at work in Sanctuary.

He searched for the right words. "You describe one of the rulers of what we call the Burning Hells. There are others, but he and his brother Azmodan rose to power after the Prime Evils were banished to our lands. I saw the great mountain fall when the Worldstone was destroyed, and I knew that although Baal and his army had been defeated, it was merely the beginning. Evil overran our lands. The signs of Sanctuary's corruption are everywhere now: the blight that has begun to overrun our oceans and forests, the tales of hellish creatures spotted in the Dreadlands and among the jungles of Torajan. People vanishing without a trace or, worse, the wasting sickness that seems to spread within certain cities. But I am afraid that the greatest threat to mankind is yet to come."

Cain described his journey to the Vizjerei ruins in the Borderlands, and what he had found there: evidence of some form of the Horadric order still alive in Sanctuary, evidence that had been strengthened by his visit with Kulloom in Caldeum.

Mikulov nodded. "We must find these men who say they are Horadrim," he said. "Yet . . . you are conflicted." He glanced across the clearing at the spot where Leah sat upon the rock.

"How can I ignore such signs, in service to a child? And yet, how can I continue to put Leah's life at risk?" Cain had done such a thing before, through his own selfishness and neglect. He could not allow that to happen again.

"The girl reminds you of something terrible you suffered," Mikulov said. "I can sense that well enough. It is natural that you would try to protect her. But she is a part of this, as much as you or I. The prophecies about the coming war speak of her role as well."

"She is only a child—"

"You must embrace this, and welcome whatever will come. What we witnessed last night should stand as a warning. Dangerous magic is at work in these lands. Such power to raise the dead is not lightly wielded. Whoever is behind this is a very powerful sorcerer, and engaged in the most destructive kind of demonic spells. And his time is coming soon, if we do not do something to stop him."

Cain found Leah still sitting cross-legged on the rock, staring at the valley below. He sat down next to her in silence and waited patiently for her to speak.

"There are no animals," she said, after a time. "Where have they all gone? And the trees. Look at them."

Cain followed her gaze out over the valley toward Kurast, huddled in the distance like a blight upon the world. In days past, the growth would have been a lush, vibrant green, but the trees grew ever more gray and stunted as they neared the city, as if a fire had run through them, turning their leaves to ash.

"I suspect the animals are in hiding, much like most of the

people," he said. "They sense that the world around us is not calm or welcoming. The trees are a part of that."

"Why aren't we hiding too?"

It was impossible to answer. In the old days, Cain might have begun a lecture about the history of evil and the rise of heroes who battled against it. *In the absence of true heroes, others must answer the call.* But something made him pause. "I was thinking," he said simply, "that it might be time for that. To find a place where you would be safe."

She looked at him sharply. "You would come with me?"

"I have my own journey still ahead of me, Leah. I must not shy away from my destiny. I will find a place for you, I promise. And I will return, when the time is right."

They sat in silence for a moment. Cain thought of the long road back the way they had come. The bridge had fallen; they would have to search for a place to cross, and even if they could find it, there was no shelter for them in Caldeum. Where else could they go? All the way across the sea, to Westmarch? There was no shelter for a little girl there, either. The orphanages were little better than slave camps. He sighed, and rubbed his itchy beard. A journey like that would take weeks, and by then it would be too late for everyone.

"I miss my mother," Leah said. A tear trickled down her cheek. "And I don't remember what happened last night. Why don't I remember?"

"Our minds do strange things sometimes. But everything is going to be all right." Even as the words left his mouth, Cain felt the betrayal, the lie in them. "The truth is," he said, "I don't know why. I don't have all the answers, although I wish I did."

Leah seemed to shrink into herself, hunching her shoulders against the world. "Please don't leave me alone," she said. She looked up at him, her eyes glimmering in the morning light. *"Please."*

"It would be best—"

"I want to go with you!" Leah suddenly leaned forward and hugged him violently, her little arms clutching at his tunic. Her tears wet his chest. "I don't know anyone anymore, I don't even know who my real mother is, and I don't want to be alone. My mother—Gillian—she trusted you; you told her you would take care of me!"

Cain sat rigidly upright, every muscle in his body tensed as Leah continued to sob. A thousand different thoughts ran through his racing mind, many of them jumbled fragments of memory that had been forced so deep inside his subconscious they had shattered like stained glass. He caught a flash of color like a little boy's laughter, and another like the sad moans of a woman in pain as a red-stained wagon wheel spun over and over in the bright, cruel sunlight.

*I cannot bear it,* he thought, *not any longer,* but instead of pushing her away he found himself gathering the little girl up in his arms and rocking her until her tears eased and the hitches in her chest began to slow.

"It's all right, Leah," he said. "I won't leave you. I promise. We shall go to Kurast together."

# EIGH+EEN

## Tristram's End

Deckard Cain clutched like a drowning man at the slippery bars that stood between him and oblivion. The cage rocked gently in a hot wind, bringing the smell of charred wood and scorched human flesh. Shame and horror twisted like a knife in his guts, and he moaned in sorrow at the memory of all the pain and bloodshed he had seen, and all he had lost.

Everything that had ever meant anything to him was gone. Aidan, the king's eldest son, whom Cain had tutored so long ago, and who had slain Diablo and emerged from the catacombs a hero, had disappeared in the night, and Hell had come back to Tristram.

"My Aidan," he whispered through cracked lips, and then gasped a plea that fell away into emptiness. "My Tristram. Please, no more. No more . . ."

His limbs shook with exhaustion, his body near collapse. He had not eaten in days. He peered with watery eyes at the last of the flames guttering among the remains of his town. They had come with little warning, returning to finish the survivors, who had barely had the chance to breathe after the Diablo's reign of terror. The people had fought valiantly with the last of their strength and taken a few of the damned with them; a bloodied goatman lay sprawled across a pathway with an axe in its chest, and the head of an imp stared vacantly back at Cain from the edge of the well, its eyes like half-lidded, foggy windows to hell.

But the people of Tristram had paid dearly for their efforts. The ground was soaked with blood; human limbs and chunks of bodies ripped and bitten littered the space where the town's bonfire had been built not long ago.

One of the limbs lying closest to him was recognizable by the jagged, half-healed bite marks along the forearm: Farnham, the drunken father of three who had emerged from the catacombs a ruin of his former self.

Deckard Cain's beloved home was gone forever.

The old man screamed, shaking the bars, his voice ragged. The horrible, crushing weight of his sins was too much. He could not live any longer with the knowledge that Aidan was lost, consumed by the spirit of the evil that he had fought against. This slaughter could have been avoided, if only Cain had been the man his mother had always wished him to be. Was this penance for his earlier transgressions? Had he brought this upon them all? He couldn't bear the thought.

"Come back for me, you filthy, murdering cowards! Come do your dirty work! I am WAITING!"

As if in answer, something moved from the shadows behind the smoking rubble of the old pub.

A man lurched into sight, dragging his right leg. He stopped, cocked his head as if listening, then lurched forward again, directly toward the square where Cain had been hung inside his iron cage and left to die.

It was Griswold, the town blacksmith. But something was wrong with him. Cain's faint hope and shout of recognition died on his lips; the man's eyes were wild, barren, and soulless, his mouth twisted in a snarl, his bloody hands up and clutching at the air. His body was bloated and pale, the color of the dead.

Griswold came nearer. He stopped below the cage, staring up with hunger on his face, his mouth working like a man looking at his last meal. He moaned, a sound like a wind through an empty, echoing crypt.

"No, Griswold," Cain whispered. He shrank back from the bars, shaking his head. "Not you, too . . ."

As the cursed creature reached out for the rope to shake the cage free, an arrow thudded into his left shoulder. Griswold howled and tore it away. Black blood bubbled up from the wound and oozed down his arm, and he shook like a wet dog, sending splatters in all directions.

Another arrow whistled through the air, narrowly missing his head. The creature looked around and then lumbered off, still screeching in pain and anger.

Cain returned to the bars. A tall, beautiful woman in full amazonian dress emerged from the cover of the scorched trees, glanced around her, and then approached the cage, slinging her bow back over her shoulder. She wore a golden helmet and armor.

She released the rope holding the cage aloft, then caught its end and lowered Cain gently to the ground. He tumbled into the blood-soaked mud, his fingers clutching the ground, his limbs trembling with release.

I am free, he thought, and I am saved. But for what?

When he looked up, several others had emerged from the trees: among them a necromancer, barbarian, sorceress, and paladin. They crossed the open space to stand next to the amazon, forming a half circle around him. He gathered himself and tried to regain his feet, but could not. The amazon took his arm and helped him up, where he stood with legs planted and shaking with effort.

"I . . . am Deckard Cain," he said, with the last of his strength. "The only survivor of this cursed place. I am in your debt."

"We have fought through hell itself to get here," the paladin said. "Spared by the grace of the Light. We are ready to fight on. But we need your guidance."

Cain's knees buckled, but the amazon caught his arm. Emotions swirled like a storm within him: thoughts of all who had died here and all who would perish in the days to come. For surely, this scourge of Hell was not over but only just beginning, and now it would spread across the lands, infecting everything in its path.

*Unless they could find a way to stop it.*

*"The Dark Wanderer," Cain whispered, the cursed name springing to his lips almost unbidden: he could not use the man's name, not anymore. The Aidan he knew was gone. "He has the demon inside him, and he is trying to release Mephisto and Baal from their imprisonment. We must find him before it is too late."*

*A scream echoed across the valley, high and shrill, and as it faded away into silence, a deeper, more menacing sound like the thunder of many feet brought chills to Deckard Cain's spine. It was not the sound of men, nor anything the others could hear.*

*It was the sound of death, coming to march upon them all.*

Cain awoke to a hand shaking his shoulder. Mikulov stood over him in the early, gray light, his face filled with concern. "You were screaming," the monk said quietly, glancing at Leah, who lay still nearby, her back to them.

They had walked for another full day, and made camp in the hills with Kurast just over the next rise. Mikulov had proven an able companion so far, scouting the road ahead for thieves and keeping them going with stories of his life in Ivgorod; Leah had grown more fascinated with him as they went along. Cain had meant to question the monk further after they had made camp and Leah had dropped into sleep, but exhaustion had taken him quickly once again, only to bring these terrible dreams of his own imprisonment and near death at the hands of the demons that had overrun his town.

Cain rolled over and took several gasping breaths, wiping the sweat from his brow. He looked up into the leaden sky as dawn broke above the mountains. The dreams were growing more vivid and more disturbing, thrusting him back into days and events he would rather forget. Even now, he smelled the filth, felt the iron floor of his cage beneath his bare feet, the heat of the fires washing over him.

The horror of the loss and the guilt over his role in the slaughter felt like a fresh wound. He remembered the pain and despair of it all—the beloved son of the king, forced to kill his younger brother. Tears overcame him.

"I dreamed of the Dark Wanderer," he said, his breath catching in his chest. "And the end of Tristram."

Mikulov squatted next to him, balanced on the balls of his feet. Cain's sense of sadness and loss made it almost impossible to speak. He lay quietly for some time, staring into the sky.

"Aidan was burdened, haunted by something terrible. I should have seen the signs right before my eyes. I had been his teacher! But I thought it was a result of what he had been forced to do to his own brother. I thought it was despair over what he had witnessed. I never thought . . . that he would shove that cursed soulstone into his own head. That he had taken on the essence of evil, and Diablo still lived inside him. That he would become . . . the Dark Wanderer."

"You pursued him across Sanctuary."

"Along with a group of brave adventurers, yes. He snuck away in the dead of night, and shortly after that, a new demon plague descended upon what was left of Tristram. I . . . I was imprisoned in a cage hung upon a pole and left for dead. Forced to watch as . . ." Cain's voice quavered and failed him, and he wiped his wet face with his sleeve. "As . . . unspeakable things happened below me. Finally I was freed, and the demon horde pushed back, but Aidan was already far away, consumed by evil and intent on releasing Diablo's two brothers from their soulstones. Aidan, our hero, my friend, was hopelessly lost.

"My heroes went after him, and I followed shortly thereafter, but we were always one step behind. We defeated Andariel beneath the chambers of a cursed monastery and fought the Lesser

Evil Duriel in the tomb of Tal Rasha. We chased the Dark Wanderer through Kurast after that city had fallen, and we vanquished Mephisto, his brother, in Travincal. Finally we pursued Diablo into the Burning Hells and defeated him. Aidan was . . . killed."

"I am sorry," Mikulov said. "Our Patriarchs teach that death is simply a chance to be reborn."

"I would like to think such a thing exists," Cain said. "But the horrors I have seen . . ." He trembled with emotion, tears wetting his cheeks. "The Prime Evils are gone. But even the Lesser Evils of the Burning Hells can destroy worlds, should they choose. Some would say they are even more dangerous. If Belial or Azmodan come to Sanctuary, may the archangels help us all."

After gathering their few things and taking only a moment to drink at a small stream nearby, they resumed their journey, the monk in the lead. They had camped a few hundred feet from the road and reached it quickly enough, setting out down the middle with grim determination.

The day was gray and cold, wind ruffling their clothes and bringing a stench to their nostrils. The smell of death, Cain thought. Perhaps Leah wouldn't recognize it, but Mikulov, he realized immediately, certainly had; the monk glanced at him with a somber expression.

They crossed a branch of the river again, this bridge intact and strong, running over rushing water that cascaded through rocks. The sky darkened, and the wind picked up, until the first drops of an icy rain fell over them. The trees had become withered and bare, the ground gray and lifeless. Once, Cain thought he smelled smoke, and they passed the remains of a fire that appeared to have been hastily doused. But there were no signs of people.

They proceeded more cautiously, keeping Leah between them. The last of the trees gave way to small, deserted shacks; piles of trash and broken furniture; and, once, the rotting carcass of a horse.

And then, opening up before them like a boil on the face of Sanctuary, was the city of Kurast.

# NINE+EEN

## *The Red Circle*

The area they had entered appeared to be deserted. Crows flapped and cawed overhead as they walked down the wide road and through the open city gates. Parchment flipped across the street, carried by the breeze, and the scent of the mudflats near the docks permeated their clothes, along with smells even fouler and less identifiable.

*The former center of power in Sanctuary, the height of learning and culture, reduced to this: a ghost city filled with beggars and thieves.* The tragedy of it all nearly brought Deckard Cain to his knees. He was catapulted back in time to the day he had arrived here after his traveling party, pursuing the Dark Wanderer. The city had been under siege then, and the people had been running for their lives. They had met the last of these people at the docks, rushing away with their belongings tied into cloth sacks: men, women, and children with haunted faces, forever scarred by the things they had seen.

Kulloom's warning about Kurast came back to him once again, like a whisper on the breeze: *The people there will take what they can from you and leave you to die on the road. And there are other things . . . Things that are not so kind.*

Larger drops of rain began to spatter down, and Leah shivered. It wouldn't be long before nightfall. They had to find shelter soon.

In the streets of Lower Kurast, all was silent. The small, communal huts were abandoned and falling into ruin, their doorways dark and empty. This had been the poorest section of the city, meant for laborers, and a good place to hide, if hiding was what you desired. Above them rose the larger buildings of Upper Kurast, the forgotten temple and reliquary looming over all. The things that had lived beneath these places the last time Cain was here made his blood run cold: underground chambers and sewers full of lurching undead and beasts, both mortal and demonic. So many of the people had been blind to the horrors that were lurking just beneath their feet, as many more across Sanctuary still were. They did not believe in angels and demons, or worlds beyond this one.

Leah moved nearer to Cain and Mikulov, the three of them closing ranks as a rat the size of a small dog skittered across the street in front of them. "Stay close, little one," Cain said. He glanced at Mikulov. "We must remember why we have come. Somewhere in this city is a man who may hold the answers to whether the Horadric order is still alive and well."

Something else moved in the shadows between two huts, something large and raw and glistening, slipping out of sight quickly. Cain stepped closer; the corpse of a woman sat propped up against one wall, maggots squirming in her empty eye sockets, her neck half missing, as if something had been chewing at her. The wound was still wet.

A sickeningly sweet smell wafted over him, and he imagined her turning slowly toward him, her wound like a second mouth, eye sockets fixated on him as she raised her arms for an embrace.

A low, distant moan drifted beyond the buildings ahead. About twenty feet away, an emaciated male figure stumbled into

the street, weaving drunkenly sideways before correcting himself and standing rather unsteadily before them. The man was
hardly taller than Leah herself, wearing ragged clothing stained
with dark blotches that might have been blood or feces, his hair
long and hopelessly tangled, his wispy beard caked with filth.
His nails were so long they curled back toward his palms, and
there were raw patches where he had cut into his own flesh with
them.

The man glanced around, muttering, his face contorting as he
chewed at his own cheek. His glassy eyes rolled wildly before he
suddenly fixated on the three travelers. He shambled forward,
hands up in supplication. "Do you have any food for us? We are
hungry. *Please.*"

"We seek lodging," Mikulov said, stepping in front of Cain
and Leah. "A place to stay for the night."

The man stared at him, openmouthed. He began to chuckle,
quietly at first, then louder, lips curling upward to reveal yellow,
broken teeth. "You want to stay . . . here?" he said, wheezing
with laughter, tears squeezing from the corners of his eyes. "Are
you mad?"

"We're looking for a man named Hyland," Cain said. "If you
take us to him, we can pay you well for it."

"It's too late for you now. It will be dark soon. Poor souls." The
man cackled again, glancing around as if afraid he might be
overheard. "We're all damned. We cannot escape. They take
from us what they need and leave nothing."

"Whom do you speak of?" Cain asked.

The man stared blankly at him. "They come from Gea Kul,
traveling far in the night. You will see." He nodded again, eyes
fixed on a point of reference that was not in this world. "You will
see."

The man tilted his head, exposing his neck. It was covered in
dark purple bruises, as if he had been gripped by giant hands.

Leah tugged on Cain's tunic, pointing to the huts. Others had gathered in the shadows, all of them watching silently. They were all as thin as this man, and dressed like beggars, faces as white as parchment. He saw a girl about Leah's age, standing by someone who might have been her mother, and another woman old enough to be the grandmother.

An old wound tugged at him, an emotion he refused to acknowledge.

Cain reached into his rucksack, removing some of the seeds he had collected back in Lord Brand's manor. "There is black magic in these," he said, extending his hand toward their visitor. "You may have them, if you help us find lodging. Plant them outside your door during the day, and at night they will grow up into a forest of roots. You must be careful, because they will grab and hold anyone within reach. But they may also protect you from what preys upon you. Black magic is not discriminating about that which it entraps."

The man snatched the seeds away. He looked around furtively, as if expecting an attack at any moment.

"Come with me," he said.

The man led them through the narrow streets without speaking, shuffling from side to side. The sky darkened as evening came on swiftly. The rain continued to patter down. They saw no others on the way, but as they left Lower Kurast and neared the docks, they began to hear music: a lyre, from the sound of it, plinking out a muffled tune, accompanied by raised voices. They followed the strange little man down a wider street, the buildings no longer quite as deserted. A light glowed from one window, and farther down was a row of abandoned shops, the windows of the largest of them filled with light.

"The Red Circle," the man whispered. "They may have rooms,

for a price. Good luck to you." He melted into the shadows and disappeared, leaving them alone.

The smell of cooking meat came from the inn. They heard the sound of something shattering. As Mikulov opened the door, more smells and sounds assaulted them, a raucous mixture of food and human sweat, off-key strumming, hoarse singing, and lots of conversation. The inn was packed with people, some of them belting out songs accompanied by a lyre in one corner, others sitting at tables over mugs of ale.

Almost immediately, one of the drunken men spied them and waddled over, taking Cain by the arm with a grip of iron and pulling him inside.

"This is no place for a girl!" the man roared into Cain's face, his beard dripping with sweat. The man gestured at Leah. "What do you mean, bringing her here?" Then he winked. He wasn't as tall as Cain, but his body was solidly built. Mikulov tensed, but Cain made a calming gesture and let himself be led forward, into the fray.

At the bar, the man grabbed a mug of ale, handed it to Cain, and took another from the bartender. "Bottoms up!" he cried, clinked glasses, and downed the amber liquid in several large swallows, wiping his beard with the back of his sleeve. "Do you know," he shouted above the din, "that a hundred years ago, this very spot was a gallows? They hung nearly fifty men where you're standing right now—neck broken, if you're lucky. If not, legs twitching, face turning purple while you choke to death. That's a slow and miserable way to go. One man refused to die, they say—hung there for two days. They poked him with a stick every few hours, and he would open his bug eyes and stare at them, gurgling. They thought he was a demon. Finally they cut him down and let him go, and he went around for the rest of his life with a red circle around his neck." The man grinned. "That's how I named this place." He stuck out his hand, and Cain shook it. "Name's Cyrus," he said. "I own the Red Circle. Welcome to the gates of Hell. Or, as some of us like to call it, Kurast."

Cain pulled a gold nugget from his sack. "We're looking for a place to stay for a night."

Cyrus hooked a thumb toward Mikulov, who stood next to Leah with arms folded. "Tell him to stand down, Grandpa. If your gold's real, I'll give you a room. Not exactly full up in here, if you know what I'm saying." He leaned forward, speaking in a lower tone. "I wouldn't go flashing it around like that, though. Likely to get your arms cut off so as they can get at your pack, understand?"

Cain glanced at the other patrons. They were a ragged bunch, almost all men except for a few prostitutes, their dresses half open in front, vacant smiles on their faces. The air of celebration had a desperate edge that worked its way through the room and into the eyes of everyone there.

The lyre stopped for the moment, and someone slammed a mug down on the top of a table and shouted for more music. After a moment, the man began playing again, the notes coming faster and sounding more frantic.

"We're full of pirates, thieves, and worse," Cyrus said. "This is what's left, after the decent folk are gone. The pirates take the waterway to the sea, then work their way over the plains to Caldeum, avoid the main road. Less of the Imperial Guard to watch for, you understand, and . . . other things that might get at them. A ship's come in tonight, full of loot from Kingsport." He waved at the room full of men. "There's less of 'em these days, though. Even thievery is a dying profession around here." Cyrus suddenly grew serious. "Gea Kul, that's what it is, and what lives there. Have to pass that hellish place to get upriver, and nobody wants any part of that."

"The port town," Cain said.

"Aye." Cyrus nodded. "It's grown up over the years from what it was, deformed as a twisted back on a cripple. If Kurast is the gates of Hell, Gea Kul is right smack in the middle of the flames."

Word had gotten around about Leah's presence, and the room began to quiet, all eyes turning to them. A woman's high, strained laughter drifted over the crowd, then the sound of a harsh slap of hand against flesh, and a muffled scream. "All right," Cyrus bellowed, "go about your drinking and your whoring, all of you! Haven't you seen a child before?"

"Tell her to step up, then," a man shouted, and a flurry of activity erupted around him as another man threw a wild roundhouse punch at his jaw.

Leah shifted closer to Mikulov. "Excuse me a moment," Cyrus said, and waded in, swinging with both elbows. The fighting intensified for a moment, and then someone gave a high, wavering cry, and the room quieted down again.

Cain and Mikulov looked at each other as Cyrus came back their way, his face even redder than before, his lower lip dripping blood. He grinned at them through stained teeth. "Told you this was no place for a girl," Cyrus said. "That's taken care of, and I don't reckon he'll be up and about for a while. Now, let me fix you a plate of food and show you to your rooms."

Cyrus brought a large bowl full of meat stew and a loaf of bread. He took them through a door and up a flight of narrow stairs to a long, dimly lit hallway, the floors worn and scuffed, the walls bloodstained and carved with knives. Thuds, creaks, and moans came from behind several closed doors as they passed.

"People tend to disappear around here, intentional or not," Cyrus said as he led the way. "Maybe you don't want to be found. Either way, your gold's as good as any other."

"We're looking for a man named Hyland," Cain said.

Cyrus stopped short and turned to stare at him. "What do

you want with that slippery bastard?" he said. "Thinks he runs this city. Nobody runs Kurast. It's a den of thieves."

"We were told that he would have some information for us."

"Ah, well." Cyrus waved his hand in dismissal. "Hyland has information, all right. Just can't tell if it's worth a damn. Most of what he says can't be trusted. But I'll let you find that out yourself. There's some gathering tomorrow morning, at the docks. Hyland'll be there, running the circus." He walked a few steps down the hall and stopped in front of a battered door. "Here's your room," he said abruptly, the mirth gone from his voice. He handed Mikulov the bowl and bread. "I'd lock it, if I were you."

Then he stalked past them and disappeared back down the stairs.

# TWENTY

## *The Docks*

The three of them shared the bowl of stew and stale bread, and slept fitfully side by side on a bed of straw. Bugs crawled into their clothes and bit at their skin. The shouting and music went into the early hours of the morning, but Cain found the silence in the aftermath to be worse: at least the noise meant they shared the night with others, but after it died away, they were alone.

The old building settled, creaking, into the dawn, and several times they heard moans and what sounded like the whispers of ghouls. Leah cried out from a nightmare once, and Cain touched her hand in the dark to reassure her. She was trembling, her skin hot as a furnace even as the temperature in the room dropped. He felt a rush of emotion for the poor girl; she had lost the only person in the world who meant anything to her, she had been taken from her home, and she was facing danger and darkness at every turn. Yet she had remained strong, even defiant, in the face of all of it.

She clutched his hand, and he hummed a lullaby he remembered from many years ago, a time long forgotten. Tears welled in his eyes. Eventually her trembling stopped, and her sleep grew peaceful, while Deckard Cain remained awake, his old bones aching and the wound in his side beginning to itch, until the gray, hopeless light of dawn began to slip through the tiny window.

Ratham was five days away.

The inn was quiet as they left for the docks. Mikulov found more bread in the small, filthy kitchen behind the tavern room, and they shared it as they walked down the empty street. The rain had fallen most of the night, but instead of washing everything clean, it had served only to carry trash out from the alleyways and form murky puddles.

Cain's back ached terribly, his skin felt slick with a layer of filth, and his tunic had begun to smell decidedly foul. The bedbugs had given him an itchy rash. Mikulov and Leah didn't look much better. They wouldn't make the best first impression, although he doubted there would be many here to impress.

In that he was dead wrong, for even before they entered the docks, they encountered at least a dozen others going the same way, men and women and children. They all walked without speaking, their faces somber, clothes hanging on their thin frames. The crowd grew larger and more animated as they approached the water and entered a wooden walkway that spanned several large floating platforms. The platforms were lined with leaning huts made of wood and straw, most of them abandoned, some perhaps inhabited by squatters who had long since left the scene, their meager possessions rolled up and tucked into corners. The remains of cooking fires sent wisps of smoke into the air, and the smell of the mudflats combined with charred wood.

A man was speaking loudly to a group of twenty to thirty people on the largest platform. He was tall and well built, gray-haired, wearing the clothes of a nobleman, made of fine silk, although they looked slightly dirty and worn. He stood on a makeshift stage built of packing crates, the ruins of a larger receiving building behind him.

"We are not prisoners here," the man was saying, looking around the crowd. "And we are not helpless. Kurast is our city, not theirs!"

Many of the people held makeshift weapons, hammers, iron bars, clubs with nails sticking out of the ends. A few voices murmured in agreement, while others shook their heads. "Forget the pirates," a woman's voice shouted. "What about the feeders?"

The crowd began to jostle each other as people pushed toward the front. The man made a calming gesture with his hands and waited for quiet. "They attack those in the jungles and swamps, picking off the weak and the sick," he said. "As long as we remain here, we are perfectly safe."

"Not true!" another man, closer to the front, shouted. "They are inside Lower Kurast now. They bring the dreams. And people have seen them. Last night, one was spotted just two streets from my home!"

More voices shouted in anger and fear. This time, when the man raised his hands, the people gathered did not quiet down to listen. Cain felt the atmosphere getting quickly out of hand.

"Get me to the front," he said to Mikulov. The monk shouldered into the nearest group and opened up a pathway. The people seemed to part before him like magic, stepping aside as they turned and saw him coming. As they made their way forward, whispers went through the crowd. Even the man who had been speaking stopped to watch them come. When they spotted Cain, people seemed to shrink away from him, fear in their eyes.

"Are you Hyland?" Cain asked as they reached the stage.

The man nodded. "What's the meaning of this interruption?" he said. "We have important business here."

"My name is Deckard Cain, and I was told by a man named

Kulloom that you could help me. But perhaps I may be of some help to all of you." He turned to face the crowd, pulling the Horadric spellbook out of his sack and holding it up for them to see. "I am a scholar from Tristram, and have studied the ways of the Horadrim."

The reaction was swift. At the word *Horadrim*, the people gasped and backed away from him, pushing each other to create more space. "A feeder, in disguise!" someone shouted.

"No, he's the Dark One himself," another cried out. A woman screamed, and suddenly there was bedlam as everyone began knocking over and trampling each other to get away. The man on the platform tried to ask them to remain calm, but his voice was lost in the din. Two of the largest men ran forward, murder in their eyes, fists raised; before Cain could move, Mikulov was there, stepping smoothly in front of him and Leah, taking one man's legs out with a kick at the knee and putting another flat on his back with a blow to the jaw.

It was over in seconds. The two men lay moaning on the boards of the dock while the rest of the crowd had disappeared.

Cain looked up at Hyland. "Perhaps we should speak in private," he said.

"Forgive my people," Hyland said. He poured a glass one quarter full of grog from a shelf and handed it to Cain. "They are frightened. The days are dark indeed, and nightmares plague us all."

The four of them had retreated to the receiving building, where Hyland had set up a makeshift office. It was dangerous there, he had said, but as self-declared mayor of Kurast, it was his duty to make a showing and not cower before the thieves who had overrun their city.

The two men who had tried to attack Cain were stationed outside the office as guards, still rubbing the bruises they had received from Mikulov's blows. Cain suspected their injuries were more to their pride than anything else. If so, Mikulov had pulled his punches.

"Kulloom sent you to me, did he?" Hyland said. "An old trade partner of mine, although I wouldn't exactly call him a friend. He didn't like it when I took control of Kurast and chose other business opportunities over his own."

Cain produced the Horadric book once again from his rucksack. "He spoke highly enough of you. He told me you might be able to help me find the people who made this."

Hyland took the book and studied it for a moment, turning it over in his hands and opening its pages. "It was likely made by a man who used to reside here in Kurast," he said. "A group of young scholars came here looking for someone who could reproduce some ancient literature, and found Garreth Rau, a scholar and litterateur, one of the finest bookmakers in all of the world. He was impressed with the great works these scholars had brought him, amazed by their potential. Eventually he joined this fledgling order and left Kurast."

"Where can I find this man?"

Hyland handed the book back, wiping his hands on his robe as if he had touched something foul. "They say he was killed by the Dark One, a powerful sorcerer who has turned the very nature of magic against itself, twisted it into a path to evil."

*The Dark One.* That name again. Cain took a taste of the grog. It did not sit well in his already-churning stomach. "The people called me that earlier. I can assure you, I am no dark sorcerer. Why did they run from me?"

Hyland swirled the drink in his own glass, then drained it and poured another one. "Because to them, you are the enemy."

"I don't understand—"

"Our city does not take kindly to the Horadrim," Hyland said. "The citizens of Kurast fear them. Some say evil has corrupted man's greatest assets, darkening even the Horadrim."

"That's not possible," Cain said. "The order has always stood for justice and light. It was the most basic tenet of their way, a directive handed to them directly from the archangel Tyrael himself. If there are any true Horadrim left in Sanctuary, they wouldn't be engaged in demonic magic. "

"So you say. But those young scholars who came to Rau brought Horadric texts with them and spoke of the order as if it were their own. The people believe that these texts, and the magic they contained, brought the Dark One here."

A chill reached deep into Cain's bones. He remembered Kulloom's warning back in Caldeum about the group of Horadrim led by a dark sorcerer: *You must do something. You must find these men and stop them . . .*

Hyland sat down on one of several old chairs, and motioned for the others to do the same. Cain remained standing, Mikulov and Leah at his side. "You're offended," Hyland said. "I can't help what my people believe. But perhaps they are right. What do you know of these matters? You're just an old man. Things in the world have changed, and not for the better."

The atmosphere in the room had grown tense. Cain felt the blood in his face, the clenched muscles in his hands. He took a half step forward, but Mikulov put a gentle hand on his arm.

"Uncle," Leah said quietly, her voice trembling. Hyland just smiled up at them.

"Please, sit," he said. "Let's discuss this like civilized men."

Mikulov glanced at Cain, who nodded, willing himself to relax. There was no reason to frighten the girl even further, and besides, Hyland had many more men at his disposal. Even with Mikulov's physical talents, they were far outnumbered.

Something bothered him about Hyland; part of him wanted to walk out on the arrogant man, yet he could not. There was important information here, at his fingertips.

"Do you know who this Dark One is?" Mikulov asked, when

they had sat down opposite Hyland. "We have heard things ourselves about a powerful sorcerer of demonic magic. But this connection to the Horadrim . . . it disturbs my friend. It is . . . his lifeblood. You understand?"

"Good," Hyland said. "Anger is power here. It is the only real currency." He glanced at Leah, who sat quietly next to Mikulov, hugging her arms to her chest. "Perhaps the girl would like something to eat? It would give us time to talk more freely."

"I'll tell you the rest of what I know," Hyland said, after Mikulov had taken Leah in search of food, in the company of one of the guards. "But now it's your turn. Who's the girl? And that one with her? Ivgorod, eh? A monk? I have heard of their ilk."

"Leah is the daughter of a good friend. I'm watching her now that her mother's gone. And Mikulov saved our lives just a few nights ago. His own path here is complicated, but no less legitimate."

"Hmmm. You said you could help us. I'm curious to hear how."

"I am trying to find any remaining members of the Horadrim," Cain said. "You're right that things have changed in Sanctuary. There is a great war looming, a demon invasion, a war between Heaven and Hell. I was in Tristram when it fell to Diablo, and I can assure you that everything you may have heard about those days is true. But what is coming soon will make them pale in comparison. I have seen the signs, read the prophecies. It is close. I suspect that the troubles that plague Kurast are related to it."

Hyland nodded. "There have been rumors of these things you describe," he said. "There are even a few old men here who claim to have been here in Kurast when it was overrun by demons years ago. And there is evil at work now, sure enough. But you think you can stop the darkness from spreading? Many warriors have tried, only to disappear and never return. You are an old man, Mr. Cain. No offense."

"If you tell me more about what is happening in Kurast, I can study my ancient texts and find a way to stop it. We don't have much time. The first day of Ratham is only days away, and we have evidence that this will be the moment of truth for all of us."

Hyland drained the last of his grog, staring at the glass as if he would discover the answer there. Then he sighed, stood up, and refilled his drink again before speaking.

"They're called feeders," he said finally, turning to face them. "They come in the night, terrorizing those in the fringe areas of Lower Kurast. Sometimes they steal children and even take able-bodied men and women, but more often they simply . . . feed on them. We don't know exactly how they do it, but their victims begin to fade away, growing weaker, list-less, and ill. They are very nearly walking corpses." He took a long sip from the grog. "People say they come from Gea Kul. Nobody goes there anymore. Kurast is a lost city, but Gea Kul is a wasteland."

It was the third time since they had reached Kurast that some-one had mentioned Gea Kul. "Kulloom told a similar story, of a trade merchant who had witnessed something like these feeders."

Hyland's gaze grew distant, his face flushed in the light that filtered in through the window. "There are rumors all over. Many claim to have witnessed feeders creeping around in the dead of night, horrible ghouls that seem to float in the air and appear and disappear at will. They are like human insects, crawling upon all fours, up walls and across ceilings—bloated, misshapen things that are so horrible to behold, they turn people mad. They say these creatures are commanded by the Dark One I spoke of earlier."

The shadows in the room seemed to grow, the air gaining a

chill. "And you think these Horadric scholars brought these creatures to Sanctuary?"

"Many here do. But perhaps the group, along with Rau, left here to travel to Gea Kul and battle the evil that was already gathering there." Hyland shrugged. "I knew some of these young men from their time in Kurast. They seemed well intentioned enough. I had no reason to think they were . . . corrupted."

"Do you know the feeders' purpose?"

"Perhaps they are simply here to drain the people's will, to make them easier to overcome. Or perhaps it is all simply a rumor started by fools and drunkards." Hyland stood up to pour himself another grog. "Perhaps I am one of them."

"I would like to speak to someone who has seen one," Cain said. "If they could tell me something of better use—"

Hyland waved a hand. "I don't think you'll find anyone willing to come within a hundred yards of you," he said. "And let's just say that most of those who have seen them are no longer interested in talking. But I've got something else." He set the glass down and began rummaging through piles of books. "I know I put it here somewhere . . . ahhh." He held up sheets of parchment. "Several weeks ago, a woman came to me in fear of her life. Her son, a talented artist of no more than twelve, was wasting away with the familiar sickness. I went to see him, and he gave me these."

He handed the parchment to Cain. The first held a roughly scratched drawing of an unsettling figure, perhaps an animal of some kind, crouched in the corner of a room. The room was dark, the angles shaded with angry marks from the charcoal from which it had been drawn, and the shape was indistinct, as if emerging from a fog.

The second was more detailed, and the creature's shape was clearer—a large, misshapen head, hunched back, distended belly, face like a black hole. But the third drawing was so strong and so terrible Cain drew in a sharp breath. It showed a humanlike creature hovering over a small child in bed, claw-like hands extended as if to caress its victim. The creature had advanced upon the viewer so that its presence appeared to fill the page, bringing with it a feeling of terrible, overwhelming dread. Its face was turned upward, wisps of hair hanging across a white, shiny scalp, and its eyes were blank holes, blindly staring with a hunger that could not be quenched.

Below the drawing, scratched so roughly the parchment had torn, were two words: *Al Cut.*

"I don't know what it means," Hyland said. "I don't think the boy did either. The strange thing was, his mother did not beg me to save her son. She asked for him to be banished, to drive the feeders away from her home. I refused, and two days later, she disappeared. The boy remains, a shadow of himself, haunting the alleys of Kurast. I have seen him since, but he does not recognize me."

Cain stared at the thing in the drawing. Even through the parchment, the evil in the creature was strong enough that it almost appeared to move, tilting its cursed, ravenous face, its long fingers slowly opening as if to reach out at him. But it was the thing's mouth, open and puckered, searching blindly in hunger for something to feed upon, that left him deeply shaken and ice-cold.

"If you remain here," Hyland said, "you may no longer need to worry about finding out more about the feeders."

He drained his glass again and looked bleary-eyed at Cain from across the room. "You'll dream of them. And I think you may see one in person soon enough."

# TWEN+Y-ᐁNE

## The Feeder

Deckard Cain found Mikulov and Leah near the water's edge, where Mikulov was teaching the girl how to skip stones. They had found nothing to eat. Gulls screamed above their heads, also searching for food. By the time they returned to the Red Circle, it was late afternoon.

There was no sign of Cyrus. The inn still slumbered, those few who remained present sleeping like the dead, the smell of stale ale and sweat drifting through the downstairs rooms. Mikulov found more rancid stew in the kitchen, and they ate what they could stomach before the first few patrons began to stumble in, bleary-eyed and sour, and wet from the rain that had again begun to fall.

Out of earshot from Leah, Cain explained to Mikulov what Hyland had told him. The Horadric scholars were apparently real, and had been close to Kurast. Perhaps they were still in Gea Kul. It was as much as Cain could ask for, considering the circumstances. But their connection with the creature Hyland had called the Dark One and his feeders was troubling. Cain had little doubt that this Dark One was the false leader from the book of Horadric prophecies that he had found in the ruins and, most

213

likely, the same man Mikulov had seen in his visions. He was probably also the "master" referred to by Lord Brand back in the village.

Had this sorcerer killed Rau and the Horadric scholars? Or were they plotting together against the people of Sanctuary?

"Al Cut," Mikulov mused. "Do you suppose it's a living man?"

"The text is quite old, and it referred to his tomb, so I'm assuming he's dead unless it is a prophecy of coming events. But I have never heard of such a person in all my years of studying history. One would think he might be written of, were he this important."

"Hmmm." Mikulov shrugged. "Gea Kul is not far from here. Perhaps a day or two's journey, if we make good time." Darkness was falling outside as they set their dinner bowls on the table near the kitchen. They listened to the sound of the wind moaning against the eaves. "At the monastery," Mikulov said, "the masters teach us to listen to the earth and sky and wind, that the gods are in all things if only you learn how to open your mind to them. They are speaking to us now."

Cain nodded. There was something heavy in the air, a presence like the promise of violence and blood. Leah seemed to feel it too; the girl had been mostly silent since the docks, keeping close by Cain's side, and once, as a group of large men came into the inn with voices raised, her small hand had snuck into his and squeezed it. Her skin was clammy, her bones as fragile as a bird's wing.

They returned to their room, and Leah fell asleep on the bed of straw. "Forgive me," Mikulov said, "but I sense something else is bothering you."

"Everyone has a history they would like to forget."

"Some more than others," Mikulov said. "The Patriarchs say that if we do not face these things, we are not whole. And we are vulnerable to the darkness."

"I've seen horrors that most other men would not recover from," Cain said. "I have seen my friends murdered, my town destroyed. I've lived most of my life with guilt because I let these things happen, and did not fight back soon enough."

*And Leah,* he thought, but did not say it: What was her role in all of this, and what did she mean to him? A chance to change things, a way to fight back against the darkness that had plagued him most of his adult life?

*You cannot change the past.*

Mikulov studied his face for a long time, as if looking for some kind of truth written there. "I sense there is more, much more. Whatever else may be inside you, it is your burden alone to carry. But should you need a friend—"

"Thank you, Mikulov." Cain removed the Horadric book of prophecies from his rucksack. "Now I must search for more answers, before the morning comes. We have only five days before the prophecies say Hell will come to Sanctuary. There is no time for this. We must rest soon, and be on our way again."

Mikulov opened his mouth as if to speak again, then shrugged and nodded. "As you wish."

Cain pored over the text until late into the night, searching for anything that might help them, but he found nothing else of substance. An increased sense of urgency drove him on far longer than he might have thought possible; time was getting away from them, and they were no closer to a solution. It was maddening.

Finally he fell asleep sitting up, the book dropping into his lap, and he dreamed he was walking down a long, dusty road lit by fire on all sides, the heat prickling his skin and turning the hairs on his arms black and twisted. Somewhere nearby there was a presence so foul, so filled with evil, it made his stomach churn with sickness. He was searching for someone he had ignored for far too long. The evil presence had taken that person from him.

He became aware that feeders were following him, flitting like ghosts on the road's edge, their pale, crab-like forms mirroring his pace. He went faster, but they grew closer, hundreds of them. As he walked down the road, he could make out two figures in the distance holding hands, one taller than the other. They walked away from him, and no matter how fast he went, they remained distant specks on the horizon.

He increased his pace until he was running, his staff banging the ground, rucksack flapping against his shoulder. But he could get no closer.

*They are mine*, a voice boomed inside his head, loud enough to make him cry out. Laughter echoed across the landscape, following him as he ran ever faster. *I took them years ago, snatched on the road to Caldeum. Now they suffer for all eternity.* The laughter raked him like claws as the fire roared up, and a tiny child's voice began screaming.

*You were blind, and now you see.*

He awoke in a cold sweat, his mouth dry, legs numb. The room was dark and filled with the faint sounds of Mikulov's and Leah's breathing. The text had fallen to the floor. He gathered it up and slipped it back into his rucksack, trying not to think about the dream. It had been more vivid than any of the others, and the voice of the evil presence had sounded real.

Cain wiped tears from his face. That was many years ago, so many years. There was nothing he could do about it now, and no way he could change the past. He had to go on. That had become his mantra, recited so many times in his own head he had come to believe in its power to erase his history and to bring about his redemption: *I must go on.*

A low moaning sound drifted from somewhere down the corridor, beyond the closed bedroom door.

Cain froze, listening. He had heard similar noises the night before, but this one seemed to rattle him even more; it was a haunted, lonely sound, that of a dying man.

The moan came again, followed by a dull thud, like something heavy falling to the floor.

Cain took his staff and opened the door, peering out into the hallway. It was filled with shadows broken only with a dim light that filtered through a single window at the far end. The night outside was a gray-blue, the color of deep water. He paused, waiting, and heard something move from behind a door about ten feet down on the right. It sounded like a heavy object being dragged across the ground.

An icy draft wafted over him, bringing chills. There was something in that room. Every instinct told him to turn around, gather Leah and Mikulov, and take them far away from this place. But he also sensed that whatever was happening behind that door could not continue. Someone was in terrible danger.

Cain crept down the hallway as quietly as possible, keeping close to the wall. As he went, he imagined fires burning all around him from his dream, pushing him forward.

The door was open a crack. Darkness loomed inside.

Another soft moan broke the silence. Cain muttered words from the Horadric spellbook, his staff taking on the familiar blue glow. He pushed the door wide.

A pale, nearly translucent creature sat hunched over the prone body of Cyrus, the innkeeper, who lay upon the floor. A few strands of hair hung from a nearly bald skull, skeletal features covered with skin as thin as parchment. Blue veins traced patterns across dry, flaking flesh.

The creature's claw-like hands were around Cyrus's neck. Its bare shoulders moved as it leaned in again to the big man's face and kissed his lips.

Cyrus's fingers twitched.

The feeder attached itself like a parasite and breathed in. Its torso swelled, filling with something that Cyrus gave up with a slow, ghostly sigh. As the blue glow from Cain's staff washed over the room, it turned to stare blindly over its shoulder at him, eye sockets black and empty, ghoulish mouth open in a glistening, toothless circle, saliva dripping from the hole.

Cyrus began to shudder, his bare heels drumming on the floor.

*What hell is this?*

Cain pulled the last of the black seeds from his rucksack and tossed them at the creature's feet. They sprang to life, tendrils digging into the cracks and sprouting up with unbelievable speed. The feeder screamed, a high, ear-splitting noise like the screech of glass against metal as the black roots lashed across the room, grasping hold of anything within reach and creating a forest of waving limbs.

Cain slammed the door shut, shuddering. Mikulov had heard the noises and was already in the hall, Leah right behind him.

"There's a feeder in Cyrus's room," he said.

From the sleeve that wrapped over his wrist Mikulov slipped a punch dagger into his hand so that it protruded from his fist. The blade glowed briefly with markings of power etched into the steel.

The noises from inside had ceased abruptly. "I'm scared, Uncle," Leah said. Cain looked down at her pale face, which shone like a tiny moon in the darkness.

"I will not let anything happen to you," he said. "I promise."

Mikulov opened the innkeeper's door to a thicket of black roots that had spread across the frame. He sliced at them with his blades. The cut roots fell, writhing like snakes before shrinking away again to seeds, which Cain scooped up. In a few moments, the monk had cleared a path, and he stepped into the room and disappeared from sight. Then Mikulov appeared at the door again, Cyrus over his shoulder.

"The thing is gone out the window," he said. "We are safe, for now."

He carried Cyrus back to their room and put him on the floor, and Cain crouched over him, looking for any obvious wounds. His neck was deeply bruised. A moment later the innkeeper opened his eyes, his gaze unfocused; his head fell to the side, his limbs unresponsive. Cain tried to get him to speak, with no luck. It was as if the man was in a trance of some kind or had been drugged.

The big man seemed smaller and thinner than before, his flesh sunken around his eyes and cheeks, bones protruding in more angles and sharp points. He appeared as drained as a piece of dry fruit, his skin cracking, a hollow husk of flesh made all the more horrifying by the way his eyes rolled loosely in their sockets and his mouth hung open, breath rasping in and out like the last gasps of a dying man.

But Cyrus did not die. Instead he remained in the same state, unresponsive, his breathing irregular, his pulse faint. Cain listened to Cyrus's rattling breath and thought about the creature he had seen, its eyeless face staring blankly at him. The sound of flapping wings came faintly from outside their room, and Cain felt a momentary darkness cross their path with a rush and a sigh, then pass out of sight again. He shivered.

The moment of truth was getting closer. Soon he would know whether the Horadrim still lived on or whether they had faded away into legend, leaving him as the last bastion against oblivion. Soon Ratham would be upon them.

*May the archangels save us all.*

Tomorrow, they would go to Gea Kul.

# TWENTY-TWO

## *The Blood of Al Cut*

Underneath the tower of stone and sea, the Dark One drew a circle around a familiar symbol: a figure eight with two pointed dagger tips at its bottom, amber gemstone in the middle. A candle fluttered in its center, but the edges of the room were shrouded in shadows, deeper than the night outside. Yet he saw everything with perfect clarity; his eyes had developed a peculiar sensitivity to light, the way a cat's eyes cut through the darkness to spy its prey. There were other changes as well that were more dramatic. It was all part of his transformation from human into deity.

His ghouls had continued to spread across the land, bringing the essence of life back to him and filling the containment chamber. He felt its power swelling beneath him, a ticking bomb ready to explode.

Only four days until his coronation. It was time to make the first contact.

Something splattered across the symbol's center. The Dark One looked up at the chained man hanging from hooks through his shoulder blades as he kicked and writhed at his bonds. Blood ran down his legs, dripping to the stone. A rune, the mark of Belial, glowed upon his upper arm like the embers of a fire.

The Dark One smiled. His master would not be satisfied to remain within his human host much longer. But the flesh was simply a vessel, and now he would call a new visitor to occupy it, a visitor he had been waiting a very long time to meet.

He went to the book propped upon the stand near the circle and read a passage aloud. It was a delicate ceremony, and it strained his abilities to call through so many years and planes of existence. The past was like a complicated series of interlocking plates that constantly shifted and rearranged themselves, marking the path through a dangerous maze of illusions; one could easily get lost inside and never return.

The candle flared up in a roar of flame, then died down again. The circle and symbol glowed red. He slid a dagger from his sleeve, held his other palm up, and pricked it. Blood welled from the wound, pooled there, and began to thread its way slowly upward like a fleshy, liquid worm, reaching for the blade and then running over it. He watched, fascinated, as the blade soaked up the blood, binding it to him forever.

He knelt at the circle's edge, reciting more words of power, and raised the dagger with both hands, plunging it directly into the floor where the man's blood had dripped, at the center of the figure eight. The blade sank to the hilt, slicing as smoothly through stone as it would through soft flesh.

At once, he felt the tremendous pulse of energy below him. The floor shuddered beneath him. Blood erupted all around the blade, spraying upward like a fountain, an artery cut clean through, spattering the Dark One's face and washing over the stones, soaking through his cloak. It arced upward, bathing the hanging man until he was barely recognizable as human. Still it continued, on and on, the blood of the dead and the damned, the blood of countless victims and warriors, slaughtered on the killing field and condemned to the depths of the Burning Hells for eternity.

The blood of Al Cut.

"*Lɪft ðə vel frəm hɪz ajz,*" the Dark One said. "The thread is bound."

His consciousness began to expand, stretching out in all directions as rivulets of blood ran like tiny rivers through cracks and seams. He was moving through space and time, linked to a thousand beasts across the land, hiding in sewers and basements and caverns, slinking through the night: wendigos, spider mages and flesh hunters, khazra and scavengers and fallen ones. He sensed the hundreds of thousands of slumbering dead, buried in the muck of seas and through the centuries, moldering away in catacombs and graves, entombed beneath the earth. All of them awaiting his command.

*Not yours,* his inner voice whispered, but the Dark One pushed it aside, refusing to let the doubt creep in. The power was his to control and wield, and his alone. The Worldstone destroyed, he was destined to bring about the destruction of humanity and the fall of all of Sanctuary, just as his bloodline had brought about its salvation centuries before. He would cut out the sickness of mankind. It was written in the prophecies, his true surname seared into history. He had seen it all himself.

Light and dark, forever bound.

*"FIND THE GIRL."*

The voice brought him back with a jerk. It thundered inside his head, soundless yet so loud it made him wince. The Dark One began to feel a familiar rage. Why would his master depend upon a child? *He* was the one who would command Belial's army; *he* would bring about the fall of Caldeum and the rule of the Burning Hells. The old man Deckard Cain was blind to his machinations. Cain's power was weak; he was a pawn in a much larger game.

The Dark One stood on the floor of a vast chamber. The hellfires raged all around him, and the screams of the damned nearly brought him to his knees. The clanging of iron beaten into the shape of weaponry rang out. Blood flowed like a river against his shins—atrocities, torture, beheadings, those skinned and burned alive, all of it happening at once. He was occupying the same space across centuries of time, a world that had existed this way for even longer than the creature that stood in his way could remember.

Belial rose up before him. The demon's yellow eyes locked with the Dark One's and held them. *"Your power is impressive,"* the beast said. *"You have conquered time. Yet you are nearly overcome. You have so much to learn, to become the master you would claim to be."*

"I can raise them alone," the Dark One said. "You don't need the girl. Let me try."

*"Try?"* Belial seemed amused. *"You show your weakness with such a word. And why should you turn away from her and her companions? Your chance at redemption is at hand. This man Cain has stained your family name with his own. Betrayal tastes worse than death, does it not? Don't you want your revenge?"*

The Dark One felt his pulse quicken. "I do, my lord."

*"I thought as much. Did you know there was demonic magic in his blood? How else do you think his ancestor overcame yours? Through charm and persistence? No, through trickery and the power of the Burning Hells. Even now, history has been revised. The world believes a lie, and the truth has been buried, just as Tal Rasha was buried beneath Lut Gholein."*

"I—"

*"Lure the girl here, bring Al Cut to life, and take your revenge on the old man. It is the right way, and the only way."*

"I understand, my lord." The Dark One was growing dizzy with the effort of maintaining his place in time; the plates were shifting with increasing speed, and he was in danger of becoming lost among them forever. He managed to steady himself long enough to focus on the great beast before him. "I must go now, and use this vessel . . . for other purposes."

Belial laughed, the sound shaking the cavern like the screams of a thousand dying men. *"Do not tell me what you must do. But very well. I shall exit gracefully. Play with your toys, but do not forget what I have told you."*

The temporal plates shifted, absorbing the blood and swallowing Belial and the cavern in an instant. The Dark One found himself in another cave, this one nearly as vast as the one before. An entire city stood all around him, and he saw every moment of every year at once. Its buildings and streets were dusty, broken, and teeming with life. A mage battle raged next to children at play, each oblivious to the other. Generations of people crossed by and through each other like ghosts.

He paused, focusing every effort of his will upon the present day and the spirit he had come here to contact. Slowly, the ghostly images faded away, until he was left with silence, dust, and decay. He could feel the blood of ages throbbing, the energy of Al Cut vast and untapped, a river dam waiting to give way.

*"Lɪft ðə vel frəm hɪz ajz,"* he said.

The ground began to glow as the rune, the mark of Belial, traced a pattern through the dusty street. The ground shuddered and split with a rumble, and he caught his breath as a skeletal hand reached up and clutched the side of the abyss.

"I have awakened him," the Dark One whispered. "He is here."

Sometime later, he opened his eyes. He was back in the chamber below the Black Tower. The blood was gone, his cloak dry. The candle flickered, nearly burned to the floor. But the connections he had made remained, a thousand bloody threads reaching out in all directions.

His army shuddered with ecstasy, waiting for him to command them.

A noise from above made him look up. The man hanging from the chains was staring back at him. But his gaze was very different now. The Dark One released the chains, letting the wheel they turned upon lower the man to the ground.

The man stared at him, a new confidence and sense of power evident in his eyes. This was clearly not Belial, nor was it the spirit of the man who had owned his fleshy shell before. The Dark One felt a shiver run through him; he had done it. Until this moment, a part of him had wondered whether it was possible. He had raised a man from the dead, but not just any man. The one who would command his troops as they marched through Caldeum and lay waste to humankind.

And he, the Dark One, was this man's master.

The Dark One smiled. "We have much to discuss," he said.

Far beneath him, something immensely powerful shook the earth with a low moan like the sound of some giant awakening beast. The final sequence had begun: the End of Days, as it had been written.

The Lord of Lies would not wait much longer.

# PART THREE

# THE LORD OF LIES

# TWENTY-THREE

## The Road to Gea Kul

*The portal closed with a hiss and snap of energy as he stepped through to the cold floor. Deckard Cain looked around in wonder. He was standing on a wide stone platform within a massive shadowed chamber, great columns and arches marching across it, and beyond them a set of huge stone steps that descended to another level marked by guttering fire pits. Beyond that lay darkness.*

*It was the most incredible thing he had ever seen. Colors shifted before his eyes, and shapes seemed to move and bend with the light. Before him was a fireplace nearly twice his height, its flames roaring like a furnace. Heat radiated outward. Swords, hatchets, and hammers had been mounted to the stone above it, shining in the flickering glow.*

*Something—someone—stood next to the fire, burning with his own inner light.*

*Cain's breath caught in his throat, and a chill prickled his skin. All these years, first spent in denial, then a gradual understanding and acceptance as his studies of Jered's texts and those from Tristram Cathedral had led him to the same conclusion: the truth of another phase of reality, the existence of a realm outside Sanctuary, ruled by beings who were not mortal. Yet there had still been a small seed of doubt within him, even as he witnessed demons overrun his town. His logical side* still sought out a rational explanation. These creatures he saw might have been born from natural mothers, suffering birth defects or some other form of mutation. He was a man of science and learning.

The archangel unfurled his wings.

Bolts of white-hot light sprung up from his back, crackling with energy and enveloping him in an aura bright enough to make Cain shield his own eyes. They were not wings at all, Cain realized, at least not the way humans would have described them, yet he recognized them from his studies. The streaks of light were in constant motion, in harmony with a sound like music, undulating as wings might under a strong wind.

"Tyrael," Cain whispered. Tears filled his eyes, making it difficult to see. "The archangel of Justice. Founder of the Horadrim."

"Welcome to the Pandemonium Fortress," the archangel said. "I knew your ancestor Jered well. I have been waiting to meet you for a long time, Deckard Cain."

Tyrael's voice was deep and soothing, reverberating through the huge chamber, echoing off stone and causing the colors of the walls to shimmer. He was stronger than any man. Yet the archangel was wounded, Cain realized, the result of a desperate battle against the Prime Evils, no doubt.

A tip of one of the tendrils of light flicked down and touched Cain's shoulder. Warmth spread through his body, nearly bringing him to his knees. He trembled but remained standing, an effort that took every last ounce of his will.

Cain took a deep breath. It was true. The archangels existed.

He shuffled forward, his staff clicking against the floor. "The rest of my traveling party will arrive in a moment," he said. "We have destroyed the Compelling Orb with Khalim's Will, and Mephisto has been contained. We seek the Dark Wanderer. Within him we will find Diablo, and defeat him, once and for all."

"You know much, but not all." Tyrael's face was hooded, blackness underneath, but staring at him was like looking into the sun. Cain glanced away, blinking against the tears. "You have done well, last of the Horadrim. But there is more to do before you face Diablo. My trusted lieutenant, Izual, was corrupted ages ago and must be released from his suffering. You must face the Hellforge and use the Anvil of Annihilation to destroy Mephisto's soulstone, once and for all, before crossing the River of Flame. And I fear there is more beyond that, much more. The prophecy has foretold a disruption in the balance of power that may destroy Sanctuary as we know it."

"When will this happen?"

"We do not know," Tyrael said. "Nor do we know that it will happen at all."

"I will do what I can to help our heroes fight back against the darkness."

Tyrael nodded. "I have no doubt that you will provide wise counsel. But someday you may be asked to do much more than that. And I fear that your own past will return to haunt you, in ways you cannot over-come."

Fingers of dread worked their way up Cain's spine. There was much he knew about the world of angels and demons, but much more still to learn. What did they know about the future? How much of it was his to write, and how much was set in stone?

"I . . . do not understand."

Tyrael waved a hand, his golden armor clinking softly. "You must embrace the truth of what you have done, and who you are, and who you have been. I will do all that I can to protect you through this quest, as I have protected all Horadrim from the moment I formed the order. But someday I may not be here, and you may face the darkness alone. When that moment comes, you must be able to trust yourself."

The fingers walking down Cain's spine increased their pressure. The flames from the fireplace rose up with a roar, then settled, dying down again. The fortress grew darker, shadows lengthening. Tendrils seemed to uncoil like black snakes all around him; a thunderous sound like the crumbling of Sanctuary itself reverberated through the structure, caus-ing dust to rain down and bits of stone to clatter off the floor. The voices *of thousands of screaming, tortured souls drifted up from somewhere far beneath Cain's feet as he lost his balance and fell to his side, his staff tumbling away from him.*

*Deep and chilling laughter grew up from nowhere until it filled his head with a raucous din that threatened to unman him. The tendrils had stretched across the entire room now, and the light of the flame had dimmed to almost nothing. Cain looked up to see Tyrael held aloft in a gigantic taloned grip, the archangel's tendrils of light whipping helplessly back and forth as he screamed in pain and fury. Above him, impossibly high, rose the torso and massive head of a demon so foul Cain had to turn away, his stomach churning at the sight.*

*"Bow before me," the demon said, its laughter shaking the foundations of the Pandemonium Fortress, its breath like the hot wind flung from the depths of Hell. "Bow before Belial, the Lord of Lies!"*

Deckard Cain sat upright on the bed of straw. Somehow he had managed to fall asleep again, after the incident with the feeder. Dawn crept in through the small window, painting the room will a dull, gray light.

He was drenched with sweat, gasping for air, the walls seeming to close in on him as he tried to orient himself. The dreams were getting worse, filling every moment of sleep and twisting the truth, binding his heart with threads of lies until he couldn't fight his way free. As they got closer to the answers they were looking for and his dreams continued to change, he could no longer remember what had really happened so many years ago. He *had* met Tyrael that day in the Pandemonium Fortress, and it had changed his life forever. But the Lesser Evil Belial, ruler of one part of the Burning Hells, had never appeared.

It was all wrong. Yet the dream had begun to sow the seeds of doubt in him, until he felt he could no longer trust his own memories.

*If only Tyrael were here.* The loss of the archangel of Justice during the destruction of the Worldstone was devastating. Meeting him in person had been a seminal moment in Cain's life; after doubting for so long, and then living through the horrors of the invasion of Tristram, to see an archangel face to face was like looking into the sun. There were those in years past who had said that the angels were as bad as demons, and that most of them preferred that humans be destroyed. But they did not know the truth. Tyrael had been a protector of the Horadrim and all of humanity when another member of the Angiris Council would have had them destroyed. He was Justice incarnate, a creature so pure in spirit, he made all others seem like moths beating against a flame.

But now he was gone, and Sanctuary was exposed and vulnerable. Who would save them now? Who would step in, when the world was at its darkest point?

Who would stop Belial from destroying mankind?

Cain and Mikulov took Leah out of Kurast before the sun had fully entered the sky. The road stretched before them like a jagged scar cut through burned flesh. The husks of trees huddled in small groups, banding together to ward off the plague that had stripped them of life; some looked blackened, as if they had been scorched by fire.

An abandoned wagon sat by the roadside, overturned, the remains of two oxen still yoked to its frame. Leah drew closer to Cain as they passed, and she sensed a tension in him; he could not look away from the wagon, and he gave it a wide birth, skirting the edge of the road.

The oxen's vacant, eyeless stare seemed to mock her. *What makes you think you can survive this?* they seemed to be saying, their rotted lips pulled away from their jaws, exposing rows of teeth in macabre grins. *There is only death here. Turn around and run away, as fast as you can.*

For a moment she was tempted to do it. But then she thought about returning to Kurast, and what might happen to her there without Cain and Mikulov. Those people they had met on the way into the city were nothing but empty shells, like ghosts. They were already dead; they just didn't know it yet. And though she hadn't actually seen anything the night before in Cyrus's room, she had the feeling Uncle Deckard had, and it had frightened him badly.

For some reason this made her think of her mother (*not your* real *mother*, Leah's mind insisted on pointing out; *your real mother left you*): Gillian making her breakfast on a sunny morning before they went to visit Jonah's market for vegetables; then they would walk down to Caldeum's gates to watch the action at the trade tents, and if she was lucky, Gillian would buy her a honey stick for a treat. Those were the good days, before Gillian's sickness had taken all the happiness away. It was all too much for her to bear.

"What's wrong?" Cain was looking down at her in concern, and Leah realized that tears were running down her face. She shook her head, watching his bearded face through a prism of colors, afraid that he would lecture her again about being responsible and strong and facing her fears, but instead he put his arm around her shoulders, and she leaned into him, smelling the dust and smoke of his tunic, and was glad to have him, so very glad, even if he was a strange old man, and even if she didn't entirely trust him yet.

To entertain them as they walked (and, Leah suspected, to distract them a little bit too), Mikulov told them stories of his homeland in the foothills on the edge of the Sharval Wilds, and his extensive training to become an Ivgorod monk—the hours of sitting motionless, learning to read the voices of the gods in all things, dissolving the sense of self and need and serving the Patriarchs. He told them of his intense physical exercises and mountain excursions, wrestling giant beasts that lurked there far away from the world of men. Even at her young age, Leah suspected that some of these stories were exaggerated, but Mikulov told them with surprising intensity and enthusiasm, and she found herself losing track of time as she listened to his voice.

Cain questioned him further about his beliefs, and Leah sensed a great sadness within him about leaving his masters and the order of monks that he had known for so long. It was a decision, he said, that might mean his own death, although she didn't quite know why. Then they began talking about the Horadrim, and at that, Leah began to drift off, losing interest. She didn't understand all of that stuff, only that Uncle was a member of some kind of mage clan and that they were supposed to do something Cain thought was important. But most of what they discussed had to do with ancient writings and prophecies. It was more than enough to bore a young girl to tears.

Leah noticed that the sky had grown darker, and in the distance black clouds obscured the horizon. The clouds seemed to be clustered in the direction they were headed. A chill settled over her bones. She tried to remember what had happened back home, during the fire. Much of that night was a black hole to her; she dimly remembered waking up to the smell of smoke, then nothing until she woke up outdoors on the ground, James's cloak over her shivering body. She knew Cain must have gotten them out somehow, but it was a mystery to her.

The same thing had happened at the evil man's house, after she had eaten all that food and fallen asleep. She had awakened to a dim sense of panic and something strange growing over her bed like black ropes, and then suddenly they were outside, running through the darkness with people chasing them. When they reached the graveyard . . . Leah sighed. She just didn't know. It was as if someone had stepped neatly into her head and taken over for a while, then had given it back again sometime later.

Leah didn't like losing control, and she liked it even less when she couldn't remember anything. What did it all mean? Could she really be crazy?

A terrible thought occurred to her: what if whatever had been wrong with Gillian was wrong with her too?

They stopped for the night some distance off the road where a huge shelf of rock formed a natural shelter against the wind and any prying eyes. Cain explained to her that they did not want to light a fire, because it might draw attention to them, and they could do without other people looking to steal what little food they had. Leah had left James's cloak behind in the strange little village when they had run away. She missed it, both for its warmth and for its safe, strong, fatherly smell.

Mikulov had brought three loaves of bread from Cyrus's kitchen and a canteen of water, and they shared some of the bread and passed the canteen around, huddling together for warmth. It wasn't much to eat, and Leah's stomach growled late into the night.

The next morning dawned cold and wet, the ground covered with dew that smelled like bad eggs. The traveling party resumed walking, with little conversation this time. They shared more bread around lunchtime, one of them occasionally saying something or pointing out a feature of the landscape, but Mikulov's stories had ended, and the last of any forced cheeriness between them had been bled away.

Eventually Leah stole a glance at Cain, who was watching the horizon, where the same black clouds seemed to boil and twist, never shifting away from the spot they had been the day before. Leah began to get the feeling that they were not clouds at all, but oily smoke or even some kind of living, breathing presence waiting for them to arrive, when it would strike.

It had been a while since she had thought of the bird pecking at the string of meat, back when the pack of boys had terrorized the old beggar. But the image came back to her now: the crow's beady eyes fixed on her own as it bent to pull, tear, and swallow the gray flesh, a clawed foot resting on the carcass for purchase, sharp, black beak going to work. In her memory the bird had grown to nearly human size, and its feathers were no longer black and shiny, but dull and thin and falling out, so that she could see right through them to the crow's skin beneath.

They watched that blackness churn as they climbed a long, slow rise in the road, finally reaching the top.

Gea Kul spread out below them in the distance, huddled on the edge of the sea, a miserable-looking town that had grown up and overrun its borders some time ago. Shanties and muddy refuse pits lined the road, which ran straight down the hill, and there were more carts and dead horses here, and even, Leah realized with fresh horror, dead people. She saw skeletal hands reaching from beneath an overturned wagon just a few hundred yards away, as if people had been trapped and had tried to claw their way out. The smell of rotting flesh wafted up to them, mingling with the scent of the ocean.

This seemed like the last place in the world they should be; if everyone from Gea Kul were trying to flee the town, why should they be trying to get in? Could these Horadrim that Cain and Mikulov were so anxious to find really do anything to stop the evil that had taken this city? If they had so much power, why hadn't they helped these people who had died on the road?

A far more terrifying thought occurred to her: what if *they* were the ones responsible?

Things were moving on the horizon, tiny black specks that seemed to swarm over the town like gnats: crows, hundreds of them, their black wings flapping as they soared and dove toward the ground.

Leah tried to calm her trembling. She could not get the image of the crow in Caldeum out of her head. *A bird's beady eye, staring at her like a black moon . . .*

She followed Cain and Mikulov down the hill. At the bottom of the long slope, they had to pass through the opening between two tall carriages, one of them overturned, the other sideways in the road. Sticking out from underneath the overturned carriage was a dead woman's arm, the skin peeling, the ends of the fingers raw, the nails torn completely off.

As she stepped quickly past, the woman's hand reached out and grabbed her foot.

Leah screamed. The woman's grip was strong and ice-cold, and her fingers dug painfully into Leah's flesh. She yanked hard enough to pull the woman out from under the carriage.

The woman opened her eyes. She stared up at Leah, her mouth working, gray tongue poking out from between cracked and peeling lips. Her face was skeletal, her hair matted, her flesh a blue-white.

"You are damned . . ." she whispered. "They will return . . . soon . . ."

Leah stared in horror at the huge, purple bruises covering the woman's neck. Something alien seemed to rise up within her, and she screamed again, and this time Cain was at her side, beating the woman's wrist with his staff until the bone snapped, and pulling Leah backward and beyond the narrow space, into the open air.

Still, the woman reached out for them, her ruined hand dangling limply, her legs caught under the carriage. She started making a strange sound, deep in her throat, as though she had swallowed a bone; after a moment Leah realized she was laughing, and the three travelers ran down the road away from the terrible sight, the woman's laughter following them on the wind until they could no longer hear her and the sound of the crows cawing overhead drowned out everything else.

# TWENTY-FOUR

## *The Horadric Chambers*

The woman had been alive.

As they approached the miserable port town, the clouds darkened overhead. Guilt washed over Cain like the threat of rain. Clearly the woman had been another victim of the feeders, with those bruises on her neck, yet he had panicked, breaking her arm to get Leah free. His desire to protect the girl was so strong, he had reacted without thinking.

The feeders were only pawns in a much larger game. They were worker bees, mindless drones carrying out a mission. But what was the mission, and who had ordered it? What had the people who died on this road been running from?

The crows were everywhere. They settled on the broken, blackened limbs of trees, pecked at the human corpses on the ground. They circled overhead, cawing and flapping, like a macabre welcoming parade under menacing skies, flitting shapes against the boiling clouds that hovered over the town. The very air seemed run through with a charge, and Leah remained so close to Cain's feet that he almost tripped over her as they entered Gea Kul.

He put a hand on her shoulder to calm her. He had sensed

something building again before he had intervened with the woman, that familiar drop in temperature that had preceded a manifestation of her powers before. They all felt the tension.

Gea Kul's streets were a maze of shoddy, decrepit buildings and confusing intersections. The stench of the sea permeated the moist air as a light mist descended, turning everything at a distance into murky, indistinct shapes. The call of the crows was amplified, the mist serving to bounce the sounds in strange and disorienting directions.

There were people here. Cain sensed them hiding in shadowed doorways, keeping out of sight; they caught glimpses of haunted, pale faces hovering in windows before ducking away, flashes of movement in alleyways, faint footsteps and scraping noises. They were more skittish than wild deer. The mist made the entire scene feel dreamlike and unsettling. He glanced at Mikulov, who slipped his blade out.

Around the next corner a young boy not much older than Leah stood in the street. The line of his ribs showed through his shirt, his eyes sunken and haunted.

He raised his arm slowly and pointed a long, thin finger at them.

Leah gasped and pressed herself against Cain's legs. Two men were standing behind them holding makeshift clubs. Several more people materialized soundlessly from the mist, all of them as thin as death itself. Cain glanced up to find that the rooftops around them were lined with crows, their black bodies fluffed against the cold, their eyes staring relentlessly, motionless.

The men with clubs shifted closer. The silence of the crowd was unsettling, the threat of violence hanging over them. Leah's grip on Cain's arm tightened painfully, her nails digging into his flesh; she was so tense she seemed to be vibrating like a struck tuning fork.

The rigging of a distant ship creaked in the stillness. A long, low moan rose up over the streets and grew to an echoing wail. The crows lifted off the rooftops all at once with a thunderous flapping of wings. The sound went on, growing louder, and the crowd scattered in all directions, fading back into the shadows until it seemed as if they had never been there at all.

A man hurried down the street. The mist made it difficult to make out his features, but he was large and white-haired, and slightly hunched. As he hurried closer, Cain could see that he carried a horn in one hand.

The man raised the horn to his lips and gave off another blast. "The streets of Gea Kul are no place for a fine young lass like this," he said. "They don't like the sound, reminds them of a feeder's call at night. But it won't take them long to return. Follow me, quickly now, my friends. You don't want them coming back on you, believe me."

They followed the man to a weathered structure with a sign hanging outside pronouncing it the Captain's Table. He opened the door and ushered them into a silent, empty dining room lit by lanterns, the surroundings as worn as the building's exterior. Thick boards had been nailed across the windows, but the room was neat and clean. "Not sure why I bother," the man said, as he closed and bolted the door behind them. "No patrons anymore, but I know no other way. 'Tis the service that taught me. Make your bunks tight enough to bounce a coin, they said, or swab the decks 'til your fingers bleed." The man stuck out his hand to Cain. "Forgive me; my manners are as rusty as the old tub sitting at the dock. Captain Hanos Jeronnan, at your service. These seas have seen plenty of me over the years. Settled here with my daughter to make a life of it, back when Gea Kul was a better place." The old man's eyes grew distant. "'Twas a long time past."

Cain sensed a kindness and strength about Jeronnan. He was

old, his face lined and haggard, curly hair and sideburns white as snow, but he was wide in the shoulders, and his grip was still strong.

"Does your daughter still live here?"

Jeronnan shook his huge head. "Lost her many years ago. I kept up the place, though. Had my reasons." He nodded at Leah, and his face softened as he looked at her. "Are you hungry, lass? A bowl of fish stew would warm your bones." He shuffled into the kitchen as the three of them took a seat in the nearest booth away from the door, and returned only moments later with three bowls balanced on a tray. As Cain began to speak, the big man raised a blue-veined, meaty hand. "Fill your bellies," he said. "Then we'll talk." He stood back and folded his massive arms.

Cain took a bite and realized he was starving. The stew was delicious. He finished the bowl in moments, and saw that Jeronnan was already on his way with more, along with mugs of frothy ale and water for Leah.

Finally the three of them sat back while Jeronnan pulled up a chair with a scrape of wooden legs and settled his bulk on it. "Nothing makes a man happier than seeing his cooking enjoyed by a group of fine strangers," he said. His energy was infectious, and soon Leah was smiling shyly too, stealing glances at the big man when he wasn't looking: apparently she'd found a new hero. When Jeronnan pulled a wrapped honey stick from his pocket and gave it to her, she beamed with surprise and happiness, as if he'd handed over a pound of gold.

"Now tell me what you're doing in a place such as this? Gea Kul's been my home for near on forty years now, but it's a cursed town. Legends tell it was built on top of an ancient mage battlefield. There were many who said I was crazy for staying through the worst of it, but I won't give up. Just don't see many others coming here voluntarily." Jeronnan looked Cain up and down. "You're a sorcerer," he said.

"I'm a Horadric scholar," Cain said.

"Ah." Jeronnan rubbed his beard. "You'll be looking for your brothers, then."

A chill raced through Cain's bones. "I am," he said. "Have you seen them?"

"Aye." Jeronnan sat back in his chair, the look on his face impossible to read. "Have a soft spot in my heart for sorcery, and there's good reason, even if you might think it's a strange one. There was a lovely necromancer who passed through years ago and sat in this very booth . . ." He shook his head, a soft smile on his big, shaggy face. "I know the very thought of necromancers makes most people want to run the other way, and most of them look stranger than a ship on dry land, but Kara was different. She was sweet, and gentle in her own way. Kara's passed on, either from here, or from this world, or both, while I remain, a bullheaded old sea captain who doesn't know when to quit."

"The Horadrim," Mikulov prodded gently. "You've seen them?"

Jeronnan nodded. "They're responsible for much of the terror that has fallen over this poor town, or so it's been said. Me, I've known many mages in my day. This one who led them . . ." He shook his head again. "I don't think the evil in him was born from any order of men."

Jeronnan went on to tell them about the group of Horadrim who had come to Gea Kul many months before, and the leader of the group, a man named Rau, who had established the order in town and had a huge, stone tower built on the edge of the sea. But soon Rau disappeared, the group went into mourning, and tragedy struck. "There was darkness all around that place," Jeronnan said. "And eventually that darkness came to Gea Kul.

"Soon enough, there were sightings of creatures that visited people's homes in the middle of the night, sucking the life right out of them. People started locking their doors and staying in with lanterns burning. Others began to act mighty peculiar, as if they were haunted—sometimes flashing eerie smiles, vacant stares, cocking their heads like they were hearing voices. It was enough to make you believe the entire town had gone mad." He shrugged. "There were other changes, too; some of them you've seen with your own eyes. Those people out there, wasting away, like walking corpses."

"How have you avoided the same fate?" Cain asked.

Jeronnan reached down to a pocket and withdrew something covered with a leather sleeve, which he carefully removed. An ivory dagger shone in the lantern light as he held it up. "A gift, from an old friend," he said. "She returned here after her adventures in the desert and gave me this charmed blade. It's a rare gift, something an old captain like me doesn't deserve. They don't like it, these feeders. They stay away from here."

The captain handed the blade to Cain. Cain turned it over in his hands, feeling the carefully balanced weight and the energy held within it. A necromancer's blade was a vital part of their magic, and they would never willingly give up their personal weapon. But this one was similar to those used by the priests of Rathma in their rituals. Jeronnan's friend must have enchanted it herself and brought it to him.

"She must have admired you greatly, to give you this."

Jeronnan smiled again, but this time it held a tinge of sadness. "Kara was like a second daughter to me. But she went off to find new adventures with that Norrec fellow, and I haven't heard tell of her in years."

Cain removed the Horadric book from his sack, placing it on the table. Jeronnan looked at the familiar symbol stamped on the front cover, a figure eight with an amber gemstone in the middle. "I've seen this," he said. "The symbol of their order. I knew two boys from town who joined with them before the feeders came. Used to carry these books around all day. They were good boys, in spite of the man who led them."

"This group of scholars," Cain said. "They're still here, in Gea Kul?"

"They picked up and left in a hurry a couple of months back, after the tower was done. But there's a hidden place in town where the order used to gather, for study. I don't know its exact location, but I can take you to the area, if you like."

The streets were empty, a fresh glaze of rain making them shimmer. Cain followed Captain Jeronnan through the mist, watching his giant back and staying close. He had considered whether to trust the captain or not; for all Cain knew, the old man could be leading him into a trap. But Jeronnan's motivations seemed pure. He had brought his horn and dagger to keep the people away, but they hadn't seen a soul. Gea Kul was an abandoned wasteland, and Jeronnan was Cain's only lifeline.

Cain had left Mikulov with Leah at the Captain's Table. As much as he had wanted the monk with him, he had been even more concerned with keeping Leah safe. The situation had become too dangerous. Cain had made Jeronnan promise to return to the inn as well, once they had reached the area where the Horadric gathering place was located.

Jeronnan stopped in a street full of rundown shacks. Garbage piled in corners reeked of old, rotted food; huge rats scurried away from the sound of their footsteps echoing through the silence. "The group met somewhere near here," he said. "I used to see some of them on this very street, but then they'd disappear, and I never knew exactly where. I don't know what you plan to do, should you find them. But we're badly in need of help. There was a time when this town saw its fair share of trade, when the taverns were full of rowdy sailors and the docks heavy with goods bound for Kurast and Caldeum. I won't say it was a place for royalty, mind you, but it was a town full of life." Jeronnan put his hand on Cain's shoulder. "I'm a good judge of character, and something tells me you're the man to bring a sense of peace back to Gea Kul."

Jeronnan handed Cain the horn. "Blow this, should you need me again. It'll keep those who have been corrupted by the feeders away, and I'll come find you with my dagger in hand and whatever force I can muster." He took Cain's hand in both of his and squeezed it. "Take care now," he said. "And good luck."

He disappeared into the mist. Cain tucked the horn into his sack. He looked around at the abandoned huts on all sides, and the now-familiar feeling of being the last man left in Sanctuary settled over him again. He was closer to his goal, yet in many ways he felt even more isolated and forlorn. The weight of the world had been placed on his shoulders, and he had no idea if he was up to the task at hand.

*I'm no hero.*

That much was true. But he would do all that he could to make up for his past mistakes, and he would sacrifice his own life, if necessary, to save this world. That would have to be good enough.

Cain studied the row of buildings again, looking for a clue to the location of the hidden entrance of the Horadric hall. The site was typical; years ago, the Horadrim were known for hiding their meeting places in plain sight, and in an area that people would least expect to find them. It would be protected by a spell of concealment, of course. Quite likely a powerful one.

He searched through his more familiar texts for something that might help him, but found nothing. The mist grew thicker, writhing across the ground as the minutes ticked past. Finally his fingers settled upon the ancient Vizjerei spellbook he had found in the ruins.

*Demonic magic, written by the followers of Bartuc, the Warlord of Blood.* Cain carefully flipped through its crumbling pages. There:

a spell meant to reveal anything that had been cloaked by magic. But this kind of incantation was dangerous. It called attention to itself, and Sanctuary was no longer protected from the Burning Hells and all the creatures that lived within that cursed place. It would light up like a beacon in darkness, drawing moths to the flame.

What other choice did he have? He could search for days and never find the entrance.

Cain recited the words of power, feeling the ground begin to thrum beneath him, and as he did so, he felt the gaze of thousands turn to focus on Gea Kul, the senses of things he did not want to know, abominations that hid in dark caverns stinking of rot and blood. Above them all loomed a black tower with what had once been a man living within it, a man who was now something else entirely—a creature that lived on pain.

The Horadric symbol, the figure eight with sharp points like fangs, glowed a blood red from the side of one of the larger stone buildings about a hundred feet away. Cain tucked the old book away and ran, his tunic flapping like a crow's wings, the mist swirling all around him, and as he reached the building, he realized that the lower right point was the handle of a door cleverly hidden in what had appeared to be a smooth wall. As the spell's power receded and the symbol began to fade again into oblivion, he grasped the handle and pulled, and it opened easily, revealing blackness inside.

The voice that came down from the Black Tower was thunderous inside his head, like the rumble of boulders across a mountain. It cried out in rage at his presence, a challenge to battle, an inarticulate scream that promised to shatter his skull.

Deckard Cain ducked into the building and closed the door carefully behind him, cutting off the scream abruptly, and turned to face whatever might be waiting for him.

A set of stone steps led down into gloom. Somewhere a candle flickered, lending a faint amount of light to the landing below. Someone was here.

A grating noise floated up to him. Cain heard nothing more, and he descended slowly and carefully through the dark.

At the bottom of the stairs was a simple room with a wooden desk and open doors on either side, enough light from the door on the right bleeding through for him to see. The desk was empty, but a tapestry on the wall behind it bore the Horadric symbol.

It had been slashed nearly in half by a sharp blade.

A waking dream came to him, of black-clad soldiers laying waste to this place, hacking with their heavy swords and over-turning tables, putting torches to dry pages of books, and these men turned into huge, hopping crows, their beaks like black daggers. Cain touched the tapestry, felt the marks beneath it, gouged into stone; it had not been slashed by a blade, after all. There were three equal tears, as if some giant creature had raked it with razor-sharp talons.

What else would he find down here? Would it lead to salvation, or to his destruction?

He slipped quietly through the right-hand doorway into a large library. The remains of a candle flickered on a table, guttering in a pool of melted wax; it had burned nearly to the bottom. Simple wooden shelves lined all four walls, most of them full of books; of these, some looked familiar, while others he had never seen before. The collection was remarkable.

On the table was an open book. It looked similar to the one he had found in the ruins.

Cain smelled something foul, like rotten meat. Another room loomed through an archway beyond this one, pitch-black inside. He heard movement, and a low, guttural snarl, accompanied by the sound of something scraping against rock. Feeling exposed in the candlelight, he flattened himself against the wall and moved as quietly as a ghost to a corner between two bookcases.

The thing that emerged from the archway was so huge and incomprehensible that at first Cain had trouble processing the sight of it. It appeared to be made of human limbs and torsos all rolled together, along with a forest of jutting spikes of what looked like rock and shards of wood. Two long arms ended in clubs rather than hands and sprouted the same shards of wood or stone. At least three separate heads emerged from putrid, swollen flesh, white-filmed eyes rolling in their sockets.

The monstrosity moved slowly and laboriously, ducked to clear the arch, more than ten feet off the floor. Its dripping shoulders nearly touched both sides of the opening as it leaned into the library, grunting with the effort. It seemed to have one main head in the center of its chest, and as it swung in Cain's direction, those eyes fixed on his face.

The creature paused, as if studying him. Then it opened its mouth and roared, the putrid stench of its breath washing over Cain as the mouths of the other heads screeched in unison.

The candle flickered and nearly went out. Fresh panic rose up in Cain as the creature took a lumbering step toward him and threatened to knock over the table, sending them into darkness. He slipped out from his hiding place and went for the door, but the monster moved with him and reached out its long, clubbed limb as if to smash him into the floor.

Cain had no time to react other than to swerve and duck, and the monster roared again. The candle went out. Suddenly he could see nothing, and sounds seemed to cascade at him from all sides. Feeling dizzy in the pitch-black room, Cain stumbled against the edge of the table. He heard the thing coming, blind now as well, and the table was shoved hard against him, throwing him backward into the bookcase.

The room flared to life again as a brilliant, white-hot light blossomed in its center. Cain blinked against it and saw a robed, hooded figure in the second doorway from the front room. The figure threw a second burst of flame at the creature's feet, sending it back as it waved its arms and screeched in rage.

Cain pushed the table aside as the stranger beckoned to him to follow. They ran past the desk and tapestry and stairs, through the door on the other side as the thing in the library howled again and lumbered after them, crashing into the table and walls, shaking the floor as it smashed its way out.

They were in a long hallway made of stone with a blank wall at the end. The man went straight to it and pressed a hidden lever, and a stone panel slid aside, revealing a new set of stairs descending into the earth. He threw another ball of light that revealed a narrower passage extending beyond the bottom step. This section seemed much older than the library, the walls cracked and covered in moss. The stranger headed down.

Cain hesitated at the top. He knew nothing more about this new arrival than he did about the thing chasing them; for all he knew, he was the Dark One himself. There could be even greater danger below. But another bellow from the creature broke his paralysis, and he took the steps as quickly as he dared, being careful of the slippery moss.

The man pressed another hidden spot in the wall, and the door at the top slid closed again with a rumble of grating stone. The noise of the creature above them was cut off abruptly. He took a torch from the wall and dipped its top in the spitting ball of light on the floor. Slender fingers rose up to slip the hood away to reveal a young man's face, as pure and white as fresh snow.

"My name is Egil," the man said. "I mean you no harm. I am a member of the First Ones—the Horadrim. Please, follow me."

# TWEN+Y-FIVE

## *The Camp*

Cain followed the man through the dripping, moss-covered tunnel, his mind filled with endless questions: how had Egil found him? How many Horadrim were left? Did they know about the impending demon invasion of Sanctuary?

Other, darker thoughts pushed their way in as well. He wondered what had happened to their leader, Garreth Rau. Could this strange young man be trusted? And if something happened to Cain, who would take care of Leah?

But Egil seemed to be in too much of a hurry to speak. Cain struggled to keep up, following the dipping, flickering torchlight as he rushed forward. Cain tried to get closer, finally catching the sleeve of Egil's tunic, making him stop and turn. The man's face was curiously calm and patient.

"What was that thing in the library?" Cain said.

"We call them the unburied, but nobody is sure exactly how or why they have come," Egil said. "They seem to be created from the bodies of the dead, along with other pieces of the landscape around them, as if someone rolled them all together and lit a spark of life. There is powerful black magic awake in Sanctuary. Perhaps this is a result."

"And what were you doing there?"

"It was our former meeting place, before . . . we left Gea Kul. I was trying to recover some of the texts. Now, I am afraid they may be ruined." Egil sighed, the first sign of any emotion he had shown. "It is a terrible loss. But it wasn't the only reason I was there."

Egil explained that the prophecies had foretold Cain's arrival on this very day and the brothers had been eagerly awaiting it for months. The order was in a transition, he said, and new leadership was needed. Many of them hoped that Cain would provide crucial information to them about the changes in Sanctuary since the destruction of the Worldstone.

"This transition," Cain said. "Is it because of Garreth Rau?"

If Egil was surprised, he did not show it. "It is complicated," he said. "We will tell you everything, I promise, as soon as we return to camp. But now we must go. This tunnel is part of a large network, built under Gea Kul many years ago, and no one knows how far it runs or its purpose. But the unburied most certainly came from here. There may be other creatures within these tunnels, or beneath them. It is very dangerous."

Cain shook his head. "I must return to a place called the Captain's Table, if you want me to accompany you. I have friends there."

Egil hesitated, then nodded. "I know of it. I can take you to them, and then we will go meet my brothers. Please, come."

The man moved with a fluid grace, making almost no sound, his torchlight flickering off an arched ceiling that seemed to close in over Cain's head. They passed several branches in the tunnel, finally taking one that sloped upward to another set of stairs leading to an iron grate. Leaving the torch burning in a brace on the wall, Egil pushed the grate aside, and Cain found himself at street level, just a short distance away from Jeronnan's inn.

When they arrived at the Captain's Table, Mikulov and Leah

were overjoyed to see him. Leah threw her arms around his neck and squeezed him tightly, while Jeronnan shook Cain's hand with both of his own. "I suppose you'll be moving on, then," he said. "You can trust this man, Egil. I know him well enough, born and educated here in Gea Kul. He's a good lad." Jeronnan handed Leah another honey stick. "A little something for your troubles, lass," he said. "Stay well."

Mikulov wanted to know more about the order, but Egil was growing desperate, warning them of the dangers of traveling through Gea Kul after dark. "We have less than two hours to be free of the town," he said. "We will have time to talk later."

The four of them said their good-byes, thanking Jeronnan profusely for his help. The captain insisted on giving them some fish wrapped in paper for the journey, though Egil said it wasn't far. Cain tried to return the horn, but Jeronnan wouldn't take it. "Remember," he said, his huge hand on Cain's shoulder. "Should I hear the sound of that, I'll come to your aid, wherever you may be. I may look old, but I'm still a match for anything that might be wanting to hurt you."

They left before night fell. In the street they saw no one other than the crows, which continued to swoop and caw loudly above their heads, the sounds traveling in the fog that had continued to thicken. Egil led them back into the tunnels beneath Gea Kul, picking up the torch again from the wall and taking them through a dizzying warren of intersections, finally emerging beyond the town through a sewer entrance.

He left the torch and took them into the wilds beyond and away from the sea, with Mikulov watching their backs. Leah remained glued to Cain's side, suspicious of their new friend and his strange looks; Cain did have to admit that Egil's colorless eyes were intense, almost hypnotic, and his white hair and eyebrows gave his face a waxy sheen. He had no other apparent facial hair, and his skin was smooth and unlined.

Beyond the town, the landscape quickly changed to a wilderness of scarred, leafless trees, slabs of rock and dead grasses sprouting in thick, razor-like tufts from patches of dry soil. They followed a narrow path winding through the tufts. Egil kept looking at the skies nervously, but the crows appeared to have lost them at the entrance to the tunnels, and there was no sign of any pursuit from here.

The ground rose gently as they entered a thicker copse of trees. It was dark and gloomy, dead branches reaching out like skeleton fingers overhead. Mikulov closed ranks in the rear, and Leah grabbed Cain's hand again as Egil slowed his pace, finally stopping completely in a small clearing. He gave a low, soft whistle. Almost immediately an answering whistle came from somewhere to their right. Leah's grip tightened as three figures emerged from the gloom, closing in on all sides as silently as ghosts in the dim light. One of them was huge, even wider through the shoulders than Captain Jeronnan and several inches taller than Cain himself. He carried a bow, an arrow notched and ready.

The figures paused. The mist drifted in and swirled around their feet.

"My brothers," said Egil, his voice trembling with emotion. "We are saved. I have found him."

# TWEN+Y-SIX

## *The First Ones*

The camp was not what Mikulov had expected. He had had a vision of a sprawling complex of wooden temples and studios and sleeping quarters, buildings rising up out of the wilderness as builders swarmed over them, while others meditated or discussed strategy or led scholarly discussions on the future of Sanctuary itself: something that fit with the grand history of the order, as it had been written.

This was nothing but a network of caves, set within the rocky face of a steep incline that led up to a cliff overlooking the town and the sea. There was little evidence on the outside that anyone was living there at all.

The location itself was the biggest problem. The Ivgorod masters had taught him about the ways of war, and the most important thing in choosing a stronghold, after its defensibility, was to have an escape route, should the battle turn against you. These caves appeared to be a dead end, and a deathtrap should they be discovered by a force stronger than their own.

The three men who had met them in the jungle were initially suspicious, but after Cain showed them his reproduction of the Horadric text, along with the other texts and scrolls he had in his rucksack, they grew more animated. The biggest one, a man named Lund, appeared to be what his masters would have called slow-minded; but he had a kind heart, and Leah took to him almost immediately. Lund was as thickly muscled as an ox, and his bow was nearly as tall as a full-grown man. Mikulov wondered how he could draw it back, but as he showed Leah its pull, he drew the string effortlessly in one fluid motion, pointing out a knothole in a tree over fifty yards away before burying the arrow in its center.

As they arrived at the cave entrance, more men swarmed around them, about thirty in all. Cain was treated like a returning king by some, and all but ignored by others. "Never mind about them," Egil said quietly, after they had a moment to speak. He nodded at the group of men who had held back when Cain arrived and were now gathered to one side, whispering to each other. "There are two divisions here: those who believe in the prophecies and the future of the Horadrim, and those who do not. For those of us who believe, you are our salvation."

"And for those who don't?" Mikulov asked.

"They may take a bit more convincing," Egil said, with a wry smile. "But they are good men. They will come around, once we have our meeting tonight. We will all hear about your journey, and discuss what lies ahead."

"I'm no savior," Cain said. "Just a scholar who has studied enough of the ancient texts to know we must act quickly. There is little time left. Ratham is only three days away."

Egil looked blankly at him. "Ratham? The month of the dead? Why should that be important?"

Mikulov tried to explain what he had found in the scrolls, but the discussion went downhill from there. It didn't take long for him to realize that these men knew very few actual details about the dangers facing Sanctuary and had only the faintest sense of what was to come.

This was a great disappointment. Cain and Leah sensed it as well, and Mikulov felt the energy that had formed when Egil had been leading them here begin to dissipate. Still, those who peppered Cain with questions seemed to think he had come here to lead them to a victory against the darkness, and they wasted little time trying to convince him of their worth.

*Perhaps I am being too quick to judge,* he thought. *We must give them a chance to prove themselves.* If they were Sanctuary's only hope, then so be it. The gods would provide the answers, in time.

More persistent questions about the group of men, and their former leader, were turned politely aside until the upcoming "meeting," which would happen after they broke bread. Mikulov sensed Cain's growing frustration at the seeming lack of urgency from the group.

But there seemed to be no immediate danger here, and inside the largest cave, torchlight flickered brightly against the walls as the smell of smoke filled the air. As the members of the order directed the travelers to sit on piles of animal furs around a cooking fire and handed them mugs full of cider, Lund lumbered in with an antelope carcass over his giant shoulder, an arrow still buried in its chest. "We eat well tonight!" the big man shouted, a grin plastered across his face, and several others cheered and clapped enthusiastically, causing Lund to do a little jig before laying the antelope down and beginning to dress it with a knife. A man named Farris, who was the leader of the group that favored disbanding entirely, grumbled at first, but then even he reluctantly joined the others.

As the celebration grew more raucous, Mikulov took the opportunity to slip out into the cool night, and he stood for a moment in the shadows of the cave entrance, tasting the air. There was a sentry stationed in the trees, and another somewhere above the cliff face. His senses had been finely tuned over years of focused meditation and training; he could hear the sentries shifting on their haunches and smell their strong male scent on the breeze, although they had not noticed him.

Summoning the power of the gods was no small matter, but Mikulov was an Ivgorod monk, and he felt their power flowing through his limbs like water over rock. It lifted him as he moved with blinding speed, so quickly that a blink of a human eye would have missed it.

The sentries never even turned in his direction. In seconds he was in the trees above the cave, climbing effortlessly up the steep slope until he reached the top. He looked out over the valley below, aglow in the moonlight. Gea Kul lay on the edge of the sea in the distance like a rotting carcass washed up by the black waves, and to the right, a tower rose up out of the rocky shoreline, dark and silent.

Mikulov remembered standing on a cliff like this one only a few days earlier and staring out over the trees at Kurast, imagining what was to come. Cain and Leah had been strangers to him then, yet he had been filled with a confidence that seemed curiously absent now.

He felt the weight of centuries beneath him, anchoring him to this place as Ratham approached. He knew that he would be challenged by something terrible. His destiny had been preordained since the moment of his birth; what role he would play in the looming battle was unclear to him, but it would come, whether he was prepared for it or not.

It was not the way of his people to question their duty, yet he couldn't help wondering what would happen if he simply slipped away, into the night, leaving all this behind. Would his path change? Or would he simply be forced back here by some circumstance beyond his control, ending up at the same place in the end?

Were his masters right? Was he too headstrong, too selfish, too eager to leave the Ivgorod monastery without their blessing? Was he not ready for this challenge?

Would his pride be his downfall?

*No.* Mikulov shook his head. Now was not the time for misgivings. He had spent years preparing for this. He had studied the ancient texts of Ivgorod, and when those had not shown him enough, he had traveled across Sanctuary to find more, some of them nearly as old as time itself. A thread had connected them all, if one only knew where to look; he had picked up that thread, following it through the centuries, a common theme that predicted the rise of a great evil, and a battle that would make all others pale in comparison. It had brought him to Deckard Cain, and he had led Mikulov to this place.

The gods would show him the way.

In the distance, above the mist that clung to the shore, the stone tower seemed to sway like a cobra about to strike. For a moment, Mikulov imagined tendrils of smoke slithering outward, writhing through the air, and he heard something whisper on the wind, words that he could not understand. The text from one of the ancient scrolls came back to him, signs the Patriarchs had interpreted about a sickness in the skies and the ground, the screams of tortured souls rising up against the gods themselves . . .

A shriek split the night, shredding entire trees in its wake, rolling forward with gathering speed, a hurricane of rage that flattened cities and emptied the seas and struck the stars from the sky. Mikulov's eardrums shredded, popping against the pressure; his eyes bulged outward, breath ripped from his chest, the blood boiling in his veins. He felt his skin begin to peel away, muscle stretched from ligament and bone, his organs squeezed like ripe fruit until they burst, and the wind took it all until there was nothing left but empty rock in an ocean of blackness.

Mikulov came to gasping like a drowning man, clawing at the ground with his fingernails. The night was silent and still. He climbed to his feet, looking around him, feeling his body as if to make sure it was whole. He was unharmed, at least physically. But he had been badly shaken.

He shivered. He had never felt such power, had never had his own body and mind possessed in such a way. He felt as if the black smoke had wormed its way inside his lungs and he was now tainted by its touch. Something within the great darkness was coming after him, and it was huge, and grinning, and wanted to swallow him whole.

He knew who was responsible for this. It was the man inside the tower: the Dark One.

Inside the caves they sat on furs around the fire, languid and slow after their heavy meal of venison. Several of the other men were cleaning up; others were asleep, but a smaller group remained awake. Lund sat cross-legged like a monstrous child, licking his fingers, Leah next to him watching open-mouthed as the giant man grinned, his mouth shiny with grease. The conversation had taken many different paths and eventually had wound around again to why they were here tonight.

This was the so-called important meeting Egil had been promising him.

Cain sighed and rubbed his itchy beard. The order was nothing like what he had expected. He needed a bath, and clean clothes, and a good night's sleep. What he had learned during the past several hours was enough to fill his heart with dread, and he needed some time to think it all over and decide what to do.

Everything Egil had told him seemed to fit, more or less, with what Hyland had said. The order had grown up out of circumstance, more than anything else. The discovery of a cache of hidden texts in an abandoned, secret Horadric meeting place in Gea Kul had intrigued a small group of scholars, who had taken ownership of the crumbling texts and attempted to get them re-

produced. They had brought the texts to Garreth Rau, a litterateur in Kurast, and a chain of events had been set in motion that
would prove to be their downfall.

Many years before, Rau had worked as a servant boy to a
member of the Taan mage clan in Kurast, and he had his own
obsession with ancient texts, after he had discovered his master's
libraries. The magic held within these texts was powerful, the
prophecies they foretold astonishing; Rau had studied in secret,
learning how to create new books out of the old, eventually leaving the sorcerer's employ and starting his own business. The
books that the Gea Kul scholars had brought him had been like
the finest wine to him, and although they had only the barest
understanding of what these texts contained, he had seemed inspired by what he read. Something had clicked into place, and
Rau had made a pact with them: they would return together to
Gea Kul, and the scholars would swear oaths to uphold the tenets of the Horadrim, to seek out more knowledge and form an
official order.

Rau had been a natural leader, and he had quickly taken over.
They reclaimed the ancient Horadric meeting hall, which had
given them a place to gather, organize nightly study sessions,
plan trips outside the town to search for more texts and artifacts,
and attempt some of the spells within the books they had found.
Rau had encouraged them to learn the Horadric ways, but he
had a raw talent and power none of the others had possessed.
The litterateur had understood the depths of knowledge that
these ancient texts plundered. The more he had studied them,
the more convinced he had become that he could use them for
personal gain.

"He called us the 'First Ones,'" Egil said, passing the bottle of
cider to Cain. "Back then, things were still good between us, and
we thought we would become heroes, leaders of a new Sanctuary
based on the Horadric principles we had embraced. At least, some

of us did. But he'd based everything on his own corrupted vision. He called himself royalty, had some idea he was descended from a powerful mage. He even showed us a crest that was supposedly from his family, although we had understood him to be an orphan. We had no idea that he had fallen so far."

"What do you mean, fallen?"

Egil sighed, looking at Lund, who avoided his gaze. It was as if the big man was ashamed—which, Cain thought, might not be far from the truth.

"Dark magic," Egil said. "We did not see it at first. We followed him blindly. He led us on more quests to find artifacts, received prophetic visions of ancient sites to explore. He instilled faith in us, even during several excursions that led to actual demon encounters, which he always handled with ease. He knew the right spells, and they would yield to him. But with each new artifact he found, he grew more powerful, his intentions darker, his obsession with the dark arts more intense. Members of our order began to disappear and then return changed, completely loyal and obedient to Garreth. He began to talk of a new vision for the Horadric tenets, holding daily lecture sessions about the future of the order.

"He believed that the original Horadrim were wrong about the nobility of Tyrael and his intentions. He spoke derisively about the archangel, who formed the Horadrim but never directly combated the Prime Evils, after all. Instead, Tyrael used the mages to do the brunt of the work, Rau told us. Why couldn't this powerful angel do battle himself, he would ask? Was humanity truly more powerful than the angels? Why were the angels considered any better than the Prime Evils, when they judge humanity so harshly?

"He spoke of humanity in the same way. Humans were inherently evil, he said, worse even than the creatures of the Burning Hells. Look how they treated each other, he said, the weakest of them, those who could not defend themselves, beaten down and destroyed like cattle. The time would come when a new order would arise to lead Sanctuary, and all those who did not embrace it would be gone. He began to insist we call him master. He had a tower built for himself in secret on the edge of the sea, by people—or other things—we never saw. It went up nearly overnight, through some kind of black magic."

So Garreth Rau had become the Dark One. It didn't surprise Cain, not really; he'd begun to suspect it since Jeronnan's story of the scholars' arrival in Gea Kul and their leader's strange disappearance. Still, it was unsettling to know that one who had studied the ways of the Horadrim so closely could have been so terribly consumed with hatred.

"The prophecies have foretold it," Cain said. "One of the Lesser Evils of Hell had corrupted him."

Egil nodded, his strangely pale eyes somber. "It was Lund who discovered the final truth."

Cain looked at the big man, who had stopped smiling, his gaze suddenly wary. "Don't like to talk about that," Lund mumbled, looking away.

"But we have to," Egil said gently. He turned to Cain. "Rau had taken to leaving our meeting place by that time, and he was gone for longer and longer periods. He had Lund run errands. Lund traveled to the Black Tower to bring him some texts and witnessed a blood ritual. A . . . sacrifice of another member of our order. Garreth had made a secret pact with the Burning Hells. Somehow, through his studies he had found a connection."

"Blood," Lund muttered, his hands nervously working at a seam in his tunic. "Too much of it. Didn't like that at all."

Egil made a soothing motion, and Lund seemed to relax a little. "There was . . . a sacrifice. We tried to bring Garreth to his senses, but it was too late. He had been lost to his darkness, perverting what he had learned from the Horadric texts and following the very demons that he had once sworn to defend Sanctuary against.

"After that, our eyes were opened. We realized we had to escape or be destroyed by what was coming. We managed to get away under the cover of night and ended up here, in these caves. The few texts we managed to bring with us pointed to the arrival of a man who would save us from the darkness we faced. We've been waiting for you ever since."

"Not all of us," one of the men muttered from across the fire. He was tall and blond, and he'd been silent for most of the meal and the conversation afterward, but Cain recognized him: it was Farris, the leader of the group of skeptics within the order.

"The prophecies told of his arrival," Egil snapped. "Isn't that enough for you?"

"And we're just supposed to believe it, now that he's arrived?" Farris shrugged and took another swig of cider. "The legends are long past, and the Horadrim, if they ever truly existed, are gone. What's left is darkness and death. We should go back to our homes and hope for the best."

There were a few murmurs of agreement from Farris's friends. "What homes?" Egil said, his voice growing louder. "Did you not see what Gea Kul has become? What the Dark One has done to us, to our land? You are blind if you think you can just go back—"

Farris leapt to his feet, his face bright red. "Don't tell me how blind I am, Egil. Your *blind* faith has kept us living out here, in these caves, while our loved ones suffer and die alone. I would rather die with them than with you."

Cain was growing ever more unsettled. He had hoped to find true mages who would help him conquer the darkness; but Egil, at least, seemed to look to him as some kind of hero, while the rest of them seemed suspicious, incompetent, or worse.

As he had suspected for so long, the Lesser Evils of Hell were at work in Sanctuary. Belial had sunk his claws into Garreth Rau.

What would happen next was unclear, but Cain could not help but feel more uncertain than ever.

Cain felt the walls of the cave closing in on him. He got to his feet and glanced at Leah, who had fallen asleep leaning against Lund's massive thigh. "I must take some air, to clear my head," he said. "Perhaps we should all take some time to think. Please excuse me."

The night was cool and silent. Cain's legs trembled with exhaustion. He tried to make sense of a world that suddenly seemed turned upside down.

How could he have been so badly mistaken? Everything he had learned through months of research had pointed him here, to these men—only to result in a dead end. The group was a disaster. He was no savior, and if Sanctuary depended upon him, and him alone, all was lost. What was more, the idea that this group could be of any help in deciphering Leah's condition and remarkable powers was laughable; they couldn't even set up a decent camp, never mind find the answers to abilities that may have been based in magic or something else entirely.

Cain felt a touch on his sleeve. Startled, he glanced over to find Mikulov standing next to him. He hadn't heard the monk arrive; in fact, he had been so absorbed in Egil's stories, Farris's arguments, and his own growing despair, he hadn't even realized until now that Mikulov had been absent for some time.

"They are not what you expected," Mikulov said. It was a statement, not a question, but Cain nodded. He wanted to remain strong, to appear as if he still held the confidence that what they were doing was right. Instead he found himself speechless, unable to describe the hopelessness that had welled up within him after meeting the men he had thought would be their salvation.

"I'm . . . I'm sorry," he said. "Perhaps we should have taken a different path. Perhaps there are others—"

Mikulov shook his head. His entire body seemed to be humming at a pitch just high enough to be beyond normal human perception. Cain could feel it like a struck piece of metal, and he was reminded of the evening he and Akarat had found the ruins in the Borderlands. It seemed so long ago.

"There is bad energy in the wind tonight," Mikulov said, staring out into the blackness beyond the cave entrance. "The gods are in hiding. There is great evil in that tower on the shore, and I fear it has found us."

"The Dark One, Garreth Rau."

He turned to Cain, his eyes shining in the faint light from the cavern. "I had a vision, just now, of his watching us. His anger was like the strongest sun, burning everything it touched to ash. I have never felt anything like it. I fear that he has already begun the rituals that will bring the undead army to march upon Caldeum."

"Then we have very little time left."

Mikulov nodded. "I, too, have been questioning our path here. I expected something different as well. But we cannot afford to stop now. The gods have led us here for a reason. We must remain strong, my friend. A great battle is coming, and any weakness we have will be used against us."

Cain sighed. The weight of the entire world was on his shoulders, pressing down until he wanted to scream out for relief. It was a burden too heavy for one man to carry. "What would you have us do, Mikulov?"

"Get some sleep." Mikulov smiled, but his face was haggard and drawn. Cain realized that he had gotten used to the monk's constant serenity and balanced energy, and now that they seemed absent, it was all the more shocking to behold. "We need to heal our minds and bodies. Things will seem better in the morning. They always do. Then we will go to work. What choice do we have? Leave now, in the dead of night? Abandon all that we have come to believe? What we know to be true?"

Cain nodded. Mikulov was right, of course. But Cain got the sense the monk was holding something else back, something that might shake him to the core, if he were to hear it.

There was something important he was missing. Egil had described Garreth Rau's descent into darkness. His power had grown with every ritual and every demonic spell. Eventually even his physical body had begun to change; he had become a mutated, monstrous shell of his former self. But he had mastered the dark arts with such precision, it seemed as if he could do anything.

Yet he had let his brethren escape. A man who wielded power such as this should have had no problem finding a small, fractured group like these men and laying waste to them. Why had he left them alone? Was there still a shred of humanity left inside that remembered what they had meant to him, something that held him back?

Or was there some other, much darker reason?

"Excuse me?"

Cain turned to find Egil standing behind them, hands clasped at his waist. Over his shoulder was a burlap sack. The young man's pale face was like a moon in the darkness. "I fear we have disappointed you," he said. "Some of the others have lost faith, like Farris. They feel that our attempt at reforming the Horadrim is a fool's game, and that the order died away for good years ago. Many no longer believe in angels or the High Heavens. They say that if Heaven exists, why wouldn't it act against the evil that is gathering here? But there are those of us who do believe, and have been waiting for someone like you to show us the way to salvation."

Egil paused, as if hesitant to speak again. "I have heard stories," he said finally. "My uncle lived near Tristram, for a time, before settling in Gea Kul. He told our family everything he had heard about the demon invasion there. He even claimed to have seen demons himself. And he told us about you. Now . . ." Egil shook his head, "he is gone, taken by Garreth and his feeders. My father and mother survive, but they no longer recognize me. They are victims too." His eyes met Cain's and held them. "Those stories about your wise counsel during the dark days of Tristram are what inspired me to study the Horadrim myself. I know you can help us. We are . . . fractured, and in need of a leader. But we are eager to learn. If you join us, the others will come to believe it too.

"I promise you, we will not let you down."

Deckard Cain stared out at the night, listening to the creak of wood, the faint sound of insects buzzing. His hearing seemed preternaturally acute—the ears of a deer as it lifts its head from feeding at the approach of a wolf, he thought, a half smile crossing his face. *I am an old man, but I am not dead yet.* The wind seemed to whisper back promises of violence: of cold, dead things reaching up from watery ground, and he knew that Garreth Rau was out there somewhere, standing just as he was, staring into the night sky. He shivered.

Egil's face was upturned toward him, waiting expectantly. Then the young man took the sack off his shoulder and dug inside, withdrawing something that made Cain suck in his breath with astonishment and wonder.

"We found this among the ruins of a monastery in Khanduras," Egil said. "We were never quite sure how to use it. But I suspect you could teach us."

Cain took the object in both hands, turned it over, admiring the workmanship. It had been a long time since he had seen one. It was a bit larger than a man's skull, and heavier than he remembered, the intricate carved wood seeming to tingle against his skin.

*The Horadric Cube.*

"You have a powerful tool here," Cain said. "Its magic is remarkable. You must use it wisely." But when he tried to give it back, Egil shook his head.

"Please, take it," he said. "Teach us what you know. Read the texts we were able to save from our library. They told us of your coming, and they may have more information that would help."

Cain's mother's voice came back to him through all these years: *The scrolls say that someday the Horadrim will rise up again when all seems lost, and a new hero will lead them in battle to save Sanctuary . . .*

And her voice again, this time as a warning: *Be careful what you wish for, Deckard.*

Cain tucked the cube carefully into his rucksack. "We have much more to discuss before we sleep," he said. "I want to know everything you can possibly remember about your time in Gea Kul, no matter how seemingly small or insignificant. There may be something important we can use."

Then he took Egil's arm, and Mikulov stepped up on his other side, and the three of them went back into the caves, where the others waited for them.

# TWENTY-SEVEN

## *Lund's Bow*

She stood on a platform that soared high above the clouds. The platform was so small she could not sit down, and its edges were crumbling away, and lightning flashed all around her, lighting up the sky with jagged cracks of purple and white. She trembled, terrified, afraid to move, afraid to even breathe. In moments she would slip and tumble end over end into the abyss.

Voices came to her through the crashing storm, a crazy old beggar and a pig-eyed bully: *"The sky will turn black, the streets fill with blood . . . where's your crazy mother? Servicing the men at the tavern? . . . we should toss you in the fountain, wash off the stink . . ."*

The sound of flapping joined the voices, and she looked all around but could not see the birds until she faced the front again and a crow at least twice her size was hovering just before her, fanning its wings, its huge, sharp beak snapping forward and nearly grazing her skin, its beady eyes fixated on her own.

She screamed as the crow began to change, its feathers melting into Gillian with crow's talons for hands, a knife buried hilt-deep in her chest; then that changed to a hood hanging over features shrouded in shadows, the talons rippling into long, bony fingers, a hunched, robed figure hovering just out of reach. It was the dark man. *YOU ARE MINE*, his voice thundered in her head, and one arm extended toward her as lightning cracked once again and thousands of horrible, skinless beasts gathered behind him. She felt herself being ripped open and laid bare, something pulled out of her like a ribbon unwinding from her stomach, and as she looked down, she screamed again because the ribbon was her own blood, coiling in the wind like a long, red snake and lit with blue fire.

Leah woke up to silence. Gray light trickled in from the mouth of the cave, and the smell of smoke still lingered, but the fire was dead. Lund slept next to her, his giant chest rising and falling slowly, and she sighed and waited for her galloping heart to slow down. The dream had been so real. She knew that the dark man and his demons meant to destroy the world. She shivered in the cold morning air.

The camp came awake slowly. Men stirred, muttered to themselves, got up to fetch water and start the fire again. Lund awoke a short time later and smiled sleepily at her, and Leah felt warmth for him begin in her chest and spread through her limbs, dispelling the chill. She didn't know why, but he made her feel safe, as if his great strength could protect her from harm. At the same time, his mind was like a child's, and he had nothing to hide. She liked that.

She looked around the cave for Uncle Deckard and found him deep in conversation with the man named Egil, two others from the camp she did not know (a tall, thin man with glasses and a shorter, round one with no hair), and Mikulov the monk. The old man's face was deeply lined and gray, his eyes ringed with dark circles. Their voices were low, but she heard the words *ennead* and *ammuit*, or something similar; they kept gesturing over a book they passed back and forth, arguing over its contents. Then Cain took out a strange, square object from his sack, pointing to its carved, wooden surfaces as if they held some great mystery. It looked like just another box, and she turned to Lund, who was sitting up, the smile on his face so wide she could not help smiling herself.

"This is yours," he said shyly, bringing something out from behind his back. It was a tiny bow made from a sapling and antelope sinew, with half a dozen arrows whittled to points blackened by the fire and topped with blue feathers at the other end.

Leah took the bow from him and held it as she might cradle a baby in her arms. Ever since she had seen him shoot his arrow through the tree trunk, she had been fascinated by his bow, the way the arrows whistled, cutting through the air, the low twang the string made as it was released. But she'd been unable to budge the tough wood when she tried to draw back the string and had finally given up in frustration after she'd almost toppled over just holding the huge weapon.

This bow was just her size. "Can we try it?" she asked. "Please?"

Lund nodded at Uncle Deckard. "Ask him first."

Lund took her out into the clearing and taught her how to stand with her feet firmly planted on the ground, how to notch an arrow to the string and sight down the shaft, squinting, then draw straight back toward her eye with one elbow bent, the other locked. Her first few arrows wobbled terribly and flew into the woods or into the ground; but on her eighth try, the arrow flew straight, missing the target Lund had painted on the tree by mere inches. Lund clapped and jumped up and down like a small boy, then ran and collected the fallen arrows for her to try again.

By lunchtime, Leah had hit the target three times. The muscles in her arms ached, her fingers had grown raw and sore, and her hands trembled, but she did not want to stop. There was strength in the bow, a way for her to take control of her fear, even master it. With a weapon like that, she was no longer powerless against the darkness.

She imagined the huge, dark shape of the crow before her, its beady eye the target. Lund showed her how to let her breath out in a long, slow hiss and hold it while she released, keeping everything else still. This time, her arrow hit near the center of the circle, and Lund finally convinced her to quit for the day.

The camp was busy, the smell of cooking thick in the air. Uncle Deckard had more men around him, and he was talking loudly and gesturing while the others watched intently, nodding or shaking their heads. They pointed to passages in books, looked at maps and objects from Uncle's sack, drew designs in the dirt. There seemed to be two different groups arguing with each other. The fat, short man with no hair (his name was Cullen, she believed) was saying something about an army of ghouls—feeders, he called them. The way he gestured, his face growing red as his voice grew louder, made her shiver. Lund took her hand and led her away.

Before dinner, they all took turns bathing in the stream that ran below camp, the frigid water making Leah gasp and raising goose bumps on her skin. She used a bar of goat's fat and flower oil that Lund gave her. It felt good to scrub away the dust and grime that had accumulated on the road, and she dipped her head under the water briefly, her breath catching in her chest, and emerged feeling reborn and new again.

At night they all ate around the fire again, and there seemed to be even more men this time, all of them focused on Uncle Deckard as he told stories about the Horadrim and their great battles from many years ago. Leah listened to the descriptions of Jered Cain and Tal Rasha, two warrior mages who battled monsters like the crow and skinless beasts from her dreams, and worse; she grew sleepy as Cain talked about the town called Tristram and what had happened there, then described his search for someone he called the Dark Wanderer and the battle at Mount Arreat with a monster called Baal.

The men listened intently. Some of the stories should have been scary even to them, but they seemed enraptured by Uncle Deckard's skill at telling. For some reason, Leah wasn't afraid anymore either. Uncle's voice soothed her, and Lund's presence made her feel as if nothing bad could possibly happen here. The fire in Caldeum, the strange village, and what had happened in Kurast all seemed so far away.

She fell asleep leaning on Lund's shoulder, more content and safe than she could remember feeling in weeks.

"There has to be more," Cain said. "The key is Al Cut. The tomb of Al Cut—what does it mean? He was mentioned in a book of prophecies I found in the Borderlands, in reference to an army of the dead. And the name was written at the bottom of the drawings of a boy haunted by feeders just a short distance away in Kurast. How are these things connected?"

The day had dawned gray and cold, the sun hidden behind a thick layer of dark clouds, and as the hours had passed, Cain's newfound enthusiasm and energy had begun to wane. Ratham was only two days away, and time was running out. The order had listened raptly to his stories around the fire the night before, and he had felt a connection growing with them; but there was so much left to learn, and so much to teach, that he felt overwhelmed and lost.

At least there had been some attempt to recreate the Horadrim in a similar way to their founding, centuries before: the fledgling scholars had dedicated a person to each of the main mage groups, just as the original Horadrim had consisted of mages from each school of magic, and these so-called leaders had taught others within their ranks in the ways of the Ennead, Ammuit, Taan, and Vizjerei. But their teaching had been erratic and often completely wrong, and Cain had found himself spending as much time correcting misconceptions about transmutation, illusion, and prophecy as he did finding out anything useful.

They had already been over everything they had in their possession, but it wasn't much. Egil had explained that before the group had escaped the town, Rau had already begun to gather hundreds of creatures around him, some of them the drained husks of the citizens of Gea Kul and surrounding areas, others much darker and more threatening. He had become a mage of considerable skill and training by then, summoning things from the netherworld that none of the other mages had ever seen or heard of before. Some of these creatures, the things they had called feeders, had spread out across the land, draining strength from the populace in a way that the rest of the order had not fully understood.

"Has anyone heard of this man, Al Cut? Either living or, more likely, long dead? Someone important from history—a mage, perhaps?"

The men who had gathered around him (Egil, Cullen, Mikulov, and another one called Thomas) remained silent. They were looking for some clue that would help them plan their attack on the Dark One's stronghold.

Cain dug into his rucksack and took out the book of Horadric prophecies that he had found in the Vizjerei ruins, the one that appeared to have been written by Tal Rasha himself. "The passage is here," he said. He read it aloud: *And the High Heavens shall rain down upon Sanctuary as a false leader arises from the ashes . . . the tomb of Al Cut will be revealed, and the dead shall lay waste to mankind . . .*"

"May I see it?" Egil asked. When he looked it over in his hands, recognition dawned in his eyes. "Is it possible?" he said softly. "It can't be . . . these ruins in the Borderlands. Was there a library below a collapsed temple, and a foul demon that guarded its contents?"

"How did you know that?"

"We were there, several months ago," Egil said excitedly, his voice rising. "In those ruins. We were chased out by a foul demon that possessed one of our order. Garreth pushed it back long enough for us to escape, but we were forced to leave some of our possessions behind. A pack with our food, and this text, as well as a book of ancient Vizjerei spells we had found there. Demonic magic."

Cain held up the book of Horadric prophecies. "*You* brought this text with you to the very same ruins where I found it?"

Egil nodded. "Garreth said we would need it on our journey, and we never questioned him about things like that. He was always right. But this time . . ." He shrugged. "The demon was not the only threat. There were sand wasps and dune threshers. We barely escaped with our lives."

A chill ran down Cain's spine. He and Akarat had followed Rau's First Ones into the Vizjerei ruins; it was their footprints he had seen in the dust, and their belongings he had found behind the temple. It seemed almost too much of a coincidence to be possible.

Cain skimmed through the text again, most of it already familiar to him. It was full of very old writings that seemed to predict Cain's own path to these caves, as well as the fall of Kurast and Gea Kul to the darkness. It was almost as if it had been written recently, rather than hundreds of years ago.

A passage near the end, just before the mention of Al Cut, told of thousands of lost souls buried deep beneath Gea Kul, a killing field from the depths of Sanctuary's history that held something terribly dangerous and important. But the book ended there abruptly, as if the scribe who had written it had run out of pages.

"I need to see the companion texts to this one," Cain said.

Egil put up his hands in a gesture of helplessness. "I do not have them," he said. "If there are more, they must still be inside our Horadric library in Gea Kul. I had returned there to try to find more answers, before I found you."

The idea of returning to that place, and having to face creatures like the unburied once again, filled Cain with dismay. He could not possibly fight something like that; he was a man of words, not weapons. Yet what choice did they have? There were no more answers to be found in this camp, and if they remained here, Cain was certain it would only be a matter of time before the Dark One and his army would come for them.

"We must go back to Gea Kul, to your meeting rooms," he said. "We need those books."

"There are other artifacts there, too," Egil said. "Or at least there were. Things we had found on our journeys—"

Cullen shook his head, jowls wobbling. "It's too dangerous," he said. "Garreth has spies everywhere. He'll find us!"

Cain held up a hand. "We cannot cower in fear anymore. Look at how you're living in these caves, like animals, while the man who used to lead you is slowly destroying this world, and you are doing nothing to stop him." He stared at Egil, Cullen, and Thomas, challenging them with his gaze. "Our enemy will find us soon enough if we do not act. You call yourselves Horadrim. It's time to embrace your destiny and prove yourselves worthy of such a name."

There was silence among the group. The three men avoided his look, staring at the ground.

"I will go with you," Mikulov said. "And fight to the death, if need be."

"I will go too," Egil said, looking up, a new glint in his eyes. "We will not let you down."

Thomas nodded. Finally Cullen did the same. "Good," Cain said. "We take our first step tomorrow, at dawn. We have two days. May the archangels be with us all."

# TWEN+Y-EIGH+

## The Possession

As the gray light of dawn bled from the sky, the small group reached Gea Kul and the entrance to the tunnels that led under the town.

Leah had remained at the camp with the others, with Lund as her protector. It was too dangerous for her to come along, and she seemed to feel at ease with the gentle giant. It pleased Cain to see them hand in hand, like two absurdly mismatched but happy playmates, and he knew that Lund would do anything to keep her safe.

On the way Cain had told them more stories about his traveling party's search for the Dark Wanderer after the fall of Tristram and the assault on Mount Arreat by Baal. He had ended with the story of Tyrael's heroic journey into the mountain to destroy the Worldstone, where he had sacrificed himself for the good of Sanctuary. Cain had meant to inspire the order with his tales, but in the end he had inspired himself as well. As he had spoken, growing more animated and dramatic as he went along, Cain had thought of his mother, the gleam in her eye as she told the children about the ancient mages and their battle with the Prime Evils. He had thought it to be madness, but now he realized that it was the passion of the righteous. To these men, they were simply stories, as inspiring as they might be, but Cain had been there on Mount Arreat, running for his life, had seen the things he had described with his own eyes. He knew what the darkness could bring.

Cain stood for a moment, looking at the row of shacks sitting silently before them. There were people inside some of them, hidden away from prying eyes, mere shadows of the men and woman they had been before. He shook his head, clenching his fists. Rage built within him like a cresting wave. Garreth Rau was bleeding the life out of the people of Sanctuary, and it had to be stopped.

A pop and blaze of light caught his attention. Egil had opened the grate and taken the same torch he had left behind just days before, lighting it with one of his bags of exploding powder.

They entered the tunnels together. Egil led them through the dank, dripping stone corridors, torchlight flickering across the walls and picking up some kind of luminosity in the moss, setting off an eerie glow. It was this same moss that, mixed with the minerals from the hills outside the First Ones' camp, caused the explosion of Egil's bags of powder. The air was frigid; Cain could see his own breath as he hustled to keep up with the others, pushing his poor old knees to the breaking point.

Several different turns and branches led to others, but Egil seemed to know exactly where he was going. Eventually they arrived at the steps leading to the secret door. They listened; all was silent beyond, and Egil pushed the hidden lever that slid back the door with a loud rumble.

The hallway was empty, the room beyond black as pitch. The door to the library had been damaged by the unburied, chunks of rock strewn across the floor. A bug the size of a small mouse skittered through, insect legs ticking against the stone, causing them all to jump. Nothing else moved.

"Give the torch to me," Mikulov said. He took the burning brand and strode forward, stepping over the rubble with Cain close behind. The old man's breath caught in his throat. In spite of the danger, he was enthralled by the prospect of the books he had caught a glimpse of on his last visit; he couldn't wait to get his hands on them. He felt sure the secret of Al Cut could be found somewhere among their brittle pages.

The library did not disappoint him. It was even more impressive than he remembered. The thrashing about of the unburied had taken several shelves down and strewn their contents about the room, but most were intact. Torchlight revealed shelf after shelf of rare texts, many of them in nearly perfect condition. The air held a faint hint of rot, but there was no sign of the creature, and the rooms beyond were dark and silent. Cullen and Thomas righted the table and began to gather the books on the floor, stacking them carefully. Egil stood in the doorway, motionless, an odd look on his face as he surveyed the damage.

Cain let his fingers drift over the spines of the nearest texts, taking some of them down to peruse more closely, losing himself in the familiar, heady scent of old paper; here were original documents from the church of Zakarum, next to texts on the history of the Horadric order, the Vizjerei, and the priests of Rathma. His heart beat faster. Some of them he had seen before; others he had not. An Ammuit treatise on illusion and the bending of planes of reality sat next to a reproduction of a Taan book on divination. There were ancient writings from spellcasters and witches; formulas for healing potions; curses, powders, and spells; and tomes on shape-shifting and elemental magic by the druids of the northern forests. Other texts were written about the umbaru witch doctors from the jungles of Torajan, outlining concoctions of tree root and herbs of which Cain was only vaguely familiar.

On a lower shelf, he found a folded piece of parchment. Bringing it closer to the light, Cain found it to be a map of the tunnels under Gea Kul. He saw the very rooms where they were standing, sitting above the spokes of a wheel-like design that stretched beyond the entire town to the sea. There were other notations that he could not make sense of at first; they looked like buildings of some kind, buried beneath the earth. The map was detailed and carefully drawn, and he tucked it into his rucksack for safekeeping.

Cain returned to the shelves and paused, astonished, staring at a volume as he drifted back through decades of memories. Could it be? He took the book down with trembling hands, blowing dust from its cover.

A history of Westmarch and the Sons of Rakkis, a copy of the same text his mother had burned in front of him when he was just a boy.

*This one is not part of your destiny . . . Your proper texts are with Jered's belongings, when you choose to read them.*

Cain was alarmed to find himself close to tears. *An old man like me shouldn't cry for what's past,* he thought. *There's not enough time left in these bones for that.*

"Rau was a scholar at heart," Thomas said, breaking the hypnotic spell that had seemed to fall over Cain as he lost himself in the library's contents. "He was always focused on the pursuit of knowledge, driving us to collect whatever we could find. He studied these texts and learned from them."

The range of knowledge was remarkable. The First Ones must have spent years collecting them, and even then, the breadth of the collection almost defied belief. Yet Rau had left it all behind. And that led to an important question: what other, more disturbing texts did he have in his possession now?

Cain could not help but see the parallel between himself and Garreth Rau. But what had caused Rau to veer off the path of righteousness? Cain had regretted the years he had lost before he had found his true calling, convinced that he could never make up for them. But perhaps they had done something important in giving him the wisdom of time and the perspective to keep from making the same mistakes and being tempted by the seductive power of evil.

*You must come to belief in your own way, in your own time.*

Mikulov had found a lantern on the wall; he lit it with the torch, handing the flame to Egil to hold. The room grew brighter, the yellow flame illuminating the rows of books. The men had brought large sacks with them, and Cain began to direct Thomas and Cullen on which books to gather up and take with them.

It was Thomas who found it. On the floor, near where the table had been overturned, he discovered the companion text to the one in Cain's rucksack.

The bindings were identical: hand-sewn leather, with the Horadric symbol branded into the cover, with the mark of Tal Rasha inside. Cain had Mikulov bring the lantern closer and opened the brittle book as carefully as he could, scanning its contents. The writing was dense, as if its author had tried to cram as much as possible onto each page. Rather than a continuation of the prophecies from the first text, much of this one was a recounting of the Mage Clan Wars and the founding of the Horadrim by Tyrael, and Cain's excitement slowly turned sour as he flipped through it.

In the second half of the book, the pages were blank.

He sighed and rubbed his eyes. The range of texts from the library could take him months to read, and there was no guarantee he would find any answers, even then.

*No.* He studied the blank pages more closely. It did not make sense that they would be empty. Words were hidden here: he was sure of it.

Cain removed the book of demon-summoning magic from his rucksack, searching for the reveal spell he had used before to locate these very chambers. He felt the dark power flow through

283

him once again as he spoke. The lantern flame guttered and then flared up, and something unseen seemed to enter the room; he heard the others gasp with fright, but he did not look up, his eyes bound to the blank page as words began to appear there, as if freshly written.

The text described an ancient battle from the Mage Clan Wars many centuries before, fought over a forgotten city. The brothers Bartuc and Horazon, leaders of the Vizjerei sorcerers, gathered thousands of followers each; light and dark clashed, and the streets ran with blood, their vast powers nearly splitting the land in two before Bartuc prevailed in this particular battle and slaughtered what remained of Horazon's followers. The two brothers escaped the killing fields, leaving the dead sorcerers to rot where they had fallen.

A short time later, Bartuc returned to the city under the cover of darkness and used his demonic powers to cover up what he had done and sink the city deep beneath the ground, burying it forever and erasing it from history with a powerful spell. But the dead sorcerers from the battle remained, entombed in the ruins of ancient buildings and tunnels that connected them.

A drawing scratched into the text's pages, this one more crudely done, filled Cain's heart with fear.

The lost city's name was Al Cut. And its location was chillingly familiar.

Gea Kul had been built directly on top of it.

The notations from the other map came back to him; they marked the spots where Al Cut's buildings lay, entombed forever beneath the sands of time.

"Al Cut," Cain breathed softly. The revelation was like a thunderbolt. "It's not a man; it's a city."

"Where's Egil?"

The urgency in the voice broke the spell that had fallen over Cain. He looked up to find Thomas looking frantically around the room and Cullen still packing books into his sack with a frenzy that made him seem almost mad with fear. Something had terrified the two men. The lantern no longer gave their surroundings a warm yellow glow; the gloom crept out from the corners, seeming to eat the light, and the cold had returned like the touch of icy, dead fingertips.

Cain remembered the odd look on Egil's face as he had stood in the entrance to the library. He glanced at Mikulov, who shook his head, then nodded in the direction of the only other way out of the library—the archway from which the unburied had appeared several days before. The torch Egil had been holding was tucked neatly into a bracket on the wall.

Wherever he had gone, he had been without a light to guide him.

"What's back there?" Cain asked.

"A meeting room," Thomas said. "And a . . . place for rituals. There's an entrance to a lower chamber, but we never used it."

The men's sacks were heavy with books. "Take these back to the camp," Cain said. "Mikulov and I will go look for him."

Thomas began to protest, but Cain raised a hand. "Go," he said. "He may have gone that way, and you can catch him. Take the lantern, and protect those texts. We'll follow you in a moment."

Thomas shouted Egil's name, but there was no response. The two men hoisted the sacks, took the lantern.

Thomas put his hand on Cain's shoulder. "Hurry," he said. "There is something evil here. I can feel it." Then they headed back to the passageway. Mikulov grabbed the torch from the wall and stepped through the entrance to the next room. Cain followed him inside.

The torchlight revealed a smaller chamber with a large, wooden table and chairs at its center. The walls were bare, and the air smelled more strongly of mold and rot. It was empty. Mikulov swept the torch down toward the dusty floor, revealing footprints leading to another archway beyond.

A frigid draft washed over them, followed by a faint, echoing moan. Mikulov looked at Cain and slipped out his blade. They moved cautiously to the next archway. Inside was an empty room with a round ceiling and a circle at the center. *A portal.* Cain could only guess where it might lead. There was a red jewel in its center, and he knelt there and pried it free, slipping it into his sack for safekeeping.

Another noise, this one like a shuffling of feet, drew their attention to an open door. Mikulov tensed, muscles going rigid as he held up the torch for a better view.

Egil stood in the doorway. He had his head down, his colorless hair nearly glowing in the torchlight, hands held at his sides. His breathing was slow and even, white clouds rising in the cold air.

Cain called his name, but the man did not move or answer. Mikulov took several steps forward, keeping the torch out like a weapon. He held his blade down, away from sight.

The two men stopped halfway across the room. "Something is wrong," Mikulov said quietly. "I don't think—"

Egil looked up, his face making Mikulov abruptly cut off whatever he was about to say. Egil's pale skin had gone gray and lifeless, blue veins running underneath like map lines. His eyes caught the fire and reflected it, like an animal's in the dark.

He was grinning at them.

Cain took an involuntary half step back. The look on Egil's face . . . it wasn't Egil, in there. This was someone else.

*"It's about time you arrived,"* the thing rasped. *"A bit too slow, I'm afraid, and still blissfully unaware. Then again, you were always the last one to see the truth, weren't you, Deckard Cain?"*

"Who are you?"

*"You know who I am."* The creature slid forward, as if floating inches off the floor, and stopped ten feet away. *"After all, you came here looking for me."*

Cain tried to calm his racing heart. *Garreth Rau.* If he had indeed been able to possess Egil's body, his skills were considerable indeed.

*"There are others here too."* The thing turned its gaze on Mikulov. *"Do you really think that what you are about to do will make any difference?"*

Cain tried to stop him, but it was too late. Mikulov moved blindingly fast, but Rau barely seemed to glance at him as green light erupted from his hands and a brilliant flash painted the room. Cain cried out and put his arm up to protect his face, and he was thrown backward to the floor, landing hard and hearing the loud crack of something breaking. He lay for a moment, stunned. When he looked up again, the torch was out, but a strange glow remained, Egil's slight frame bathed in it as if his own flesh was on fire.

Mikulov was on the floor against the wall, motionless. He didn't appear to be breathing.

Cain crawled to the fallen monk's side, cradling his head in his arms. Mikulov's eyelids fluttered, and he moaned softly.

*"Deckard?"*

The voice was different now, lighter, touched with fear. Familiar. Cain looked back, and Egil's face had changed, the jawline softening, cheekbones more pronounced, eyes large and dark as pitch.

*"It's cold here, Deckard. I can't get out of this place. Please."*

Cain's own blood turned to ice. *It can't be.* The pain came rushing back like a freezing river, chilling him to the bone.

"Amelia," he said. The words were ripped out of him like a hand twisting his insides. "No."

His dead wife, gone thirty-five years now, vanished from his life like a phantom. He had buried the truth for decades, pushed it down so deep it had nearly disappeared. The pain was too much for him to bear. But there was more, so much more, and to even begin to think of the rest of it meant madness.

"*We thought it was safe. We needed someplace to go. My mother, she begged us to come. I . . . you weren't there, Deckard. I tried to reach you, but you were lost with your books; you weren't there . . . You were never there.*"

"You aren't real—"

"*They took us, Deckard. They hurt us. Please don't let them hurt us anymore. Don't let them hurt your son.*"

Egil's face rippled, changed again, flesh melting like wax forced to the flames, a screaming, blood-soaked mask of pain that re-formed itself, becoming smaller and rounder, softer yet, plump cheeks and smooth brow. The face was someone else's now, someone who had haunted Cain's dreams for decades, a young boy who had learned to run before he could walk, who had never slowed down enough to listen to a word his parents said, a wild, trembling ball of pure energy and a true force of nature.

"*Daddy!*" The boy was crying hysterically. "*I don't like the monsters, Daddy! Please come get me!*"

With a strangled cry, Cain launched himself at the possessed figure, the walls he had erected around these memories during so many long years suddenly crashing down all at once, and the flood of pain and suffering pouring out like rushing water over a broken dam.

"*A letter for you, sir.*"

*Deckard Cain looked up bleary-eyed from the table where he had fallen asleep. The empty bottle and glass, still crusted with wine, stood in silent witness to his despair. He glanced at the door, where Pepin stood framed by sunlight. "It was open," Pepin said. "I thought I'd deliver this. Thought it might be important."*

*The healer stepped forward too quickly, setting the envelope down on the table and rushing back to the doorway, as if Cain might have* a contagious disease. It was uncharacteristic behavior. But he could not be blamed. Cain had shut everyone out, even his family, so absorbed in his scholarly pursuits, he had left no time for anything else.

And so his wife had left him, taking his young son. He was thirty-five years old and alone. He had no friends left in Tristram.

"Get out," he said.

"I—"

"Out!"

Pepin stepped back across the threshold and closed the door, leaving him in silence.

His head ached from drink. "Amelia," he whispered. He wasn't quite sure why. They had fought bitterly several nights before, the same argument they had had for years now: he was always locked away among his books, she said, always more attentive to them than to his students, his wife and son, or anyone else, for that matter. Why had they named the boy after his famous ancestor when family apparently meant so little to him, she had asked? Where had he been when his little Jered had spoken his first word, taken his first steps? Where had he been when the boy had nearly died from fever? Where was he when she needed him?

He had retreated from her tears and her pleadings, going to his library and locking his door, leaving his son standing in the hall, looking after him with his tiny hands clenched into fists. When he had come out again, she and Jered were gone.

What had he done?

Deckard Cain's hands trembled as he reached for the envelope. It was stamped with the royal seal of Khanduras, marking it as an official missive from the local lord's men. He tore it open, removing the thin parchment from within and scanning the contents with growing horror.

Dear Schoolmaster Cain: We regret to inform you . . .

As he reached the thing that had taken Egil, it closed its fingers around Cain's throat, holding him like a small toy, their faces inches apart.

The thing's features had changed again. This time, what was revealed was not man, woman, or child, but something inhuman. Raw flesh stretched shiny-slick across knobs of bone surrounded a gaping maw full of sharpened, bloody teeth.

*"They cry for you,"* Belial spat at him, his breath like rotting flesh. *"You never could look at their bodies, could you, Deckard? See what we did to them on that empty road? Yet their physical pain was nothing—only the beginning. We took their souls and made them slaves, and they have been suffering under the watch of my loyal servants ever since. You ignored them for so long for your precious books, you hardly noticed what they meant to you until they were gone. And now you have brought us another one to play with, just in time. We thank you for doing our bidding, even if you weren't aware of it."*

Deckard Cain saw a flash of an empty, overturned wagon upon the road to Caldeum, the splash of blood across the spokes of the wheel. Red-stained shapes under rough blankets that men had draped over them. "You . . . lie . . ."

The demon roared, throwing its head back and howling at the ceiling, its laughter shaking the foundations of the building like an earthquake. *"Everything is a lie, old man. All that you see, all that you believe. Your family was a lie, your sad little life of solitary study, your loneliness and anger. Even your pathetic little quest to find us. You think all that you've done, the things you have found along the way, the signs that brought you here—all that was your doing?"*

Cain's legs gave way, and he sagged against the creature's arms as its fingers tightened around his throat. Everything seemed to click into place: Akarat's discovery of the texts that had led them to the ruins, and the Horadric prophecies he had found there that had been left by the First Ones seemingly by accident, texts that had eventually led him to Caldeum, Kurast, and finally to Gea Kul. So many coincidences, so many close escapes.

*"Even now, you do our bidding, old man. This shell we inhabit will die in a moment, yet you will be too late to stop what is happening."* The thing grinned at him. *"The little girl. You left her alone, didn't you? Left another one alone again. You thought she was safe. You poor fool. Check the book. You—ahhhhh."*

The creature sighed, eyes suddenly growing dim and fixed, face re-forming, features bubbling back to their original shape as its hands went slack and Cain dropped, gasping, to the floor. Egil slumped, already dead, falling toward Cain and wetting his face with blood.

He looked up as Mikulov slid his punch dagger back out from the base of Egil's skull. Mikulov stepped back, breathing hard, his eyes wild, as the green light that had bathed the room began to fade into darkness. Cain pushed Egil's body off him, scrambling backward as the blood soaked through his tunic, wetting his skin. He fumbled in his rucksack, pulling out a bag of Egil's powder and throwing it against the wall. The pop and flare filled the room with light once again, and Mikulov retrieved the torch and lit it.

Cain found his staff in one corner, snapped in two. The cracking sound he had heard when he had fallen earlier came back to him, and as he gathered the pieces, a deeper fear spread through his limbs and urged him on. His fingers touched the piece of parchment paper in the hidden pocket of his tunic, the edges old and crumbling, its message seared once again across his memory: *We regret to inform you . . .*

"Wait!" Mikulov cried, but Cain ran as fast as his trembling, nearly useless legs would carry him, careening through the shadows with the torchlight following behind and Mikulov continuing to call out. Egil was dead, poor Egil, another young man who had trusted Deckard and had paid the bitter price for it, as had Akarat, the young paladin who had been filled with such confidence. Used like all the rest.

*I will not let you down,* Akarat had said, back at the Vizjerei ruins. Egil had said much the same thing before they had come here. And they had not let him down, but Cain had been unable to protect them in return, as he had promised himself he would. And now he feared the worst for someone else under his care and protection. Someone he had promised to keep safe.

*The demon lies.*

Yes, of course it did. But lies were often wrapped in truth.

Deckard Cain reached the library, Mikulov close behind with the torch. The room was silent and empty and shrouded in shadows, the remains of their search strewn in piles on the floor. The book of Horadric prophecies was still open on the table. *Check the book,* the demon had said. Cain flipped through it with trembling fingers, all the hidden text still legible as Mikulov stepped to his side and the flickering torchlight brightened its pages.

"What is it—?"

Cain let out a small cry, stepping away from the table and the book. But it was too late. He had already seen what had been scrawled across the last two pages, written in blood, still fresh and wet.

The words were seared into his brain:

*The girl is mine.*

# TWENTY-NINE

## *The Warning*

Long before they reached the caves, they could smell the smoke.

Cain and Mikulov had caught up with Thomas and Cullen before the two men left the tunnels. They had been slowed down by their heavy burden of books, while Cain and Mikulov had been propelled ever faster by their fear of what they would find when they returned to camp. The two men sagged as Mikulov explained briefly what had happened to Egil, Thomas leaning on Cullen for support. Thomas and Egil had been close friends, Cullen explained, as Mikulov assumed Thomas's sack of books for him. It was a tough blow to take.

But it was nothing compared to what they found when they reached the clearing.

Black smoke billowed from the cave's entrance. The bodies of men and other creatures still lay scattered across the ground, many of them with arrows buried to the fletching in their necks and chests.

What drew their eyes was the huge wooden cross that had been erected in front of the cave, and the thing that hung there.

Lund's chin rested on his chest. The huge man was naked, his hands and feet lashed to the wood, rope digging cruelly into flesh the color of white marble. But Lund was beyond any pain now.

He had been split from throat to groin, his innards spilling out and hanging down to the dusty, blood-soaked ground.

The crows had been at work on him. One still remained, perched upon the right crossbar above Lund's fingers, a gigantic black bird with glossy feathers and curved talons. It pecked at his fleshy thumb, pulling loose a string of meat, and cocked its head at them, peering, as if deciding whether they were a threat. Then it opened its beak and cawed, the sound echoing across the hillside like the scream of the damned before it flapped its wings and rose, still screeching, up and over the tops of the dead trees and out of sight.

Thomas fell to his knees in the dirt, a high wail bursting from deep within him. Cullen closed his eyes and looked away, then was violently sick. Cain's apprehension turned to a full-blown, galloping panic as he shouted Leah's name over and over and received silence in return.

Cain held the sleeve of his tunic against his face as the smoke washed over him, along with another smell that made his stomach churn: burning flesh. The heat from the fire inside the cave nearly beat him back, but he pressed on, shouting Leah's name again and hearing nothing in return but the crackle of the flames.

He got close enough to the fire to see the remains of charred bodies, clawed hands reaching upward as if searching for salvation, before his eyes threatened to boil in his skull and the hairs on the back of his hands started to curl and burn. There was no hope of finding her in here; he had to turn back. But the smoke was thick and swirling all around him, filling his lungs, and he lost his bearings, stumbling in the searing heat until someone grabbed him with strong hands and pulled him back out into the cooler air as he gasped and coughed and spat into the dirt, tears streaming down his face.

*The girl is mine.* The words had kept running through his head as he'd hobbled into the cave's entrance. Garreth Rau had Leah. He felt it in his heart, like a black hole that threatened to swallow him up. He remembered a night not so long ago when James had pulled him and Leah out of the burning house in Caldeum. This time it was Mikulov who held him up.

"She's not in there," Mikulov said. "Listen to me. They saw her being taken away. She's alive, Deckard. She's *alive.*"

Slowly, Cain came back to his senses. He looked up to find a small group of men gathered around him; along with Mikulov, Thomas, and Cullen, there were perhaps a dozen more, most of whom he recognized from the camp, many of them with injuries of some kind. He saw a man with a lacerated cheek, as if he had been clawed, and another with a maimed arm. All had the haunted, beaten look of abused dogs, their eyes darting here and there in anticipation of another attack.

Cain set his trembling legs back under him and wiped his face clean, bringing himself back under control with tremendous effort. His eyes still smarted from the smoke, and his lungs were burning. But now was not the time to panic; if Leah had any chance at all, it would be because he remained calm and rational. Every single moment, every move he made, was crucial.

"We tried to fight, but there were so many of them," Farris said. They were still gathered in the clearing, and Cain was asking those who remained to tell him exactly what had happened. The youngest and strongest of those who were left, Farris also seemed to be the only one who could speak of the massacre that had occurred without breaking down. "They came with no warning. There were townspeople from Gea Kul carrying knives and pitchforks, and other . . . unspeakable creatures. We saw goat-things and fallen ones, and some kind of monstrous walking dead. Some of us were able to escape into the woods during the madness. I watched from the hill as they surrounded Lund and the little girl. He fought them back with his bow, killing many." Farris nodded toward the smoke pouring from the cave. "They began burning those who had fallen inside. Some of those bodies in there are not ours but were killed by Lund's arrows."

A few of the remaining men muttered their agreement, all of them avoiding looking up at the body of Lund that still hung over them, a stark symbol of their failure.

*They made an example of him,* Cain thought. *A warning to us, should we choose to fight back.*

"Tell me what happened to Leah," he said.

"They killed Lund in front of her. The crows . . . they attacked him, and they were so fast, and there were so many. He could not hit them with his arrows. When he was finally overcome, the townspeople tried to take her, too." Farris shook his head, his eyes haunted by the memory. "But she fought back. I don't know how she did it, but she used powerful magic and killed several. It was like an invisible hand was battering them. I saw one who was picked up and crushed against the rocks like a doll. Then they used some kind of dart and drugged her. They dragged her off with them."

"Was she hurt? Tell me!"

"I . . . I don't know," Farris said. He looked around the small group, his bloody face growing flushed with anger. "But this should serve as a lesson to all of us! Many of us wanted to end this long ago, but we were convinced to wait, that help was on the way. Look at what that help has done for us!"

Farris pointed up at Lund's broken body, then back at Cain. "You are no savior," he said. "No true Horadrim would have allowed this. That way of life is long gone, and many have lost their lives pursuing it. Sanctuary has changed, and not for the better! It's time for us to stop playing at fantasies, stop pretending to be something we are not. We would all be well served to accept the truth, run far from here, and live out what time we have left before they come for us again."

The other men nodded. Mikulov started to speak, but Cain held up a hand to stop him. "You are all good men," he said. "I thank you for your bravery here today. I am no Horadrim, and never was. I'm only an old scholar. Perhaps Farris is right: perhaps you should all get as far away as you can. I'm sorry."

Blinded by fresh tears, Cain stumbled, nearly falling to his knees without his staff before catching himself and continuing on, away from the group. It was no use carrying on like this anymore. They had been outsmarted at every turn; what was worse, it appeared quite possible that his entire search for his Horadric brothers had been orchestrated by Rau and Belial. He was like a puppet, and they had been pulling the strings.

He pulled the parchment from his hidden pocket and unfolded it carefully, his fingers shaking. He had spent more than thirty years banishing everything that had happened from his memory, erecting such strong walls around the disappearance of his wife and son, it was as if they had never existed at all. But it was all crashing back down upon him, every moment, every emotion, his overwhelming guilt, his rage, his sorrow, and he was not strong enough to stop it anymore.

*Dear Schoolmaster Cain:*

*We regret to inform you that a wagon was found abandoned and heavily damaged yesterday on the road to the east, one that we have confirmed was carrying your wife, Amelia, and four-year-old son, Jered. Their bodies have been discovered at the scene, along with that of the wagon's driver. From their conditions, foul play is suspected.*

*We will be sending representatives to gather more information from you shortly. Please be assured that we will not rest until we have uncovered the truth about this unfortunate incident.*

*My sincerest condolences,*
*Thomas Abbey, Captain, Royal Guard*

Cain folded the parchment with the upmost care and returned it safely to his pocket. The lord's men had suspected bandits, but they had never discovered who had done it. Justice had not been served, not for all these years.

Sometime later, he was not sure how long, Mikulov was at his side. "You cannot mean what you say," he said in a low voice. "All you have fought for, all we have been through—"

"Is for nothing," Cain said bitterly. "There are no Horadrim left in Sanctuary. I am not even Horadrim, just a crude shadow of what I might have been. If I had listened to those who loved me, if I had embraced my destiny, I could have stopped this. I could have been strong enough. But I am not.

"We must face the truth." He stopped, and grabbed Mikulov's arm, holding on like a drowning man. "We are alone, and Ratham is upon us."

# THIR+Y

## *Blood Ritual*

The tower was trembling.

The man formerly known as Garreth Rau placed his blue-veined palms upon the moist stone of the interior chamber wall and closed his eyes. It had been built for him in less than seven days by inhuman hands, under his very specific instructions, for a purpose only he fully understood. The tower was perfectly straight, each seam of rock flawlessly smooth and strong, its circular interior exact in its measurements, down to the width of a human hair.

It was made to channel the lifespark of the living directly into the arms of the dead. Its shape would harness the demonic magic he called into existence, magic that existed deep within the ether and had been banned in Sanctuary for generations.

The Dark One smiled. The stone hummed under his fingertips, slight enough to be barely noticeable. But he felt it. He was in tune with the vibrations, acutely aware of their power. The tower was a conduit, a focal point of sorts, built upon the well of power he had spent so many months preparing, and upon the graves of thousands of dead mages, buried where they had fallen among the cursed streets of Al Cut.

"You are playing a dangerous game."

The Dark One turned from the cold stone to face the man who had spoken. The man stood with his hands clasped behind him, still dressed in the same clothing the villager had worn. Physically, this was the same man who had hung above the blood ritual just two nights before, but his spirit was vastly different. The body was only a vessel.

Anuk Maahnor, Bartuc's captain and one of the thousands who had fallen in the great battle of Al Cut, had returned to serve him.

"Your abilities are strong," Maahnor said. "Calling me to this bodily shell took skills I have seen in only one other man: Bartuc himself. But demonic magic is wild and powerful. You may control it, and eventually realize it is controlling you. And you will require far more than that to call the rest of our army back to life."

"Feel this," the Dark One said. "Touch the pregnant belly that will give life to your brothers."

Maahnor walked over to the stone and put his own possessed hands upon it, closing his eyes. A moment later, a slight smile creased his lips, and he breathed in deeply. "It is good," he said. "But still not enough."

The Dark One nodded. "I have more," he said. "A nearly endless supply."

Only in the course of the battle at the camp in the hills had the reason behind Belial's orders become clear to him: the girl's pure power was breathtaking—even, the Dark One was loath to admit, stronger than his own. She had tossed about his demon horde like kindling, and only the dart filled with Torajan root had taken her down. If his archer hadn't acted so quickly, he didn't know what might have happened. Perhaps she would have cracked the world in two. It did not matter; the important thing was that her abilities would provide the ignition for the vast well of energy he had gathered with the help of his feeders. Once ignited, this lifespark would raise his undead army.

"Commune with the spirits of your men, Maahnor. Get them ready. Come tomorrow, they will regain the strength to rise and walk, and you shall lead them into battle once again."

"I will speak to them," Maahnor said. "But they serve me, not you. Should they choose to go to battle, they will fight at *my* side, for me."

Rage erupted inside the Dark One, making the blue veins pulse in his forehead. "Your return to the living plane has given you a false sense of your own talents, Maahnor. You are bound to me by the blood ritual—a thread that connects us through the centuries. You are duty bound to obey."

"Perhaps," the man said, walking around the bulbous face of the containment chamber, "or perhaps I shall take control right now, and awaken them myself."

"Not even the Lord of Lies himself could break such a contract."

Maahnor smiled. "You have much to learn, my poor little friend."

The Dark One felt the familiar twinges of inadequacy and fought against them. That was the old Garreth Rau, a helpless child who had let others take advantage of him. Those days were gone.

He had to teach this insolent man a lesson.

The Dark One raised his arms, summoning the element of fire. Blue arcs like lightning flew from his fingers, striking Maahnor in the chest. But the man did not cry out or fall back, as the Dark One had expected; instead he smiled again and raised his own hands, cupping the blue fire and holding it away from him.

Shame and fear rushed through the Dark One. He was the strongest mage in Sanctuary. Belial had told him so, and he had demonstrated his talents many times. This could not happen.

Maahnor took a step toward him. The Dark One faltered slightly, falling to one knee. But just as he thought all was lost, a fresh wave of power flowed through him. He regained his feet and struck back with a mighty blast of fire, sending Maahnor flying across the room, where he crumpled in a heap.

The Dark One stood over the man, who looked up at him in shock. "Do not defy me again," he said, "or your new life will be far shorter than you think."

The Dark One climbed the long steps to the ritual room at the top of the tower, flush with the success of battle. But a small part of what remained of Garreth Rau felt discomfort. He did not understand what had happened in the containment chamber. Why hadn't he been able to wield such power at first? How much of this talent did he control?

It did not matter, he thought. *Garreth Rau is no more.* There was only the Dark One, lord of Sanctuary. There was no room for indecision and failure.

Outside the stone walls, he could hear the crows.

There were countless numbers of the birds now, blanketing every surface. Some were his servants; others had simply flocked here on their own, perhaps feeling these very same vibrations from miles away. Called home to join the battle, they swooped and darted through the slate-gray skies above the heads of other things cavorting in the surf: his children, born of darkness, blood, and fire.

The old man had done exactly what he had been supposed to do. *The fool.* Everything the Dark One had put in motion had worked flawlessly. His spies had followed Cain and the girl for the remainder of their journey, keeping out of sight unless they had been required to provide a little push. The remaining First Ones had played their roles, willingly or not.

Possessing the body and soul of Egil had been particularly sweet, even when he had been forced to yield it to the Lord of Lies himself.

Yet the plan had not truly been the Dark One's own, he had to admit. He was a conduit of sorts, too. Belial had been the one to whisper in the Dark One's ear about the girl's importance. He had been the one to suggest this deceit: all the clues he had placed in Cain's path had been Belial's work—the appearance of the demon in the ruins, the books the First Ones had left there for Cain to find, the man in Caldeum he had possessed for long enough to point the old man to Kurast.

He took his hands from the stone and turned away, walking across the empty floor to where his captive lay alone and motionless. *No.* He might be serving his lord for now, but soon enough he would rule this world and order the deaths of thousands of guilty men, women, and children. He was in control. Sanctuary would be his prize, in return for opening the gates of Hell. Belial had promised it to him.

From below, in more hidden rooms populated by devices too unspeakable for humans to fathom, he heard the distant screams of those he had imprisoned and tortured. Their pain helped feed the insatiable need of the tower for energy, just as his feeders drained the people of their lifespark and brought it here, where it gathered like a building electrical storm.

But Maahnor was right: it was not enough.

He stared down at the girl, still heavily drugged. All this had been necessary because of her. She was the key to awakening his slumbering army. Yet her power was so dangerous, he could not have brought her here had he been acting alone. She had been protected by something he only faintly understood.

The Dark One slid the familiar blade from the sleeve of his robe. It had tasted his blood and found it satisfactory, and it would taste the blood of many others before the final deed was done. The girl would provide the spark that he required. He could sense it, feel the pulse of energy from her even as she slept.

It was time to test her.

The Dark One shivered with anticipation. He brought a small corked vial from the pocket of his robe and knelt next to her in the shadows. Removing the stopper, he waved the bottle under her nose, then sat back and waited. A moment later, she began to stir. He smiled. She stretched against her bonds, but the chains that bound her held strong. Judging by what had happened at the camp, he had little faith that such a thing would contain her once she was fully awake. But in her current state, with the drugs still thick in her veins, she would have little energy left for a fight.

As she moaned softly and her eyelids fluttered, he quickly bent forward again, slipped his blade up against the ball of her right thumb, and let it bite down, holding the vial under her skin to catch the blood as it dripped.

He never would have expected what happened next. Leah opened her eyes, her gaze fixing vacantly on his face. The Dark One immediately felt the temperature in the room turn to ice, and at the same time he felt a sudden heat on his skin, like the sun beating down on him.

Something invisible yet immensely powerful exploded out of her. He felt as if an unseen hand punched him in the chest, lifted him into the air, and threw him against the wall. He tumbled to the floor in a heap as pain radiated throughout his body. Fear flooded his limbs, and he scrambled to his feet, fumbling in his robes for what remained of the drug he had used to keep her still.

As he moved toward her once again, he felt his master stir.

*The girl is strong.* Belial's voice thundered in his head. His hunger for her was like a ravenous beast's. The Dark One felt the demon's need rush through him, propelling him back toward her like a slavering madman before he stopped himself with every last ounce of strength he had left. Her eyes had rolled back into her head, and her mouth was working soundlessly.

He sensed her power waiting for him, and he also sensed that if he tried to feed upon her as he fed upon the others, she would destroy him.

The thought filled him with fresh terror. Quickly he knelt and pierced the skin of her arm with the needle, then stepped back again as she began to rise up from the floor, her mouth opening as if to scream, before she sank back into silence and sleep.

The Dark One tried to calm his thudding heart. How had she reacted to him with such brute strength? The drug was barely containing her now. There had been two incidents in which his strength had been put to the test, with worrisome results.

He had to prepare the more elaborate ritual to tap into her power and focus it properly. A new blood ritual. He held up the small vial with a few drops of her precious life's essence. He had to prepare further. The ancient Vizjerei magic, Bartuc's legacy written in blood, would hold the key.

The Dark One felt Belial slowly contain his raging hunger. Even the true ruler of the Burning Hells understood what had to happen. The Dark One smiled. Once again, he felt in control. When he'd been just a boy in Kurast, he had been ordered around, ridiculed, and beaten mercilessly. After all, what was a simple servant boy compared to the great sorcerers of Sanctuary?

They had not known the truth: that he held the blood of legends in his veins, and that his destiny had been foretold centuries before.

The Dark One went to the window and looked out at the creatures below, more than three hundred of them now, and more coming. He felt them return his gaze, their calls of excitement rising up to him. He held out his arms and screamed into the frigid air, and the creatures responded in kind, their cries growing to a frenzy of mindless lust. He watched as several of them turned upon one of their own and tore it limb from limb, bathing in the demon's blood. The cries rose up to him through the mist, echoing off the surface of the water and causing the crows to lift into the air in a deafening symphony of flapping wings. The wind washed over his face, and he closed his eyes.

The old man was on his way, along with the monk: he could feel it. He welcomed the challenge. This was what he had been waiting for, a clash of epic proportions, and revenge for his ancestor, who had sacrificed himself for the greater good and been condemned to entombment for all eternity with a demon. Jered Cain had been responsible for that, and his offspring would pay the price. Belial had already baited Deckard with the thought that his wife and young son had been tortured and killed by demons, their life's essence dragged off into the Hells to suffer for all eternity; did it matter that this was a lie, that this could not have been possible? *No.* It did not matter how they died; the truth was irrelevant. The important thing, as Belial had taught him, was how you used the information and, in this case, Deckard Cain's pain and suffering.

*Let them come.* His plans were almost complete. They were entering the month of Ratham, he held the lifespark of thousands within the tower, and the girl was here. The old man had no army; even if he made it this far, his life would end quickly. The Dark One almost felt disappointed at the thought. Deckard Cain still had a role to play in this game, even if it was short-lived.

When he opened his eyes, the creatures below were battering themselves against the base of the tower, trying to get in. Their ranks seemed to grow even as he watched. But this was nothing compared to the legions of faithful servants he was about to call back to life. Together they would spread out across the land, claiming Sanctuary for the coming of their lord, and to hell with anyone who stood in their way.

The Dark One turned from the window to begin his final preparations for the end of this world and the birth of his new kingdom.

# THIR+Y-⊕NE

## *A Plan Emerges*

Cain stood under the trees on the edge of the clearing, leaning heavily on a crude piece of wood he had found for a walking stick. Every bone, every muscle in his old body ached terribly. He was falling apart like an old wagon, the sides cracking, wheels coming loose from their axles.

*I am no warrior.* The old man barely managed to sigh at the thought. He had never pretended to be one. Wasn't his journey across the wilds of Sanctuary something for much younger, stronger men to do? How had he ever thought that he had a chance to defeat this terrible evil, with or without assistance?

The truth was, he had never thought such a thing. His hopes had been built around the promise of finding a surviving brotherhood of Horadrim, men stronger and more resourceful than he was, who would take up the battle for him.

Instead, he had found this.

Mikulov had gone to pray to the gods for answers, and Cain was alone. Across the clearing, the remaining members of the First Ones were gathering the few personal items that remained. The fire inside the cave had finally died down enough for them to enter, but most of what had been inside was so badly burned or damaged by smoke, it was useless. The men had piled the meager supply of weapons to one side, but Cain had a feeling they wouldn't be needed; Garreth Rau had crushed the group beyond repair, and against his strength the remaining members of the order were like flies battering themselves against a lantern. Those who were left would be gone soon, returning to the shattered remains of their homes or simply disappearing into the hills, slinking away in the night like beaten animals from the slaughter.

When he thought of Leah, his panic returned with a vengeance—a galloping, savage terror that threatened to overwhelm him. He remembered her anger and fear when they had first left Caldeum, the night at the bridge when he had told her about her real mother; how she had run from him, into the hills; their escape from Lord Brand and the things beneath the graves; how she clung to him as they entered Kurast. Her distrust had slowly changed to something else as they went along. And he, in turn, had learned something from her: he was capable of caring about another human being far more than he cared about himself.

He hadn't felt this way since the loss of his wife and child, so many years ago. Yet it had come far too late for his salvation.

*She called me Uncle.*

Cain wiped fresh tears from his eyes. He realized with a start that his objective had changed. He was no longer driven to save Sanctuary from the invasion he knew was coming; his purpose had become much more personal. There were thousands of ravenous creatures between him and the girl. There was no hope of reaching her. But he would go anyway, and he would die trying.

He watched as Farris argued over a blackened cook pot with Thomas, the two men growing red-faced and heated. This could not be where it all ended. He remembered the stories of the Horadrim his mother had told when he was a boy, and how he had questioned the truth of them, while a part of him had remained a believer in the nobility, the ethics and bravery of the order. Even then, he had *wanted* to believe in the legends. He had spent the last decade of his life dedicated to the order, immersing himself in the lore, trying to make up for lost time. He was an old man, but he was not helpless.

Something stubborn set itself inside of him, making him shake his head. *It cannot end here,* he thought again. He was not strong enough alone, but the men who remained could still fight. Who was to say they couldn't rise to the occasion? They had fancied themselves Horadrim once. Why not now?

Wasn't that his true talent, finding the strength within others?

Cain hobbled across the clearing. Someone had cut down Lund's body, but the cross remained intact, the bloody rope still wound around the bar. He stopped underneath it, waiting. Eventually, the conversation died down, as the men began to notice him. He stood patiently.

It was Thomas who spoke first.

"Are you leaving us now?"

It could have sounded petulant and angry, but it did not. Cain pointed up at the cross. "An intimidation tactic," he said. "As old as time itself. A show of strength, meant to break your will. But we cannot be broken. We are part of an ancient order formed to defeat the dark forces that plague us."

"We are no Horadrim," Farris said bitterly. "It's better that we just leave. You said so yourself."

"You may not be, in the way the mages of old would have described them. But have you studied the ancient texts of the schools of magic? Do you know the legends, understand the teachings of the order?"

Cain looked around the small group. "Have some of you performed magic in the spells you have found, even small magic?" Several of them nodded, while others looked away. "So have I. But this alone does not make you Horadrim."

He hobbled over to Cullen and put his hand on the man's shoulder. He had taken off his glasses, and his face had become softer, more expressive. He looked like a boy. "You are gentle," Cain said, "yet you hide it deep inside yourself. Let your mercy and kindness come through." He turned to Thomas, who kept his gaze cast toward the ground, and waited until the man looked up at him. "You, Thomas," he said. "You've lost someone close to you, and your friendships run deep. You are loyal to the end, and your loss enrages you. This is a strength, not a weakness. Use it to your advantage."

Cain looked at Farris. "You are a skeptic," he said, "always questioning the truth of things. But deep inside, you have a burning desire to believe. I was once like you, Farris. Instead of embracing who I was, I hid from it until it was almost too late for me. You must let your faith come through and trust in others, and in what you know to be true. The ability to become more than who we are lies within all of us, but we must seek it out and strive to be better than we ever thought we could be."

Others in the small group were nodding now, glancing around at each other. Cain recognized two of them as former members of Egil's inner circle, but one man had formerly been aligned with Farris.

"But what hope do we have?" one of them said, a man named Jordan who had cuts to his face from the attack. "We are a dozen men, and some of us are wounded. There arc hundreds, maybe thousands of those demons out there. And our former master is a powerful mage. What can we possibly do against such a force?"

"You have me."

The voice came seemingly out of nowhere. Cain turned to find Mikulov standing behind the group, at the foot of where the ground rose up to meet the cliffs. The monk had his muscled arms folded across his chest, and he stared at the small group with a fire and energy that seemed to lift him up and make him appear larger than before.

Mikulov's eyes flashed. He was only one man, but he looked able to take on an entire army. He reached out his hand, and Cain clasped it.

"You have found your gods once again," Cain said. "They have given you strength."

Mikulov nodded. "With them on our side, we will not fail."

Cain hesitated. The voice of his long-dead wife and son, channeled through Egil, came back to him, and he felt as if his heart might break. He knew that it was far too late for them. But Leah had become a physical representation of all he had lost. She was still alive; he could feel it in his bones. He could not lose her, too. It seemed as if his entire life had come down to this single moment in time: all that he had been, and all that he had wanted to be, coming together to point him in a direction he was destined to go.

"The Dark One will have a force like nothing we have seen before," he said, looking at the men around him. "I have learned enough from the texts to suspect an army of the risen dead, entombed beneath Gea Kul, in the remains of what was once a city called Al Cut. There will be other foes as well, human and demonic. But we are not helpless. Whether you are Horadrim does not matter; whether we are willing to face our fears, and refuse to let them win, is what matters now. We must use our wits and our own particular strengths to fight through hell and pierce the enemy's heart."

Cain described the plan taking shape even now within him, a way to use the tunnels of Gea Kul and turn the small size of their group into an advantage. He could only hope that the others would not see how thin the plan was, how fragile. He noticed more of them nodding as he went on, warming to what he was saying. There was hope yet, and he meant to use every bit of it.

Finally Cain knelt in the dust, slinging his rucksack down before him, feeling the men's eyes upon him. What they needed now was a symbol, something that would inspire them to embrace their fear and use it. He withdrew the pieces of his shattered staff that he had collected after the encounter with the possessed Egil in the Horadric chambers, laying them out in the dirt. His aches and pains had faded to a distant throbbing now, as his pulse began to speed up. He took out the jewel he had pried from the portal, then removed the Horadric cube and slid the items into it, one at a time, the pieces of the staff disappearing with a low thrumming of energy into a space that should have been far too small to contain them.

But the space inside the artifact was infinitely larger than it appeared. The inner workings of the cube were a mystery long lost to time. It could transmute certain objects into others far more valuable, combining magical traits in a way that led to a more powerful whole. This staff, and the portal jewel, would be transformed.

He had not used one in a long time. But he felt the familiar thrill as the cube did its work.

There was a buzzing crackle and what felt like a surge in the air, as the hair on Cain's arms raised up. Then he reached in and removed the new object. It was taller than the old staff, the wood whole and strong. Intricate designs had been carved like flames along the wood's surface. Blue fire licked over the shaft, then faded. Cain could feel the energy held within it.

Cain got to his feet, waving off Mikulov's offer to help. He set the bottom of the staff in the dirt, leaned upon it, and stared out at the men, who looked back in astonishment. The staff was his talisman, a source of power that would lead them all like a beacon through the blackest night. But they would need far more than that to prevail.

"True Horadrim," Thomas whispered. He had dropped to his

knees in the dirt, his eyes sparkling with tears. "You are the one from the prophecies, just as Egil said."

Cain went to him, and put his hand on Thomas's shoulder. "Get up," he said. "I am no hero. *You* are. I am nobody to kneel in front of, certainly, and I am old, but you are not. Be strong. We are not alone in this fight, and we have a few tricks left."

The others followed him as he climbed the slope. It took him a long time, with his old bones protesting again and his muscles cramping as he went. But he would not hold onto Mikulov or anyone else. This was something he needed to do on his own.

While they went, he asked the First Ones to describe exactly what had happened when Leah had been hit by the dart. The plan was progressing in his mind into something stronger. Finally he reached the top, and the skeletal trees ended on the edge of the cliff. Deckard Cain hobbled to the edge and looked out over the valley, through the mist toward the sea. He could just make out Gea Kul gathered there, the hunched back of a sea serpent with the Black Tower rising up like the head of the beast.

They needed more allies. He had no real reason to trust Jeronnan other than blind faith. But something told him the old sea captain would come through.

The others remained behind him as he removed the horn and raised it to his lips.

The sound rose up like a low moan of a mortally wounded beast and grew into a wail of the damned. It echoed over the tops of the dead trees, amplified through the mist, reaching out across the valley. Cain slammed his staff down on the rock, and a crackle of energy and power rippled outward with a flash of light. A moment later the distant screams of others came from somewhere beyond the trees, as if in answer. Friend or foe, he could not tell.

Cain turned to the others as the sounds echoed and died away. "I need you to find a type of root that grows near here," he said. "And bring me your shovels and pickaxes. We have some more digging to do." He took out the folded parchment that contained the map of the tunnels under Gea Kul.

"This is our way in. And then we go to war. But not in the way you think."

# THIR+Y-TW⊕

## *The Tunnels*

As he had promised, the old sea captain came searching for the source of the horn's blast. Cain met Jeronnan on the edge of the jungle and explained what he needed to do. The only way for them to have a chance of victory was through trickery and deceit, and Jeronnan would provide a distraction. The captain eagerly agreed, ready to fight for his beloved town.

They studied the map of tunnels that led directly underneath the Black Tower. Cain took careful notes of strategic locations to place his charges, while the others dug for the root he needed and the right minerals to fill his sacks. The plan fell into shape. A spell of concealment would hide them long enough to get underground and away from prying eyes. From there, while Jeronnan led a march on the tower aboveground with the few remaining citizens who were not under the sway of the feeders, their party would slip in secret beneath the streets and infiltrate it from below.

If Cain was right, they had until the sun rose before Ratham would begin.

Thomas knew the upper tunnels even better than Egil had, and he wasted little time getting them to the right entrance. He led the small group under the cover of darkness through knee-high dead grasses to a separate sewer grate away from the town's main gate, well hidden by a mound of refuse and mud. They pulled the grate aside, entered the narrow hole, and climbed down an iron ladder to the stone floor, where Thomas lit his lantern, bathing the passage with yellow light.

The tunnels were dark and empty, dripping with moisture. They smelled like moldy graves. Cain prayed they would not become his tomb.

The remaining First Ones had pitchforks, swords and bows, kitchen knives and hammers. It was a sad army of perhaps twenty-five people, several of them wounded. Mikulov was at the lead with Thomas and the lantern, while Cain brought up the rear with Cullen. Farris remained aloof, but he had agreed to come, and his small, loyal group had joined him. Cain was not quite sure whether he could be trusted. But there was little choice now.

They shuffled forward until the last of the glow from the entrance had faded away. Then they paused, huddled close together, as if trying to remain bathed in the light. The lantern's glow penetrated the darkness only a few feet.

The sound of scratching came from somewhere down in the tunnel. Thomas held the lantern up. They saw nothing at first, and then, just beyond the circle where the light penetrated, something moved. A ghostly moan drifted up to them, followed by a thud and a bone-shivering crash.

"Cover the light!" someone hissed, and Thomas threw his cloak over the lantern, plunging the tunnel into darkness. Another thud shook the walls, dirt and small pebbles trickling down to the floor.

The thuds came again, closer this time. "Footsteps," whispered Cullen in the dark, his voice full of fear.

A foul stench overwhelmed them. Thomas uncovered the lantern again and held it up.

An unburied stood about thirty feet away, its massive girth nearly filling the tunnel. The smell of rotting flesh washed over them once again as the thing fixed multiple sets of filmy eyes on them and roared, charging down the tunnel as if it meant to crush them under its bulk.

The men erupted in panic. Thomas turned to run, and the lantern nearly went out in the ensuing bedlam. Mikulov darted forward, and suddenly there was a flash of bright light, and the unburied roared again as the sound of fists striking flesh followed another bone-shaking crash. Cain shouted at the men to wait, holding out his arms in the tunnel as they came toward him.

Thomas stopped, his face as white as parchment, before he set himself and turned back.

The creature slumped sideways against the tunnel wall. One gigantic limb had been torn from its body, and oozing gashes gaped like new mouths in its torso. Mikulov's movements were a blur as he attacked again, slicing at the thing's meaty neck with his blade. The unburied roared in pain or anger and tried to turn, lashing out with the spikes of its good arm, but it was slow and clumsy in the confined space, and the blow crashed into the stone wall as Mikulov moved lightly on his feet, dancing out of range before darting in again and pummeling the soft flesh with his fists and blade.

The monk cried out as he struck, and a wave of power exploded from his palm, causing the creature to fall back as its many fanged mouths opened and closed, hissing and dripping dark fluids.

With a small cry of his own, Cullen ran forward, raising his pitchfork and thrusting it straight into the monster's side. Another man released an arrow from his bow, which sank deep into the unburied's back.

As it lumbered around again to face the rest of them, Mikulov swung his blade, slicing deep through the monster's neck with one mighty blow.

Foul dark fluid spouted from the wound. The creature's head tilted to one side, exposing a stump of rotten, writhing meat. Its swollen, putrid body trembled, Cullen's pitchfork quivering like a tuning fork.

Mikulov stepped forward with his palm thrust out and struck once again with blinding speed, unleashing a wave of pure energy directed straight into the unburied's chest.

The creature exploded.

Bits of dead flesh flew in all directions, covering the closest men with gore. Chunks of rock rebounded off the tunnel walls and rolled to a stop at Cain's feet. Part of an arm came to rest next to the rock, twitched once, and was still.

The lantern flame guttered with the blast but did not go out. Thomas held it up again, revealing a scene of such carnage it was almost impossible to believe. Pieces of flesh still wriggled like the legs of a dead insect. One of the disembodied heads opened its fanged mouth, white-filmed eyes rolling blindly in a suppurating skull, before Farris crushed it under his boot with a sickening, wet crunch.

The tunnel was silent for a long moment. "We . . . killed it," Thomas said wonderingly.

"Can you kill something that's already dead?" Cullen said, grinning like a madman and wiping gore from his glasses.

They all looked at each other. Several of the men shouted and clapped one another on the back. But Cain could not share in their celebration. They had little time to waste. He imagined Leah chained in a dark room, with Garreth Rau preparing the demonic ritual that might cost Leah her life.

After he had received the letter about his wife and son, Cain had gone to visit the place where the accident had happened. The stretch of road on the way to Caldeum was unremarkable— a place where the road narrowed with thick trees on either side, providing cover for whoever had surprised them, perhaps. But a road like any other. He had never actually seen the overturned wagon; that had been long gone by the time he arrived. But he had imagined it lying there on its side in the weeds, one wheel still spinning lazily in the hot sun while Amelia and Jered were dragged away into oblivion. He hadn't been able to help feeling as if the entire world had changed in that moment, and from then on the sound of a wagon's wheels on cobblestones had always left him cold and empty.

Thomas led them on, through one tunnel and down another branch until he reached a point where he said none of the First Ones had ever been. He consulted the map, finding his way deeper, into more unfamiliar spaces and toward the center of the vast and complex tunnel system.

The air grew colder as they descended. Thick green moss grew everywhere, and at one point they had to wade through knee-deep brackish water that felt like ice on Cain's skin. Shortly after, they heard the soft patter of tiny feet. Dozens of rats rushed toward them in a panic, running under the men's legs.

There was something else up ahead. Something moving in the dark. The lantern revealed a familiar ghostlike creature, low to the ground and moving on all fours. The creature's face was contorted into a snarl, its bald head shiny in the lantern light, eyeless sockets glaring blindly out at nothing. It hissed at them.

"A feeder," Cain breathed softly. "We must kill it, quickly now, or it will tell others, and we will be overrun with them."

The men drew back in shock as the feeder turned and climbed up the wall, its claw-like hands gripping the stone, then turned to them once again, hanging upside down like a bat, before crawling away and disappearing into the darkness.

Mikulov took the lantern. "Wait here," he said, and raced off down the tunnel. The rest of the men were plunged into darkness so thick and absolute, they couldn't see their own hands in front of their faces. Cain cautioned them to be quiet and still, and spoke the words of power until the jewel in the head of his transformed staff began to glow, and light bathed the faces of the men around him, as if they had been touched by flame.

A crackling flash came from somewhere in the distance, along with an inhuman screech of pain. Cain led the party forward. They found the lantern on the floor, and Mikulov standing over the mangled bodies of three feeders. "There were others," he said. "They got away."

Cain's blood ran cold. They were surely scouts for Rau, and any left alive would scurry back to him and report their position, if they didn't simply lie in wait and ambush the First Ones at some upcoming bend in the tunnel.

"We must be careful," he said. Thomas regained the lantern, and Cain took up the rear. He expected to encounter a horde of ghouls around every corner, but the tunnels were empty. He did not know whether to be relieved or concerned.

They went deeper still. He felt something as they got closer to the center of the wheel of tunnels—an almost undetectable thrumming from the ground beneath their feet.

Then, far beneath the surface, the ceilings of the tunnels finally opened up to a cavernous space so vast it defied the imagination. They stood upon the edge of a silent, black hole, the light from Thomas's lantern swallowed up by the shadows, the dust of generations thick upon every surface and the smell of closed tombs in the air.

They had found it, at last: the lost city of Al Cut.

# THIRTY-THREE

## Al Cut

Thomas led them through an empty, shattered street. Al Cut had been impressive once, a showplace of ancient Sanctuary. The streets were wide and paved, the buildings mostly made of stone and brick. They stared in wonder at the structures lined up and silent as graves: long-abandoned homes of the people who had lived here centuries before. The damage caused by the mage battle was still apparent, as scorched rubble lay across scattered and broken walkways, and many houses leaned drunkenly, their foundations weakened by whatever magical forces had struck them.

The scope of the lost city was staggering. The strangeness of discovering it down here, so far belowground, made it almost impossible to process; the ghosts of its past inhabitants seemed to float at the edges of Cain's vision, disappearing when he turned to look.

"I have seen this place," Mikulov said. "I have been here in my dreams. It is a city of the dead, burdened with the weight of thousands of lost souls."

Nobody else dared to speak. The sense of some unnatural power gathering under their feet had increased, and the need to hurry along with it. The dust lay everywhere, but more chilling were the footprints that led through it. Some of them appeared human, but many others did not.

"Dawn is coming," Cain said. "We must not waste any more time." He sensed movement from an alcove on the right, but when he turned to look, the space was empty save for a huge spider on a web. The creature, the size of his fist, sat defiantly, staring back at them with multifaceted eyes, hairy legs twitching.

They continued through the street, skirting a place where a wall had collapsed, wandering through more deserted buildings. They remained silent, as if to speak here would disturb the dead. The size of the space swallowed the lantern beams; the city went on and on, the cavern's ceiling stretching so far above their heads it disappeared like a starless sky. They passed several crumbling Vizjerei libraries and a monument to some ancient, long-forgotten leader or war hero.

It seemed to go on forever. But where were the bodies? The legend had told of the remains of Vizjerei mage warriors left to rot where they fell. Had they simply been carried away by scavengers, or was something more sinister at work?

Finally the ground began to rise gently, and the small party passed through the far edges of Al Cut. Cain saw the ceiling of the cavern come back into view, arching downward to meet the far wall, where a new tunnel loomed, its entrance as black as pitch.

Water sluiced down the center of the floor, through a groove in the stones, and out from the tunnel's entrance. Cain could smell the brine.

This was the spot he had been waiting to find.

They entered the tunnel. "We're close," Thomas whispered, as they moved along. "By my calculations, we should be beyond Gea Kul now." The mood among the men had grown tense;

Cain's plan had worked flawlessly so far, but once they had broken cover, they would no longer have the luxury of surprise.

Cain consulted the map before directing the others to place the packages they had carried with them into strategic locations along the tunnel. The group made slow progress, continuing forward. The sea was just beyond them, separated by a layer of rock. If he could only—

*Deckard Cain.*

Cain whirled around, searching the dark, his skin prickling. The voice had sounded close by his ear, yet he saw nothing dancing through the shadows, no demon face, no ghostly apparition. The other men acted as if they had heard nothing.

A familiar moment from the distant past returned to him: standing in his room as a boy after a fight with his mother, the smell of burned pages still thick in his nostrils, staring out at the dark as something whispered his name.

*Come find us, and learn the truth about this world. Your destiny awaits, as does mine. We are linked, you and I, through history and legend. We are more alike than you care to believe. I am a scholar, as you are. I am descended from those you would call heroes. But they were blind, as you have been. You can change that.*

Cain gritted his teeth. He dared not respond. The others would surely panic, if they knew they had been discovered. The Dark One was powerful indeed, to find Cain down here, but there was a chance he did not know their true location and was only sending out his thoughts into the void, hoping to engage his enemy.

Still, Cain could not help wondering. Were they truly alike? Were their paths intertwined, forever bound, and did he have a choice in all of this? He had to believe that he did. Humans were born of angels and demons, and the battleground between Heaven and Hell lay within their own souls. The desire to act with selflessness, charity, and love was in a constant battle with greed, anger, and jealousy. Sanctuary existed within mankind itself, and as such, humans held a special power that could be harnessed for either great good or great evil.

*Your sea captain is dead. The little girl is dead. The gates have already been opened. There is no use resisting any longer.*

*Join me in welcoming our true master to Sanctuary.*

Cain's heart raced. It could not be true. He would not believe it. He must not listen to the lies—

"We are here," Thomas whispered. "If I am right, we are under the tower itself, or close to it."

Cain came back to himself with a jerk. The men were standing at the foot of another ladder, its rusty rungs moist and covered with slime. Far above them, faint gray light trickled down, along with a steady rain.

He realized he had broken out in a cold sweat, and his breaths were coming fast and shallow. *The demon lies. You must not listen.* If Leah were dead, he would feel it; he had to believe that. Rau was toying with him, trying to bring him out where he could be slaughtered.

Yet another voice nagged at him, a darker voice. In spite of his better judgment, he had used the book of demonic magic. He had opened the door to his own soul, just as Garreth Rau had done.

Had he let something terrible in?

They were close now. The Dark One could feel them. Deckard Cain was coming, along with his pathetic little army of castoffs and misfits, those First Ones he had not seen fit to use himself.

All except for one. The easiest to possess.

The Dark One watched through another's eyes as the men began to climb the ladder, rising up out of the depths of the tunnels one by one. Climbing right into his web. The iron rungs were slick and corroded from the ocean air. *Carefully now,* he thought. *Don't slip. We wouldn't want an accident to happen, not when you're so close.*

It was sad, really, that Deckard Cain had come so far, through deserts and mountains, over so many miles, only to be lured into a trap like any other useless human. For the mortals of Sanctuary were indeed useless; they were cruel, vicious, a plague upon the world, and the coming of the Burning Hells would wash all of them away like a cleansing fire, leaving mindless husks in their wake.

The Dark One would rule over what was left, as he had been born to do.

Rau opened the ancient book, his fingers trembling. It was time.

As he began the ritual, he could feel Belial waiting like a trembling, multi-limbed god, ready to burst forth in all his glory. The Dark One sensed a power so immense it was like looking into the sun. The demon's thought tendrils were already weaving themselves around his mind, becoming one with his own, caressing him, cradling him with promises of the riches that awaited his chosen ones, after the coming storm.

The Dark One could feel the pulse of his demon horde outside. They had made short work of the sea captain and his pathetic group of allies; there had been perhaps thirty of them fighting through the streets with makeshift weapons, the last remaining citizens of Gea Kul who had resisted the feeders' hypnotic pull before. But they were easy prey for the huge flock that had gathered in service to their dark lord. The captain had been the last to fall, a man who might once have made a forbidding adversary, but who was now old and frail. The Dark One had watched through others' eyes as the old man had disappeared under a wave of feeders, his last image a hand thrust up through the writhing, bloody shapes, clutching at the air as if waiting for a salvation that would never arrive.

War had come to Sanctuary, but the battle was one-sided. This was only a small taste of what was destined to happen. Soon the final spark would be lit; then, the true army would rise. *A legion of undead sorcerers, commanded by me.* There were cities to conquer, entire territories to overcome. The possibilities made the Dark One shiver with anticipation.

Belial's mental tentacles squeezed his mind, bringing him sharply back to himself. The Dark One returned to the book he had been reading. He took a bag of powder from his robe and drew a symbol around the girl, who was still drugged and lying motionless in the center of the room. Even in the depths of her stupor, he could feel her breathtaking, raw power—her mother's gift, passed down and magnified. She would be sacrificed for the end of the world, her essence the final spark to light the fuse below his feet. What better way to serve your lord and master?

The Dark One muttered the spell he had practiced so many times, his voice low and rhythmic. The activity of the creatures gathered outside grew more frenzied. He had to time this perfectly; as the energy began to build around him and he felt a wind come up within the smooth walls, he felt he had finally reached the pinnacle of his craft. The feeders screeched their love for him, swooping and darting around the tower. He was commanding the armies of the Burning Hells, bending them to his will, just as Bartuc had so many years before.

The floor had been designed with grooves to catch the girl's lifespark and channel it; it would rush down through the center of the Black Tower and soak into the waiting space below, joining the energy of countless others.

The Dark One bent to his work.

# THIR+Y-F⊕UR

## *The Courtyard*

The men climbed the slippery rungs of the ladder, one at a time. Mikulov looked at the feet of the one in front of him, Farris, who had insisted on going first. The monk's heart, normally slow and calm even in the midst of battle, had sped up, and a cold sweat had broken out across his skin. The moment he had trained for his entire life was coming, and he was afraid that when he came face to face with the void, he would hesitate, just long enough for it to matter.

*You are not ready.* The voices of his masters returned to him, as if in a dream, their accusation sharp and judgmental. They sat in their chamber upon the council seats in ceremonial robes, their long, white beards and smooth heads nearly identical. *You must remain here for more training, until you overcome your pride and impulsiveness. If you do not, you will make a terrible mistake.*

Yet Mikulov had left, vanishing like a thief in the night, while the others slept. Now his day of reckoning was here, and he was as frightened as a small boy.

*Perhaps my masters were right, after all. Perhaps I have been a fool.*

Mikulov had meditated back at the First Ones' camp and had found the gods once again. He had regained the strength and confidence that had propelled him through this long journey. Yet, as the sounds of a demonic army grew louder just above them, that strength seemed to bleed away once again, leaving him alone.

Farris had reached the top. Water dripped steadily down upon them all, wetting their clothes. The light that bled through the grate was a sickly gray. "I can't move it," Farris whispered down, after heaving at the iron with his shoulder. "It's too heavy—"

Something yanked the grate up and away, nearly causing Farris to fall backward. A monstrous clawed hand reached down from above and grabbed him around the neck, pulling him through the opening and out of sight.

One of the First Ones shouted a warning from below. Mikulov looked down and saw hideous creatures at the foot of the ladder, forcing their way up just below the rest of the traveling party.

*A trap.* He scrambled up the last rungs, his fear suddenly forgotten in the rush of energy that washed over him, and thrust himself out, going into a roll and regaining his feet in a smooth, powerful burst, his weapon up and ready.

He had emerged onto a huge, stone courtyard. A cold, stinking rain pattered down from leaden skies.

The courtyard was seething with creatures from the depths of Hell itself.

A group of skinless, muscled beasts approached from the left, slinking on all fours, their doglike, snarling faces dripping acidic fluid. Mikulov spotted several female demons with their swords extended, sensual curves carelessly exposed between blue-veined patches of flesh. There were huge beetle monsters and a swarm of airborne insects with six-inch stingers, and beyond their ranks, hundreds or perhaps thousands of the feeders, advancing upon all fours with their moonlike faces turned skyward.

Farris had been pulled out of the tunnel by a red-skinned overseer, a leader of the dog-beasts—the horned, heavily muscled fallen ones, their eyes glowing with demon fire. The overseer threw its head back and howled at the sky, beating its bloated chest with clawed fingers, and snapping a long barbed whip over the backs of its minions. Mikulov expected to see Farris ripped limb from limb, but the creatures parted as he walked forward, smiling.

"Welcome to hell," Farris said, spreading his arms wide. Behind him, the demon horde screeched with excitement, the sound nearly deafening.

Thomas had cleared the hole and was standing next to it, blinking into the gray light, a stunned look on his face. "You?" he said. "No. Not you, Farris."

The man was grinning. His pupils were dilated and fixed, his face slightly flushed. "He is under the control of another," Mikulov said quietly. "Possessed, like Egil in the meeting room."

Farris turned his hypnotic gaze on Mikulov. "You thought I was going to just sit by and wait to die, with all of you? It was my choice to join the Dark One."

"The Dark One?" Thomas said. "Garreth Rau?"

Farris nodded. "It was their choice, as well." He pointed to the hole, as three others climbed out. Farris's crew. They quickly took up positions around the tunnel opening as Cullen, then several more First Ones, and finally Cain emerged, laboring more slowly from the climb. Farris's men were surrounding him, closing in. Cullen looked around in confusion, but Cain seemed to realize immediately what had happened.

*Betrayal.* Mikulov hesitated only a moment, and in that single flash, everything that he had done in his short life, everything he had learned on this journey came together in a moment of singular clarity. His impossible choice to leave the monastery had been the right one. The gods spoke to him all at once as lightning split the sky and thunder crashed; the sea whispered and wind blew, relaying their message of faith and strength.

The thousand and one gods had guided him with a steady hand. His sacrifice was for the greater good, and he would make it willingly, knowing that at the last moment he would once again become one with all things.

*You are not ready . . . until you overcome your pride and impulsiveness. If you do not, you will make a terrible mistake.*

Mikulov glanced at Cain. The old man's eyes widened, and he shook his head, reaching out a hand and starting to speak, but Mikulov was already gone.

Deckard Cain watched helplessly as the monk gave him a slight smile and a nod, then turned to the demonic army looming all around them. He knew what Mikulov meant to do, glimpsed it in the determined set of his face, and felt it in his bones.

They were surrounded, outplayed and outmatched once again. Farris had given them away. *I should have seen this,* Cain thought. *I should have stopped it when I had the chance.* His love and his fear for Leah had blinded him to the truth.

Mikulov screamed, a low, guttural sound of triumph as he launched himself headlong into the snarling mass of demonic flesh. The monk's fists and feet lashed out with breathtaking speed, his blade flashing as he slashed and hacked at the enemy, drawing them away from Cain and the First Ones. The demons responded en masse, their bloodlust raised to deafening levels as they attacked, but Mikulov held his own, whirling in a blur of energy as a wave of blue light crackled out like ripples in a pond and felled dozens more, pushing the rest back.

He was opening a path that led toward the Black Tower, in the process almost certainly sentencing himself to death.

Cain glanced down at the hole from which they had emerged.

Feeders and other beasts were swarming up the ladder, their features contorted into terrifying snarls. He turned to Farris. "This is not the way," he said. "You are making a terrible mistake."

"I don't think so," Farris said. He motioned to Cain, Thomas, and the half dozen other First Ones who stood clustered together. "Secure them," he said to his men.

The three men hesitated, looking uncertain. "You cannot trust a demon," Cain said to them. "Whatever you have been promised, it is a lie. Remember what I said around the campfire. The Dark One and Belial will tear you apart once you have done what they want."

"Farris," one of them said, glancing at the beasts all around them, several of which had started to advance once again on their position. "I don't think—"

"Enough!" Farris shouted, his face flushing red. "Take them now!"

The men hesitated again, giving Cain the chance he needed. He took the last bag of Egil's powder from his sack and threw it at the tunnel opening.

The powder exploded in a blinding flash just as the first feeder stuck its head out of the hole; it fell back, screeching and on fire, taking several others with it as it careened back down the ladder. At the same time, Thomas lashed out with the side of his shovel, catching Farris in the temple. The man dropped without a sound.

The other three were now badly outnumbered. They put their hands up, shaking their heads as Cullen leveled his pitchfork at them.

"Hurry," Cain said. Mikulov's path was littered with the torn and broken bodies of dead creatures, but it was closing again quickly. They had only moments to spare.

The remaining men rushed through the opening, toward the Black Tower.

Mikulov was on fire. The gods' power flowed through him, encased his limbs, and gave him the strength to fight through a sea of vicious, snapping demons. Elemental energy crackled and flashed with each blow. He moved too quickly for the human eye to process, hitting monsters from everywhere at once, slashing at them with his holy blade. Dozens fell, gushing black blood, arms and legs severed and twitching, heads rolling across the slippery stone.

But for each creature that fell, ten more took its place. In spite of himself, Mikulov began to tire.

As he decapitated a howling, red-faced overseer and its head toppled from its muscled shoulders, a scavenger's claws raked his back, drawing blood. He turned and sliced off its arm, sending the monster howling and stumbling away, spouting gore across the backs of the fallen ones that had crept up from behind. Three of them rose up, snarling, before he whirled and sent a crackling burst of focused energy directly at them, turning their faces into black, smoking ruins.

As they fell back, shuddering, a flying insect darted in and sank its stinger into Mikulov's shoulder. White-hot pain raced through his arm and across his chest, causing him to gasp and stagger. His heart stuttered; there was poison in the stinger. He sliced the insect in two with his blade, then crushed what was left beneath his feet.

Two more flew at him, and he used one arm to slash them both in two, his other arm hanging useless at his side. An unburied lumbered through the midst of the fallen imps, roaring with its multiple heads and raising its arms like rock-studded anvils ready to crush anything in its path. Mikulov ducked under its killing blow and delivered a series of lethal slashes to the creature's back and legs, bringing it toppling to its knees. But as he

moved to cut off its stinking, dead skull, it swung wildly backward with one arm and caught him in the side.

The blow was like a wagon colliding with a tree. It lifted Mikulov in the air and sent him sprawling. The monk's skin, thickened through years of training and physical punishment, was
tough enough to withstand almost anything, but his bones beneath were not. He felt a rib snap as he landed upon the backs of
more scavengers, their sharp fangs nipping at him as they flung
him to the ground.

Mikulov lashed out at them, making the creatures scatter,
then lay on his back, gasping for air. He couldn't seem to catch
his breath, not anymore. The stinger's poison continued to work
its way deeper; he felt it racing through his veins, each pump of
his heart pushing it along. He looked up into the sky as rain fell
on his face, burning his parched throat with a sour, metallic
taste. Even the rain was tainted here.

The small space around him was closing quickly, feeders advancing on all sides. There was a moment of calm when the gods
all became silent within his head and everything slowed down
to a crawl. Time ceased to matter. He was a small boy, running
through the mountains, ducking under the cool shade of trees,
and splashing across brooks filled with trout. Something was
chasing him: a man, playing a game of tag. But the man changed
as Mikulov ran, and Mikulov changed too, growing taller, stronger, his body thickening with the weight of years, and the thing
chasing him wasn't a man at all, but a beast with a black hood
and the wings of a crow.

Mikulov closed his eyes against the advancing demon army,
shutting out the brutal, ravaged faces. He called to the gods and
drew their energy from the air around him. He held it deep
within himself, as if taking a huge, deep breath; a warmth began
in his chest, soothing at first, and then it grew into the heat of a
raging fire. Still he held on, feeling the power filling him up,

spreading through his limbs as the gods accepted his gift and returned it to him tenfold.

The monk opened his eyes, the fire alive and writhing like a dragon within his chest. The creatures were upon him now.

He smiled, and let it all go.

Deckard Cain was halfway to the Black Tower when the world exploded.

It began with a soft pop, and then a ripple of blue fire burst outward from where Mikulov had fallen, a wave of light. The pop was followed by a thump that Cain felt deep within his core as the ring of fire expanded, taking down everything in its path. A whisper of heat washed over him, and then the shock wave hit, knocking him off his feet and taking the breath from his lungs.

Cain drifted for a moment, as if a wall of water had collapsed over him and sent him tumbling through the deep, before he came back to himself. His head ringing, he sat up as the wave passed, looking around in shock and horror. A cold shiver ran down his spine, a sense of doom overwhelming him. Nobody could have survived such a blast.

But he had already known that would happen, hadn't he? He had known it as soon as the monk had met his gaze, back at the tunnel hole. Cain had seen it in his eyes, a quiet, steady purpose, as if he had met his fate already and come to terms with it, and the rest was simply a matter of time.

Most of the creatures standing within one hundred yards of the explosion had simply vanished, turned to ash; those farther away were either dead or mortally wounded. But at the edges of the blast zone, others were regaining their feet. An overseer threw back his head and roared into the leaden sky, and his minions howled in return.

Mikulov had given Cain's party an opening, but he had not stopped all of the demons. A new resolve gripped Cain, an almost frantic determination, a need to hurtle himself forward. He pointed at the Black Tower and shouted at the remaining First Ones to hurry. Then he stood and stepped over the scattered bodies as quickly as he dared.

His staff seemed to hum under his fingers as he went, the ruby top glowing softly. He had recited no spell, called nothing into life. Yet it had been activated in some way, like a lightning rod in a storm. In fact, the air around him had begun to vibrate.

He had no time to puzzle over that. The noise of the demon horde had begun to grow once again. He glanced to his right and left, and saw feeders coming fast on all sides like giant white crabs, moving forward in packs. They would be upon him in seconds.

As one leaped at him, a whistling arrow caught it in the side of the neck, and it went down without a sound. Cain glanced back to see Thomas with another arrow notched and ready, Cullen at his side with his pitchfork.

"Go!" Thomas shouted, waving at him. "We'll hold them off!" Then he turned and shot at another feeder as it rushed at him, taking it down with the thwack of an arrow through the chest.

Cain turned toward the Black Tower, running the final few feet to the open archway at its base and disappearing inside.

The archway led to an inner wall and a huge wooden door with the symbol of the Horadrim engraved in it. But the symbol had been altered. Demonic runes had been added that foretold the end of the world: the fall of humanity and the age of demons, a foul corruption of the sign of goodness and light, and a clear warning to all who entered.

The door swung open with a low whine, revealing a dark and

empty hall. He ducked through and shut the door against the raging creatures outside.

Whatever happened now, he was alone. His friends were sacrificing their lives to give him precious time. They had turned out to be true heroes, after all. The urge to rush forward came over him again. All his life, he had stood on the sidelines as others fought, choosing to remain in the background. At first his excuses had to do with his scholarly pursuits and, later, his advancing age, but all had had the same result. He was a coward at heart, was he not?

This was the time to act. Yet an inner voice began to question all of that once again, seeds of doubt creeping back in. He was an old man, and not prepared for a fight like this. He had never wielded a sword. What would he do, once he reached the enemy? What kind of skills did he possess to face such a horror?

*Leah.* He was the little girl's only hope. And that, more than anything else, was what finally got him moving again.

The staff's light illuminated a set of stairs. The stairs were circular and ran around the edges of a dizzying open shaft that reached up far beyond the edges of his light, with a column of stone at its center. From somewhere above, he could see a faint gray glow.

His heart pounding in his throat, Cain began the climb. The stairs went up forever, and his breath began to labor, his chest burning, knees protesting, the familiar ache in his back unbearable. He felt his mind enter an entirely new state, as if he were hovering just outside himself and watching the progress, and it seemed his entire life was playing itself out once again through this final act: his mother, watching from beyond the edges of the fire, her eyes filled with sorrow mixed with hope; his days as a young schoolteacher in Tristram, more absorbed by scholarly texts than anything the children did; his wife and child walking hand in hand into the distance, leaving him forever; and finally, alone with his books at the End of Days, old and broken, waiting to rejoin his family in a place of peace and hope, a place beyond all imagining.

Beyond the tower walls, the demons had fallen strangely silent. Cain heard the call of a single crow, echoing across the courtyard like a harbinger of doom. He pictured the remains of the First Ones, gutted and hung from their feet from the archway, blood pooling on the stone. The image was so strong, he almost believed he was having some kind of vision, and his stomach churned from the truth of it. He must not stop, must not let the horrors that had already happened distract him from his goal. Above him was Leah, and somewhere close was the Dark One, waiting for him.

He only prayed he was not too late.

# THIR+Y-FIVE

## The Ritual Chamber

Leah swam upward through ocean water, the color as black as night. Somewhere far above her head was a hint of blue, and she struggled toward it, her lungs aching, her eyes growing blurry and sightless as she pushed against the void.

At some point the hint of blue changed; it became something else, a black hole, the pupil of a giant unblinking eye. It was the crow from the streets of Caldeum, pecking at ruined flesh and pulling it taut, cocking its head at her as the muscle snapped.

*Silly little girl,* the crow said. *You think you have free will. What you do has no consequence here. I own you.*

At that, the voice changed, and the eye melted into the beggar, shouting about the End of Days, his voice ragged and cackling. *The sky will turn black, the streets fill with blood! You are doomed. The Dark One is powerful, I tell you. He will raise a demon army! The dead will walk among us!*

The beggar melted into Gillian. She stood over Leah with a knife in her hand. *The dead are restless,* Gillian said. *The demons, ready for blood. They want it, Leah. They* bathe *in it.*

And that changed into the image of her real mother, but her face was shrouded in shadow, and she stood silent and motion-

339

less. No matter what Leah did—begging and pleading, screaming, crying—her mother did not move, did not react, only stood
in the darkness like a statue.

When she opened her eyes, she did not realize at first that she
had left the dream. Her surroundings were dark and silent, and
the black pupil that had watched her was still there. But as she
regained her bearings, Leah realized that what she was seeing
was the hooded face of a man, standing before her.

She had no idea how she had gotten here, who the man was,
or what he might want from her. The last thing she remembered
was being at the camp outside the cave, and the things that had
come for them through the trees. Had she been taken by some
sort of monster?

Where was Uncle Deckard? Fear prickled her flesh. *Why hadn't
he come for her?*

The man was chanting something, his voice a low, even tone
that brought chills. The floor vibrated all around her, shaking
her to the bone. Then she felt something: a gentle pressure
against her waist. Deeper fear made her pulse speed up, but her
heart fluttered strangely, like a dying bird in her chest, and she
felt light-headed.

She looked down at herself.

A creature climbed up her body like a wriggling snake, its
hair matted and thin, shoulders nothing but skin and bone. It
hunched over her, its claw-like hands pulling at her like the
crow with the scrap of dead meat; when it looked up with its
black holes for eyes and its purple, cracked lips, she barely recognized the horror of its face. In her mind she saw Gillian again,
and the air had become threaded with lines of blood that danced
and curled through it like charmed snakes around Gillian's
head before they sank through a hole in the floor and disappeared.

Something came awake in her, something huge and powerful,

and before she lost consciousness again and fell down a dark, endless well, Leah gathered the last of her dying strength and screamed, the sound echoing through the stone rooms and beyond, before fading away to the sound of crows, cawing and beating their wings against the walls of the tower like the thunderous applause of an audience waiting for her end to come.

Deckard Cain heard Leah scream.

The sound brought chills, yet it gave him hope. The sound of her scream meant he still had a chance. He redoubled his efforts, and when he glanced up, he was near the top of the staircase and facing a small landing and another closed door. The light came from here—an open window that looked out over the gray sea, where white-sapped swells like the endless movement of time washed onto the rocks.

Cain stood at the window and gasped for breath. Every muscle in his body cried out in agony; every bone ached with each beat of his heart. He had never felt so old and broken; he had no idea how he had been able to climb so high.

When he placed a hand on the wall, he could feel the energy within the tower itself.

It came up through the stone from deep within the ground, or perhaps it was flowing the other way; Cain could not tell. His staff glowed brighter, seeming to feed off the energy as it raced through Cain's fingers, up his arm and down the other.

He listened to the other side of the door and thought he could hear the sound of movement. A soft thump and a scraping noise drifted out, then, so shockingly loud it made him stumble back, a low, bone-shaking moan of something inhuman.

For a moment Cain could not place why it sounded so familiar, before it suddenly clicked: Jeronnan's horn.

There were feeders inside.

Cain tried the door and found it unlocked. He swung it open to madness.

The room beyond was circular, taking up the entire circumference of the top of the tower. It was empty of any furniture or other decoration, save for two low, flickering torches set in wall sconces shaped like skeletal hands.

But that was not what held Cain's gaze. Fingers of dread walked their way down his spine as he looked in horror at the scene before him.

Leah lay face up on the floor in the center of the room, her arms and legs shackled. Feeders were at work on her wrists and ankles, neck and lips, their misshapen, ghoulish bodies writhing in ecstasy, their scalps glistening wetly through strands of white hair. They had latched their purple, worm-like mouths upon her like leeches. Cain could hear the sounds of them sucking at her as their shoulders moved, bones jutting out like wings from their backs.

They looked like giant, featherless birds. *Abominations.* He shuddered.

Leah's eyes had rolled back into her head, showing the whites. Her skin was too pale, her breathing fast and shallow, and her flesh seemed to collapse upon itself, as if she was being hollowed out.

Cain ran forward with a small cry, disgust and rage mixing within him as he raised his staff and spoke words that burst from somewhere deep within him. His staff came to brilliant, sparkling life, and before its red glory the feeders hissed and shrank back, one of them making that low moan again. As they hopped to the windowsill, their features changed, feathers growing from flesh, noses turning to black beaks. They flew away, flapping into the wind.

Cain crouched next to Leah, touching her face; her flesh was cold and clammy, and she did not stir. But she was not dead, not yet; he could feel the faint, feathery pulse in her wrist. Outrage washed over him again as he cupped her head gently to his chest. *They will pay for this.*

Something else moved at the edge of the room. Cain looked up to see a dark, hooded figure seem to congeal from thin air and step right out of the stone wall itself, his hands hidden under long sleeves of his robe. The figure appeared to float forward like an apparition.

Leah suddenly convulsed upward, her back bending until it seemed it would break, and the tower began to tremble.

"I have been waiting for you, Deckard Cain," the figure said, reaching up with long, bone-white fingers and slipping the hood away from a face that came from the depths of Hell itself.

Eyes glowed like coals buried deep within pockets of bruised skin above a black hole where a nose should have been. Its lips were drawn back from toothless gums, its slick, suppurating flesh crossed with blue veins that pulsed with each beat of its heart.

"Garreth Rau," Cain said. He got to his feet. "You don't know what you've done—"

Rau spread his arms wide toward the window and the bruised sky. "The way of the Horadrim has long since passed, and a new era has begun, one that will embrace the Burning Hells and all that are birthed from its hellfire. I will lead the way, and you will be the last witness to a dying world, imprisoned here forever. How fitting that will be!"

"Belial has corrupted your thinking," Cain said. "You must listen to me, Garreth. You cannot believe his lies. He will use you until he no longer needs you, eat you alive, consume your soul, and then he will cast what is left of you out."

Rau smiled. "Clever," he said. "Using my name. Gaining trust, and trying to make me remember who I am? Then perhaps you should address me as Tal Rasha."

"I don't understand—"

"My true ancestor and namesake, one I have taken for my own. Imprisoned forever in Baal's tomb by your flesh and blood, Jered Cain. Betrayed by the only one he really trusted." The Dark One's face had twisted itself into a vicious grimace, and his eyes burned even brighter than before. "Or don't you remember?"

Cain shook his head. "Tal Rasha was not betrayed," Cain said. "He chose to take Baal within himself, to save Sanctuary."

"That's the story the world has been given. Lies, spun to hide the truth. Your Jered Cain was no hero. He used demonic magic to trick Tal Rasha, and shoved the soulstone into him against his will. He turned his back on his friend and left him to rot for all eternity. Instead of saving him, Jered chose to sacrifice him so he could escape with his own life. He was a coward."

"Jered and Tal Rasha were *colleagues*. Both of them were Horadrim, selected by Tyrael himself to lead Sanctuary from darkness. They were—"

"*I know the histories!*" the Dark One shouted. "Do not pretend to lecture me, Deckard Cain. I have read the secret scrolls, the texts that tell the truth about what happened." He whirled and picked up a text from a stand, showing Cain the crest branded into its cover. "This is the crest of the Tal Rasha family. And this—" he took a piece of torn paper from his robe, showing the same crest—"this is from my own parents, who died when I was just an infant."

Cain shook his head. The entire idea was preposterous; Tal Rasha had never had children and certainly had never had a family crest. "You're wrong," he said. "There is no Tal Rasha family tree. There never was."

The Dark One's face grew more furious, and Cain caught a glimpse of the petulant little boy he must have been. "You dare to try to tell me this," he said. "When your own family felt so abandoned by you, they ran away, only to fall victim to demons? Do you know their souls still suffer, crying out for you? And you still cannot and will not act. Still you turn a blind eye to their suffering. And once again, you cannot protect a child who depends upon you. It is too late. Your precious Leah will die, in order to give life to the destruction of Sanctuary itself."

"No." Cain shook his head. "Belial has lied to you yet again. My family was attacked by bandits. It was a robbery, nothing more. They—"

Rau reached out a hand. Blue fire coursed from his palm across the space between them, catching Cain in the chest and throwing him backward, pinning him to the floor. As he lay on his back, helpless, the trembling of the tower increased until the sound of thunder threatened to drown out everything else.

The Dark One turned his attention to Leah, washing her with fire. She convulsed again, and something exploded from deep within her, a flash of power so strong and bright that Cain could not hear or see anything but the beating of his own heart and the rush of his blood.

The wave of power raced through the Black Tower, flowing down into the ground where the containment chamber sat, pregnant with the lifespark of thousands of mortal men. The chamber exploded in a flash of light, energy racing through stone tunnels in all directions.

Far below, within the silent catacombs of Al Cut, a man stood waiting. Anuk Maahnor spread his arms wide and smiled as things long buried in the earth began to stir.

Bones creaked; sinews cracked; leathery muscle and skin, mummified over years of entombment, returned to an approximation of life.

But this life was unnatural. Creatures dead for centuries rolled in their graves, hidden from view until they burst through walls and into open spaces.

The power continued to course down the tubular center of the Black Tower and through the grid of tunnels beneath it. The symmetrical pattern of the tunnels themselves lent strength to the spark, feeding upon itself in a circular pattern with the tower at its center.

Veins regrew on top of bone and sinew, and black fluid flowed like blood. The dead marched with purpose, joining together in lines that grew longer as more joined the others, their moldy, eyeless sockets staring blankly forward, hairless, patchwork skulls oozing. Jaws worked soundlessly, teeth cracking together as if they attempted to speak. But their throats and vocal cords had long since rotted away.

They marched, led by Maahnor, toward the surface.

*The woman and child ran hand in hand through the high grass. Their clothing was torn, and there was blood on their faces. The woman tried to comfort the small child with soothing words, but the carnage that still lay behind them in the road told the real story: a wagon overturned, wheels askew, the two oxen that had led it slaughtered, their innards spilling into the dust. The man who had driven the wagon lay nearby in two pieces, his head ripped from his shoulders as the creatures dragged him into the brush.*

*The woman's face registered shock. She stumbled and almost brought the boy down with her. He was crying in the way that small children did, his chest hitching, but he kept up, his little legs churning.*

*The goatmen behind them gained ground quickly. There would be no escaping them, the woman seemed to realize, and at the last moment she sank to her knees and gathered the boy to her chest, wrapping both arms around her child as if she could protect him with her own body.*

*But the creatures did not tear the woman and boy to pieces. They surrounded them, howling up at the darkening sky and clawing at the ground as if in ecstasy or pain. The woman glanced back at the road, hoping for a miracle, someone to come along and save them; but the road to Caldeum remained empty.*

*"Deckard," she whispered, tears running down her cheeks, "I'm—"*

*Whatever words she might have spoken were cut off abruptly, as the ground before them trembled and split. The shuddering landscape threatened to throw them headlong, as a glowing, smoking cavern appeared where moments before there had been nothing but grass. The cavern swallowed up the land until it reached the woman and child, and then it stopped abruptly.*

*The creatures shrieked and beat themselves against the ground in a kind of religious fervor, as something monstrous reached up from below and began to pull itself free. Huge clawed appendages gripped the earth. A bony carapace loomed over a skull three times the size of the woman. Eyes that glowed like hellfire fixed upon the two humans before it, and the creature opened a maw that stank of death and destruction, laughing into the hot wind.*

*The souls of your wife and son came to live with the creatures of the Burning Hells long ago,* the voice thundered inside Cain's head. *The archangel Tyrael, that stinking beast, is here with us as well, as our prisoner. Now you will join them and bow to me, Belial, ruler of Hell and all who live within it, and soon to be ruler of Sanctuary and the High Heavens above.*

Belial, the Lord of Lies, loomed over him like a giant ready to crush anything in its path. Cain squeezed his eyes shut tight, returning to the place in his mind that had kept him sane after the loss of Amelia and his son, so many years ago. He focused on the teachings of Jered Cain, who had written that the true nature of a warrior lies in his ability to remain focused within the storm of battle. He was in his mother's home, sitting at his old desk under candlelight; his hands were young again and unmarked, his eyes strong and his heart filled with the ecstasy of a man who had found his life's passion. The pages of Jered's books and the familiar smell of dusty old paper calmed him.

But the image would not hold. It dissolved into the motionless bodies of his wife and young son, ravaged by the goatmen that had chased them down and dragged them into the brush.

*Ah, their wounds were painful, but even now, they still suffer, unable to pass beyond the Hells, waiting for a hero who will never come. Their hero did not exist. But you know that, do you not? You have known the truth for a long time, and still you choose to ignore it.*

The vision switched to a landscape filled with the screams of the damned. Fire licked at the feet of humans bound and hung across a vast chamber, while others were forced to labor under the eyes of demon masters. Overseers lashed their bloody backs with cruel whips, driving them forward; they pulled carts full of molten iron to forges that burned hot enough to peel the skin from their limbs. Others beat long swords and armor into shape with hammers. Pile after pile was stacked along the walls of the cavern as the people carried them from the forges and placed them there.

*We prepare for the coming war,* Belial said. *Garreth Rau has opened himself to me, and soon I will control his mortal form. First Caldeum will fall and then the rest of Sanctuary's cities, and when the undead army has finished its work, we will unleash a new army of our own, using Sanctuary to storm the Crystal Arch, taking Silver City and the High Heavens themselves.*

Cain stared at the hundreds of people, their bare feet raw and bloody, their faces filled with pain and suffering. His heart broke.

The souls of his wife and son flitted among them.

When Deckard Cain opened his eyes, the vision vanished. It was a vision, nothing more—a lie fed to him by Belial, a master of manipulation. He knew this, knew that the souls of his loved ones could not have been spirited away like this. Yet fingers of doubt continued to creep in, no matter how hard he tried to force them away, plucking at his sanity.

He was jolted back into the room at the top of the Black Tower, where the Dark One stood over Leah, hands outstretched, as the thunderous sounds of thousands of undead soldiers grew louder far beneath them. Cain imagined line after line of them marching to the surface, their faces half formed and horribly twisted by unnatural forces, rusted weaponry clutched in their bony hands.

The power continued to flow from Leah, through Garreth Rau and the tower, into the caverns below. It popped and crackled like fire, yet it was not, and though Leah was not conscious, something else within her continued to respond to Rau's spell.

He must not let Rau and Belial turn him away from what he had to do. *You must act, and do it now.*

Cain struggled to his feet. His staff was close. He picked it up and hobbled around Leah's shuddering body, then swung the staff with every last ounce of his strength.

The wooden shaft shattered across Garreth Rau's temple, snapping his head back. Black blood flew from a gash in his forehead, and his hold over Leah seemed to be broken. Cain did not hesitate; he gripped the end of the staff with both hands and raised it over his head, driving the jagged end down into Rau's chest.

A gout of thick blood sprayed from the wound as Rau staggered back, clutching at the wood protruding from his flesh. Cain felt the tower shift, as if swaying in a strong wind, and the sound of the demonic horde outside quieted for a moment.

He rushed back to Leah's side, cradling her head again. She had definitely been drugged, as the First Ones had said; if he was right, there was only one drug that would have this powerful an effect.

Cain slipped his hand into his rucksack and took out the liquid he had prepared from the root the First Ones had gathered a few hours before. It was the only known antidote for the Torajan formula that he believed the Dark One had used—the same drug he had used to calm Leah back when he had first met her in Gillian's home and she had gone into one of her trances. Nothing else could have kept her under like this.

Gently, he touched Leah's lips with the liquid.

A few moments later Leah moaned lightly, her eyelids fluttering. Cain worked at the chains that bound her but could not release them. The girl's skin was pale, her face sunken, her limbs nearly skeletal. Chills washed over him, and fresh anger at what she had suffered.

A noise made him turn. Garreth Rau had regained his feet. He drew the wood from his chest, an inch at a time; when the last of it had emerged, his skin had already closed around the wound.

"You'll have to do better than that," Rau said, tossing the shaft aside. His smile revealed blood on his teeth. "Belial comes to greet his army soon. The girl's power draws him here."

"Then he will take full possession of your physical form," Cain said. "You will cease to exist, pushed out of yourself and into the void, while the Lord of Lies inhabits your body and uses it for his own."

"No." Rau shook his head, but Cain saw a flash of doubt. "He has promised me that I will rule alongside him—"

"Belial cannot be trusted," Cain said. "You really think he will allow you to remain in control? He has told you lies about your ancestry, Garreth, to manipulate you into doing what he wants. He has told you lies about me. But when the time comes, he will not hesitate to cast you aside."

He thought of what he knew of Rau's childhood, growing up as an orphan, very likely starving for something to hold on to and give him hope. Belial would prey upon that, making him feel strong and in control, using this to gain a way in. "Possession is often slow and insidious," he said. "Think about your powers, how they manifest themselves. Have you ever felt as if they are not completely your own?"

"You are frightened, old man. Your words betray you."

"Belial has very likely already manifested his power through you, used you as a conduit. He is brainwashing you, testing the bonds, weakening your interior defenses. He means to overthrow this world, in preparation for an assault on the High Heavens. Once he has used you to gain access to this realm, just ask yourself one thing: why would he need you any longer?"

Rau seemed about to speak again, but his expression changed to one of puzzlement and, finally, a trace of fear. He seemed to be struggling with something.

"No," he said, shaking his head. He shivered. "It can't be. I won't let you. I won't . . ."

Cain was no longer sure whether the man was talking to him or someone else. Suddenly Rau screamed, gasped, and screamed again, scratching at his own face and drawing rivulets of blood. His features rippled and changed, bony plates growing up from his forehead, his eyes yellowing.

Finally he relaxed, a thin, haughty smile playing about his lips. Garreth Rau was no more.

"Deckard Cain," the Lord of Lies rasped, the breath rattling in his lungs, "you *are* resilient, for your age. I must thank you for your assistance in bringing little Leah to me. But I'm afraid your job is complete, and so is hers.

"It's time for you and your little friend to die."

# THIR+Y-SIX

## *The Walking Dead of Al Cut*

Mikulov came to, one moment at a time.

He was lying on his side, covered in the remains of vaporized feeders and imps. He found himself in the middle of utter devastation: a small crater marred the stone floor, with him at its center. The stone had cracked nearly all the way to the tower, revealing a deep, wide crevasse that fell away into darkness. Farther away, bodies of demons and feeders littered the courtyard in all directions. Several mortally wounded creatures were writhing in their death throes.

But, incredibly, he remained unharmed.

Mikulov's head throbbed, and his mouth was dry as cotton. He sat up, shaking off the ash, and looked around more fully. What he saw chilled him to the bone. Seemingly everywhere, the dead were emerging from the ground: through tunnel exits, climbing from the huge crack and other, smaller fissures that ran across the courtyard. There were hundreds already, and more kept coming. They hooked bony fingers over the stones, wave after wave, pulling themselves up and gaining their feet, standing motionless in rows with weapons at their sides, all of them facing the Black Tower.

A man stood before the tower doors. At first glance, he looked unremarkable—in peasant dress, middle-aged and worn. But his eyes glittered in deep-set sockets, and his posture was straight and strong as he assessed his army.

Mikulov made his way through the ranks of the dead. They did not move, did not even turn their heads as he passed, even when he brushed against their slippery flesh. He kept his pace steady, his eyes straight ahead. If he could just reach the front of the crowd . . .

The ranks of the walking dead seemed to go on forever. The strange man watched him without speaking. When Mikulov had come within twenty feet, he held up his hand. "Do not come closer," the man said. "Who are you, and what is your business here?"

"I am Mikulov, of the Ivgorod monks," Mikulov said. "My business is my own."

"I am Anuk Maahnor, captain of the army of Bartuc, Warlord of Blood, and keeper of the tower. I will ask you again: what is your business?"

"Get out of the way," Mikulov said.

"I think not." Maahnor smiled. "You are one man. We are all mages here, trained in the dark arts by our master himself. You shall not enter in this lifetime."

"Not one man!" The voice came seemingly out of nowhere, but a moment later, Thomas and Cullen pushed through, shivering as they brushed against the strangely still, silent ranks of the dead. "Three, at least," Cullen said, at Mikulov's side. Cullen grinned at him, but his hands shook as he gripped his bloody pitchfork.

Mikulov smiled back. He felt no fear; a strange calm had descended upon him. He felt a peace his masters had spoken of many times, one he had not known before. A harmony with the gods, an acceptance of his fate, and an understanding of his own strengths and limitations.

"So be it," he said. "We will take on your army."

Maahnor looked surprised; then he smiled once again. "I accept your challenge," he said. He raised one hand, then dropped it in a slashing gesture. Immediately, the undead soldiers leapt into action, raising their weapons and charging forward.

Other than their footsteps thundering on the stone, they made no sound. Cullen gave a cry and lifted the pitchfork. Thomas tried to fit an arrow to his bow, but his hands fumbled, and he dropped it.

Then the soldiers were upon them. Mikulov felt the power of the gods coursing through him as he lashed out, catching the nearest one by the arm as it thrust its sword and turning with it, using the weapon's momentum to cut several of its brethren in half. He moved in a blur of fists and feet, crunching bones and skulls, leaving piles of bodies behind him.

The undead were slow and clumsy, but as they fell, more took their places, and Mikulov realized with dismay that those on the ground had begun to reassemble themselves and stand up again.

"Keep fighting!" he shouted at Cullen and Thomas, but the men were terrified, and he could tell it would not be much longer before they were overcome.

*Help us,* Mikulov prayed as he fought desperately for an opening, trying to work his way forward. *Let the gods hear my cry.* But the undead kept coming, wave after wave, relentless as the ocean tide, as Maahnor stood watching silently at the tower's entrance, waiting for the end.

Cain looked at Leah. Her eyes had come open, pupils flat and black as pinpricks. The chills he felt deepened; something had come over her, the way it had that night at Gillian's house and again in Lord Brand's manor. He had released something that he did not know how to control, and for the first time, he wondered if it had been the right choice.

Leah sat up with one fluid motion, tearing the arm shackles

from the floor effortlessly, then yanked her legs free and stood. The temperature in the room dropped quickly, and the now-familiar buzz of energy swarmed around her.

She paused, and looked around, her gaze finding Belial. The two of them observed each other for a long moment, and some spark of recognition seemed to come over them both.

"I know that face," Belial whispered. "Who—"

The sound of crows drowned out everything else. They blackened the windows of the tower, blanketing every inch of the outside walls as Belial released a thunderbolt of power that was met by Leah's own. A crackling flash erupted, blinding Cain for a moment. He blinked against it, trying to find his bearings as the crows' wings continued to beat against the stone walls, their cries growing louder.

Cain caught a glimpse of something huge and inhuman across the room, where Garreth Rau had stood; later he was never sure whether it had been real or only imagined, for when he looked again, he saw Rau at the window, writhing in place as if gripped in a titanic inner battle. Leah stood with her arms out and her head up, eyes blazing, and as she looked at him wildly, he saw the real Leah for just a moment, and the terror in her eyes was so raw and horrible he wanted to comfort her. As soon as he took a step toward her, he was held in the grip of her power, immense and immovable; as it squeezed him, cutting off his breath, he cried out, pointing to the hole in the floor and willing her to release the energy there.

He wasn't sure if she understood him or was even capable of controlling it. But Leah let him go and cried out, and something huge and invisible seemed to leap from her, barreling down the hole and through the center column of the tower, into the ground below.

For a moment, nothing happened. Then a series of muffled booms occurred, one after another. The Black Tower shuddered.

Directly below them, if Cain had calculated correctly based on the map, were the charges made up of Egil's powder he and the First Ones had set in place against the tunnel walls. Leah's blast had ignited them, as he had hoped. He imagined the implosion below them, the sea crashing inward with tremendous force, washing through the lost city of Al Cut and crushing everything in its path.

Garreth Rau stood framed in the open window, looking back at the two of them with surprise, his features rippling and changing, and then changing again; he stared into Cain's eyes, the pain and anguish seared into place.

"You . . . were right," he whispered, his voice cracking. "They were lies . . . all of them."

With a single, strangled cry, he threw himself backward out the window and disappeared from sight.

For a long moment, nothing happened, and then there was a faint, muffled boom, and the tower shook more violently. "We must go now, Leah!" Cain shouted. This time, when he took her hand, she allowed herself to be led easily to the door.

Stones began to crumble, falling from the ceiling. Cain risked one more look back; crows had come through the window, their bodies beginning to change, feathers retracting, ghoulish features protruding before Cain pulled Leah away from the room and down the stairs, away from their mournful, hungry cries.

Mikulov had nearly come to the end of his strength when he happened to glance up at the tower. What he saw shocked him; a figure tumbled head over heels through the air, robes flapping like a bird's wings as it plummeted to the ground. At first he was filled with horror, imagining it to be Deckard Cain. But as it hit the ground with a tremendous boom, he realized it had to be the Dark One himself.

How it had happened he did not know, but the body's impact set off a shock wave of power that rushed through the courtyard like an ocean swell. The effect was immediate and dramatic; almost as one, the undead soldiers dropped lifelessly to the ground like puppets with their strings cut. The connection that had bound them, the magic threads Garreth Rau had created, had been severed.

Mikulov turned back to the tower. The body Anuk Maahnor had occupied was lying motionless on its back—what was left of a simple villager, bleeding from the eyes and mouth.

The stone courtyard shuddered, and a rumbling sound came from beneath their feet. Cullen pointed up at the tower, which was swaying back and forth. "It's going to come down!" he said, as more cracks appeared around them and the rumbling grew louder. "Run!"

They raced downward, stumbling several times but somehow never falling as the tower trembled violently. More stones came loose above them, plummeting down through space and crashing into the floor below. The steps grew shakier as they went, but they reached the bottom without getting hit.

Cain pulled Leah by the hand through the entryway and out the door, into the courtyard under blackened skies. The entire world seemed to be coming to an end; the ground was littered with bodies, and the stone beyond the steps had split in multiple places, exposing jagged, gaping holes in the earth.

Cain led Leah around the crevasses, then scooped the docile girl into his arms and ran as fast as he could, driven by pure adrenaline as a loud groaning noise came from behind them and the ground began to tremble even harder. He risked a glance back; the Black Tower started to lean as the stone underneath it buckled and twisted, frothy spray exploding up through cracks and sending rocks, dirt, and bones flying many feet into the air.

As the tower teetered on the edge, seemingly forever, Cain sensed a presence rise up above the crows that circled and flapped away from the structure, a great evil that watched with unblinking eyes as the walls came down.

He kept going. They were perhaps one hundred feet away when the bottom of the tower imploded with a tremendous earth-shaking roar. Cain stopped again and turned as the top half toppled over and fell, hitting the ground in an avalanche of stone and mortar. Pieces of rock flew like shrapnel in all directions as a gigantic hole opened up and the base collapsed into the ground, burying the tunnels and caverns beneath it in debris. A geyser of seawater shot fifty feet into the air, and a wail of rage from that unseen presence rose up over everything before slowly dying away, leaving nothing but the last few crows circling aimlessly in a dead sky.

# THIR+Y-SEVEN

## *Gea Kul, Resurrected*

"Over here!"

Cain was startled to find Thomas and Cullen waving franti-
cally at them from across the courtyard, where they stood with
Mikulov and a small group of people. Cain was overjoyed to see
Mikulov alive; he had thought the worst.

Captain Jeronnan was among them as well. The big man
waved too; although he was covered in blood, he appeared to be
more or less unharmed.

Thomas hurried over to them and tried to take Leah from
Cain's aching arms. "No," he said, hugging her fiercely to him.
He kissed the top of her head as tears wet his cheeks. The girl
was unresponsive but breathing evenly, and color had started to
return to her face. Everything seemed to come to the surface at
once, and a torrent of emotions poured from him as he fell, sob-
bing to his knees, cradling Leah to him like a baby.

"You're all right," he said over and over, and in his mind he
was speaking to his wife and son as well as Leah. "I promise
you, everything is fine now. You're safe."

Eventually, Cain allowed Thomas to take Leah from him, and he sank back, utterly exhausted, before Mikulov helped him gently to his feet.

They limped over to the others. Cain clasped Jeronnan's huge hand in both of his, managing a smile, although he felt like he might collapse at any moment. The man embraced him.

"How did you—"

"'Twas the necromancer's blade," Jeronnan said. "The creatures met us in Gea Kul, and we put up an honest fight, but they had me by the throat, and they took me down to the ground with them. Thought I was done for. But I managed to get Kara's knife in a few of their bellies while we struggled, and they ran from it, the cowards. Most of them came this way, looking for the real battle, I would guess. We followed them here."

"Is it really over?" Cullen interrupted anxiously, peering at Cain's face. He was bleeding from a scalp wound, and the pinkie on his right hand appeared to have been bitten off. He clutched his hand to his chest and blinked through broken spectacles, his eyes bloodshot.

"I don't know," Cain said. "I think for now, perhaps it is."

He looked back at the ruins of the Black Tower. Somewhere in the rubble lay the remains of Garreth Rau, who was surely dead, having spent the last moment of his life finally standing up for himself in a way he never had before, and saving the world in the process. It was almost enough to make Cain believe in humanity again. But other thoughts were more unsettling.

What had appeared there as the tower collapsed? Had it just been his imagination, or had it been Belial himself, there to witness the end of his plans?

Perhaps, Cain thought, he had been there to witness the beginning.

After exploring some of the ruins left behind by the collapse of the Black Tower, and finding nothing left alive and no signs that the demon horde would return, the small group left for the Captain's Table. There were perhaps fifteen of them in all; Jeronnan's group had sustained heavy losses, and those citizens who had survived were wounded and dazed, as if just coming out of a deep sleep.

The day began to lighten as they walked, and when they reached the streets of Gea Kul, a single ray of sunlight broke through the gray clouds, shining directly upon the Horadric meeting place like a beacon of strength. Beyond it was a ruin of collapsed buildings, but this one remained standing. Thomas whispered to Cullen and pointed it out to Cain, who nodded. That, more than anything else he had yet seen, gave him hope that the worst was over, at least for now.

By the time they reached the tavern, the sun had broken through completely, and people were starting to emerge from their houses and hiding places, blinking in the bright light like terminally ill patients who had been given a reprieve from death. Most were emaciated, with telltale bruises on their necks, and they did not seem to respond to anything other than the sun's warmth. They craned their heads to peer up into the sky, squinting, traces of vacant smiles upon their sunken faces.

Leah, however, remained unresponsive. Mikulov carried her for the first few minutes, and then Cain, in spite of his utter exhaustion, insisted upon taking her in his arms for the rest of the way, while Thomas and Cullen walked beside him. He put her head on his chest and listened to her soft breathing to assure himself that she was still alive.

"I will not let you go," he whispered to her. "I promise." For a moment he thought he might have heard her try to speak, but she remained silent and still.

Gradually, almost imperceptibly, Sanctuary began to return to life. The sunlight brought more people out into the streets, and a celebration of sorts began to spread from neighbor to neighbor as the citizens of Gea Kul realized the reign of terror had ended. Many had been lost during the collapse of the caverns beneath the town, but those who had seen the ruins of the Black Tower themselves returned to tell others, and rumors of the Horadric heroes who had defeated the Dark One grew, until a small crowd began to gather outside the Captain's Table. Eventually Thomas and Cullen went out to speak to them, and a roar of appreciation rose up as the last of the day's warm rays bled from the sky.

Cain remained inside, sitting with Leah and holding her hand. Her wounds had been cleaned and covered, and he had dressed her in fresh clothes Jeronnan had given him. They were some of his daughter's childhood clothes, Jeronnan said, that he'd kept for all these years. The captain insisted there wasn't a more fitting person to wear them now.

Cain couldn't find anything physically wrong with Leah. She had lost a lot of blood, certainly, but her color was good and her heart strong. And so he waited patiently by her side, refusing to clean his own wounds or allow himself to sleep.

Eventually, in spite of himself, he nodded off in his chair. When he snapped awake sometime later, she was looking at him, puzzled.

"Uncle?" she said. "Where am I? What's happened?"

Emotions rushed through him, choking his voice: "What's the last thing you remember?"

"I . . ." Leah looked bewildered. "I remember we stayed at an inn, and met a man . . . I remember you were kind to me. You watched after me. But I don't remember anything else."

"You're safe, and that's all that matters," he said, warmth

blooming in his chest. He decided not to tell her exactly what had happened during the past few days, no matter how much she begged him. Her childhood would be better without these memories to haunt her, and if he had learned anything through this ordeal, it was that childhood was a precious gift, not to be taken lightly.

He was alarmed to find himself close to tears. "I love you, Leah. We are family now."

She sighed and nodded, and her eyes drifted closed. Cain sat and watched her for some time, the ghost of a smile on his face. He thought of his wife and son, their bloodied bodies under the blankets the men had spread in the ragged brush. For so many years, it had haunted him, his inability to lift those blankets and see them one last time. The idea of how they had suffered had remained with him like a ghost, buried deep beneath his con- sciousness until it had become a black, bottomless well. Belial had used that pain to his advantage.

But Cain knew now that they were at peace, that whatever they had suffered had ended long ago and it was time to put them to rest, once and for all.

Eventually he was able to close his eyes again, and this time, his sleep was dark, calm, and deep.

# THIR+Y-EIGH+

## *The Road Ahead*

The next few days were bright and sunny as life came back to
Gea Kul.

About half the town was gone, swallowed up by the
ground. But the people began to clear the streets that remained intact of the debris that had gathered there, unchecked, over many months. There were more spontaneous
celebrations, and more than a few times Deckard Cain left the
Captain's Table only to find a small crowd waiting for him
outside, like religious pilgrims. They were respectful enough,
but they made him nervous; he was never one to accept adora-
tion gracefully.

Still, they seemed to consider him some kind of hero. "You
are that, you know," Mikulov said, when they left one day and
found more than two dozen waiting outside, asking to shake
Cain's hand. "A hero. The last of the Horadrim."

"I hardly think—"

"It takes all kinds," Mikulov said. "You don't have to carry a
sword to be heroic." He smiled. "For a smart man, you seem to
have missed the point. You led us to the edge of death and back
again. You were the only one with a plan, even at our darkest

point, when we wanted to give up. Without you, we would have been lost."

"And without you, Mikulov, we would have been lost. We're all heroes, then. Every last one of us."

"If that is so," Mikulov said, "then you are responsible for it."

They walked in silence for a while. Their mission today was an important one, and something they had to do quietly, and alone.

Cain had done a lot of thinking during the past few days, a lot of it about Leah. She was a special little girl; there was no question of that, and yet she had suffered almost unbearable trauma, enough to have blocked it all out. She seemed to remember almost nothing of what had happened, during not only the battle in the tower but much of their entire adventure. It was as if her mind had completely erased anything she had been unable to process.

He, of course, remembered everything, and his latest revelation had to do with Leah, and with the true meaning of the battle between darkness and light. Garreth Rau had been defeated, at least in part, because he had not taken into consideration that Leah had her own free will and the ability to make a choice to fight back for good instead of evil. And he had not understood the power of human relationships—the good in them. Cain hadn't either, not for a long time, but Leah and Mikulov had changed all that. They had helped make him whole again.

Cain and Mikulov walked through the streets until they reached the Horadric meeting place. Cain was nearly certain that the Dark One's army had been destroyed. But he had to be sure.

The building still stood, but it had been badly damaged. They managed to get down the stairs to the place where the tapestry hung in tatters on the wall, but the tunnel entrance was choked with debris, and the rooms beyond the library were gone, collapsed into the floor.

They returned to the surface and walked beyond the building to find that this part of the town had simply vanished, swallowed by the earth below and leaving a crater filled with stone and murky water. It was as he had hoped, Cain thought. The lost city of Al Cut, and all it contained, was gone.

"Using Egil's formulation to destroy the tunnel walls and bring in the sea?" Mikulov shook his head, a look of admiration on his face. "That was the move of a brilliant strategist. None of us really understood what you were doing when you had us dig for the mineral vein. Even when we put the bags against the walls where you told us, we didn't think it would work." He shrugged. "But how did you ignite them?"

"It was Leah who did it," Cain said. "I had witnessed her power before. I knew from studying the map that the caverns were vulnerable if we placed enough of the explosives in the proper areas, and the moss was present to cause the chemical reaction we needed. And I knew that the tower was some sort of focal point above the lost city that we might be able to use like the wick of a lantern."

They stood and looked out over the destruction. Cain thought about Garreth Rau, and how Belial had twisted whatever vulnerabilities existed in the man to his advantage. And that led to other, more disturbing thoughts. Belial was not one to give up so easily. Cain began to wonder whether it was over, after all. He had come to realize that the prophecies could be interpreted in different ways. Perhaps this was only the first stage in a much larger, much more dangerous plan.

He had to know more, to be sure.

"Thank you, Mikulov, for everything," Cain said. "I will have to leave here soon, but I will never forget what you did."

"Nor will I forget you," Mikulov said. They clasped hands. "I must leave as well. The members of the Floating Sky would have me executed for leaving the monastery, if they could, and may be searching for me even now. But my fate is with the gods. Perhaps we will see each other again, someday."

They returned to the inn, where Cain told Cullen of his plans. "What?" Cullen blinked in surprise. "But we have so much to do! We must recruit more brothers to the order! You said—"

"You will be fine here," Cain said gently, putting a hand on Cullen's shoulder. "You and Thomas are more than capable of leading others to the light. You have both studied the texts; you understand what is required. I would only get in the way."

"Nonsense." Cullen shook his head, his jowls jiggling comically. "You are the only true Horadrim left in Sanctuary!"

*If that's true,* Cain thought, *it's even more important that I seek out answers and learn the truth of what the Worldstone's destruction really means for all of us.*

Cullen protested even more, but Cain's mind was made up. They went outside in time to meet Leah and Thomas, who had gone searching for saplings to make a new bow and new arrows for Leah. Although she did not remember Lund or anything about the camp, something had remained with her, and she was eager to try to shoot again.

"There's new growth out there," Thomas said, his face full of hope. "The trees are already returning! And we saw more animals, too. Life has come back to Kehjistan."

Thomas and Cullen went into the inn, talking animatedly about what they had both seen. Cain took Leah's hand. This was the moment he had been dreading; he would have to find a place for her where she would be safe. He would have to explain why he had to leave her, and he felt as if his heart might break.

They sat in the shade near the docks. "Where will we live, Uncle?" Leah asked. "Will we have our own house?"

In a halting, uncertain voice, Cain told her about what he had to do. It was a nearly impossible task, and in the middle of it Leah stood up and began skipping rocks across the water. He could not tell if she was angry or sad, but he continued to explain himself as best he could. The world was an uncertain place, and as much as it hurt him to say it, he had responsibilities that he could not avoid. If not he, then who else would do it?

"I want to go with you," Leah said.

That stopped him short; it reminded him of when he had considered finding a safe place for her before, on the road to Kurast, and how she had refused to let him then. But this was different. It was not just a journey, but a way of life.

He stood up and joined her at the water. "You don't know what that means," Cain said. "There are . . . dangers in Sanctuary, things that I may not be able to protect you from—"

"I don't care!" Leah shouted, and when she turned to him, there were tears streaming down her face. "You're the only family I have now, and I want to be with you! Please don't leave me, Uncle!"

Once again, she buried her face in Cain's tunic. They had formed a bond that could not be broken, and he realized with sudden shock that he could not leave her behind, any more than she could bear to be without him.

"All right," he said, tears welling in his own eyes. "I was wrong, Leah. You will travel with me, and we will never be apart again."

He began to think about writing everything down, creating a book of his own, for her benefit. She was not yet ready, but someday, perhaps, she might study the Horadric ways, just as he had. If this was their destiny, he would embrace it, and when the true demon invasion came, they would be ready to face the enemy together.

The two of them sat that way as the water lapped against the docks, and Deckard Cain imagined his wife and son sitting next to them. For the first time in as long as he could remember, he felt at peace.

# EPIL⊕GUE

## *The Lord of Lies*

Far beyond the mortal plane, among the raging fires of the Burning Hells and deep within his realm of illusions, Belial screamed his frustration. The walls shook with his fury, and his demons cowered before him, fearful of being caught by his wrath.

He had been so close to tearing apart the very fabric of Sanctuary and accomplishing the first phase of his plan, but then that useless waste of a man had caught him by surprise. He had never expected Garreth Rau to defy him in that way, and certainly never thought he would sacrifice himself in the battle for control.

*Perhaps I acted too quickly,* Belial thought. But the temptation had been too great; the human shell had been his for the taking, and destroying Deckard Cain had been an extra incentive to assume control immediately.

*I am still the Lord of Lies,* he thought, *ruler of the Burning Hells, and I shall not be denied.*

"My lord," a voice said. Belial looked down to find one of his minions at his feet—a beautiful, golden-haired female, strong and tall and proud, her full, red lips holding a hint of a smile. "I must speak with you—"

Belial snarled. He was not in the mood for games. He reached

down with a massive clawed hand to pick up the demon, bringing it to his face as its physical shape rippled and changed, the
illusion broken; a skinless, oozing nightmare stared back at him
from lidless eye sockets.

The creature squeaked in pain, squirming against his grip.
"Please, my lord!" it said. "I bring news. A seer has had a vision,
one that will please you. There will be . . . a birth, in the east! A
boy emperor shall come to Caldeum!"

Belial set the creature back down, the urge to rip its head from
its shoulders fading. A new curiosity piqued his interest—a boy
emperor in Caldeum? This was very interesting indeed. His plan
had been dealt a damaging setback. But perhaps there was another way to find the particular object he so craved.

"The birth shall come within five years," the creature said,
bobbing its suppurating skull. "It is not too long to wait, not for
you . . ."

"Have your brothers torture this seer," Belial said. "Take no
chances. I want to hear more. There is much to discuss."

The demon nodded and scampered away. Belial smiled. *Much
to discuss, indeed.* He began to think that his entire approach had
been wrong from the beginning. He was not about brute force;
he was about cunning and deceit.

There were many ways to approach the problem, but only one
goal: the destruction of Sanctuary and the fall of the High Heavens itself. The Lord of Lies would not rest until it was done, and
he ruled over all that was left.

*Patience.* Soon enough, his time would come.

# ACKNOWLEDGMENTS

The *Diablo* universe is amazingly complex and exciting, and there were many people who helped me navigate through the waters. I'd like to thank my editor at Simon & Schuster, Ed Schlesinger, for all his hard work and unwavering support. He's one of the good guys. Another huge note of thanks must go to Micky Neilson and James Waugh, two of the finest people I've met in this business, and everyone else at Blizzard Entertainment, one of the most incredibly creative places on the planet (I'd name everyone, but the list would be very long). Finally, as always, to my wife, Kristie; my children Emily, Harrison, and Abbey; and the rest of my family and friends: I thank you all for your support. I couldn't do it without you.